A BETTER LOVE NEXT TIME

Florence Philpotts defies her family and boyfriend to take a position as an apprentice hairdresser. It is a career she feels sure she was born to succeed in, although her apprenticeship is spent avoiding the attentions of her boss, Mr Tony. In the midst of a glorious local scandal, the opportunity arises to take over the salon but her parents refuse to lend her the money to do so. Tony's brother, Cliff, offers her marriage in return for her own salon. Is this a step too far even for impulsive, ambitious, Florence Philpotts...?

A BETTER LOVE NEXT TIME

by

Doreen Edwards

Magna Large Print Books
Long Preston, North Yorkshire,
BD23 4ND, England.

British Library Cataloguing in Publication Data.

Edwards, Doreen
    A better love next time.

    A catalogue record of this book is
    available from the British Library

    ISBN   0-7505-1495-7

First published in Great Britain by Judy Piatkus (Publishers) Ltd., 1999

Copyright ' 1999 by Doreen Edwards

Cover illustration ' Richard Jones by arrangement with Artist Partners

The moral right of the author has been asserted

Published in Large Print 2000 by arrangement with Piatkus Books Limited

Magna Large Print is an imprint of Library Magna Books Ltd.

Printed and bound in Great Britain by
T.J. (International) Ltd., Cornwall, PL28 8RW

In tribute to my very good friends Helen Smail and Don Allan for their tremendous help given to me whilst writing this book. I am very grateful.

CHAPTER 1

Swansea 1948

It's now or never! Florence Philpots stood on the edge of the pavement in the High Street, hesitating to take that first step into a new world, a world of independence where her dreams had every chance of coming true.

'Well, Flo, do it, then, if you're going to. But I bet you won't.'

Rita Bevan, her cousin, stood by watching her. There was a knowing little smirk on her face that Florence didn't like.

'I will, don't worry!' Florence said, with a defiant toss of her head. 'I'm not a scared little rabbit like you, tied to your mother's apron strings.'

'I'm *not* scared of my mother!' The corners of Rita's mouth turned down. 'I've just got a bit of common sense, that's all. The trouble with you, Flo, is you're too irresponsible, too reckless, by half!'

'Oh, listen to you, then!' Florence snapped, her lip curling with disdain. 'You sound more like forty-eight than eighteen. You're a stick-in-the-mud, Rita, and always will be.'

Rita sniffed. 'You're being horrible to me!'

Florence sighed with irritation, lifting her eyes to heaven.

'Oh, for goodness' sake, Rita! Stop being so touchy, will you? You Mammy's girl!'

7

She looked at her cousin's face. It was becoming pink and blotchy, a sure sign she was about to burst into tears, and Florence suddenly felt remorseful. She wasn't normally spiteful. She and Rita got on very well as a rule.

Today, though, Florence was jumpy and a little scared, too. She'd planned this move for so long; her strike for freedom, as she thought of it, and now suddenly she was afraid and uncertain.

Not that she doubted her own ability, she reminded herself sharply. It was just that she'd never openly defied her parents before; had never been openly rebellious.

'I'm eighteen today,' she told Rita as well as herself. 'I can do as I like from now on. I can be anything I want to be and no one's going to stop me. So there!'

Those were brave words. Florence felt her head spin a little with excitement and nervousness. Now that she was grown up, could her parents prevent her from taking charge of her own future? Surely not, but still she hesitated.

'Your mother will kill you, Flo,' Rita said, dabbing at the corner of her eye with a small square of lace-edged linen.

Florence thought of her mother and gulped.

She'd be furious. No, livid! There'd be one heck of a row. Florence might be able to twist her dad around her little finger, but her mother Edie had a will of iron. Florence knew she must put some metal in her own backbone when the clash came. Did she have enough courage for that confrontation?

'I'll live!' she said, trying to sound confident.

8

She wouldn't be put off! This was the most important decision of her life, so far. She *had* to find the courage from somewhere, otherwise she'd be second-best in her parents' eyes for the rest of her life.

She readily admitted she wasn't as brilliant as her older sister Amy, up at university, or clever like her younger brother, Tommy.

But, so what? She knew she had depths to her being that others couldn't see. She could make something of herself if only they'd give her a chance. That's all she needed, she told herself firmly. One chance!

'You don't know what it's like, Rita, you being an only child.' Florence said bitterly. 'Amy and Tommy are doing so well. Mam and Dad think I'm second-rate by comparison. They think I'm too feather-brained to be a success. But I'll show them!'

Florence ground her teeth in irritation. Why wouldn't they listen to her? Why wouldn't they believe in her? She knew the answer to that. They thought her flighty and shallow and didn't understand her at all.

'What will Ken say, though?' Rita asked.

Florence thought about her boyfriend, Ken, as she did so often these days.

'He'll stand by me,' she said with confidence, lifting her chin. 'He will, Rita!' she went on when her cousin looked doubtful.

Ken was the one person whose support she was sure of. They'd been going out together for almost a year now, and she was excited at being in love.

He was so good-looking and self-assured. He was clever, too, and ambitious. He would understand how she felt about making the most of her life; working at something which really interested her.

'How will he like you being just a hairdresser, though?' Rita persisted. 'His family are a bit posh, aren't they?' She touched Florence's arm. 'Listen, Flo. You've got a good job now. You'd be daft to give it up.'

With disgust, Florence thought of the stuffy office where she and Rita worked as shorthand typists. It had been her mother's idea to give Florence a commercial education. As if office work was the last hope if you didn't have brains to do something better.

David Watson and Palmer might be the most prestigious law firm in town but she hated the work. It was a reasonably well paid job, and she knew she'd earn much less as an apprentice hairdresser, but that didn't worry her. Office work was boring and she felt chained to her typewriter. She couldn't take much more of that, and she wouldn't, not now she was eighteen, grown-up. She'd show everyone what she was made of.

'It's not daft to want to do better for myself,' Florence said hotly. 'I'm not planning to be an apprentice hairdresser all my life for goodness sake!' She tossed her head. 'One day I'm going to own my own business. I'll be a success.'

'That's a long way off yet,' Rita said, cuttingly. 'You're having good money now. We're saving up to go to Butlins in Pwllheli next summer, remember? We won't be able to do that if you're on less money, Flo.'

Florence sniffed scornfully.

'Don't kid yourself, Rita. Your mother'll never let you go anyway, so what's the difference?'

Rita looked cross, and turned her head away.

Florence felt peeved at her cousin's lack of enthusiasm for her new venture.

'Well, Ken will stand by me, if you won't.'

Florence hesitated a moment, uncertain whether she should reveal her other secret dream. Well, why not? She could trust Rita. And after tonight she could tell everyone.

'I think Ken's going to ask me to get engaged,' she said, half shyly. 'He'll probably ask me tonight as it's my birthday.' She felt her face flush up. 'Promise you won't say anything to the family just yet.'

She was thrilled at the thought of getting engaged. Engaged to be married *and* taking up a new job, one that really interested her. Who could ask for more?

'He's taking me to the Grand Theatre tonight to see a play. We'll have a meal first at the Burlington. I'm thrilled.'

Florence had the satisfaction of seeing the fleeting look of envy in Rita's eyes.

The Burlington was a high-class restaurant at the top of Union Street. She and Rita always wished they could go there for coffee and cakes, but it was too expensive on their pocket money.

'Well, if you're not going to do it,' Rita said petulantly. 'Let's get back to the office. I'm hungry. I want my sandwiches.'

11

'I'm going to do it. Don't rush me.'

Florence glanced across the street at the windows of Terri's High-class Hairdressing and Beauty Salon, where glossy photographs of young women sporting various fashionable hairstyles hung above glass shelves filled with colourful toiletries and fancy bottles of perfume.

'It looks really classy, doesn't it?'

'They're all fake, you know,' Rita said scornfully. 'Those scent bottles and things.'

'I know that!'

Even though the war had been over three years, toiletries and perfume still couldn't be had for love or money, unless you knew someone who was well in with the black-market.

But fake or not, it made no difference to Florence. She'd always dreamed of being a hairdresser; longed for the chance. The idea of owning her own beauty salon one day filled her with excitement. She intended to make a success of her life. Then her parents would *have* to be proud of her, wouldn't they?

Florence sighed deeply. As from today no one could dictate to her, not if she were strong and showed she was determined. And she was determined to go after what she wanted. All she had to do was cross the street, walk into the shop and ask them to take her on as an apprentice. It was as simple as that.

Brave words! Florence thought wryly, hesitating again, her feet teetering on the kerb.

'I think you're too old for an apprenticeship at eighteen,' Rita said. 'And anyway perhaps they only take girls with a high-school education?'

'Well, I won't know till I try, will I?' Florence retorted.

She couldn't back down now and throw away all her dreams. Why let silly doubts stand in her way? She'd waited too long already.

'I'm going in there now. Coming with me?'

'No fear!' Rita shook her head emphatically. 'I'll wait by here, but don't be too long, mind.'

The High Street was busy this lunchtime. Florence paused while a red double-decker bus trundled by, then a coalman's horse drawing a cart piled high with bags of coal. At a break in the traffic she dashed across.

She lingered outside the shop a moment more, peering through the windows. The window-dressing was very well done, she thought admiringly; alluring and glamorous. She was well aware that hairdressing itself was no glamorous job. It was hard work, and probably very tiring, but she wasn't afraid of hard work despite what her mother thought of her.

At that moment the shop door opened and a tall woman in a long sleek fur coat came out, blonde hair immaculate in a marcel wave. The woman had a self-assured air, with a little arrogant lift of her chin. She clipped across the pavement on high-heeled strapped shoes of patent leather and, with a flourish, opened the door of an Austin Seven parked at the kerb and climbed in.

Fascinated, Florence watched her drive away, and for some reason felt her confidence returning in full measure. That's the way *she* intended to be. Self-confident and sophisticated.

Mistress of her own fate and future. She *would* make it happen.

Florence glanced across the street at Rita and waved, then willing the butterflies to stop fluttering around in her midriff, she squared her shoulders, pushed open the shop door and went straight in, to find herself in a small reception area.

The receptionist, a young woman with bold eyes, rouged cheeks and smooth dark hair, stopped filing her nails to look at her. The enquiring smile on her lips didn't have much warmth in it.

'Yes?'

Florence glanced round at the thick pile carpet, the shiny chromium-plating on door handles and reception desk, and the black leather-upholstered chairs, and was awed despite herself. The air was faintly perfumed, and somewhere a wireless played dance music. A samba. Sounded like Edmundo Ross.

'I ... I'd like to see the proprietor.'

The receptionist looked down her nose.

'What for?' Her gaze was as cool as her smile had been.

'I...' Florence hesitated, then remembering her resolve to be self-assured and sophisticated, lifted her chin defiantly. 'It's private.'

'Oh, all right.' The girl didn't look too pleased at her sharper tone. 'What's your name, then?'

Florence gave her name, wetting her lips, feeling nervousness steal over her again.

'Wait by here,' the girl said, regaining her superior expression. 'I'll see if anyone's got time.

We're very busy, mind.'

She disappeared through a multi-coloured wooden bead curtain. Left alone Florence couldn't help fidgeting. Suppose she was on a wild goose chase? She'd feel a real fool if they turned her down flat. What would she do then? An apprenticeship in a less fashionable establishment didn't appeal to her at all. From today it was going to be first class all the way, she'd see to that.

She looked around again. It was all very posh here, though. Perhaps a shade too posh?

The receptionist returned through the bead curtain, and right behind her was a tall, well-built man with dark curly hair. He was in shirt sleeves and still held a pair of scissors. He smiled widely at Florence, even teeth very white against his tanned face.

'Well, Florence!' he said, his tone familiar as if he'd known her for years. 'What can I do for you, sweetie?'

Florence was disconcerted at his familiarity and didn't know how to answer. He was eyeing her up and down in a way that made her face start to burn. At the same time he held out a hand, and she felt obliged to grasp it, her confusion deepening. His over-friendly reception wasn't what she'd expected at all, and she didn't like it. He gripped her hand tightly and for too long, and she tugged it away, embarrassed.

'You won't forget Mrs Price-Hopkins, will you, Tony?' the receptionist interrupted loudly, glaring at Florence. 'She's only got another five minutes in the rollers, mind.'

'She's all right, Hazel, sweetie. Stop fussing, will you?' he said evenly, his gaze lingering on Florence.

'Are you the proprietor?' she asked, trying to ignore the furious expression on Hazel's face.

He put the scissors in the breast pocket of his shirt and leaned towards her.

'I'm Tony Longford, sweetie.' His voice dropped in tone to a deeper level. 'What *can* I do for you if you'll let me?'

Florence averted her gaze from the glint in his eyes.

'I'd like to apply for an apprenticeship here,' she said, pretending not to understand the *double entendre*. 'I'm eighteen, but I'm very keen to learn.'

'I'll bet you are!' His smile was crooked as his eyes slid over her.

Florence felt her colour rising again. She didn't like the way he was looking at her. It made her feel very uncomfortable and uneasy, but, at the same time, he wasn't turning her down flat. And that had to be good, didn't it?

'I work in an office at the moment,' she went on, swallowing her discomfort. 'But I want to learn the hairdressing trade. I'm sure I can give good references if you need them.'

He smiled widely. 'I think we can skip the references.' He put a finger to his top lip, inclining his head. 'Have we met before?' He shook his head. 'No. I wouldn't forget a stunning girl like you.'

'Tony!' For some reason Hazel was seething. 'You've got another client in five minutes...'

Tony ignored her. 'Come into the office. We can talk in private there.'

Taking Florence's arm, he propelled her through the bead curtain as Hazel gave another furious shout.

'Tony!'

The salon itself was much smaller than she'd expected. There were three cubicles on either side, each containing a washbasin and chair. The cubicles were screened from each other by curtains, and Florence glimpsed three or four clients where these were only partially drawn.

A thin girl with frizzy ginger hair, younger than Florence, was busy sweeping up hair cuttings. She looked up with curiosity, her glance darting from Florence to Tony Longford and back again. Florence smiled at her in a friendly way, but the girl's freckled face remained stony.

In another cubicle an older girl, willowy tall and blonde, was carefully plugging a client's hair rollers into electrical sockets hanging by flexes from a devilish-looking machine suspended from the ceiling.

Florence stared at the contraption in amazement. She'd never seen anything like it before. It didn't look at all safe. Florence glimpsed the client's face reflected in the mirror. She looked serene, not at all worried that her head was wired up to the electricity supply!

The blonde girl, preoccupied with her task, didn't glance at them until Tony called to her as they passed.

'Nancy! Be a pet. Rescue Mrs Price-Hopkins, will you? I'm going to be busy for a bit.'

She turned limpid eyes, the colour of purple pansies, in his direction, her tone languid as she replied:

'Okay, Tony.'

As Florence walked past the furthest cubicle, the curtain was pulled aside quickly, and an older woman, probably in her early forties, grinned impudently at her. She wore the same kind of overall as the others; royal blue with a fine pinstripe, but it did nothing for her tall, big-boned frame.

'You watch *him*, love,' she said loudly to Florence. 'He's got more arms than an octopus. And, he can't keep his hands to himself, either.'

Florence was startled, and even more bewildered. She glanced quickly at Tony to see his features darkened with fury.

What kind of a place was this where employees spoke about the boss in that insulting way, and to his face, too?

'Shut your big mouth, Marge!' he spluttered. 'And get back to work.'

Ignoring him, Marge winked at Florence, making her feel even more uncomfortable. She hoped Tony Longford wouldn't attach any blame to her for this. When he'd asked her to come to the office she'd begun to hope she might be successful in getting the apprenticeship after all. Now she was in two minds. The atmosphere here was charged in some way; very different from the blandness of the solicitor's office. She was beginning to feel out of her depth amongst these people.

It's no good feeling like that, she told herself

sternly. Of course she'd find things strange at first, but she'd better get used to it. This was her big chance. She'd be a fool to let anyone put her off.

'I'll only be by here, love,' Marge went on. 'If he tries any funny stuff, give us a shout.'

Florence felt her face redden, and was afraid to look at Tony again, but she was sure he cursed under his breath as he pushed her through the doorway into a small, untidy office. It was big enough to take a desk and a couple of chairs. Another door stood open behind the desk which, Florence saw, led to a storeroom.

Tony sat down, his expression still dark with anger. He pointed to the other chair.

'Have a seat.' His tone was harsh, but she could see he was struggling to regain his composure. 'Don't take any notice of Marge. She's past it herself, and she's as jealous as hell of the other girls.'

That was a peculiar explanation of an employee's behaviour, Florence thought, and hesitated to sit down. She still couldn't get over the disrespectful way Marge had spoken about him. Again she was conscious of undercurrents ebbing and flowing.

She wouldn't be put off chasing her dream, but did she really want a job at Terri's after all? There *were* other places, she reminded herself. But Terri's was the best, there was no getting away from that. And she did want this chance to make a change in her life, to make her dream come true. And besides, she wasn't a girl anymore, was she? She was eighteen, grown-up, a woman now.

Nevertheless, inside her head a cautious voice was telling her she hadn't met a man like Tony Longford before, and she needed to be wary.

She studied his face. He was smiling now, his anger seemingly forgotten. Clutching her handbag more tightly under her arm, she took a seat, automatically pulling the hem of her utility skirt down over her knees as far as it would go. He noticed the action and grinned widely at her.

'No need to be nervous, pet. I won't eat you.'

He took a cigarette from a packet of Craven 'A' on the desk and lit up. Florence watched him nervously, despite herself. Her legs felt jumpy as though primed for flight.

Don't be silly, she told herself sternly. This was her golden opportunity at last, and she must snap it up if she could. She didn't want to ruin her new start before it had even begun.

'So, sweetie, you want to be a hairdresser, eh?'

Florence gulped.

'Yes, very much. I believe I'm suited to the work. I know I'll find it interesting.'

He was silent for a moment, letting smoke rings drift to the ceiling, his gaze intent on her face, obviously sizing her up. She thought about Marge's warning. He *was* a bit of a wolf, obviously, but at eighteen she could handle that, couldn't she?

He tapped cigarette ash into a cut-glass ashtray which already contained stubs stained with bright lipstick. She wondered whose they were.

'Where do you work now, Florence?' he asked at last.

Florence explained about her present job in the

20

solicitor's office, and how much she was earning.

Tony raised his eyebrows, obviously surprised, and leaned back in his chair.

'From typist to apprentice; training all over again. That's a big step, sweetie. You'll miss the drop in wages. Are you sure it's what you want?'

Florence took a deep breath, her heart beating quickly, sensing she might be on the verge of a new venture.

'Money isn't everything, Mr Longford...'

He laughed, as though at a private joke.

'Call me Tony. Money is damned important, kid, especially if you haven't any. What about your family? Is your father working?'

Florence sat a little straighter, annoyed that he was asking irrelevant questions, though she tried to keep her feeling out of her expression.

She was applying for the job, not her family. She didn't like strangers prying into her private life, and was tempted not to answer. But maybe he was just naturally nosy. Caution warned her not to get too independent. She wouldn't want him to think she was a troublemaker.

'Yes, my father's employed ... er ... Mr Longford.' She wouldn't tell him her father ran his own business or say too much about her family. Somehow it didn't seem a good idea. And she had no intention of getting on familiar terms with him, either. 'I'm sure my parents will be understanding about my keep.' She thought that was very unlikely. 'I don't need a lot to get by.'

Tony leaned forward, cigarette dangling from his lip, and picked up a fountain pen, making a few notes on a pad before him.

21

'So they're fully prepared and able to pay the premium, then?' he asked.

Florence stared at him in dismay.

'Premium?'

She was expected to pay a premium? She felt a chill of disappointment go through her. This was something *she* wasn't prepared for, let alone her parents. If only she'd taken the trouble to make enquiries.

He looked at her speculatively, eyes squinting against the rising cigarette smoke.

'The premium at Terri's is one hundred and fifty quid, pet. They can manage that, can they?'

Florence's jaw dropped open.

'As much as that!' she managed to gasp at last. 'That's an awful lot of money, Mr Longford.'

It was enough to put a deposit on a house and secure a mortgage, as she'd heard her office supervisor, Miss Hopkins, saying to Mr Watson only last week.

'It is for a three-year training period, sweetie,' Tony went on. 'They probably ask lower premiums elsewhere, but weekly wages will be considerably lower, too, and you won't have the prestige of Terri's training at the end.'

He looked smug. 'I trained with Alexander of Paris before the war. Nancy trained in London. We both paid very high premiums for the privilege and prestige of training with top-drawer hairdressers. Consequently, training at Terri's is highly thought of everywhere.'

When she didn't speak he looked at her keenly.

'You did realise you'd have to pay a premium, didn't you, kid?'

Florence gave a confident toss of her head.

'Of course,' she said. 'But I didn't think it would be so much.'

One hundred and fifty pounds. Where on earth would she get hold of a sum like that? Certainly not from her parents.

A mental picture of her maternal grandfather came into her mind. Poor old Gramps. He had a heart of gold, but he'd never had two pennies to rub together in his life. Granddad Charlie Philpots, on the other hand, had plenty, but he'd never part with it, and she'd never get up enough courage to ask him, anyway.

'What are the weekly wages, Mr Longford?' she asked, trying to sound confident again. She felt sure she wasn't fooling Tony, though. He was too astute.

It was all so hopeless, but she wasn't quite ready to let go of her dream yet, even though she could see cracks appearing and it might collapse any minute.

'Let's see, now,' he answered, making some calculations on the pad. 'One hundred and fifty pounds over three years will give you fifteen shillings and sixpence a week for the first year...'

He paused as Florence gasped in dismay.

She couldn't help it. Fifteen and six was less than half of the wage she was getting at David Watson and Palmer. After her mother had taken the usual amount for her keep, she'd be left with nothing. Nothing at all!

Her mother was going to be angry enough, already. There was no way Florence could see Edie agreeing to take less for her keep, even if she could persuade her to fork out one hundred and fifty pounds.

Tony waited for Florence to speak. When she didn't, he went on explaining.

'The wage will rise to eighteen and six the second year, and twenty-one shillings the third year.'

Florence sat there dumbly. She didn't know what to say next. She felt numbed, too. She'd been so full of hope and dreams. She'd thought she only need reach out her hand and grasp what she wanted. Now her dream was collapsing like a Christmas balloon on Twelfth Night. She sat without moving, her future looking bleaker than ever.

She was aware of Tony watching her, but she couldn't look at him. She felt such a fool. All she wanted now was to get out of the office and the salon. She'd go with her head down, beaten before she'd started. She could hear Rita's, 'I told you so' even now.

'Your face is a picture, pet,' Tony said. 'Your family haven't got the money, have they?'

Florence kept her gaze lowered.

'No.' It was easier to lie. She couldn't and wouldn't explain it to him.

She rose awkwardly from her seat, still unable to look at him. 'I'm sorry for wasting your time, Mr Longford.'

She began to shuffle toward the door.

'Sit down again, sweetie,' he said persuasively.

Startled, Florence glanced up at him, wondering why he wasn't angry.

'You want to be a hairdresser, but your family

24

can't afford it. Okay.' He shrugged. 'There are other areas you could try. Take wig-making, for example.'

Florence stared.

'Wig-making?'

He waved her to the chair again, smiling at her astonished expression. Florence sat down. She was more curious than anything else.

'Terri's has a big reputation in wig-making,' Tony said. 'We make wigs to order, and we produce the best this side of Cardiff, perhaps even this side of London.'

'But who...'

'Lots of people want wigs.' He anticipated her question. 'Fashion, vanity, but mostly for medical reasons. You'd be surprised, kid.'

'I had no idea.'

'Look, we were going to advertise next week for a girl to train in the art and craft of wig-making at our workrooms in Dillwyn Street,' he went on quickly, 'But since you're here now, we're prepared to consider you for the post. There's no premium required and we pay a reasonable wage. What do you say?'

Florence shook her head, opening her mouth to speak, but Tony lifted his hand to forestall her refusal.

'Yes, I know, it's not quite what you had in mind, but you'd be training with the best there is, and you'd be in the hair and beauty business. Why don't you think about it, sweetie?'

Florence drew in a deep breath of disappointment mixed with desperation. It was second best again. What *was* it that fate had against her? No matter which way she turned she couldn't escape it.

She'd planned and dreamed of being a hair-dresser for so long. Could she really lower her sights now? A trainee wig-maker! It didn't seem anything much at all. The idea was crazy! She couldn't do, wouldn't do it.

'How much is the wage?' she was astonished to hear herself ask.

Tony grinned, obviously pleased.

'Shall we say nineteen and six to start? We supply the overalls, you launder them.'

'I can't decide right away,' Florence said hesitantly. 'It's a big step.'

He shrugged.

'No more so than going from typist to hair-dresser.'

Florence swallowed hard.

'I need time to think it through.'

She must weigh up the pros and cons. It would mean changing her whole way of thinking. Giving in to the idea of being second best. How could she do that? This was the fight of her life so far, she felt it.

And yet, what was the alternative? She had no hope of raising the premium. It was either take up wig-making training or give up altogether.

Florence felt real pain in her chest at the thought of giving in, surrendering to fate, capitulating to a future as a nonentity.

No! Going back to her boring office job was impossible now. She hated it, was weary of it. She couldn't do that anymore. There *had* to be some kind of a change in her life. Not the one she'd

26

dreamed of, longed for, but there had to be something better.

Tony leaned back, his smile gone.

'Well, kid, like I said, we'll be advertising for a girl to train next week. I don't know when a chance like this will come again.'

Florence felt she was being torn two ways. Let the dream go, a small voice inside was urging her. Take what you can get. After all, it might prove worthwhile.

Florence lifted her chin, making up her mind.

'All right, Mr Longford, I accept the post,' she said, trying to sound happy and grateful at the opportunity he offered. 'How long is the training period?'

She had decided and *was* glad. It was childish to be muddled and indecisive. She was grown-up, in charge of her life, and she had to be able to take chances, gauge risks.

'Usually two years,' he said, smiling again. 'Okay, Florence, pet, when can you start?'

Florence swallowed hard, taken by surprise at her own sudden decision. She'd done it! She was on her way. She felt a sudden burst of elation which seemed to wipe away her earlier dis-appointment and despair, but tried to control her expression, not wanting to seem like a silly kid in front of him.

She had to swallow a couple of times more before she could answer.

'I'll have to give a week's notice to my present employer. I could start a week on Monday, Mr Longford.'

He made a note in a diary lying on the desk,

27

then stood up, grinning.

'Right then, sweetie.' He came round the desk and opened the office door. Florence stood up too, eager to get outside to tell Rita the news. 'Report to the workrooms in Dillwyn Street a week Monday,' Tony said. 'Nine on the dot, mind.'

Florence wondered if Rita would laugh at her for taking less than she'd aimed for. Well, let her, Florence thought haughtily. Let them all scoff. At least I'm making my own decision, living my own life.

She'd made her momentous decision and nothing was going to stop her now, Florence told herself, yet her legs trembled as she walked through the doorway into the salon. She wasn't looking forward to the inevitable row with her mother over leaving her job. And wait until she learned there would be a substantial cut in her keep. Nineteen and six wouldn't stretch far, not with fares up from the Mumbles, and a little bit of food during the day.

Florence sighed. Goodbye to that New Look two-piece suit she'd been planning to have made. It would be make-do and mend with a vengeance from now on.

The salon had grown busier since she'd been in the office. Now there were more clients, smartly dressed women, seated in the waiting area reading magazines. No one took any notice of her as she walked out on shaky legs.

In the front reception area Hazel was still tending her nails. She lifted her nose in the air and sniffed disdainfully as Florence appeared.

'How did you get on, then?'

Florence had the impulse to tell her to mind her own business, but she didn't want to get off on the wrong foot with anyone. Hazel had probably worked in the salon a long time, and might try to turn Tony Longford against her.

'Monday week I start learning the art and craft of wig-making, if you must know,' she answered as civilly as she could, pulling on her gloves and pushing her handbag securely under her arm.

'Oh! Well, I wouldn't count on it, like,' Hazel said with a sneer. 'You don't want to listen to anything Tony says. He's not the boss around here, mind.'

Florence was about to open the street door, but stopped short, staring at the other girl.

'What do you mean?'

'Lillian's the boss here. What she says goes. She's the master wig-maker at Dillwyn Street. If she don't like you, you're out. Double quick, too, I can tell you!'

'Who's Lillian?'

'Lillian Longford. Tony's wife. She owns Terri's, lock, stock and barrel. He's just a hairdresser around here, like the others, see. Lillian likes to pick her own trainees, so don't be surprised if she shows you the door come Monday week.'

Florence felt her heartbeat slow down rapidly, assailed by sudden doubts again. Had she been foolish, duped? Was it all a pipe-dream after all?

She stared hard at Hazel, seeing the triumphant gleam in her eyes, and was partially reassured.

'I don't believe you!' she said forcefully.

Hazel was only saying that to be spiteful,

Florence decided. For some reason the girl had taken an instant dislike to her, though she couldn't think why. Florence wasn't after *her* job.

Hazel looked disdainful again.

'Well, suit yourself! Only don't say I didn't warn you.'

Rita was nowhere to be seen in the street. Florence, glancing at her wristwatch, wasn't surprised. She hurried up High Street towards the bus stop outside the station to catch a bus across town to the office.

She was cutting it fine already, and she had a lot to think about before she got there. To start at wig-making on Monday week meant she must give in her notice this afternoon.

Her heart fluttered at the prospect. Mr Watson might be put out. She quite liked him and didn't want to upset him. He was a friend of her father's. It was through her father's influence she'd got the typist's job at David Watson and Palmer in the first place. And that had galled her, too.

Giving in her notice would be the final step. It would be burning her boats good and proper.

She thought about Hazel's warning again. The receptionist had been exaggerating for her own mysterious ends, Florence was sure, and she wouldn't let the girl's spiteful words upset her.

By the time she boarded the bus, her mind was firmly made up. She would stake her all, and take her chances on Tony Longford's word, because no matter what her reception might be at Dillwyn Street a week Monday, she was finished with her old life.

Perhaps her dream of being a hairdresser was beyond her. Well, never mind! There was nothing stopping her learning how to be a master wig-maker. She'd be the best, the very best!

CHAPTER 2

Florence sniffed gently at the aroma of freshly brewed coffee permeating the air of the Burlington café, and sighed with deep pleasure. Ordinarily the delicious smell would have given her an appetite like a horse, but this evening she was far too excited to think about food.

From the tip of her nose right down to her toes, she tingled with excitement, and couldn't keep still on her seat. There was a permanent silly grin on her face, and she'd noticed Ken glancing at her from time to time in puzzlement, but she couldn't help it. The grin was set firm.

She *was* now feeling very happy and pleased with her day. A new future was opening up before her; opportunity and independence, and she'd made it happen by her own efforts.

She couldn't help feeling proud of herself. Yes, proud! She had every reason to be proud that she'd risen above her earlier bitter disappointment. Everything would turn out for the best, she was certain of it. She'd make the most of any opportunity she was given.

And that wasn't all of her pleasure, either. She was sharing a wonderful evening out with Ken, and the occasion seemed just perfect for him to ask her to get engaged. Maybe the ring was nestling in his breast pocket this very minute!

She felt the tingling excitement again as she

33

watched him consult the menu. He looked so handsome and immaculate in grey flannel slacks and navy blazer with the badge of the Dunvant Cricket Club on the breast pocket. His blond hair, neatly trimmed, gleamed like gold. She knew her friends envied her having such an attractive boyfriend. Rita for one. She sighed again, feeling smug as she imagined how wonderful he would look in formal attire for their wedding.

Craning her neck, she looked around at the other people dining out at the Burlington, wondering if they too were celebrating something exciting.

'Stop gawking and fidgeting like a silly child, Florence, for goodness sake,' Ken said in a lowered voice, handing her the menu. 'People will think you've never eaten out before.'

She smiled widely.

'Well, I don't often, do I? This is a real treat for me, Ken. Thank you. I'm really excited.'

She was about to say she didn't have much appetite, either, but this meal was part of his birthday present to her, so she wouldn't spoil it for him. She'd taste everything just to please him.

'And don't talk so loudly,' he said in an undertone. 'People are looking at us.'

'It's my birthday and I don't care.'

'Well, I do,' he replied. He straightened the knot in his tie, glancing around at the other diners out of the corners of his eyes. 'You're eighteen today, so act grown-up for goodness' sake. People will think we don't know which fork to use.'

34

Florence wanted to laugh out loud at his obsession with other people's opinions, but suppressed the urge because she knew he wouldn't like it.

He eyed her suspiciously.

'Let's have some decorum, Florence,' he said, though his lips hardly moved. 'You're showing me up.'

She straightened her face with difficulty. Ken took life so seriously, and sometimes she forgot. It would be different when they were married, away from his parents.

She had to admit Bernard and Ursula Henderson were rather snobbish and uppity, but Florence was confident that, once married, Ken would soon settle into *her* ways.

He was staring hard at her again and she quickly turned her attention to the menu, going through it very carefully. Even though she wasn't hungry, she wanted to remember this special meal all her life; remember the wonderful evening when Ken proposed. He would be very correct about it, she knew that, correct and solemn. She hoped she wouldn't start giggling at the crucial moment. Ken would never forgive her for that.

She still hadn't made up her mind what to order when the waitress came to their table. Florence was taking one last look at the menu when Ken gave a hushed, but definitely irritated cough to attract her attention.

'Florence?'

She looked up, beaming at him.

'Yes, darling?'

His face flushed, and he darted an embarrassed glance at the waitress.

'Give your order, please.'

When the waitress was out of earshot, having taken their order, Ken looked at Florence, his mouth a straight line.

'I wish you wouldn't be familiar with me in public, Florence, especially in front of the waitresses. I particularly dislike that endearment. It sounds so vulgar and common, and I have a position to keep up, you know that.'

'Oh, Ken!' Florence wanted to laugh out loud again, but held herself in check. 'You're not on the town council yet. I don't suppose anyone here has even noticed us.'

He looked smug.

'Of course they have. My family is well-known in this town. Respected and influential, too.' He gave a furtive glance around the room. 'I expect there're quite a few here who know who I am.'

'Why don't you relax, Ken?' Florence said, with a toss of her head, suddenly impatient and speaking more sharply than she intended. 'Let's enjoy ourselves. It's my eighteenth birthday!'

'Then start acting your age,' he said in a low voice, his face still flushed. 'You're making me look a fool.'

It flashed through Florence's mind that he was ashamed of her, and for a moment she was shocked and hurt.

'Perhaps you'd rather be here with someone else?' she asked, her voice rising.

'Keep your voice down!' he hissed angrily, leaning forward slightly to emphasise his words.

'Of course I don't want to be with anyone else. But you might be a little more considerate, Florence. Be a little more sophisticated, like your cousin Rita.'

'*What?*'

Florence couldn't help letting out a hoot of derisive laughter, which made Ken squirm on his seat.

'Our Rita, sophisticated! You don't know her very well, then.'

'Well, she knows how to behave in public,' Ken muttered angrily. 'I noticed particularly when we were having tea at your mother's the other Sunday.'

'That's not sophistication, Ken,' Florence burst out. 'That's timidity. Our Rita is scared of her own shadow. Talk about a white rabbit!'

It was true. Poor Rita. They were best friends as well as cousins, but Florence always felt sorry for her. Auntie Sybil dominated her daughter, hardly letting Rita have a single opinion of her own. Florence knew that if she had Auntie Sybil for a mother, she'd have left home long ago. She wouldn't be able to stand it. At least her own mother might treat her lightly, but she didn't try to run Florence's life for her.

'Rita's a mouse,' she went on. 'She doesn't know how to stand up for herself, but I do. Catch me kow-towing to anybody, I don't think!'

Those were brave words, Florence knew. She still had to tell her parents what she had done this very day. Her insides churned each time she thought about it, so she wouldn't let herself think, not this evening anyway. This evening was for fun and enjoyment. She had grown up at last.

Ken said nothing, but looked sulky, the way he always did when he lost an argument. It was Florence's policy to ignore such behaviour in him. When they were married he'd learn to be different.

The meal came and they ate it in relative silence. Florence longed to chat, but Ken kept his gaze on his plate, his expression warning her she must curb her exuberance, at least until they were at the coffee stage. Then she'd tell him her news.

The waitress brought their coffee at last. Florence watched Ken spoon sugar into his cup, searching her mind for the right words to begin. Now she was on the point of telling him, she hesitated. He seemed moody tonight and ill at ease. Maybe she could guess why, she told herself gleefully. It wasn't every day a man proposed to a girl. It must be nerve-wracking.

'Ken?' she began. 'Remember how I've always been on about going into hairdressing...'

He looked up from his coffee.

'Oh, not that again! You have a respectable and good-paying job with David Watson and Palmer. In a few years you could be managing the typing pool. You have a future there.'

'No I haven't, Ken,' Florence plunged in. 'Because I've chucked it in today.'

He looked at her for a moment, then smiled for the first time that evening. He has a gorgeous smile, Florence reflected dreamily, momentarily distracted from her purpose of confessing all.

'This is mid-September, Florence, not the first day of April. Your little joke has backfired.'

'I'm not joking, Ken.' She shook her head, solemn now. 'I went to see about an apprenticeship today.'

She wetted her lips, swallowing hard, hating having to admit to him that she'd failed.

'I didn't get an apprenticeship, but I did get something better.'

It *was* better, she told herself firmly, and she had to believe that. She'd make a success of it. She could do it!

'I start as a trainee wig-maker a week Monday,' she went on hurriedly. 'I gave in my notice to David Watson this afternoon.'

Ken was staring at her speechless, his mouth open.

'Working in the hair and beauty business is what I've always wanted, Ken, you know that,' she said defensively. 'I was never happy in that office. It's stifling. I'm going to work at something that really interests me. You're always telling me you intend to go after what you want in life. Well, me too!'

She paused, staring at his stunned expression, thinking he was bound to be surprised at first.

'Aren't you going to congratulate me, then?'

'Congratulate you?' He stared wide-eyed. 'Are you mad, Florence?' His mouth tightened into a straight line. 'You must be, if this isn't some kind of stupid joke. *Wig-making!* For God's sake! Are you really serious?'

Florence flicked back her hair, annoyed at his derisive tone.

'Well, of course! You must have realised how serious I am about it.'

She'd expected him to be surprised, but then she'd also thought he'd be as excited as she was about her new future. She'd talked about it often enough, hadn't she? Of course, it wasn't what she'd planned, what she'd always wanted, but never mind.

But now he was looking at her as though she were just a big kid, the way her parents often looked at her. It was disappointing, to say the least. Why did she feel the need to defend her actions, especially to Ken? She'd counted on him as her one ally.

'I start at Terri's workrooms in Dillwyn Street a week Monday,' she said defiantly.

'Terri's!' Ken was aghast. He almost rose from his seat. 'That's where *my* mother has her hair done, for God's sake.'

'Yes, I know, but I won't be in the High Street salon...'

'I don't care! I won't have it, Florence.' He shook his head emphatically. He was more upset than she realised, because his voice was rising. Heads were turning in their direction, and he hadn't even noticed. 'It's out of the question.'

'Ken!'

He pushed his half-filled coffee cup away from him with an impatient gesture.

'First thing Monday morning, you'll tell David Watson you've changed your mind,' he went on firmly. 'Tell him you want to withdraw your notice. It'll be all right, because he knows your father.'

Florence felt her jaw drop open. She couldn't believe what she was hearing. Not only was Ken opposing her, he was trying to dictate to her, as well. Much as she loved him, she wasn't having any of that!

'I'll do no such thing!' she retorted, tossing her head so vehemently that her hair, in a sleek pageboy style, swung around her shoulders.

'Yes, you will, Florence, or...'

Ken's jaw jutted forward aggressively. Florence stared. She'd never seen *that* kind of expression on his face before. It was hardly one of a man about to get engaged. She'd been so certain he'd ask this evening. Now she'd got him into a tizzy, and knowing him, he'd sulk for hours.

She felt keen disappointment, but, at the same time, his attitude was getting her back up. They'd had little spats before, lovers' tiffs, as she liked to call them, nothing serious, but this looked as though it might spoil her special evening. Even so, she couldn't let it go unchallenged.

'Or what, Ken?'

He took a deep breath, as if trying to be reasonable this time, and her hopes rose a little. Could she talk him round after all? She was sure she could.

'Florence, being a ... a wig-maker, or a hairdresser for that matter, just isn't a suitable occupation for a politician's wife.'

'*What?*'

He fingered his tie again somewhat nervously, while Florence held her breath in anticipation.

'I was building myself up to ask you something this evening,' he went on. 'Something important to both of us.'

'Oh, Ken, darling...!'

'Hush!' He glanced round.

Grinning from ear to ear, because she couldn't help it, Florence leaned across the table and grabbed excitedly at his hand.

'What were you going to ask me, Ken? What? What?'

He eased his hand away from her grasp, embarrassed.

'I thought it time we made it official, you know what I mean, our future together, but now, Florence, now I have to stop and question.'

Florence leaned back slowly in her seat, staring at him. Was that it? Was that what she'd been waiting for? She'd never pretended to herself that Ken was in any way romantic by nature, despite his admirable looks, but was this the best he could do? He sounded as though he was addressing one of those boring political meetings he forever attended, rather than asking her to get engaged. And what did he mean – he had to stop and question?

'Question? Ken, what are you trying to say?'

'I would've liked us to get engaged, Florence, but...'

'But! But!' She felt heat rise in her neck and face, and fought hard to keep her temper in control.

'Keep your voice down, will you! We're attracting attention again.'

He glanced at his watch, then picked up the bill from the table where the waitress had left it.

'We'd better make our way to the Grand,' he went on. 'I don't want to rush getting into our seats. Latecomers at the theatre always make fools of themselves.'

Florence was speechless.

Ken got up from the table and, without looking at her again, made his way towards the cash till. After a moment staring open-mouthed at his back, Florence rose hastily and followed.

They walked down Union Street. Usually they went arm in arm, but this evening Florence stepped stiffly at his side, keeping daylight between them.

He'd like to get engaged, but... The words kept ringing in her ears. She'd never felt so flat and let down in her life. Serve him right if she refused to get engaged after all!

As they passed the wide bow window of the Number 10 public house at the bottom of the street, Ken turned to look at her for the first time since leaving the café, his expression aggrieved.

'I should have thought you'd understand my position, Florence. You know what I want to do with my life, what my ambitions are.'

'What about *my* ambitions?' she asked hotly, as she stalked along beside him.

Her legs felt like sticks now, stiff and awkward. She wasn't sure she wanted to sit for the next hour and a half watching some silly play. Everything was spoiled, and she had been so looking forward to the evening.

'Don't be silly, there's a good girl,' he said deprecatingly. 'I'm talking seriously, now. A man's image is very important when trying to get on in politics. People expect high standards. I was quite happy for you to work as a shorthand typist whilst we're engaged, but as soon as we're married, I'd expect you to be at home, running my household.'

'What?'

'So you see, Florence, don't you, this idea of yours to become a trainee wig-maker or whatever, is out of the question? I'll have to insist, dear, that you withdraw your notice as soon as possible or...'

There it was again! That veiled threat. Florence was growing hot with indignation, yet for the moment words failed her. And that was really something unusual for her, she had to admit. She was stunned. She had to admit that, too.

They'd reached the Grand Theatre on Singleton Street, and walked past the queue waiting to go up into the 'gods'. She and Ken, of course, had very good seats in the circle. They might as well have been seats in the nearby bus station for all the joy she was getting out of it, she thought peevishly.

All the pleasure she'd expected to feel at this moment was missing. The anticipated thrill of being asked to get engaged was conspicuous by its absence. What a wretched evening this was turning out to be. Her new disappointment was like a fishbone stuck in her throat. She was almost choking on it.

They took their seats with plenty of time to spare. She was conscious of Ken sitting very still beside her. There was plenty of energetic conversation going on around them, but they were silent, and the longer the silence went on the more difficult it was to break, Florence found.

He would never take her hand until the lights went down anyway, but tonight she knew there would be no such closeness between them. She felt a tension building up inside her and longed to relieve it by clearing the air between them. It gave her just enough courage to speak at last.

'What did you mean, Ken?'

Out of the side of his mouth he muttered: 'This is neither the time nor the place, Florence. Enjoy the play.'

She opened her mouth to protest but at that moment the house-lights went down, and on stage the curtains parted.

Feeling more like a zombie than a human being, Florence sat motionless. What the play was about she had not the slightest idea. All she could think of was Ken and his unspoken threat to their future.

When the first interval came he startled her by asking, coldly, she thought, whether she would like a drink in the bar. Florence paused, suddenly remembering that from today she could, respectably escorted by a gentleman, enter a bar and have a drink. But she shook her head. There was nothing to celebrate tonight, and she only drank lemonade anyway.

'Do you mind if I go and have one?' he asked.

Florence straightened her spine.

'You do as you please, Ken,' she answered, in a spiky tone.

He was away from his seat perhaps only ten minutes, but they seemed endless to Florence. She was half-tempted to get up and walk out. That would teach him a lesson!

But she still sat there. She couldn't leave without knowing exactly what was in his mind, and she was determined that before the evening was over, before they said goodnight, she would have it out with him. They'd had minor spats before, but never an outright row, and this was what they needed now, she was convinced. It was what *she* needed anyway.

At last the final curtain came down. Florence felt irritable with the slowness of the audience in leaving, longing as she was to get outside to the relative privacy of the fresh air.

Ken took her arm as they descended the staircase, the merest pressure on her elbow, and she guessed it was more for appearance than anything else.

He'd borrowed his father's car for the evening and had parked it on cleared ground opposite the Number 10, where the Exeter public house once stood before the Blitz. They walked towards it, the silence still wrapped tightly around each of them separately.

When they were travelling along the Oystermouth Road towards the Mumbles, Florence found more courage to speak out.

'Ken, we have to talk...'

'Not now, Florence, I'm driving. There's a time and place for everything.'

As they approached the driveway of her mother's guest house, Florence spoke again, her tone sharpened by the determination she was feeling. This couldn't be allowed to go on, and she'd be a weak little fool if she let it.

'Don't go up the drive, Ken. Park on the road.

I'm going to have my say whether you like it or not.'

He pulled in at the kerb, applied the hand-brake, then just sat staring through the windscreen.

Florence swallowed hard, feeling a thickening in her throat. Despite her determination, tears were not far away. She fought hard against the threat. She wouldn't make an exhibition of herself by bursting into tears, like a child. They had to discuss their disagreement sensibly and calmly. Ken must understand how strongly she felt about the change she'd made in her life. She would make him understand.

'I've no intention of withdrawing my notice from David Watson and Palmer,' she began, willing the tremor in her voice to steady itself. 'I've waited for years to do this; years.'

'You're only eighteen now,' he said, irritably.

She viewed his irritability with some hope. At least he was finished with that cold silence, something she'd been unable to break through. A healthy argument was what they needed.

'You know what I mean, Ken. The hair and beauty business is something I really want to get into. I hate being a typist. I'm lucky to be taken on as a trainee wig-maker at my age. I thought you'd be glad for me.'

He turned his head towards her, but it was too dark to see his expression.

'But *wig-making* of all things. It's ... absurd, and it's common, as well.'

There was such disdain in his voice that Florence felt a spurt of irritation herself. It

47

blotted out any possibility of tears now.

'That's nonsense, Ken!'

His parents' snobbery had certainly rubbed off on him. She wondered how long it would take for her influence to eradicate it.

'Hairdressers and wig-makers are decent, respectable, hard-working people. Anyone would think I was taking a job as a dance hostess, or something.'

'Don't be facetious, Florence. It doesn't flatter you.'

'Look, Ken,' she tried a placating tone. 'It's what I want to do. I'll make a success of it, I know I will. And think what a feather in your cap it would be to have a successful businesswoman for a wife.'

'Bloody hell, Florence!'

She jumped at the violence in his voice. Ken never usually lost control of himself enough to swear, not out loud anyway.

'Are you such a dim-brain that you don't understand?' he rasped at her. 'You're talking absolute rubbish. How can *you* make a success of anything? Your head's too full of childish day-dreams.'

'How dare you speak to me like that!'

'Huh! It's the way I speak to a naughty child, Florence.' He calmed down suddenly, as though remembering himself and his blessed image. 'You're eighteen, but I'm wondering if you'll ever grow up.'

His tone was still one of deep contempt, which made her even more furious.

She fumbled at the door handle, struggling to

open it, but her fingers seemed awkward in her fury. He reached across and did it for her, and Florence clambered out onto the pavement at ungainly speed, leaving the door swinging open.

'Well, close the door, then,' he shouted.

'You're so damned clever, Ken, close it yourself!' It gave her a lot of satisfaction to swear.

She stalked up the drive, then heard him climb out and walk around the car to close the near door.

She turned.

'I won't thank you for a lovely evening, Ken, because it was horrible. And you're horrible! Goodbye!'

CHAPTER 3

Florence rose with a headache, dull and heavy. Her legs were heavy too, as she swung them out of bed. What was wrong? Then she remembered the events of last night, and tears began to swell as she sat hunched on the edge of the bed.

She'd quarrelled with Ken, and she still had her mother's wrath to face.

How bitterly she regretted losing her temper with Ken, and stalking off. How stupid she'd been; how childish. She'd ruined what should've been a wonderful, exciting evening. Her behaviour had solved nothing between them. Despite everything they'd said, she longed to see him again to make up. He was probably sorry, too. He'd telephone her before she left for the office, she was certain.

Having washed and dressed, she heard the quarter to eight gong sound for breakfast. Although it was September the guest house was still full. She usually took breakfast in the big dining-room with the guests, liking the company, the chatter, and the excitement that exuded from people on holiday. It usually set her up for the day. This morning, though, she couldn't face that cheerfulness. Nor did she want the isolation of the Philpots' private kitchenette adjacent to their back sitting-room. Instead she chose to have breakfast in the big pleasant kitchen, where her mother was supervising the cooking of guests' breakfasts, and organising the staff of three.

Florence flopped onto a chair at the scrubbed table, and put her elbows on it, dejectedly.

'What's the matter with you, then?' Edie Philpots asked, 'You've got a face like a wet weekend in Skewen.'

Florence glanced warily at Vera Pugh, standing at the stove. She was such a nosy parker, Florence was loath to say anything in front of her.

'Where's Dad?' she asked evasively.

'He was up early,' Edie said. 'Had his breakfast ages ago. He's looking at that faulty cistern on the top floor. You'd better get a move on with your breakfast, my girl, if you want him to give you a lift to work.'

Breakfast! The idea made her feel sick now. She was only hanging about in case the telephone rang.

Her mother regarded her keenly.

'Florence? What *is* the matter?'

She was saved replying by the entrance of Tommy, whose hair was standing on end. He'd obviously tumbled out of bed and shrugged straight into his clothes. Taking a closer look, Florence could see a grubby line on his neck almost hidden by the collar of his shirt. Florence thought he ought to know better at fifteen, and had previously complained to her mother about her brother's scruffiness.

'Don't rush him,' Edie had said, wistfully. 'In a couple of years he'll discover girls, then everything will change.'

He grabbed a kitchen chair now and plonked himself down on it.

'Any chance of two eggs this morning, Mam?' he asked.

'Very funny!' said Edie, with a sniff. 'You and Florence will have to share one between you this morning. I haven't had time to get the rations.'

'Oh, Mam! There's a bowl of eggs in the larder, mun,' he said, aggrieved.

'Those belong to the guests, bought off their ration books, as well you know, Tommy.'

'He can have my half,' Florence offered despondently. 'I don't feel like breakfast, anyway. I'll manage with a cup of tea.'

Edie tutted. 'Breakfast is the most important meal of the day, Florence. Have some toast anyway.'

She ate half a piece of toast just to please her mother, but it tasted like cardboard in her mouth. She leaned an elbow on the table as she ate, chin in hand, disconsolate.

Tommy was eyeing her warily as he tucked into his boiled egg and thinly cut bread with a scraping of butter and margarine blended together.

'Have you got a cold, our Flo? If you have, keep away from me. The scouts' jamboree is next week. I don't want to miss that.'

Florence glanced at him frostily.

'No, I haven't got a cold,' she said. 'I'm grown up now, with grown-up worries; something you wouldn't know anything about.'

Edie turned from the stove to stare at her. Vera Pugh turned from the washing up, too, eyes suddenly bright with curiosity.

'What worries have *you* got, then, except being late for work?' Edie asked sharply.

Her eyes on Vera, Florence shook her head.

'Nothing that won't keep, Mam.'

'Tommy!' Edie said hastily. 'If you've finished your breakfast go up and wash that dirty neck, for goodness sake!'

She looked at Vera.

'Go and check the dining-room, will you, Vera, lovey. See if there are any latecomers waiting for breakfast, and collect the crockery.'

Obviously disappointed, Vera left the kitchen, her glance darting from Edie to Florence and back again, as though those glances might glean more information.

'Now then!' Edie said when Tommy and Vera had gone. 'What's troubling you, Florence?'

Before she could stop herself, Florence burst into tears. Edie came immediately and put an arm around her shoulders, her voice gentle and sympathetic.

'Lovey, what is it?'

'Ken and I have had a terrible quarrel, Mam.'

'Oh, is that all?' Edie turned away, with an impatient tut, moving back to the stove. 'I thought it was something serious.'

Florence sniffed miserably. 'It is serious to me, Mam! It's ruined my life ... well, almost. Ken was going to ask me to get engaged, and like a spoilt child I ruined it. He made me cross and I said some awful things to him.'

She hoped her mother wouldn't ask her the reason for the quarrel. She hated lying to her mother or even being evasive. It went against the grain. But she sensed the time wasn't right to drop her bombshell. That could wait a few more days, or even a week, or maybe…

'Engaged?' Edie came back to the table, and pulling out a chair, sat down. 'To Ken Henderson?' She shook her head. 'No. Your father and I wouldn't approve of that, Florence, so it's just as well you didn't commit yourself.'

Florence sat up straight, her mother's words making her forget her wretchedness for a moment.

'I'm eighteen, Mam, don't forget. I can do as I like.'

'Don't count on that, Florence,' Edie said, pulling in her chin, her lips tightening. 'Until you're twenty-one and while you're living under our roof you'll do as your father and I say.'

'That's not fair, Mam!'

'Fair or not, that's the way things are. You're too young yet. There's plenty of time for you to meet others, plenty of time to get engaged.'

'Others? I don't want others,' Florence said defiantly. 'I … I'm in love with Ken. I'm going to marry *him*.'

Edie shook her head again. The gesture had a finality about it that suggested the issue was not open for debate.

'I don't think so, Florence.'

Florence could feel her temper rising and tried to quell it. Her mother was trying to dictate to her. It was Auntie Sybil and Rita all over again. Well, she wouldn't stand for it!

'What could you possibly have against Ken? He

55

comes from a good family. He's very...' She was going to say handsome, but something told her Edie wouldn't be impressed by that attribute. 'Very presentable and respectable. He's clever and ambitious. He'll be someone important some day.'

'Your father doesn't like him.'

'*What?*'

'In fact, he dislikes him a lot,' Edie said firmly. 'He doesn't even approve of you going out with him. I told him it'll blow over in time and I was right, wasn't I?'

'Blow over!' Florence burst out, her hackles rising again. 'Mam, I'm not a child, you know. I haven't just got a crush. I'm in love. Surely even *you* understand about love?'

A look of anger flashed across Edie's face.

'Better than you do, my girl,' she said sharply. 'Your father's got good reason to dislike him. He's sure Ken's...'

She paused, averting her face.

'Ken's what, Mam?' Florence sat up straight, ready to defend him against all slurs.

Edie wetted her lips, a guarded look crossing her face.

'Ken's...'

She paused again.

'He's not turned communist, Mam, if that's what you're worried about,' Florence cried out. She knew it was fashionable for young people today to spout that rubbish, young and not so young, too. 'Ken's got more sense.'

Edie looked impatient again.

'Don't be silly, Florence. It's not his politics.

56

Huh! If only it were that…!' She hesitated, then rushed on, 'He's … he's not good enough for you, that's what,' she said firmly and loudly. 'And I'm glad you've finished with him.'

Florence jumped up from the table, thoroughly angry.

'Not good enough? That's utter tosh! How can you say that with his family background?'

She flounced to the door, suddenly feeling a very defiant and independent streak coming on. She'd worried so much about her parents' reaction when they discovered she'd chucked her job, but the last thing she'd expected was their opposition to her getting engaged to Ken. Being grown up was more complicated than she'd realised.

'I have *not* finished with him!' she said emphatically. 'We had a disagreement, that's all. We'll make up soon.'

She paused at the door, glaring back at her mother still sitting at the table.

'Tell Dad I don't want a lift with him this morning. I'd rather catch the Mumbles train.' She sniffed. 'And, I *will* marry Ken! So there!'

CHAPTER 4

Rita Bevan neatly folded her napkin and placed it beside her plate, at the same time giving a reassuring smile to her father sitting quietly at the table just finishing off a second cup of tea. She glanced at her mother who was putting the last crumb of *teisen plât* into her mouth. It was quite pleasant this Saturday dinnertime, quite restful really, just the three of them at the table.

When the whole family sat down at mealtimes it often made her head ache listening to her grandfather, Charlie Philpots, continually grumbling and sniping either at his wife, Hilda, or at Rita's father; mostly at her father.

Nag, nag, nag! And poor old Da didn't deserve it. She often wondered how he put up with it. He was too easygoing, that was the trouble. Too easily dominated. Like she was herself. Florence was always urging her to get out from under her mother's thumb, now that she was eighteen and grown-up. If only she could! But she wouldn't know where to begin.

Rita couldn't help blaming her mother for letting it happen; letting Granddad Charlie get away with making Da's life a misery. Da served long hours in the shop, but Granddad was never satisfied; never had a good word for him.

The annoying thing was, her mother Sybil was a match for Granddad any day of the week. On

59

the very rare occasions when they did clash, Sybil always came off best. Well, Rita reflected sadly, they were cut from the same piece of cloth, weren't they?

'Rita!' Sybil's grating tones made her jump guiltily. 'If you've finished, leave the table properly. Don't just sit there daydreaming.'

'Yes, Mam.'

Sybil tutted irritably. 'And don't say mam. That's common, that is. Say mother. That's proper. You don't hear me calling your grandmother mam, do you?'

'No, Ma ... Mother,' Rita answered wearily.

She'd learned quite early in her young life that, where Sybil was concerned, it was wise to think first before speaking. Her mother could get crotchety very quickly, just like Granddad, and then life wouldn't be worth living for hours after, sometimes days.

Rita often wished, in moments of despair, that Granddad would pop off, even though he was only in his early sixties. She felt no guilt at thinking these dark thoughts about him. He ruled their lives with his domineering ways, and though Sybil could put him in his place when she wanted to, she wouldn't challenge him too often, and Rita knew why.

It was Granddad's ironmongery business. Da's job, their livelihood, depended on her grandfather's whim. And the most important factor of all, at least to Sybil, was that Granddad had promised to will the business to her, but being such a cantankerous old devil he could change his mind any time. And probably would anyway, just for spite! Then Uncle William would get the shop, and that frightened her mother stiff.

It would be better if Uncle William did get it, Rita mused. The shop hadn't progressed in thirty years. That's what her father said anyway. It was still a dark and dingy old-fashioned ironmongers. Nothing for her mother to be hoity-toity about.

Uncle William had the knack in business. He'd bring it up to date, and make something of it. Then they'd all benefit, because Uncle William was a fair man. He wouldn't let his sister be the loser.

She glanced warily at her mother. She ought to say something nice about the meal because in fairness to Sybil, she managed well on the rationing and was a good cook.

'That was a lovely dinner, Mother, thank you.'

Sybil's small mouth pursed itself into a tight prune-shape of disapproval.

'Lunch, Rita. Lunch, not dinner. Only common people call the midday meal dinner.'

Rita checked a sign of irritation, knowing better than to let it show. Her mother had started this silly affectation since striking up a friendship with the wife of the town clerk, whilst on a WI outing. Rita had found secret amusement in it at first, but now the joke was wearing a bit thin.

She'd be glad when she met some nice boy, got married and had a place of her own. Getting away from her mother had been her dream since she was about ten years old.

'Where's Gran and Granddad today, anyway?' she asked, hoping to side-track her mother's thoughts.

'Down the Mumbles at your Uncle William's. That Edie invited them to din ... lunch.' Sybil sniffed. 'I know what she's after, though. She must think I'm cabbage-looking or something.'

Sybil always referred to Florence's mother as 'that Edie', which was very unfair, Rita thought, because Auntie Edie had shown them nothing but kindness. Uncle William was always popping up to Brynmill with spare vegetables for them from his market-garden. With food shortages still so bad, her mother ought to be grateful. But not her!

'They're trying to talk my father into changing his will,' Sybil went on, her cheeks reddening. 'That's what they're up to.'

'Now, Syb,' Ronnie said gently. 'You're being suspicious for nothing. They *are* William's parents as well, mind. I'm only too glad he's trying to make it up with his father after all these years, especially for Hilda's sake. It doesn't do for a family to be split. Besides, it's a change for them.' Under his breath he added, 'And a bloody good change for us, as well.'

Sybil's sharp ears caught it.

'Ronnie! If you've finished your lunch, get on with the washing-up.'

It was a pity her mother couldn't see further than the end of her nose, Rita thought angrily. And what a nose! Not for the first time was she thankful she followed her father in looks. Sybil had inherited Charlie Philpots' beak-like nose as well as his hawk-like temperament. Whenever they sat down at the table together, Rita couldn't help comparing them to birds of prey. Or, she thought, with malicious fancy, two vultures feeding off other people's weaknesses.

Sybil turned to Rita.

'I want you to help me lengthen my black skirt before the next WI meeting. Mrs Prosser-Rees is a very smart woman, mind. I notice her skirts are quite long. I don't want her to think I'm old-fashioned.'

'Ouch! Watch where you're sticking those pins, Rita!' Sybil exclaimed irritably. 'You stuck one in my leg, then.'

'Sorry, Ma ... Mother,' Rita mumbled through a mouthful of pins as she squatted on the mat in the living-room. Her mother wouldn't keep still, that was the trouble.

There ought to be something better for an eighteen-year-old girl to do on a Saturday afternoon than alter her mother's skirts, Rita thought peevishly. If only she had a boyfriend, like Florence. It wasn't as if she hadn't been asked out, but her mother wouldn't let her go, not unless the boy was from a family she approved of. It seemed to Rita that money and prestige was all her mother valued. She was always harping on that Rita should get someone like Ken Henderson. Chance was a fine thing! It was very frustrating.

Rita wondered then if Florence and Ken had made up their quarrel. It had been a tearful Florence who'd poured it all out to her during their tea-break at the office that morning. Rita tried to feel sympathetic, but couldn't.

Florence was *too* rebellious. Throwing up a

perfectly good job, and then defying Ken. If she was in trouble with him and her family, Florence had only herself to blame. That was Rita's opinion, anyway.

Still, she often envied Florence, she couldn't deny it. She often wished she were more like her in many ways, but now her cousin had gone too far.

'Have you nearly finished?' Sybil asked sharply. 'I'm getting dizzy standing by here on this stool.'

Rita thankfully took the last pin out of her mouth, put it into the material, then pushed herself to her feet.

'All done, Mother. It just needs sewing up now.'

'I hope you've got the hem straight,' Sybil said tartly, as she stepped down. 'There's nothing worse than a crooked hem. By the way,' she added in a casual tone that didn't fool Rita for a moment, 'Did Florence say anything to you about Gran and Granddad at the office today?'

'No. As a matter of fact, all she could talk about was Ken and the awful quarrel they'd had.'

The expression in Sybil's blue eyes sharpened with sudden avid interest.

'Ken Henderson? Now, as I've said before, that's the sort of boy you should be going out with, Rita. His family are business people, like us.'

She slipped out of the skirt, handing it to Rita.

'Is the quarrel serious? What was it about?' Her tone was too casual again.

Rita nodded.

'Quite serious, I think.'

She mulled over the cause. Florence had

64

behaved irresponsibly, and in truth she didn't blame Ken for his reaction. Florence was always telling her about his political ambitions. If Rita were in Florence's shoes she'd help him all she could; be the wife he wanted her to be, instead of behaving like a silly hothead, losing it all.

Up until the time they both left the office at one o'clock Florence hadn't heard from Ken. In Rita's opinion Florence's goose was cooked, but she couldn't or wouldn't believe it.

'I knew it wouldn't last,' Sybil said with a satisfied sniff. She gave Rita a slanting glance. 'Florence isn't ... well ... in the family way, is she?'

Rita was aghast, staring at her mother, a blush rising to her cheeks at the very thought. Florence might be rash, but she wasn't stupid.

'Good heavens, Mam! Of course not. What an awful thing to say about my cousin. Uncle William wouldn't like to hear you say that.'

Sybil stuck her beaky nose in the air.

'With a mother like that Edie, it wouldn't surprise me. I remember only too well the way she chased after your Uncle William. I thought it was disgusting. William could've done much better. Her father was only a plumber, you know. Just a tradesman, and always in and out of work.'

'My father's not even a tradesman, is he? He works behind the counter of someone else's ironmonger's shop,' Rita retorted tetchily, astonished at her own courage to speak up. 'But he's not an inferior man for that. He's worth twenty of the likes of Granddad.'

'Rita!' Sybil's mouth dropped open, and her

cheeks reddened in anger. 'Don't ever let me hear you speak disrespectfully of Granddad again.'

But Rita's new-found courage was still bubbling up, brought to near boiling point by the thought of the way Charlie Philpots bullied her father.

'But the way he talks to Da is unforgivable,' Rita blurted out, determined now to have her say. 'And you stand by and let him do it, Mam. How can you? You ought to be sticking up for Da.'

Sybil's lips tightened.

'Don't talk to me about your father. He's a fool,' she said disparagingly. 'A topflight professional footballer, he was, with a cap and all when we were first married. All the clubs wanted him, but Sheffield United were willing to pay the biggest money, they were...'

She paused, a little sob of bitter frustration escaping her. Rita suppressed a sigh of impatience. She'd heard it all before. Sybil never stopped harping on it, particularly when she was dissatisfied. Which was often.

'I ... we could've had it all,' Sybil went on, the bitterness in her voice reflected in her eyes. 'Money, prestige ... your father had the sporting world at his feet, and what does he do? He goes and crashes his motorcar, ruins his legs. Our whole rosy future gone.' Sybil snapped her fingers. 'Just like that!'

'Gran says it was *you* who made him buy the motorcar in the first place,' Rita blurted. 'You can't blame him for everything.'

'Yes, I do!' Sybil flashed back, her eyes glinting.

'He did me out of what was rightly mine. Lots of professional sportsmen go on to better things. We'd have had a nice house by now instead of living in rooms with my parents. We'd have had money in the bank.'

'Gran says you spent Da's money as fast as he earned it.' Rita was fired up. 'She says you were always flashing money about on posh three-piece suites, motorcars and the like. Always showing off, Gran says.'

'My mother's a silly, stupid old woman who knows nothing!' Sybil shouted, her nostrils flaring with rage. 'She's as thick as two short planks. And don't you go repeating the nonsense she talks, my girl. She's always been jealous of me, she has. She's never done anything or been anywhere. It's no wonder my father loses patience with her, and tells her off.'

Beaten, Rita was silent, biting her lip. Her grandmother had never had much of a life with Charlie Philpots. Poor Gran. But at least she had Uncle William and his family.

Sybil might be disparaging about them, but Rita had been very conscious of the happiness in Auntie Edie's household. There was warmth and love there. Rita had felt it, and was always acutely aware that that feeling was absent in her own home.

Charlie Philpots was cold and unloving to his wife, his children, his grandchildren. Uncle William had wasted no time in getting out when he was just a teenager, Rita reminded herself. They would never be happy as a family while they were under his roof.

'Why do we have to live here with Granddad, Mam?' she exclaimed at last. 'Why can't we get rooms somewhere else?'

She wouldn't mention the possibility of renting a house from Auntie Edie. Her mother would be affronted at the suggestion.

'Let's get away from Granddad, like Uncle William did.'

Sybil pulled in her chin, looking down her nose.

'Don't talk so silly, Rita. You forget, I'll own the shop one day, if that Edie doesn't cheat me out of it. We're staying right by here to make sure I get what's mine. I won't be done out of what's mine again. Though–' she smiled broadly-'my father's no fool. He's never approved of Edie.'

'Then what are you worrying about?' Rita asked, turning away to reach for a needle and cotton, suddenly weary and depressed by it all. If only she had Florence's courage, she'd get away herself. But she wouldn't leave her da on his own in this house. They were pals and secret allies, and needed each other's support.

'It's that Edie's underhandedness, isn't it? I can never tell what she's going to do next. She's so sly.'

Rita kept her mouth shut. Defending Auntie Edie to her mother would be like putting her head in a lion's mouth. No matter how kind and considerate Auntie Edie was, her mother would never change her opinion. A badly mistaken opinion, Rita knew. And it was a shame, because if only her mother would unbend she'd find her sister-in-law a good friend.

Rita's father came into the living-room at that

moment, pushing down his rolled-up shirt sleeves, and buttoning his cuffs.

'Have you finished the washing-up, Ronnie?' Sybil asked sharply.

'Yes, Syb.' His tone was gentle and patient.

A gentle giant, her father was. He was six-feet-four in height, and powerfully built, and she frequently wondered how it was that Sybil, who was barely five feet, could dominate him so thoroughly.

Rita often tried to picture him in his heyday, as one of the brightest stars in the football world. Her mother was always carping on about what she'd lost after his accident, but what about Rita's da. His dreams had been smashed too, but she never heard him bemoaning his fate.

He had a lot of love in him, she knew that, and knew she could rely on him for sympathy and understanding, something she would never expect from her mother. Her father would do anything for her, and that thought filled her with warmth.

She watched her father fondly as he walked over to the wireless set on the sideboard, and started fiddling with the knobs, producing a cacophony of sounds. He loved listening to the wireless. It was one of the few pleasures he had. Ignoring him, Sybil put on another skirt, then glanced in the mirror over the fireplace, her hawk-like nose elevated. She twisted her head this way and that as she viewed herself as though she wholeheartedly approved of what she saw.

'I could do with another marcel wave,' she said, fingering the stray wisps of hair around her ears.

'Mrs Prosser-Rees has her hair done at Terri's in High Street. She recommends Mr Tony. Says he's a wonder. I'll make an appointment next week.'

Rita was startled.

'Terri's?'

Florence had asked her to say nothing, especially not to family, about her change of job. She wanted to break it to her mother gently. But Rita had been careful not to promise to keep quiet. If Florence was so afraid to face her mother why had she acted so rashly in the first place? Rita decided she had no patience with her cousin's foolhardiness.

'About Florence's quarrel with Ken Henderson,' Rita said, head bent over her sewing. 'As a matter of fact, Ma ... Mother, she's done something very silly. She's thrown up her job with David Watson.'

'What?' Sybil turned from the mirror, staring at Rita in astonishment. 'Why, for heaven's sake?' She frowned. 'Are you sure she isn't in trouble?'

The cacophony Ronnie was making got suddenly louder, and Sybil rounded on him angrily, colour flooding her cheeks.

'Ronnie! Stop fiddling with that blood ... that blooming wireless, for God's sake! You're giving me a headache.'

Ronnie switched off the set immediately, looking crestfallen.

'Sorry, Syb, love.'

Sybil tossed her head. 'I should think so!'

Ronnie picked up a newspaper, and sat down in an armchair.

Sybil turned to look at Rita again, the colour in

70

her cheeks seeming to run into her nose, making it look more like a beak than ever.

'Now, where was I? Oh, yes, Florence is in trouble, I wouldn't mind betting.'

'Not the kind of trouble you mean, Mam,' Rita replied through clenched teeth, barely able to contain her anger at the way Sybil had spoken to Ronnie.

If only he would turn on her once in a while, reassert himself. But after twenty years of marriage to Sybil, of giving in to her bullying, perhaps it was too late for him to change? But it wasn't too late for her, Rita decided. She shouldn't let her mother dictate and control her life. She should make a stand soon, as Florence was doing. If only she could find the courage.

'Well? What trouble is she in then?' Sybil asked impatiently.

Rita swallowed hard against her anger, berating herself for her own lack of backbone.

'Florence will catch it in the neck when Auntie Edie finds out what she's up to,' she said finally.

She told her mother then about Florence's wig-making training at Terri's, and her failure to secure an apprenticeship in hairdressing itself.

'*Wig-making!*' Sybil screeched disparagingly.

She sat down on the sofa, a vindictive little smile playing around her mouth, and Rita felt a quiver of remorse for betraying Florence's secret, but it passed quickly. She hadn't promised anything, and in any case, Florence would have to face the music sometime or other.

'Wig-making?' Sybil said again, with a chuckle. 'Well, there's a comedown, if you like! She's a

71

wilful little madam, that Florence. But what can you expect?'

By her derogatory tone, Rita knew her mother considered wig-making or even hairdressing on a par with being a housemaid or a dance hostess. Or a waitress in a café, as Auntie Edie had once been. Rita could almost hear her mother saying it. Nice girls didn't stoop to that kind of work.

'It's no wonder Ken Henderson has thrown her over,' Sybil went on. 'He's seen through *her* all right.'

Sybil's eyes fixed themselves on Rita with such intensity that she felt a little quiver again, but this time of apprehension. She fancied she could hear the cogs in her mother's brain turning as she manufactured a new scheme, and quailed.

'Rita, you must ask Ken Henderson over to tea next Sunday.'

'Mam! I mean, Mother, I can't do that!'

'Of course she can't, Syb,' Ronnie chipped in. 'I don't like that bloke Henderson, anyway. There's something about him...'

Sybil ignored him as though he hadn't spoken.

'Why not?' Sybil's eyes were glowing with expectation. 'There's nothing wrong in asking a nice young man to tea.'

'Nice young man, my arse!' Ronnie muttered.

'Ronnie! Don't be so vulgar! And keep quiet, will you?' Sybil snapped. 'This doesn't concern you. I'm trying to do the best for our daughter. If I left it to you, she'd get mixed up with any old riffraff.'

Rita could have kicked herself for opening the floodgates. Now she wouldn't have a minute's peace.

Why not? There were quite a few reasons why not. Although she rather admired Ken, he was *so* good-looking, and liked the idea of having him for a boyfriend, it seemed wrong to try to steal him from Florence.

But *could* she steal him from her cousin, anyway? She doubted it. She couldn't match Florence's vivacity, no matter how hard she tried. She just didn't know how.

And the last reason was the strongest; her own mother. Sybil tended to put on the most absurd airs and graces with people she thought important. It made Rita squirm with embarrassment. She didn't want to be shamed and made to look a fool in front of Ken of all people.

'Don't make a face like that, Rita,' Sybil said sharply. 'Anybody would think you were ashamed of your family. I'm as good as the Hendersons any day. Gran remembers the time Bernard Henderson's father had a stall in the market.'

'I can't play such a dirty trick on Florence,' Rita said defensively, astonished that her mother could read her mind so well.

'Don't talk so soft, will you?' said Sybil. 'Florence and Ken aren't suited. He'll come into his father's business one day. And there's that beautiful house on Gower Road. I can't see Florence coping with any of that. She's too flighty, by half.'

'She isn't flighty, Mam,' Rita said, feeling that, out of fairness, she had to defend her cousin. It was the least she could do if she were going to steal her boyfriend, if she could. 'She's just a bit rash, that's all. Acts without thinking.'

Sybil sniffed.

'Like I said, they're not suited. But you, my girl, know how to behave like a lady. I've seen to that, Ken will soon see the difference. You'll have him eating out of your hand.'

Ronnie rattled the newspaper impatiently, but was silent.

'Married to Ken Henderson you'll be set up for life,' Sybil said with satisfaction. 'And you deserve it, Rita.'

By the avid look in her mother's eyes, Rita knew it was Sybil who considered herself most deserving, and her heart sank. Her mother wouldn't rest now, and wouldn't let anyone else rest either, until Ken was snared.

CHAPTER 5

'Nine o'clock, girls!' Miss Hopkins told them brusquely. 'Covers off machines, please!'

Florence, just putting a comb listlessly through her hair, groaned mentally at the sound of the supervisor's loud voice. She hated Mondays at the best of times, but this Monday looked to be the worst yet.

Reluctantly, Florence pulled the cover off her typewriter, folded it and put it into the bottom drawer of her desk. The machine was sitting there in front of her, like some great hungry animal demanding to be fed, and she was sick to death of it. The days ahead of her stretched out endlessly. Working her week's notice was going to be murder, sheer murder.

Feeling dismal, she put an elbow on the desk and laid her chin in her hand, trying to stifle a yawn. She'd cried so much for Ken over the weekend, she'd hardly slept at all, and now her head was aching fit to shatter. She could well do without Miss Hopkins and her corn-crake voice, Florence thought peevishly.

'Are we keeping you up, Florence?'

Miss Hopkins was peering at her over the top of her spectacles.

'No, Miss Hopkins,' Florence muttered, immediately straightening and glancing around self-consciously at the other girls.

Rita had her eyes downcast. Sonia was making a big show of inspecting the work in her in-tray, but Brenda was smirking at her openly, obviously delighted at her discomfort.

Florence scowled back furiously, tempted to stick out her tongue. They'd never liked each other. Brenda was one workmate she definitely wouldn't miss.

The typists' room was small and stuffy with the five of them in it. The desks were too close together, and the supervisor sitting facing them saw every blink of the eye.

'Well, get busy then, Florence, please,' Miss Hopkins went on with energy. 'Working your week's notice doesn't mean you can start slacking, mind. Here's a batch of conveyances for you to type up before lunch.'

Harridan! Florence thought spitefully, as she got up to fetch the work from the supervisor's desk.

Florence knew Miss Hopkins wasn't *really* old, though, and, surprisingly, she was even engaged to be married to a bank clerk who worked in Wind Street.

But it just wasn't fair, was it? Miss Hopkins, at least twenty-eight, if she was a day, was engaged, with a lovely ring on her finger, and Florence herself, eighteen, madly in love, was no nearer getting a ring on her finger than she had been last Monday.

And now she'd quarrelled with Ken, with not one word from him over the weekend to make it up.

What should she do? she wondered miserably.

She'd have a chat with Rita during the lunch break! Perhaps her cousin could suggest something, anything, to get Ken back. Oh, Ken! On whom she was pinning all her dreams.

Well, not *all* her dreams, she reminded herself, cheering up a bit. She felt a little thrill of excitement snake up her spine, despite the Monday morning gloom.

She was going to the hair and beauty business. Not as a hairdresser as she'd hoped, of course, but nevertheless, it was wonderful! She'd soon be free of this place. She'd hang onto that happy thought, she told herself. It might just get her through this awful week.

She worked steadily through the conveyances, though her mind wasn't on it, and had to use the eraser more than a few times, feeling Miss Hopkins' eagle gaze on her.

Her inability to concentrate wasn't only due to Monday gloom and Ken's silence, she had to admit to herself. She'd tried, repeatedly, over the weekend to find the courage to tell her parents about her new job. But her quarrel with Ken had sapped all her spirit, and she couldn't bring herself to face the inevitable row. Without a strong nerve and a pinch of courage she dare not attempt facing her mother. It was going to be a fight, a terrible bust-up, she knew that.

A commercial education at Clarke's College didn't come cheap. She'd been at the college all of four years, and that added up to a substantial amount in fees. So, there was little hope of Edie paying the hairdressing premium, as well.

Stop thinking about that! Florence ordered

herself sternly. She should be thankful she had the wig-making job. It was a wonderful opportunity, and it might turn out to be the best thing in the end. After all, she was glad she wouldn't be working in close contact with Tony Longford. He was far too pushy.

Her mother would be furious; enraged with her at the wastage of college fees, but she wouldn't let herself feel guilty about it, Florence decided, with a defiant lift of her chin. It was *her* life after all. She was very conscious that the fight with her mother would decide how the rest of her life would be. A success or a miserable failure.

And she couldn't put it off much longer. She'd tell them tonight after tea, she promised herself. And who knows, after the initial explosion, if she stood her ground, it might all blow over in a couple of days. Picturing her mother's strong face, Florence knew instinctively there was little hope of that.

'Let's not eat our sandwiches in the staff-room today,' Florence suggested to Rita when lunchtime eventually came. 'I want to talk about Ken.' She lowered her voice. 'And I don't want that Brenda to hear.'

They sat on a low wall in the small flag-stoned back yard of the offices, where the staff lavatory was. Florence was glad of her cardigan because September was beginning to turn a little chilly. Or was it her own apprehension at facing her mother that kept her chilled?

'What do you think I ought to do, Rita, to get him back?'

Rita shrugged, saying nothing, holding her head low, and unwrapping the grease-proof paper from around her Spam and brown sauce sandwiches.

'Well, you're a big help, I must say!' Florence said loudly, pouting, annoyed at Rita's lack of interest. 'Some friend *you* are.'

'Well, it's your own fault, isn't it?' Rita snapped irritably, jerking up her head, and glaring at her. 'What do you expect me to say, anyway?'

Florence stared, genuinely astonished at the heat in her cousin's voice. There were two pink spots on Rita's cheeks, too, as though she were overwrought about something.

As Florence continued to stare, Rita turned her glance away abruptly, concentrating on her sandwiches again, though she didn't attempt to eat them.

'I'm not withdrawing my notice,' Florence said firmly. 'If that's what you're thinking. There must be some other way.'

'Wouldn't do you any good anyway,' said Rita, petulantly. 'It's too late. Frankly, Flo, I think you've had it where Ken's concerned. You're ... unsuitable for him.'

Florence looked down her nose, feeling put out. She wasn't used to Rita being so forthright, having such firm opinions. Even if she was completely wrong.

'What do you mean, unsuitable? That's a daft thing to say.'

Rita was silent, turning her glance away again. Still making no attempt to eat, her nervous fingers were pulling her sandwiches to pieces.

Florence watched, puzzled. Rita's evasion was making her feel uneasy. Her cousin was so open usually, so easy to read. But there was something in her attitude today, something like hostility. In anyone else, like Brenda for instance, she'd have put it down to jealousy. But Rita wasn't like that. She didn't have enough spirit in her to be jealous.

'You don't know anything about being in love, Rita,' Florence went on archly, deciding that her cousin was too naive to understand what she was feeling. 'I'm in love with Ken and he's in love with me. Madly in love, we are. We've had a tiff, that's all. A difference of opinion.'

The withdrawn look on her cousin's face made her angry, and Florence bit savagely into her own sandwich. A fine friend Rita was! Just when she needed a bit of advice and support her cousin was turning her back on her, even turning against her.

Although she was trying to throw it off, Rita's words were worrying. Ken's silence was hurting her more than she let on, more than she'd admit, even to herself. It couldn't be all over between them. Ken was part of the wonderful future she'd planned for herself. She pictured him, tall, blond, good-looking, with a well set-up figure, good family background. Ken was every girl's dream of a husband.

Every mother's dream, too, she'd always thought, until Edie had astonished her by declaring that Ken was not liked. But that was just her mother being awkward, as usual. She had no intention of being put off by that. She *would* get him back, somehow.

'Have you told your parents yet, about the job, I mean?' Rita asked stiffly, breaking into her thoughts.

Florence sighed. 'Not yet.'

She caught a fleeting expression on Rita's face which looked rather sheepish, and was instantly suspicious.

She grabbed at her cousin's arm.

'You haven't told your mother, have you? You haven't blabbed on me?'

Rita pulled her arm away roughly, and wouldn't look at her. Her face was set and stubborn, her lips compressed together. Florence had never seen that look before and was dismayed.

'Oh, Rita! You promised.'

'I didn't promise anything!' She rounded on Florence with energy, taking her by surprise again. 'I don't keep secrets from my mother. I've got more respect than that.'

Florence was furious. 'Oh, what tosh! You mean you let her worm it out of you. You *wanted* her to find out!'

She stared at Rita, suddenly filled with misery. She'd taken her future into her own hands, and now she'd lost control.

'You stupid, thoughtless, little fool, Rita. What have you done?'

Angry as she was, she was frightened, too. For reasons she'd never been able to fathom there was a great deal of animosity in Auntie Sybil towards Edie. Did it extend to her? she wondered. Would Auntie Sybil give her away before she had time to put things right herself?

She suspected her aunt would like to make

trouble in the Philpots' household if she could, and now White Rabbit Rita had handed her enough ammunition to start World War Three!

Florence rose abruptly, leaving Rita still sitting on the wall, not trusting herself to speak again. She felt betrayed. She wouldn't be surprised if Rita had done it on purpose, but for the life of her, she couldn't understand why.

She walked back to the typists' room on shaky legs. The afternoon stretched out endlessly. She couldn't wait now to get home to tell her parents.

Where she couldn't find the courage before, fear now provided courage for her. Fancifully, she imagined a time bomb ticking away somewhere, which she must find and disarm before it went off, blowing her dreams to smithereens.

Back in the typists' room Florence was annoyed to see the only person there was Brenda. She was sitting at her desk admiring her reflection in the mirror of her powder compact, twitching her curly hairstyle into place.

She looked up when Florence came in, that irritable knowing smirk on her face again. Florence ignored her and sat down in front of her typewriter.

'Your boyfriend's given you the elbow then,' Brenda said loudly. 'Packed you in for good.'

Florence whirled round, glowering in rage.

'Who told you that?'

Brenda sneered, patting her snub nose with a tiny powder puff.

'A little birdie.'

Rita! Florence ground her teeth, almost beside herself with rage and humiliation.

'Your boyfriend gave you a good wigging, then, did he?' Brenda giggled loudly. 'Wigging? Wig-making? Get it?'

'Oh, shut up!' Florence flared. 'You're pathetic, you are!'

She turned her back on her tormentor, not wanting Brenda to see just how wounded she was. Rita had betrayed her good and proper. To think she'd trusted her cousin with all her secrets and dreams. Well, that was it! She'd never speak to Rita again as long as she lived.

Why let Brenda think she'd got one over on her, Florence thought dismally. She'd be damned if she'd lose face in front of *her*, of all people. A little white lie never did any harm.

Rallying her courage, she turned to face the other girl again.

'And you heard wrong about me and my boyfriend, see!' she lied, pushing her chin in the air haughtily. 'I'm seeing him at the weekend. We're getting engaged.'

And it wasn't a complete lie. It might be true. If Ken didn't get in touch before, she'd go around to his home and see him on Saturday afternoon. It was all a misunderstanding. They'd soon make it up. She'd even apologise if necessary. She'd talk him round. They'd be back together in no time.

Florence was relieved when five-thirty came at last, and Miss Hopkins told them to cover their typewriters. She felt exhausted with the anger and fear that had been tormenting her all afternoon, and the tensions between herself and

83

the other girls, which were almost tangible, and which, Florence was sure, had not gone unnoticed by Miss Hopkins.

She and Rita usually travelled home together either by bus or the Mumbles train. This evening she hurried to be the first out of the office, deciding she'd sprint to the bus stop in Oxford Street, well ahead of her cousin. She'd had enough of the awkwardness between them for one day. How she'd get through the rest of the week she didn't know.

She pulled up short when stepping out of the front door she saw her father's Austin Seven parked at the kerb, and her father sitting behind the wheel, reading the *Evening Post.*

'Dad, what are you doing here at this time?' she asked him, her heart in her mouth.

He didn't usually finish work this early. Had Auntie Sybil blown the whistle on her already?

'Going up to Brynmill, I am, to see Granny Philpots,' her father said, pushing his spectacles further up the bridge of his nose. He sounded more anxious than angry, Florence noted with relief. 'Thought I might as well give you and Rita a lift home.'

Florence's relief was shortlived. She looked hastily over her shoulder for a glimpse of Rita before scrambling into the front passenger seat.

'Let's not hang about, Dad,' she said breathlessly. 'Let's go straight home. Rita can catch the bus.'

'Don't be *twp*, Flo.' Her father frowned at her. 'Of course we'll give Rita a lift. What's the matter with you, mun? You two had a tiff, have you?'

Florence compressed her lips. If only he knew! But it wasn't only her quarrel with Rita that was bothering her. She didn't want to go anywhere near Auntie Sybil, not before explaining the situation to her parents herself, in her own way.

'What do you want to see Granny Philpots again for, anyway?' she asked peevishly. 'You only saw her Saturday, Dad. Quick! Let's go.'

'Your grandmother's bad in bed,' William said, and Florence could hear the tremor of worry in his voice grow stronger. 'Your Auntie Sybil phoned me at work. Got some vegetables for them as well, I have.'

'I *have* quarrelled with Rita, Dad,' Florence said desperately. 'We're not speaking. I'll be mortified if you give her a lift. Oh, come on, let's go.'

'There she is now, look,' William said. He hastily got out of the car and tipped the driver's seat forward. 'Rita! Rita, love. Over by here!'

'Oh, Dad!' Florence felt like shrinking down in her seat.

Rita stood hesitating on the pavement and Florence thought for a moment her cousin would refuse the offer, then she stepped forward and scrambled into the back seat.

'Thanks, Uncle William,' she said, her tone subdued.

I won't speak to her, Florence thought determinedly. Family or no family, they were finished as friends.

William chatted on the drive to Brynmill, asking Rita about her grandmother. Florence could tell he was really worried, and for a moment she felt selfish and callous.

Her dad was so very fond of his mother, Hilda, who was a lovely woman, generous and cheerful. So different to Granddad Charlie. Dad didn't get on with him at all. And no wonder. Granddad Charlie was a proper old misery guts! Even Rita admitted that.

Auntie Sybil was too much like him. Florence felt her heart rise to her mouth at the thought of facing her aunt. She'd stay in the car. She wouldn't go in. Her conscience pinched her, though. It would seem awfully mean, with her grandmother ill.

When William brought the car to a standstill outside her grandfather's ironmonger's shop, Ronnie Bevan was just closing up.

William got out and went over to shake hands with him. He always did that, Florence noticed. She was sure it was a symbolic gesture; a show of solidarity by son and son-in-law against Charlie Philpots, the tyrant.

The men stood on the pavement chatting a moment. Rita got out without a word or a backward glance at her, and stood on the pavement listening to their conversation. She too, seemed reluctant to go into the house next door to the shop. Guilty conscience! Florence thought.

She continued to sit, hoping she'd be forgotten. But one glance from her father got her moving.

'What the eucalyptus are you still sitting there for?' he asked sharply.

It was no good making more trouble for herself, she decided, hastily scrambling out. She was in enough of a jam already.

They filed into the house, the men going first. Rita trailed behind and Florence caught up with her.

'This is all your fault, Rita,' she hissed, infuriated. 'I only hope your mother knows how to keep her mouth shut.'

'Don't blame me,' Rita retorted hotly. 'I'm not the one who's a fool to herself.'

Grandmother Philpots was in bed. Florence followed her father up the stairs and into the front bedroom. Hilda looked very small in the bed, with the bedclothes pulled up around her face. She did look poorly, white and drawn. But as ever, she managed a smile at the sight of them.

'William, love. Florence. Oh, there's lovely to see you both.'

'How are you feeling, Gran?' Florence asked, her conscience still troubling her.

'A bit mouldy, love.'

'It's cold in here, Mam,' William said. 'We ought to get a fire going,' he said to Sybil as she came into the bedroom.

'Can't yet,' his sister replied. 'We'll have to wait for the restrictions against lighting fires to end. Somebody might see the smoke coming out of the chimney and report us.' She lifted her beaky nose in the air. 'People are so jealous of us round here.'

'Can't get the coal, anyway,' Hilda said from the depths of the bedclothes. 'I dunno. Things are going from bad to worse, aren't they? Sometimes I wonder if we *did* win the war.'

'Come on,' Sybil said, lifting an arm to

87

shepherd them out. 'Let Mother get her rest now. The doctor's been. She's had enough for one day.'

In the living-room Granddad Charlie was sitting reading the paper. He gave them only a fleeting glance as Florence and her father came into the room.

'How are you, Father?' William asked, stiffly, almost formally. He was trying hard, but Florence couldn't help noticing how brittle his tone was.

Granddad Charlie's response was a non-committal grunt, and he went on reading, ignoring them.

Florence glowered at her grandfather, feeling her hackles rise, forgetting for the moment her own peril. How dare he ignore her father like that, as if William were unimportant, a stranger? It gave her no consolation to know, as Rita had often told her, that Charlie Philpots ignored everyone except perhaps Sybil.

'We'd better be going,' William said quietly to his sister, his gaze still on his father's disgruntled face.

'Oh, stop and have a cup of tea,' she said. There was almost a warmth in her voice, making Florence immediately suspicious.

'Dad, we can't,' she said hurriedly. 'Our meal is waiting at home. Mam'll be wondering where we are.'

'Don't you want to hear what the doctor said about Mother, then?' Sybil asked her brother archly.

It was blackmail, sheer blackmail, and Florence

ground her teeth in vexation.

Sybil's eyes flickered over her for a moment, sparking a challenge. And looking back at her, Florence forgot her irritation and began to quake instead.

The gimlet eyes, the beaky nose that seemed to get sharper every moment; Auntie Sybil was like a hawk. No, that was too noble a bird to describe her. A buzzard! That's more like it. A buzzard swooping down for the kill. Her aunt was going to spill the beans, and there was nothing Florence could do about it.

She held her breath, waiting for her father's decision.

'Of course I want to hear about Mam, and I *could* do with a cup of tea, Sybil,' he said. 'If we're not putting you out, like.'

Granddad Charlie grunted something inaudible, and rattled the newspaper.

'Sit down,' Sybil invited, with a little smile that froze the blood in Florence's veins.

'Ronnie!' Sybil screeched at her husband in the kitchen. 'A pot of tea in by here, please.'

Florence sat on the sofa next to her father, while Rita handed out small plates, and Ronnie brought in a *teisen lap*, and began to cut it into slices. It was a cake Florence was particularly partial to, and Auntie Sybil was famous for her *teisen lap*. Even Edie couldn't bake a better one.

Today, though, Florence didn't feel at all hungry, but she took a slice of the cake for appearances' sake.

Uncle Ronnie grinned at her encouragingly, and she tried to respond. She liked her Uncle

Ronnie a lot. He was a big, amiable, clumsy man, who despite being handicapped by Sybil's acid tongue, and Charlie Philpots' awfulness, could always muster a little joke. She felt sorry for him, too, because he'd given in, capitulated to his lot.

She would never do that, she told herself with renewed determination. She intended to fight every step of the way. And that fight would probably start any minute now!

She only half listened to what her aunt was saying about the doctor's visit. Perhaps she could ask to go to the lavatory out in the back yard, and stay there until the visit was over.

That's a coward's way, she told herself sternly. That's the way kids behave, and she wasn't a kid anymore. She was a grown-up, independent young woman. She wasn't going to let Auntie Sybil frighten her.

'How's work going, then, Florence?' Sybil asked suddenly.

Florence felt her face go fiery red, and almost choked on a piece of cake, the crumbs clogging her windpipe, causing a fit of coughing.

Her father patted her back trying to ease her.

'Doing well she is,' he said through Florence's coughing. 'I was talking to David Watson only last week. He's very pleased with her work. And Rita, too, of course,' he added.

'Oh!' Sybil inclined her head, her brows rising. 'You surprise me, Will.' She sniffed loudly. 'I know our Rita likes working there, and they think the world of her, don't they, Rita, dear? But I understand Florence is not happy at all.'

The gimlet eyes turned on Florence and she

90

felt herself sinking down deeper into the sofa. If only she could disappear altogether.

'In fact,' Sybil went on relentlessly. 'Florence is thinking of leaving. In fact, she's already given in her notice last Friday.'

Florence felt rather than saw her father's astonished eyes on her. But she couldn't turn and look at him. She dreaded seeing that expression of disappointment in his soft brown eyes, behind horn-rimmed spectacles. She could face her mother down, battle with her, but her dad was different. He was gentle, loyal and kind, and he hurt easily. Her mother had told her that, a long time ago; warned her.

'Don't talk eucalyptus, Syb,' William said, but his tone was faltering. 'She'd have talked it over with me first, wouldn't you, Flo, love?'

'Dad! I wanted…'

'Going in for *wig-making* she is, Will,' Sybil interrupted brutally. '*Wig-making,* mind? Of all things. There's a comedown, isn't it? And after all that expensive commercial training you and Edie paid for, as well.'

She pulled in her chin, looking disdainful.

'Tsk! You can sacrifice your all for some children, but they're never grateful, are they? It's enough to break a mother's heart. Thank God our Rita has more sense and more principle.'

William stood abruptly, his cup and saucer rattling as he put it on the side table.

'Hope Mam will be better soon,' he said. His voice sounded strange, as though he was speaking through clenched teeth. 'Give her my love, won't you, Sybil. Try to call in to see her tomorrow, I will.'

Then he marched out without another word, leaving Florence still sitting there. She felt chilled to the bone, and wretched. Auntie Sybil had humiliated her, but what was even worse, even harder to bear, *she* had been the cause of giving her aunt the power to hurt and humiliate her father.

Florence rose to her feet. Oh, Dad!

Auntie Sybil was staring at her, gimlet eyes glittering triumphantly, a small spiteful smile playing around her mouth.

'Bloody hell, Syb!' Uncle Ronnie said quietly but with deep disgust.

Florence flashed a look at Rita, who was staring at her open-mouthed; appalled perhaps?

'Satisfied now, are you, Rita?' Florence cried out passionately. 'You mammy's girl, you! Knuckle under once too often, you will, mark my words!' Florence curled her lip. 'Once a White Rabbit always a White Rabbit. I'm sorry for *you!*'

'You'd better go,' Auntie Sybil said coldly, her mouth austere and prune-shaped now. 'Your father's waiting.'

With one final wild look around at them all, Florence fled.

CHAPTER 6

As soon as her father braked the motorcar outside the front entrance of the guest house, Florence scrambled out, and without a glance at him rushed inside. She didn't wait to use the backstairs as family normally did, but careered up the main staircase, shooting up and down passages where the guests' rooms were situated, to reach the refuge of her own bedroom in the annexe.

She threw herself on the bed, breathless and deeply exhausted. The ride home with her father had been in total silence. He obviously couldn't bring himself to speak to her, and Florence couldn't find the courage or the words to offer an apology or even start a conversation.

That awful silence had been unbearable. That had never happened between them before. Their relationship was easy and loving. No one could quarrel with her father, he was too good-natured. Now she'd taken advantage of his loving nature, and been the instrument of his distress and humiliation.

She'd have to apologise to him soon. She couldn't bear being at odds with him. She was shocked at the rift that had opened up between them, knowing it was her own fault, but cursing Auntie Sybil and Rita, too.

Damn! Damn! Damn! Florence beat a fist into

the pillow. Why hadn't she found the pluck to speak up before? Anyone would think she hadn't the courage of her convictions.

Florence swallowed hard, imagining what was going on in her parents' sitting-room and she quailed at the thought. William would drag Edie away from the business of serving the guests' evening meal, telling her everything, every last little awful detail.

As soon as the rush was over, Edie would be waiting for her to appear to explain, but she wouldn't go down, Florence decided. She didn't know if it was cowardice or good tactics that prompted this decision, and she didn't care. There'd be a right old bust-up, no doubt about it. She'd rather face up to it here, in her own room, than on her mother's territory. Of course, it would make her mother even more angry to have to come to her, but at this point Florence felt she had nothing to lose.

Her own mealtime came and went. Her stomach rumbled, gnawing with hunger, but her mouth was as dry as a chip. She'd never be able to swallow food anyway.

It was just on eight o'clock when, with a perfunctory tap at the door, her mother walked straight in. Florence jumped off the bed like a jack-in-the-box.

'Mam, now listen...' Florence began defensively, then pulled up short at the look on her mother's face.

Edie was white and stony, her mouth set in a straight line, hard in its severity. Florence couldn't remember such a look on her mother's face before, and felt her legs begin to tremble.

It was going to be more difficult than she'd supposed; but she mustn't weaken. She must fight!

Florence straightened her spine, and set her own features firmly. This would be a battle of wills between them. She *had* to meet strength with strength, and would *not* be intimidated. Eighteen, grown-up, a woman, her mother's equal; this was something she must remember.

'Dad's told you, then?' she said, moderating her voice, trying to keep it firm and controlled.

'Is it true?'

Florence lifted her chin defiantly.

'Yes, Mam, it is. I'm doing what I've always wanted to do.'

Well, that was partly true, anyway, Florence thought. Wig-making wasn't exactly what she'd dreamed about, but it was the closest she could get. And just as important, it was her own decision.

Edie's mouth tightened even more, the expression in her dark eyes accusing.

'Deceitful! After all, we've done for you...'

'I didn't deceive you!' Florence blurted, suddenly flustered at the accusation. 'At least, not intentionally, Mam. I was going to tell you both tonight, honest! Auntie Sybil had to poke her nose in though, didn't she?'

'I don't care what you say, Florence, it was underhand,' Edie snapped. She shook her head. 'I don't know where you get it from. No one in our family is like that. Who *do* you follow?'

'I don't follow anyone, Mam.' Florence tossed her head. 'I'm myself, an individual ... like you.

You wouldn't knuckle under to Mam-gu when you were a girl, would you? You told me about it often enough, anyway.'

It was true. Edie always reminisced about her days as a young girl; how she'd left home rather than submit to her mother's demands to work her fingers to the bone for her.

Edie was a fighter, but Florence was a fighter, too, and she would prove it.

She saw that she'd scored a hit when Edie's face reddened, and her mouth worked with new anger.

'Don't be cheeky and impudent, Florence!'

'Impudent, I might be, Mam, but I'm too old to be cheeky. You went out and made a future for yourself when you were a girl. Why deny me the chance?'

'That's an entirely different thing, Florence,' Edie said stiffly. 'I've never put upon you, never made you skivvy for me. You've had an easy life. You've never had to work hard or go without. And I've been fair. I haven't favoured any one of my children; I've loved them all equally.'

'There's other things besides love, Mam,' Florence retorted scornfully. 'What about worth? You and Dad dismiss me as though I have no worth.'

'Huh!' Edie gave a deprecating sniff. 'What nonsense you talk!'

'It's not nonsense,' Florence said through clenched teeth, enraged that her mother was doing the very thing of which she was accused, and denying it at the same time.

'If you and Dad had more faith and confidence

in me,' Florence rushed on, 'I'd have discussed it with you beforehand. But, no. You always dismiss my opinions and ideas, and I'm fed up with it!'

'Can you blame us? Wilful and flighty, that's you, Florence, my girl,' Edie said, pulling in her chin and looking down her nose at her daughter. 'Look what you've done now. You've thrown up a good job with prospects, and for what? To be a wig-maker. A *wig-maker!*'

She shook her head as though bewildered.

'It's ludicrous, laughable. At least, I *would* laugh if it wasn't so tragic.'

'You sound as snobbish as Auntie Sybil, you do,' Florence retorted, stung by the scornful tone in her mother's voice. She'd never thought of Edie as being a snob before.

'Don't you say that! I've got nothing against wig-makers or hairdressers, for that matter,' Edie snapped back. 'But there's no future in it for you. You're not capable of it, Florence. You just managed to scrape through your shorthand and typing exams by the skin of your teeth.'

'That's because I hated it,' Florence flared, affronted by her mother's scathing words. 'I don't want to be buried in a stuffy office for years, chained to a typewriter. It bores me stiff! And what prospects? You mean winding up like Miss Hopkins? My God! There's a lovely future to look forward to, isn't it?'

'Don't you be sarcastic with me, my girl. I won't have it.'

Edie stalked to the window overlooking the vegetable gardens and the trees beyond, where the road sloped down steeply to the village.

'Why wig-making, for heaven's sake?' she asked in a flat tone.

Florence wetted her lips.

'There's a premium to pay for a hairdressing apprenticeship. A hundred and fifty pounds.' She swallowed hard. 'Will you give me the premium, Mam? I'd much rather be a hairdresser than a wig-maker.'

Edie turned to stare wide-eyed at her, obviously astonished at Florence's temerity.

'*What?* Throw good money after bad?' Edie shook her head. 'You must think me a fool.'

Edie turned back to the view from the window. Florence knew that view so well. For a moment she wished she were climbing that steep road towards home this very minute, as she had done so often before, to be greeted with love and warmth from her family. Perhaps she never would again?

'You're irresponsible, Florence,' Edie went on with vigour and without turning to look at her daughter. 'I've always said it. Irresponsible!'

Florence was fuming now, glaring at her mother's back, stiff and unrelenting. She wished now she hadn't asked about the premium. She'd known all along it was useless. Her asking, and her mother's refusal had somehow changed their relationship in some fundamental way. She felt a coldness between them and was suddenly afraid. She'd always counted on her mother's love.

But it was no good feeling soft and sentimental. Those childhood days were gone. She needed more than love now. She needed her family's respect.

Florence pulled back her shoulders defiantly. She was getting a roasting, but she was ready for it. This was the time to show her mother what she was really made of. Standing up for herself was the start of her bright new future. She wouldn't knuckle down, because that was what her mother was leading to. She *wouldn't* give in.

'You're wrong, Mam,' Florence said firmly. 'There'll be a future for me all right, because I'm going to be a success. I will!'

'The waste of it!' Edie turned to look at her as though her daughter hadn't spoken, and Florence fumed even more.

Typical, wasn't it? Her mother wasn't even mildly interested in Florence's hopes and ambitions. She'd always be second best in her family's eyes unless she pulled out all the stops to prove otherwise. If she'd ever had a fleeting moment of doubt about her decision to strike out on her own, it was gone forever.

'It wasn't easy, during wartime to find the college fees,' Edie went on, ignoring Florence's angry expression. 'The guest house wasn't doing at all well in those years. We relied on your father's salary, and his business wasn't booming, either. We struggled to pay those fees, and this is how you repay us.'

'I didn't want commercial training, Mam. I told you that over and over again,' Florence said, almost wearily.

She walked over to the dressing table, fiddling with the trinkets there. It was no good her mother trying to make her feel guilty about the money spent, because she wasn't guilty. It had been her parents' choice, not hers.

'It was what *you* wanted, Mam, not me,' she went. 'You and Dad arranged it. I wasn't consulted, yet it was my life you were organising between you.'

Edie pressed fingers against her forehead as though she had a headache.

'Didn't want you serving behind a shop counter, or waiting on tables, like I had to,' she replied. 'I could see from the beginning you weren't going to get ahead like Amy and Tommy.'

'There you go again, Mam! How dare you?' Florence flared, spinning round from the dressing table, to glare at her mother, angry that Edie's lack of faith in her was being openly spoken about, with no thought as to how it made *her* feel. 'How dare you belittle me?'

Edie looked confused for a moment, uncertain.

'I'm not belittling you, Florence,' she said at last, her tone softening. 'I'm being realistic. Your father and I are concerned for your future. We wanted you to have sound training you could rely on. This wig-making is fanciful and silly. There's no future in it.'

She came away from the window, walking towards her daughter. Florence moved away abruptly, anticipating Edie's intention of giving her a hug. Florence wouldn't be treated like a child, to be coaxed and cuddled into submission. Her mother *must* see she was a woman now, and should be treated with respect.

'Then give me the money for the premium.'

She hadn't meant to ask again. She was ashamed she might sound desperate, thereby admitting she'd made an awful mistake. She *was* doing the right thing, she told herself, sternly, and she *had* to believe that herself.

Edie hesitated, frowning at Florence's retreat. The sharpness was back in her voice when she spoke again.

'No, Florence. I'll not give you the money. I'd be irresponsible myself if I did. Look,' she said gently, 'we wanted to help you all we could, that's why we decided on a commercial education. It'll be difficult for this country to get back on its feet again after all we've been through. Restrictions may go on for years. Times are going to get harder. Money will be in short supply. You need security.'

'Then let me do what I want to do, Mam,' Florence burst out. 'I can be as successful as Amy or Tommy in my own way.'

'We've tried to help you, and we know what's best for you.' Edie shook her head, and her mouth tightened again. 'But I can see you're un- grateful and stubborn. What I *can't* forgive, Florence, is the way you've upset your father.'

This was a score for her mother. Florence turned her head away, biting her lip. How bitterly she regretted hurting him. It made her heart sore to think of it.

'I'm really sorry I upset Dad. It's the last thing I wanted.' She jerked her head around to flash an angry look at her mother again. 'It's all Auntie Sybil's fault. Damn and blast her!'

'Mind your language!' Edie snapped. 'And it won't do, blaming her, either. You've only got yourself to blame. This is what happens when you disobey your parents.'

'Disobey! I'm eighteen, for goodness sake! I can do as I like.'

'Not in this house, you can't,' Edie thundered. 'You're still under age. You can do as you please after you're twenty-one.'

'Piffle!' Florence spluttered. 'You can't dictate what work I do. This is still a free country last time I looked. I'll … I'll leave home, that's what I'll do, so there!'

Edie's face was set as they glared at each other.

I'm winning, Florence thought, feeling a little dizzy. I've weathered the storm. It's nearly over. She wouldn't acknowledge the disappointment that the last hope of finding the premium was dashed.

With a deep sigh Edie moved to the door. She stood holding it ajar, looking back at Florence.

'You'll withdraw your notice first thing tomorrow morning, Florence,' she said in a stern voice; her expression warning that she would tolerate no further disobedience. 'Your father will patch things up with David Watson. Then we'll say no more about this silliness.'

'*I will not!*'

The line of Edie's mouth hardened, and her dark eyes looked stony. Suddenly Florence felt as though someone had slammed a door in her face, leaving her alone and cold on the outside. It was a frightening sensation, and she quailed for a moment, then rallied.

No, not even this would turn her away from her purpose. No one would take her dream from her.

Edie was about to close the door, when

Florence remembered something.

'Oh, by the way, Mam,' she said loudly and boldly. 'There's something else.'

Edie paused, looking back at her.

Florence swallowed hard, her boldness evaporating, but she forced herself to go on speaking.

'There'll have to be a drop in the money I give you for my keep,' she said. 'I shan't be earning as much as I used to. I'll let you know how much I can afford.'

Edie stared at her coldly a moment before turning and slamming the door behind her.

Disturbed by feelings of remorse for hurting her father, Florence got up extra early the following morning determined to see him before he left for work. There was no opportunity to speak with him the night before, and she didn't know whether she could anyway. The knock-down drag-out fight with her mother left her sore and battle weary. Even so, she considered herself the final victor, despite not getting the premium.

In his shirt sleeves, collar neatly buttoned already, but no tie yet, he was stirring porridge in a saucepan in the small kitchenette adjacent to the family back sitting-room, where they made tea and breakfast.

'I'll do that for you, Dad,' Florence offered eagerly, coming forward to stand beside him.

'It's all right, Flo,' he answered, without turning his head to glance at her. 'I can manage.'

'Oh!' Florence withdrew a little, conscious of the rebuff in the flatness of his tone.

'There's early you're up,' he said then, perhaps sensing her withdrawal.

'Wanted to see you before you go to work, I did. I'm sorry, Dad. I'm sorry you had to find out like that. Auntie Sybil had no business...'

'Don't blame others, Flo,' her father reproved. He turned at last to look at her. He wasn't smiling as he usually was when greeting her. 'You've been very thoughtless. There's disappointed in you, I am.'

Florence said nothing. She was having difficulty swallowing, because a lump of misery was forming in her throat. Her mother could never make her cry, but her father was a different matter.

She turned quickly to fill the kettle and put it on the gas ring. A few moments passed before she could speak calmly, without showing her weakness.

'I thought you might be on my side, Dad,' she said evenly. 'I thought you of all people would understand.'

'Now why the eucalyptus would I support you in disobeying us, Flo?' he asked, an underlying irritation in his tone.

He poured the hot porridge into a dish, scraping the remains from the saucepan with a wooden spoon; filled the saucepan with cold water and placed it in the sink.

He pulled out a chair to sit at the table. Florence, eager to be of service, handed him the milk jug and sugar basin from the pantry shelf.

'Because you did the same thing yourself, didn't you, Dad?' she said.

'*What?*'

'When you were seventeen,' she reminded him. 'Granddad Charlie wanted you to work in the shop, but you left home rather than obey him. You defied him. Isn't that right, Dad?'

William pushed his spectacles further up the bridge of his nose, and looked at her, his expression confused for a moment.

'That was completely different, Flo,' he began. 'I'm...'

'Don't say it, Dad!' Florence exclaimed quickly, inclining her head to emphasise her warning. 'Don't tell me it was different because you're a man and I'm just a silly girl who doesn't know her own mind.'

She quickly pulled out a chair and sat down next to him. If only she could get him on her side, then she wouldn't feel so left out in the cold. This awful feeling of isolation was growing and it made her very miserable.

'It's not that simple...' He was waffling, uncertain.

'No, Dad,' Florence said firmly, leaning her elbows on the table, and gazing at him earnestly. 'There can't be different standards for men and women.'

He put a spoon in the porridge and began to swirl it around almost absent-mindedly.

'You know there are,' he said at last. 'You're grown up enough to realise that. It's the way of the world.'

'Oh! Piffle!' Florence cried out, pushing her chair back and jumping to her feet. 'I won't accept it. I've got every right to live my own life any way I want to.'

'You can do as you like when you're twenty-one.'

'It'll be too late then!'

William sighed deeply, as though they had reached an ending, and Florence felt a sense of sadness overwhelm her.

'It's mistakes we're trying to save you from, Flo, love,' he said.

'And who's to judge whether I'm making a mistake? You? Mam? No! I can only do that for myself – like you and she did years ago.'

William's head was bent over his breakfast. Looking at him Florence's heart was filled with regret. He was the best father in the world, loving and generous. Why couldn't he see how much she needed his support now?

'Dad, I *am* sorry for the worry I'm causing you, and Mam, but...'

'Are you?' He looked up at her, his soft brown eyes a shade darker, a touch colder, perhaps?

'Yes, and I want to apologise.'

'Can't accept your apology, Flo,' he said, his tone flat yet desolate, 'because I can't believe you're sincere.'

'Dad!' Florence was affronted. 'I am sincere! More sincere than I've ever been in my life.'

'Then why don't you be sensible and make amends?' He shook his head. 'Your mother's very upset.'

'You want me to back down, throw away all my dreams, knuckle under,' Florence cried passionately. 'Well, I won't! Oh, Dad, I don't want to quarrel with you. But I'm not giving in.

I won't be second best to Amy and Tommy anymore.'

Without being able to stop herself tears began to swell in her eyes. She turned away, not wanting him to see her cry like a big kid.

'Florence, *cariad!*' His tone softened. 'You're not second best, my lovely girl.'

He rose from the table, pushing back the chair, and she ventured to look at him. He stood with his arms held out to her.

'Come by here, my chick. Come to me.'

'Oh, Dad! I'm so sorry.' With the cry of a child, Florence rushed to him, into his safe embrace. She put her arms around him and held on as though clinging to a life-raft.

'Listen, *cariad,*' he said as he nestled her close, smoothing her hair. 'Your mother and me, we love you very much. You know that, don't you? You're our youngest daughter, our beloved girl.'

Florence, her face pressed against her father's shoulder, sniffed back her tears.

'But you and Mam don't value me, Dad, not like Amy and Tommy.'

He held her away from him, frowning down into her face.

'Now, that's *twp,* that is!' he said.

His brown eyes behind his spectacles were rather shiny, as though he was close to tears, too. He has a tender heart, she reminded herself, and I'm careless of it.

'We only want the very best for you,' he said, with a catch in his voice. 'That's why we're so concerned. We've lived longer, Flo. We know best.'

Florence stepped away from him. How could she make him understand without hurting him more? She couldn't. There was no other way than to be forthright.

'You're thinking like Granddad Charlie, now,' she blurted.

'Flo!' He looked hurt, and her heart ached for saying such a thing. But in a sense it was true.

'Granddad Charlie thinks he can rule his family's lives,' Florence rushed on, eager to prove her point. 'You stood up to him, didn't you? You defied him and trained with Meurig Davies in market gardening. Now you own the business and more besides.'

She paused for a moment, trying to gauge his expression. Was he looking more thoughtful?

'And when Mam went to train as a cook in the Gower at seventeen Mam-gu said she'd never stick it, but look what happened. Mam built up a flourishing café business and this guest house.'

Florence touched his arm pleadingly.

'Dad, why can't I have the same chance? That's all I ask.'

He looked at her searchingly for a moment in silence. Florence held her breath, sensing that her argument may have had an effect on his thinking after all.

'Flo, love,' he said at last. 'Our success didn't happen overnight. It took years. Very hard work, it was, too, and for a long time we had nothing to show for it. Very often your mam and me didn't have two pennies to rub together. We don't want you to go through those hard times. We love you too much.'

'But I've got as much in me as you and Mam,' Florence cried desperately. 'And if you don't believe in me, Dad, what good is love?'

'Oh, Flo!' He sounded wounded. 'You know so little about life or love.'

Florence stepped up to him and putting her hands on his shoulders, kissed his cheek. Her heart felt overflowing with love for him. She only wished he could understand her and her dreams.

'Dad, when you were my age did you ever have a dream?'

He smiled, then, the pain going from his face. 'Yes. To marry your mother.'

She smiled back. 'An ambition, then?'

'Of course, *cariad.*'

'Then let me reach out for mine, Dad. I don't want to disobey you and Mam, so give me your blessing for my new venture.'

He gave her a big hug.

'All right. All right, then,' he said at last, holding her away again and looking into her face. 'I give you my blessing, but as your father I must do more than that. I'll give you the premium, too. You'll get your hundred and fifty pounds.'

Florence stared at him, speechless with astonishment for a moment. She could hardly believe it. It was such a lot of money.

'Oh, Dad! Oh, thank you!'

She hugged him energetically and kissed his cheek.

'This is wonderful! Really, really wonderful!'

Then a sobering thought struck her.

'But what about Mam?' She stared at him aghast. 'What'll she say? She's very cross with me. She'll never agree.' She felt disappointment drain away her new happiness. 'She'll be very angry with you, too, Dad. I don't want to cause trouble between you.'

William rubbed his thumb against his jaw thoughtfully. His gaze looked beyond Florence, as though into the past rather than the future.

'Leave your mother to me,' he said at last. 'She's not an unreasonable woman, Flo. I'll talk to her. She'll come round.'

He glanced down at the table.

'Oh, damn it, mun!' he said. 'My porridge has gone cold. Well, there's no time to make more now. I've got to get to work, and so have you, my girl.'

Florence was startled, thinking about Miss Hopkins' reprimand if she was late. Then she remembered it didn't matter anymore.

She was going to be a hairdresser!

'Dad, when...'

He grinned at her, his brown eyes twinkling.

'I'll give you the cheque tomorrow, *cariad*.'

Florence smiled fondly at him, at the same time struggling not to let tears start again. But they were tears of happiness this time. Her father believed in her. That knowledge was worth more than anything in the world.

CHAPTER 7

Florence stepped off the bus at the bottom of Sketty Lane, knowing she had quite a walk to Ken's home on Gower Road. The long trek would give her plenty of time to think about what she'd do and say when she saw him. So many questions were buzzing in her head.

Surely, when Ken knew she was taking up hairdressing and not wig-making, he'd change his mind about it?

Wig-making! Florence smiled to herself. It *had* been a rather absurd idea at that. Comical, really. But she'd been so desperate.

Tony Longford was surprised to see her last Wednesday lunchtime, eagerly clutching her father's cheque for the premium. Surprised and taken aback, she'd thought.

She'd signed the important-looking document he'd shown her without even reading it, so anxious was she to get the deal settled. She'd been hoping to meet Lillian Longford, too, but Tony's wife was away, he said.

Still, it was all signed and sealed now, and her future as a hairdresser secure.

As Florence turned the corner into Gower Road she was assailed by sudden doubt. Why hadn't Ken been in touch? All through the past week she'd been determined not to be the first one to make the move towards reconciliation. In her opinion it was lowering for the girl to chase the man. It was Ken's place to seek her forgiveness, she thought airily. The gentlemanly thing, and all that.

However, knowing his attitude on saving face, it was likely she'd have to make the first move after all. Perhaps she should've shelved her silly pride and acted sooner?

Florence chewed on her lower lip in agitation, remembering her anger and the bitter words that had passed between them. She *was* worried, even though she couldn't believe he'd taken their quarrel so seriously not to want to see her again. A lovers' tiff it was, that's all. And they *were* in love. Practically engaged.

Suppose he *did* want to finish with her, what would she do?

She'd quarrelled with Rita. And as for her family, she was still feeling very much isolated and she didn't like it at all. Her father had forgiven her, it was true, but her mother was merely polite. She couldn't win her mother round as she had her father, and Florence missed the warmth of their previous relationship.

Surprisingly, Edie had taken William's decision to help Florence with equilibrium. Florence knew it was their deep love for each other which had cushioned Edie's anger. No rift had come between her parents over it, as far as she knew, for which she was thankful. But family feeling, at least towards her, was not as it had once been, and never would be again. She still needed support.

If only she could get Ken back.

Florence lifted her chin as she strode on purposefully. Both of them had cooled down now; both had had time to think. She walked down the tree-lined Gower Road, past elegant houses standing amid lawns and well-tended gardens, set back off the road behind stout walls. Her mother always said that when walking on Gower Road it was hard to believe there'd been a war at all, that the country was near enough bankrupt, with crippling shortages and restrictions. Gower Road looked as it always had, prosperous and out of reach.

Arriving at the house at last, she pushed open the tall wrought-iron gates and walked resolutely down the drive that curved away to the front entrance, hardly able to quell the flutterings in her midriff. She wasn't so apprehensive at facing Ken, she decided, as squaring up to his mother. Mrs Henderson could be formidable.

Her ring at the door bell was finally answered by Ken himself. He stared at her as if she were the last person on earth he expected or wanted to see, Florence thought with a jolt.

'Hello, Ken.' She forced a beaming smile to show that all was forgiven.

'Florence!'

He continued to stare, not standing back to welcome her as she'd expected. A moment of panic engulfed her as she felt he might well be on the point of turning her away.

She felt flummoxed for a moment, her fingers nervously fiddling with the collar of her jacket. She hadn't expected a warm welcome to start, but at least a welcome of sorts, yet he was staring

113

at her as though he hoped she'd just go away by herself. Well, she had no intention of meekly retreating.

'Thought we ought to talk, Ken,' she said at last, her tone firmer. 'Clear up this silliness between us. I've missed you.'

He wetted his lips, and ran his fingers through the golden strands of his hair.

'Yes, of course,' he said vaguely, then, as though offering a reason for not asking her in, went on: 'I'm here alone. My parents are out. Michael's playing tennis.'

Florence suppressed a sigh of relief. Mrs Henderson always looked down her nose at her, as if to imply that a guest-house keeper's daughter was hardly up to the standards she expected for her eldest son.

'All the better, Ken,' she said brightly. 'We can talk in private.'

She was glad Ken's younger brother wasn't here either. Michael was all right in small doses, but was spoiled and could be irritatingly bumptious at times.

'Florence, I...'

'Aren't you going to ask me in, Ken?' She couldn't help putting a sting in her voice, piqued at so cold a reception.

Obviously reluctant, he moved back, opening the door wider. Florence stepped into the wide oak-panelled hall with its parquet flooring and Chinese rugs.

Ken continued to stand, hesitating, but Florence, not waiting for him to lead the way, walked into the vast and elegant lounge. She'd been in this room before, but not too many times. Invitations were few and far between. The room always looked to her as if it belonged in one of those glossy magazines. A set. Unlived in. Sterile.

Without waiting to be asked, she sat on a deep armchair covered in a dark blue velour, removed her gloves and hat, and placed them on the table beside her.

Ken remained standing, his hands in the pockets of his grey flannel slacks. There was no smile on his face. In fact, Florence saw with dismay, no expression at all, except perhaps a faint crinkle of irritation around his eyes.

'How are you, Ken? Have you missed me?' she asked coyly.

She beamed up at him again, fluttering her eyelashes hopefully.

'Quite well, thank you,' he said, his voice stiff and distant.

Florence felt a moment's uncertainty. Was she making a fool of herself, being pushy when she was no longer wanted? The thought made hot blood rush to her face. She despised girls who chased after men.

But this was different, she told herself. She and Ken were in love! They were on the point of getting engaged. She'd counted on having a ring on her finger by Christmas. It would be perfect.

Perhaps he was still a little angry with her? She hadn't told him her news.

'I've given up wig-making, Ken,' she said eagerly. 'My father gave me the premium for a hairdressing apprenticeship. Isn't it wonderful?'

115

He didn't answer, and wouldn't look at her, his expression stony.

Florence forced a cheerfulness in the face of his silence.

'Well, I think it is, anyway.'

She fidgeted, wondering what to do or say next. She usually didn't initiate physical contact between them, except perhaps holding hands. It was Ken who usually asked if he might kiss her. Obviously, today *she* must make any advances, or they wouldn't get anywhere. It was going to be difficult, though. It didn't feel at all right.

Taking a deep breath first, she said: 'Aren't you going to kiss me, Ken? We haven't seen each other for over a week.'

'Look,' he said, running his fingers through his hair again, and backing off a few steps. 'I was in the kitchen when you rang the bell. Making myself some tea. The kettle will be boiling away...'

'Oh, I'd like some tea,' Florence said eagerly, subduing the embarrassment at having her advances rejected, but glad too, that the moment had passed. She jumped to her feet. 'I'll give you a hand, darling.'

He hesitated, shuffling his feet uncertainly. With a fixed smile on her face, Florence walked past him back into the hall, and down a passage at the far end, leading to the kitchen.

Reaching him was proving harder than she'd expected. She could hardly believe what was happening, that she'd actually asked him to kiss her. Was she being fast? Would Ken think the less of her?

116

But she had to do something to repair their relationship. It was so important to her. Was it important to her? She was beginning to wonder.

He could be moody, she knew, but she could usually jolly him around. Today, though, something was missing between them. She might almost imagine he'd stopped loving her. But how can you stop loving someone just like that?

The kettle was on the stove, but the gas hadn't been lit.

'Oh, just like a man!' she said, trying to lighten her tone, but it sounded brittle in her ears.

She reached for the box of matches on the windowsill and lit the gas.

'There!' she said. 'You sit at the table, Ken, darling. I'll make the tea, and be "mother" as well. Now, where do you keep the tea?'

Ken pointed to the cupboard next to the stove. Inside Florence found an opened packet of Lipton's tea.

'How many spoonfuls do you like, Ken? One for you, one for me, and one for the pot?'

'There's no need for you to do this, Florence,' Ken muttered. His expression was still shuttered.

'Don't be silly, darling,' Florence said, too brightly. 'I'll be doing this all the time when we're married.'

Pulling out a chair she sat at the table waiting for the kettle to boil. It was then she noticed the black and white snapshots arranged on the tabletop.

Florence picked up the nearest one and looked at it. It showed a dark-haired good-looking young man in a bathing costume at the beach, half-reclining on a rock. In the background she recognised the rugged cliffs of Bracelet Bay and the Mumbles Lighthouse on its rocky island.

'Who's this, Ken?'

He astonished her by snatching the photograph from her fingers, his face turning a dull red. Was it anger or embarrassment? Florence couldn't tell.

'No one you know,' he grated.

'I can see that,' Florence said, lifting her chin, annoyed at his sharp tone. What was the matter with him? Why was he so tense all of a sudden?

He scowled, his eyes downcast, avoiding hers. Florence wavered between annoyance and anger, yet her curiosity grew as she watched him hastily gather up the remaining snapshots and push them into his trouser pocket.

'But who is he?'

Ken wetted his lips.

'My ... cousin from Manchester,' he said. 'He was down on holiday in the summer.'

'What's his name?'

His mouth tightened.

'Why are you asking so many questions, Florence? He's nobody; just my cousin, that's all.'

Florence lifted her brows.

'Why didn't I meet him? I mean I think I ought to meet members of your family, Ken, now that we're...' She inclined her head coyly. 'Well ... we *are* engaged, darling.'

'We're *not* engaged, Florence,' he declared loudly, pushing himself up from his chair, and turning from the table. 'I don't know where you've got that absurd idea from.'

118

Florence jumped to her feet, too.

'Ken!'

She watched him stride out of the kitchen and followed quickly on his heels. He didn't go further than the hall and the front door.

'You'd better leave,' he said stiffly, opening the door wide. 'Your behaviour is childish and embarrassing. I thought you had more pride than to throw yourself at a man.'

Florence was open-mouthed, appalled. 'I'm not throwing myself at you!'

'Well, it seems like it to me,' he said. 'I believe you're trying to trick me into marrying you. The way you're flaunting yourself, it's revolting and indecent. You're behaving like a loose woman.'

'How *dare* you say that to me, Ken!' Florence retorted hotly, spluttering in her humiliation and anger.

She'd never been so affronted. No one had ever said such terrible things to her before. It made her feel dirty and common. It was a horrible feeling, and she knew she could hate him for it.

'You have no claim on me, Florence,' he said, shaking his head emphatically. 'I've never once mentioned marriage to you. Never.'

She wanted to hit back now.

'You liar, Ken! Call yourself a gentleman? You and your pompous, tin-pot politics! You're a laughing stock.'

His lips compressed in rage, his expression dark and grim. He looks far from handsome now, she thought fleetingly. A nerve throbbed in his temple, and Florence watched it with growing alarm.

'Oh, I see now what your dirty game is,' he said harshly. 'You're trying to get me for breach of promise. That's it, isn't it?'

'No!' she cried out, dismayed at his terrible accusation.

Shocked to the core, she wished the ground would swallow her up and close over her head. She couldn't believe the venom in his tone, the awful way he was glaring at her, as though he'd like to strike her.

'You think I'm an easy touch because my family's well-off and have a reputation to uphold. Well, you can think again, Florence. You'll get nothing out of me!'

Florence could only shake her head, speechless.

'My mother's never liked you,' he went on savagely. 'She says you're a scheming little minx. I can think of a less polite term for you.'

Florence opened her mouth wide to retort, defend herself against his monstrous accusation, but words wouldn't come. She could only stare at him, horrified.

The nerve in his temple still throbbed wildly. She hardly knew him anymore. He seemed beside himself, deliberately driving himself into a deeper rage. Instinct told her to leave now.

'Get out!' he ordered, opening the door wider.

Florence stumbled through the door onto the gravel outside.

'Wait!' he said, disappearing for a moment to return with her hat and gloves. He almost flung them at her.

'Take your belongings. I don't want to see or hear from you again. Got that? If you pester me, or start any breach of promise nonsense, Florence, you'll get a letter from my father's solicitor. He knows how to deal with the likes of *you*.'

As he slammed the door in her face, Florence heard the scream of the whistling kettle coming to the boil in the kitchen.

CHAPTER 8

It was raining on Monday morning, a fine misty rain that penetrated right through outer clothing. The temperature had dropped too, and walking down the High Street from the bus stop Florence was damp and chilled by the time she reached Terri's, a few doors from the Mackworth Hotel.

Her wet stockings clung uncomfortably to her legs, and she wondered if there'd be a chance of drying herself off before she started training.

The weather was miserable and it fitted her mood exactly. Over the weekend she'd not been able to get over Ken's terrible outburst; his savage attack on her feelings, the rage and hatred in his face. She could hardly believe it had happened; that he'd finished with her. It was so brutal. She'd never have believed it of him.

Had he ever had any real feelings for her? Had he ever loved her as she'd thought? She'd never been in love before. Had she expected too much of him?

Were all men like that? she wondered. She thought at once of her father. He was loving, kind and sympathetic, but then he was her father, so it was natural. But what of other men, those she might meet later? Would she ever be able to trust any man with her feelings in the future? Remembering Ken's rage and hostility, she doubted it very much. She never wanted to be hurt, disappointed and humiliated like that again. Someone should have warned her!

There was no one to talk things over with now. Her parents had already voiced their dislike of Ken, so she'd get no sympathy there. Talking to Rita was out of the question. She'd proved herself the very opposite of a friend and confidante. For the first time Florence really missed Amy. Her sister could be critical, but at least she listened.

Florence stood outside the door of Terri's for a moment, winding up what was left of her courage. It seemed every relationship in her life had been damaged in the past week. The apprenticeship was the only thing left. She prayed nothing would go wrong there, too. She'd work hard, she told herself. She'd struggle and strive. She'd *make* it go right.

Florence couldn't help remembering the receptionist's sneer as she warned her there was every chance she'd be thrown out before she'd even started wig-making training. But she wouldn't let herself worry about Hazel's warning anymore. It couldn't happen now. They'd taken her premium. She'd signed an agreement.

Florence straightened her back. She wouldn't let negative ideas get her down. If the un-thinkable *did* happen, and her dream backfired, she still had her shorthand and typing skills to fall back on, she reminded herself. But what a comedown that would be after all the fuss she'd raised about making a great success of her new life as a hairdresser!

Florence swallowed hard, but at the same time lifted her chin high in defiance as she pushed

124

open the salon door.

The reception area was empty, Hazel nowhere in sight. She'd half expected to meet the formidable Lillian Longford waiting for her, but there was no one. A bit of a let-down, really.

Nothing appeared as it had the day she'd applied for the job. There was no perfumed air this morning and no music. In fact the air smelled stuffy and heavy with the odour of stale ammonia.

Florence could hear voices beyond the bead curtain. After a moment's hesitation, pushing her handbag more securely under one arm, and clutching her string bag containing sandwiches and a wet umbrella, she marched resolutely through the curtain.

She'd forgotten that on the other side of the curtain was a small lobby where clients' coats were hung. It was too early yet for clients so there were no coats, but a couple of wet umbrellas leaned against the wall. Florence added hers, then marched through the open door into the salon.

Marge was there, struggling to get her ample frame into her pinstripe overall. She grinned broadly when she saw Florence.

'Hello, kid! So you turned up then. Hey, Nance!' Marge called to the tall willowy blonde Florence remembered from her last visit. 'The new girl is here, look.'

Nancy turned her purple pansy eyes on Florence, her smile slow but not unfriendly.

'Hello. You can put your things in the kitchen, out by there.' She pointed to a door in the far corner of the salon, partially hidden by a partition. 'I'll find you an overall.'

She spoke languidly which befitted her leisurely and graceful movements as she went in search of an overall.

'Thanks,' Florence called after her.

She took off her hat and coat, which she hung damply over her arm. She wished she had a towel to wipe her legs down. Her mother always warned her not to get her feet wet.

'What's your name, love?' Marge asked, struggling to button the overall across her generous chest.

Florence told her, gazing around the salon. It looked different this morning. Not so glamorous or shiny posh. The flower-patterned linoleum covering the floor of the cubicle areas looked clean enough, but it also looked as though it had been down some time. The piece of red carpeting running down the centre of the salon was clean, too, but a bit threadbare in places.

'If you want to use the lavvie, kid,' Marge said helpfully, 'it's out the back yard, through the kitchen.'

Florence smiled, shaking her head.

'I was just wondering where I could dry my coat?'

'Row of hooks in the kitchen,' Marge said. 'That's where staff put their things. Give it here, kid. I'll do it for you just for today, like.'

Marge disappeared into the kitchen and reappeared a moment later, accompanied by the young red-headed girl Florence had seen sweeping up hair cuttings on her previous visit.

She was shorter and smaller than Florence, with thin spindly legs.

'Glenys, love, meet Flo, our new girl,' Marge said. 'Glenys is an apprentice, too, aren't you, kid?'

Glenys nodded, regarding Florence in solemn silence. The fine rain hadn't done her frizzy red hair much good. It stood up around her small head like a thin fuzzy halo, and Florence couldn't help staring, thinking briefly that the girl's hair was hardly a good advertisement for such a high-class salon.

Glenys's round greenish eyes regarded Florence with what looked like apprehension.

'Hello, Glenys,' Florence said, smiling at her in a friendly way. 'Nice to meet you. Have you been training here long?'

'Six months,' Marge answered for her. 'But she'll get the hang of it soon, though, won't you, Glenys, love?'

Glenys didn't answer, but stared at Florence, her apprehension now unmistakable.

Nancy returned with an overall.

'Try this for size,' she said to Florence.

To Glenys she said: 'Better start putting towels in the cubicles, Glenys, before Tony comes in. He'll get mad if you forget again today.'

Glenys looked startled and immediately scuttled back into the kitchen.

Florence shrugged into the cotton overall. It fitted her quite well, she found. She looked hopefully at Nancy, who appeared to be in charge for the moment.

'What shall *I* do?'

She caught the look that passed between Nancy and Marge but couldn't interpret it.

'Give Glenys a hand if you like, for the time being,' Nancy said. 'We'll have to wait for Tony and … Lillian before we know what's what.'

Florence felt a quiver of apprehension herself at the mention of Lillian's name. She had nothing to worry about, she told herself sternly, now that she'd paid the premium.

Yet she was conscious of an uneasiness, an uncertainty. Her agreement with Terri's had been sanctioned by Tony alone. Florence wished suddenly that she'd insisted on meeting Lillian Longford before parting with her father's money. Could Tony be trusted? Could anything go wrong at the last minute?

Following in Glenys's footsteps to the kitchen, her mind was alive with questions. She'd definitely had the impression that Marge and Nancy were humouring her, pretending everything was all right for the moment.

Suppose Lillian objected to someone being taken on in her absence? Could they cancel her agreement, hand her money back?

That would be unfair, perhaps even illegal, Florence thought angrily. But it was no good speculating. She'd have to wait and see what fate had in store.

In the kitchen Glenys was busy taking folded towels out of a large airing cupboard and stacking them on the table.

'Let me give you a hand,' Florence offered, stepping forward.

Glenys turned, her small face contorted.

'Don't need your help, do I? Leave me alone!'

Florence stepped back, astonished.

'What on earth's the matter, Glenys?'

'As if you didn't know!' She burst out again. 'Lillian'll give me the push now 'cos you're here. You've stolen my job!'

'*What!*' Florence could only stare at her, open-mouthed.

Glenys's face crumpled and tears started to roll down her cheeks.

'Tried and tried, I have,' she sobbed. 'Work hard, I do. It's not my fault if I'm clumsy ... Marge is all right and Nancy. They're kind to me and help, but Tony and Darlene...'

She gave a massive sob that shook her small frame, then looked up at Florence, glaring, her snub nose pink, her complexion a blotchy-red, all at odds with the colour of her hair.

'Dreaded this morning, I did,' Glenys said, her lower lip still trembling. 'Hoped you wouldn't turn up.' Her face crumpled again. 'But you have! Now I'm out of a job, and I did so want to be a hairdresser.'

Getting over her shock, Florence stepped forward and put an arm around Glenys's shoulders. She could feel sobs still shaking the girl's body. Glenys made an attempt to shake her off, but Florence was determined, and clutched the girl's shoulders even more firmly.

'Look, sit down by here a minute,' Florence said kindly, pushing Glenys down onto a chair at the table, taking the other one herself.

If anyone else came in now it would look as if they were slacking, the pair of them, but she couldn't help that. She was shaken at the girl's unexpected accusation.

Was it Glenys's imagination, or was there some truth behind it? If there was, she'd have to think again about her own position here. She could never take another girl's job and live with herself afterwards. She'd have to get to the bottom of this.

'Who told you you'd get the sack?'

Glenys sniffed, wiping her nose with a small handkerchief.

'Hazel.'

'Hazel!' Florence exploded. 'That little pipsqueak!'

'You know her, then?'

'No, I don't,' Florence said, emphatically. 'But I know her sort. I've met her kind before.'

She thought briefly of Brenda back at the solicitors' office. Hazel was another troublemaker. Well, she'd soon sort *her* out, Florence decided.

A cautious inner voice brought her up short. Be careful, the voice said. That was wise advice, she knew. She had no idea how influential Hazel was at Terri's; where she fitted in. Perhaps she did have inside knowledge of Glenys's future at the shop? Even so, Florence was horrified at the idea that she'd dashed someone else's dream.

'Has ... Lillian ... Mrs Longford said anything to you?' Florence asked.

Glenys sniffed again, though she seemed to have calmed down a little. Her shoulders were still hunched miserably as she leaned her elbows on the table.

130

'Lillian was away most of last week. Don't know when she's due back.'

'What about Tony?'

Glenys shook her head.

'He only shouts at me because he says I'm slow and awkward. I'm trying hard, though!'

Florence patted the girl's arm as tears seemed about to flow again.

'Hazel is making this up to upset you, Glenys,' she said firmly. 'You've paid your premium, haven't you, and signed your agreement?'

Glenys nodded again.

'Then they can't sack you.' Florence tried to sound convincing, but she didn't even convince herself. 'I'm sure they can't.'

Her own future was dicey enough, she reflected, especially if the agreement she'd signed *could* be broken on the whim of an employer.

'I haven't met Lillian yet,' she went on. 'For all I know she won't approve of me. If anyone is going to get the push it'll probably be me.'

And she hadn't even had a chance to prove herself, she thought sadly. Was fate planning to play another dirty trick on her?

'Who's Darlene, by the way?' Florence asked cheerfully, deciding she must look on the bright side for the moment. It was no good searching for trouble.

'She's horrible!' Glenys said, wrinkling her pink nose. She was obviously making an effort to gulp down further sobs. 'Especially to me. Calls me names and orders me about.'

'What does she do here, then?'

'London-trained hairdresser, like Nancy. None

of 'em have been here as long as Marge, though, not even Tony. Marge and Lillian go back years. They're like this.'

She held up a thumb and index finger tightly pressed together.

'Tony'd like to get rid of Marge. She never had top-drawer training, see, like the others,' Glenys said. 'But Lillian won't hear of it. Marge tells her everything.'

'Spies for her, you mean?' Florence was shocked.

'Well, only on Tony, like.' Glenys wriggled uneasily on her chair. 'He's ... well, he likes the girls, you know.' Glenys lowered her gaze. Under her freckles and through the mottle of her skin, Florence could see she was blushing.

'Yes,' Florence said with irony. 'I gathered that much.'

'*Glenys!*' A new voice screeched through the open kitchen door. 'Get in here with those bloody towels. Now!'

'Darlene!' Glenys jumped to her feet, almost knocking her chair over in her haste. 'Oh, God! She's starting on me already.'

She made a fumbling attempt to gather up the stack of towels from the table, but only succeeded in knocking the pile over.

'Hold on!' Florence said firmly, getting to her feet. 'You go and wash your face, Glenys, love. I'll take the towels in. I'll say you're in the lavvie.'

'Oh, I dunno.' Glenys put her fingers to her mouth in consternation, hesitating.

'Well, I do,' Florence said staunchly. 'I've got to meet Darlene some time. Might as well be now.'

Florence gathered up the towels and marched to the door. She didn't like the sound of Darlene. Even her voice made her seem like a nasty piece of work.

Florence wasn't going to let Darlene boss her about, though. The sooner she made that clear the better. She wouldn't let any of them push her around. She might be only an apprentice, if she was lucky, but she was due some respect, as poor Glenys was.

Her whole future here was hanging in the balance, as far as she could tell, so what did she have to lose by standing up for herself?

She recalled the look passing between Nancy and Marge earlier. It wasn't the horrible Darlene that could give her the jitters. No, it was the thought of Lillian Longford. *Her* fate was in Lillian's hands.

There were no clients in the salon yet, Florence was glad to see, so it really wouldn't matter if there was a scene.

A young woman was standing facing the kitchen door, waiting, hands on hips, the toe of one shoe tapping the ground impatiently. She was in her late twenties, Florence judged, with bleached-blonde hair done up the style of Lana Turner. The style certainly didn't flatter the hardness of her features.

She still wore her coat, Florence saw, a camel-hair wrap-over with a tie belt. It looked like it had cost a pretty penny, not to mention the coupons.

Darlene's mouth dropped open at the sight of Florence. She turned her head to glance at Nancy, jerking it towards Florence.

'What's this then, when it's home?'

'My name's Florence,' she announced quickly before anyone else could speak. She dropped the towels on a chair nearby, then stood up as straight as she could, looking Darlene defiantly in the eyes. 'I'm the new apprentice.'

'What?'

'Tony took her on,' Marge volunteered. 'Last week.'

Darlene lifted her chin, smirking, nodding knowingly.

'Oh, I see!' She looked Florence up and down. 'Does Lillian know yet?'

'No,' Marge replied heavily. 'But it's not what you're thinking, Darlene.'

'I'll bet!' She continued to appraise Florence. 'How long have you known our Tony, then? I must say you're a bit young to be his latest bit of stuff.'

Affronted, Florence's mouth fell open with shock.

'How dare you?' she managed to splutter.

Darlene laughed out loud.

'Oh, get her! Butter wouldn't melt, if you could get it. And listen to the way she talks. Got a plum stuck in her mouth, sounds like. Where you from, then?' she asked with a curl of her lip. 'Sketty is it, or Derwen Fawr?'

Florence tossed her head, thoroughly annoyed with herself for letting Darlene upset her. She'd have to learn to be shockproof if she wanted to get on with this crowd, she warned herself. She'd left behind the safe, dull haven of the solicitors' office for a wider, rougher world. She'd have to learn how to survive; and she would, too.

Darlene was a bully, and there was only one way to deal with them. Florence jutted out her chin belligerently.

'Mind your own damned business!'

Darlene stared, momentarily startled, but she quickly recovered.

'Oh, mouthy little bit, isn't she? Listen, you,' she said nastily to Florence, wagging a finger in her face. 'Don't think you can come in here, hoity-toity, throwing your weight about just because you're Tony's bit on the side. That don't cut no ice with me or the other girls, either. We won't stand no favouritism, see.'

'Pack it in, Darlene, mun,' Nancy said, in a languid warning that had little force behind it. 'Florence's paid the premium. Everything's above board.'

'Oh, yeah!' Darlene's lip curled with scorn. 'Nice little touch of camouflage, that. But I'm not stupid like the rest of you. Tony's got more tricks up his sleeve than I've had Spam sandwiches.'

'It's true!' Florence cried hotly.

'I wasn't born yesterday, mind.'

'Darlene!' Nancy exclaimed. 'Our first client'll be here in a minute. We'll all be in trouble if Lillian hears about a row between the staff.'

Hazel came through the bead curtain at that moment. She stopped and stared at Florence and Darlene face to face.

'Is that new girl making trouble already?' she asked of everyone. 'I knew Tony was making a mistake.'

135

'Never you mind what we're doing in by here, Hazel. None of your business,' Darlene replied waspishly. She jerked her head towards the outer door. 'Get back to reception where you belong, nosy-parker!'

Hazel turned to go, her face scarlet, and for a fleeting moment Florence felt sorry for her. Then she remembered the receptionist's spiteful taunts to Glenys.

Well, now she knew. Hazel's standing was lowly in the hierarchy at Terri's, while Darlene was top dog, or thought she was.

'Now, listen you!' Darlene turned her attention to Florence again. 'Don't want no more lip from you, see...'

'What the bloody hell's going on here?'

Tony was standing at the bead curtain, his tanned face stony as his glance swept from one to another. He looked down pointedly at his watch.

'It's gone nine, Darlene. Are you late again?'

'No, Tony. I...'

'Well, get your coat off, then,' he snapped. 'What do you think this place is? Butlin's holiday camp?'

He looked at Florence, frowning. For one awful moment she thought he didn't remember her. Then he glanced at the pile of towels dumped on the chair.

'Well, don't just stand there, Flo,' he said, irritably. 'Get those towels sorted.'

Florence was relieved that Tony's presence had cooled the temperature in the salon. The process was complete when the first clients arrived, and the staff settled down to business as usual.

She was still a bit shaken, though. Her stockings had dried on her legs, but she still felt chilled through. It was nerves, she told herself firmly, shock at the hostility she'd met with from Darlene. What was wrong with the woman, anyway? She couldn't understand it. Was it going to be like this every day?

She felt a little nauseous at the thought; had she bitten off more than she could chew in coming to Terri's? It certainly felt like it, but it was done now. Florence set her jaw in determination. She'd made her choice, and she'd stick by it. She wouldn't let a bully like Darlene spoil it or turn her from her purpose. Enough was lost already; her mother's support, her friendship with Rita, and, she thought with a gulp of self-pity, Ken's love.

With a determined air she made herself useful with the broom, sweeping up hair-cuttings, washing out the basins after each client, collecting wet towels and pushing them into a canvas bag for collection by the woman who did the daily laundry for Terri's.

Glenys was helping Nancy, handing her curlers one at a time as the willowy blonde wound them tightly into the customer's hair. Glenys glanced woefully at Florence from time to time, the reproach in her eyes quite disturbing.

Florence couldn't stand it any longer. She must speak to Tony. She had to know where she and Glenys stood.

When he went into the office she followed him, standing just inside the door. He'd obviously come in for a cigarette.

'Mr Longford?'

He looked up, smiling, letting blue smoke curl to the ceiling.

'Well, kid? Darlene getting to you, is she?'

'No, Mr Longford. I was wondering...'

Florence hesitated, not knowing how to form the question.

He looked her up and down.

'You look snazzy in your overall, pet,' he said. 'You've got a very nice figure, very nice. Mmm! I wonder how you'd look in a bathing costume or...'

'Mr Longford,' Florence went on again hastily in an effort to get his mind on a new track. 'It's about Glenys. Will she lose her job now that I've been taken on?'

Tony didn't answer immediately, but tapped cigarette ash into a glass tray.

Florence's heart sank. Where did that leave her? She thought her dreams had come true in getting this apprenticeship, but the price was too much to pay. How could she ever make a go of it, knowing she'd stolen someone else's job?

'It's not fair, Mr Longford, that Glenys must go because of me.'

'It's not because of you, sweetie,' Tony said. 'Glenys has no flair for hairdressing. She'll never make a go of it. I can't let her family fork out hard-earned money for nothing. They'll get the rest of it back, and no harm done.'

'Glenys is not getting a fair chance,' Florence said forcefully. She came and stood in front of the desk. 'She's got Darlene on her back most of the time. She's scared out of her wits. Is it any wonder she's ... clumsy?'

'What do you care what happens to her?' he asked in an offhand tone. 'You've got your apprenticeship.'

'I care a lot! And so should you,' Florence flared, forgetting in her passion that she was speaking to her employer.

He raised his eyebrows, obviously surprised at her sharp tone. His smile was a little crooked when he said:

'You've got plenty of guts. I like a girl with spirit. You'll do all right here, kid. Tell me, does our Darlene frighten you?'

Florence straightened her spine, lifting her chin defiantly. She might as well start as she meant to go on, if there *was* a future here for her.

'There's very little that frightens me, Mr Longford, except, maybe, your wife.'

Tony jerked forward in his chair, his features thunderous for a moment, and Florence knew she'd gone too far.

'What do you mean by that!' he asked, his tone gritty.

Florence wetted her lips, but kept her gaze level and steady. Inexperienced as she was, there was no doubt in her mind that Tony Longford was a man who would swiftly take advantage if he could. She'd set him straight immediately, and if he decided her face didn't fit after all, then that was that. But she wouldn't be browbeaten by Darlene or him.

'I'm young, but I'm not a fool, Mr Longford. It's plain the way the others are behaving, things they've said...'

'Who said what? Was it that bloody Marge?' he demanded furiously, thrusting his face forward.

'No it wasn't. And does it matter?' Florence evaded, stepping back.

Her legs were beginning to tremble now, and she longed to get out of the room. Why had she started this in the first place? She'd met Glenys only a few hours ago, so why care what happens to her? Yet she did care. Apart from the fact that she was sorry for the girl, it was the principle of the thing.

It struck her forcefully then that Tony Longford was a man pretty short on principle. She couldn't trust him an inch. The new knowledge made her feel vulnerable.

'Your wife doesn't know I've been taken on,' she went on. 'I've been told she may kick me out as soon as look at me, even though I've paid my premium.'

Surprisingly his face cleared, and he grinned again.

'You're a mouthy piece, there's no doubt about that, but I like you, Flo. Look, don't worry about Lillian. I can handle her. As for Glenys, well, maybe I'll think about it again. Give her another chance, perhaps.'

He jerked his head toward the salon.

'Now get out there, Flo, and start your training. After all, your parents are paying through the nose for it, aren't they?'

Florence was glad to escape. Whether she'd done any good, she didn't know, but at least she'd tried.

The salon was busy for the rest of the morning,

keeping Florence on the run. She didn't mind at all. Tony appeared to have forgotten his earlier anger with her, and allowed her to wash his clients' hair. This was more like it, she thought, cheering up. But if it was this busy on a Monday, what would it be like at the weekend? Surely there was enough work here to keep two apprentices going? She hoped Tony would come to that conclusion.

Florence gave Darlene as wide a berth as possible during the morning. She wouldn't give the older girl a chance to humiliate her in front of clients.

She was amused to see the way Darlene smiled so sweetly at clients. None of them would believe she was a holy terror, Florence thought, suppressing a smile.

She almost laughed out loud when, sweeping out the cubicle next door to Darlene's, she heard the posh accent the older girl was putting on. She sounded so false and silly that Florence could feel her own face turn hot in embarrassment for her.

'Would modom lake a cup of tea?'

The client must have agreed because the next moment Darlene was swishing back the curtain between the cubicles, her waspish glance falling on Florence.

'Hey, you! Whassaname? A cuppa by here, and be quick!'

It was on the tip of Florence's tongue to refuse, but she thought better of it. She wouldn't put herself in the wrong. It was a reasonable request; part of her job as a lowly apprentice. If only

141

Darlene would be more pleasant about it.

The highlight of Florence's morning came when she was helping the same client on with her coat. The lady pressed a sixpenny piece into her hand, and smiled.

'Very nice cup of tea, dear.'

Florence was overwhelmed, staring at the sixpence in her palm. A tip! For a moment she didn't know whether to be pleased or embarrassed. She decided she must be pleased. She couldn't afford to be anything else on her wages.

She dropped the coin in the pocket of her overall. How much could she hope to make in tips during the day, she wondered with excitement.

She glanced around the busy salon. Terri's was obviously a nice little business, and she vowed that one day she'd own one just like it.

Just on a quarter to twelve a client entered the salon and Florence recognised her immediately, despite having had but one brief glimpse of her previously. It was the tall, elegant woman in the long fur coat; the one who'd inspired her the day she'd applied for the apprenticeship.

Mindful of tips to be earned, and delighted she had a chance to speak to the personification of her ideal woman, Florence rushed forward to greet her, her hands reaching forward to take the coat from the woman's shoulders.

'Can I help you, madam? Shall I take your coat?'

The woman turned and stared at her. Being reasonably tall herself, Florence found she was eye to eye with her blonde ideal.

'Who the hell are you?' the woman asked in a loud, rather coarse voice.

Florence stepped back, startled and uncertain. What had she done wrong?

'Florence. I work here, madam.'

The woman pushed back the edges of the fur coat to put both hands on her hips, glancing around the salon at the others.

'Since when?'

The coarse voice had an authoritative edge to it. Florence suddenly registered how quiet the salon had become all of a sudden, and felt the hairs on the back of her neck stand on end. She *had* made a terrible mistake.

'I said, since when, miss? Are you deaf, or what?'

'I...'

To Florence's immense relief, Marge came rushing forward.

'It's okay, Lillian,' she said breathlessly. 'Flo started this morning. Tony took her on as another apprentice last week.'

Lillian's eyes glittered suspiciously.

'Oh, did he, now! Well, we'll see about that.'

She pointed a long bony finger, tipped with a vividly red fingernail, at Florence.

'You! In the office now!'

She swept away towards the rear of the salon, the skirts of her fur coat flying out behind her. As she passed Tony's cubicle, she paused only briefly.

'Tony! I've got a bloody bone to pick with you.'

CHAPTER 9

It's over! Her dream was finished, shot down in flames.

Florence, frightened and bewildered, stumbled behind Lillian along the length of the salon towards the office. Disappointment and frustration threatened to overwhelm her, and she struggled not to burst into tears. She *wouldn't* cry in front of the others, especially not that awful Darlene.

She was all too aware of their curious stares, the shocked faces of clients and, perhaps worse than anything, Darlene's triumphant laugh. That made her face burn with humiliation. It flashed through her mind that her flushed complexion would make her appear guilty to Lillian, as though she did have something to be ashamed of.

Lillian sailed imperiously into the office, slinking out of her coat as she went, throwing it onto a chair. She stepped behind the desk and sat down, immediately taking a cigarette from the packet on the desk. She lit up, inhaled deeply, then sat back to look at them.

Florence could see suspicion sparkling in her eyes like neon lights as she flashed glances from one to the other.

Tony stood beside Florence, shuffling his feet like a naughty schoolboy caught out in a misdemeanour.

'Listen, Lillian, pet…' he began.

'Shut up! Close the door.'

He turned swiftly to close it as Lillian fixed Florence with a stare so full of venom she flinched as though she'd been slapped in the face.

'How long have you known my husband?' Lillian's tone was gritty and hard, the coarseness of her voice underlined by the fury in her face.

'I don't know him!' Florence cried out, shaking her head emphatically. 'Why does everyone keep asking me that? I never set eyes on him until I came looking for an apprenticeship the week before last.'

'Yes, well…!' Lillian gave a loud sniff of disdain. 'You would say that, wouldn't you?' She tipped her nose high in the air. 'I'm not a fool, mind, whatever your name is…'

'It's Florence Philpots,' Florence interrupted quickly, 'and I don't know why you're acting like this.'

'Come off it!' Lillian's eyes narrowed, glaring at her. 'You're his latest bit of stuff. Why else would you be here?'

'*What!*' Florence's mouth fell open with shock. She couldn't believe she was hearing those words from Tony's wife, a complete stranger to her. She'd been angry with Darlene for making such awful, uncalled-for remarks, but put it down to sheer spite. To hear the accusation spoken by Lillian Longford was unbelievable. How could she think such a thing?

'Lillian, sweetie, listen, will you?' Tony tried again.

'I said, shut up, Tony!' she snapped, throwing

him a glance of irritation. 'You're in enough bloody trouble already. Don't dig yourself in deeper. I've warned you before, haven't I? I won't have your fancy pieces here.'

Florence realised, hearing the slight change of tone when speaking to her husband, that Lillian was less angry with him than with Florence herself. Lillian was directing the force of her anger against her, and that was appallingly unfair when she had done nothing wrong.

'Please, Mrs Longford!' Florence pleaded, stepping forward to the desk. 'You've got this all wrong. I don't know Mr Longford...'

'*Mr Longford.*' Lillian gave a bitter laugh. 'You're a good little actress, I'll give you that. You'd do better on the stage than in hair-dressing.'

'This isn't fair, I tell you!' Florence cried out again. 'I've done nothing wrong.'

She was less frightened now, and more angry, furious, in fact. Her voice was raising uncontrollably. Everyone outside could hear, but she didn't care just then. Having to defend herself like this was disgusting, humiliating. She wouldn't put up with it any longer. Who did Lillian Longford think she was, anyway?

In growing anger, Florence straightened her back, and lifting her head high, clenched her jaw in determination. She wouldn't put up with this, and she'd give as good as she got. If Lillian wanted a slanging match, she'd get one.

'Whatever disagreements you have with Mr Longford, they're nothing to do with me,' Florence said loudly and scathingly. 'Don't make me part of your disgusting squabbles.'

'Disgusting squabbles!' Lillian jumped to her feet, her scarlet mouth working in fury. 'Well! Of all the brass-necked hussies, you take the biscuit.'

'I'm not a hussy, you stupid woman!' Florence blazed out, feeling really worked up.

Lillian's preposterous accusation was the last straw. So many things in her life had gone wrong lately she wanted to, needed to hit back at something or someone.

'It's not my fault you can't trust your husband, is it?' Florence shouted at her. 'It's not my fault you're blind with jealousy.'

Lillian's mouth dropped open, and she looked speechless at Florence's audacity. Florence was stunned at her own words, too. She'd said something unforgivable. Lillian Longford was a stranger.

She opened her mouth to apologise, but the words wouldn't come. She *had* been abominably rude, but she was in the right, too, she reminded herself. Lillian had no right to treat her this way. It was all Tony's fault. Why wasn't he speaking up now?

Florence and Lillian continued to stare at each other for a moment more, holding each other's gaze as though neither would be the first to give in. Florence wondered why on earth she'd ever considered this woman the epitome of elegance and sophistication. Her glamour was thoroughly tarnished now.

Perhaps she'd overstepped the mark, but she'd had good reason. How dare Lillian call her names? There was no reason to hold back. She must go on defending herself. This was the real world, and she intended to survive in it.

'I want to do my apprenticeship at Terri's because I think it is the best hairdressing establishment in town,' Florence said at last, feeling breathless with anger. She tossed her head haughtily. 'Am I wrong! I didn't realise it was Bedlam in disguise.'

Lillian's face turned red. She lifted an arm and pointed at the door.

'Get out!' she shouted. 'Go on! Get your hat and coat and get out.'

'Not without my hundred and fifty pounds,' Florence cried out, enraged. Disappointment had a bitter taste, she found, and wanted to spit it out. 'Or you'll be hearing from my father's solicitors.'

As soon as she'd blurted out the threat she knew it was an empty one. Getting David Watson and Palmer, her former employers, involved in her affairs was the last thing she wanted. Imagine it! She'd be a laughing stock.

Nevertheless, empty as the threat was, it sounded good. It made her feel better and gave her a sense of some control.

'Hold on a minute, Lillian, for God's sake,' Tony spoke again at last.

Moving closer to his wife, he grasped her arm.

'You're giving the clients some lively entertainment with all this yelling and bellowing.'

He glanced at Florence in anger. 'And you shut up as well, Flo.'

Fuming, Florence wondered why was she staying here to be insulted? She had the money

149

for the premium now. She could go elsewhere.

Lillian tried to shrug him off, but he held on, sliding an arm around her waist, his fingers spreading over one silk-clad hip.

'Lillian! Listen to me, will you? The kid's telling the truth,' he went on in a soothing tone. 'Don't know her from Eve, or Adam for that matter. She came in off the street the other week, looking for a job. Honest to God!'

He tightened his arm around Lillian's waist, easing her closer to him. It was such an intimate gesture, Florence had the impulse to look away, but steadied herself.

This was *her* future they were arguing about; these two people, possibly her employers for the next three years. She must steel herself to cope with them, and unwanted glimpses of their private lives; the way they lived; where they touched her own life.

'The cheque's in the safe, Lil, sweetheart. Wouldn't kid you, would I? I know I can't get away with anything. You're too clever, for me, Lil.'

Lillian was still for a moment as she looked up into Tony's face.

'You'd better not forget that, either, Tony.'

Her tone was more reasonable now, obviously pacified. It was evident that Tony Longford was no good, Florence thought with contempt, but perhaps he was the one to make Lillian see sense.

'The kid wanted an apprenticeship.' He was still speaking in that soothing tone to his wife. 'And I thought, why not? She's clean, tidy, dead keen to learn the business. She speaks nicely.

Might impress some of our snooty clients.'

Lillian was silent, turning her still glittering eyes on Florence.

'If you don't believe me, Lillian,' Tony went on, 'ask Marge. She watches my every flipping move, as well you know.'

There was a touch of sarcasm in his tone, and Lillian glanced up at him, just a little guiltily perhaps. She wetted her lips.

'I do the hiring and firing around here, Tony,' she answered flatly, easing herself from his clasp; reluctantly, Florence thought.

Lillian looked a little less certain of herself, and Florence became suddenly more hopeful. She didn't want to lose this opportunity.

Call it stubbornness. Her training at Terri's wouldn't be easy, that was certain. She'd have to fight every inch of the way. But she still felt it would be worth it. If only Lillian would trust her. But would she forgive Florence for the things she'd said?

'Of course you do, darling,' he said cajolingly. 'But you weren't here, were you?'

'She's insolent, Tony,' Lillian replied plaintively. 'How can you let her speak to me like that? A cheap bit, like her.'

Florence was livid. She'd been prepared to forgive everything that had been said so far, if need be, to preserve her apprenticeship, but she'd take no more insults.

'Now look here...!' she spluttered.

'Shut up, Flo!' Tony snapped an interruption, glaring at her warningly.

To Lillian he said:

151

'You're right, darling, of course. There's nothing to get upset about. And it's not too late. She's only been here a few hours. We'll give her the cheque back, if you like, tear up the agreement, and say no more about it.'

'Now wait a minute!' Florence burst out, determined not to be silenced. 'And I won't shut up, Mr Longford.'

Suddenly it was vitally important that she hang onto this apprenticeship. Going home to confess to her parents that she was unable to hold down a job in her chosen career for less than a day was unthinkable. Imagine the pitying looks she'd get as she was forced to eat humble pie! And what would she do instead? Find an inferior hairdresser? She'd never be satisfied with that.

'You agreed to take me on as an apprentice,' she went on, speaking loudly to hide the desperation in her voice. 'I paid my premium in all good faith and I signed the agreement. As far as I'm concerned, that's binding. You can't break our agreement just because your wife's got a suspicious mind. I warn you, I *will* have my father's solicitors on you, if you do.'

Lillian's lips thinned, but she said nothing. Tony opened his mouth but Florence forestalled him, determined not to let go of the advantage, fixed on having her say in full.

'You've got a salon full of clients.' She flung up an arm to point to the closed door. 'I'll go out there now and announce to the lot of them that I'm getting the sack because Lillian Longford can't trust her husband.'

Florence paused, gulping, watching their

startled expressions. It was blackmail, but at that moment she didn't care. She'd set her heart on being a hairdresser and had sacrificed so much already. She wouldn't be beaten now.

Florence swallowed hard.

'Get Marge in here,' she went on, 'as Mr Longford suggests. You'll believe her, Mrs Longford, won't you?'

After a brief pause Lillian nodded and Tony opened the door, calling Marge, who was in the room in a flash, as if she'd been waiting for the call.

Florence stood trembling as Lillian cross-questioned her old friend. It was still humiliating not being believed, as though she were some criminal or loose woman.

Lillian owed her an apology, though she knew she wouldn't get it.

Her employer looked at her finally, her expression still tight and disapproving.

'All right, Florence or whatever your name is,' she said stiffly. 'Against my better judgement I'll let things rest as they are for the moment.'

She lifted a hand and pointed a red-tipped finger at Florence.

'But I'll tell you straight to your face. I don't like you. You're a troublemaker if ever I saw one. I'll have my eye on you, mind; every minute, so watch out!' Her eyes glinted with malice. 'One false move, miss, and you're out on your ear, agreement or no agreement. Get it?'

Florence nodded, swallowing hard.

'Yes, Mrs Longford.'

'Right!' Lillian jerked her head towards the

door. 'Get out! Get back to work.'

Florence went, her face burning with humiliation. Her dream was costing her so much, much more than she'd ever realised possible. Her feelings and her pride were taking a beating, but no one would dampen her spirit, she promised herself. She'd stick, and no one would shift her, no matter how hard they tried.

She'd never get an apology from Lillian, but she'd get recompense some other way, she decided. She'd learn everything she could, work hard, then one day it would be her turn to hire and fire.

Someday, somehow, she'd meet Lillian Longford on equal terms.

CHAPTER 10

Friday! She'd made it to Friday, at least. It'd been touch and go a few times in the week, when Lillian's glinting eyes turned on her. But she still hung on to her job by the skin of her teeth, even if she hadn't got over that awful scene with her employer last Monday. Savage wasn't the word for it!

She wasn't used to people behaving like that. First Ken and now Lillian. Although her natural rashness allowed her to answer Lillian back in kind, she knew she must curb that instinct now if she were to survive. But she could also give herself a pat on the back. She'd weathered that, so she surely could face anything else fate threw her?

During the week Florence was careful, very careful, working hard, showing she was willing to do anything asked of her. She'd even put up with Darlene's taunts and bad temper, steeling herself not to mind, schooling herself to hold her tongue and not speak out recklessly as she usually did. And she'd kept well away from Tony, too.

Had it paid off? She didn't know. But it was Friday, pay-day, and the day to get the chop if it was going to happen. If she could get through today unscathed, she might make it through the rest of her life, and make her dream come true into the bargain.

Yet her survival might still mean the end for Glenys. Tony had said he'd think about it again, but hadn't mentioned it since. She was doing her best to keep as much distance between them as possible, and wouldn't dare tackle him again on the matter. She must mind her own business now, and wait and see.

It was early, but from the pavement outside the salon Florence could see the glint of lights in the salon, so someone was there already. She hesitated a moment, then pushed the door open. It wouldn't be Tony. It was far too early for him.

Marge was in the kitchen holding a mug of steaming tea, her big frame straining at the buttons on her overall. She grinned at Florence.

'Hello, Flo, love. There's an early bird you are.'

Florence pulled off her tam and took off her coat, getting ready to slip into her overall.

'Likewise,' she answered, grinning back at the older woman.

She liked Marge and knew she could learn a lot from her, even if she hadn't been trained by a top-notch London stylist. Marge knew her stuff, and had a flair all her own.

She was a bit rough and ready, and had some outrageous sayings, but, Florence sensed, deep inside Marge was really the salt of the earth, and she could understand Lillian's complete trust in her.

'Always here early Friday, I am, to see to Mrs P,' Marge told her.

'Who?'

She took a long swig of the hot tea.

'Mrs Patterson,' she said, wiping a hand across

156

her mouth. 'The old girl who does the dirty towels for us. Cheaper she is, see, than the laundry, and reliable as well.'

Marge grinned.

'She's a character, mind. Lives up by the Palace Theatre. Never seen her crack a smile, yet. Her old man gives her hell by all accounts.' She sniffed disdainfully. 'If he was mine, I'd kick his arse from here to the bottom of Wind Street. The old bugger!'

Marge finished off the tea at one gulp.

'When I think of the likes of old Patterson,' she said bitterly. 'No bleeding good to nobody, least of all his poor missus, escaping the bombing, and my Bill, with a heart of gold, ready to give his last farthing, copping it when the bloody Luftwaffe bombed the docks. Well! It makes me wonder!'

She glanced at Florence. There was a hint of tears glistening in her eyes.

'It's his birthday today. He'd have been forty-five, see.'

'Oh, Marge!' Florence immediately put an arm around the older woman's shoulders, and hugged her. 'I'm so sorry. You must miss him dreadfully.'

She didn't know what else to say. She'd never lost a loved one, not to death, anyway.

Marge gave a big sniff.

'I'm a silly bugger myself,' she said, her tone lighter. She eased herself gently from Florence's hug. 'Silly and sentimental. The past is the past. We can't go back. Make the most of now, that's what I say.'

Florence's sharp ears caught the faint clacking of the wooden bead curtain and she darted out of the kitchen, always on the alert for Lillian, determined her employer wouldn't catch her unawares.

A small thin woman stood in the salon. An old felt hat was pulled down around her ears, and her coat's dipping hem hung almost to her ankles. Bony hands gripped the handle of an ancient pram, scratched and rusting.

Florence stared for a moment, bewildered, then she saw the canvas bags piled in the pram and recognised them as belonging to Terri's.

Marge came out of the kitchen.

'Morning, Mrs P,' she said cheerfully, the sadness of a moment ago completely evaporated. 'How's life treating you, then, kid?'

'Terrible.' Mrs Patterson had a high, squeaky voice that Florence somehow associated with frailty, yet the canvas bags were weighty even for her as she lifted them out of the pram.

'Flo, love,' Marge said. 'Fetch those bags out in the yard. Put them in the pram for Mrs P, while I get her a cuppa before that bloody Darlene gets here.'

When Florence was finished, Marge and Mrs Patterson were still sitting in the kitchen, Mrs Patterson holding out her mug for another fill-up.

Marge winked at Florence.

'Go in the office, kid, and get Mrs P's money. It'll be on the desk in a brown envelope.'

The envelope was on the desk as Marge said. Florence picked it up and was about to return to the kitchen when a sound in the storeroom startled her. Who else was here this time of the morning? Not Tony or Lillian; and no one else had any business in the storeroom right now.

Florence felt her heart rise bumpily to her throat. Had someone broken in?

Cautiously, she tiptoed to the storeroom door and peered around it. The office safe in the storeroom was open, and a man was stooped down, rummaging about inside. The back of his dark curly head was immediately recognisable.

Florence let out a long breath of relief, her pulses slowing and her heart settling back down in her chest.

'Oh, Tony! I mean, Mr Longford, you gave me a turn. I thought we were being burgled.'

He stood up immediately and turned around, when Florence got another shock.

'Oh!'

She stared. It wasn't Tony Longford, after all. From the back she could have sworn it was him. This man had the same build and colouring; he had even features like Tony, but the whiteness of his skin, the deep lines around his mouth and eyes made him look older, much older.

Florence opened her mouth to shout a warning to Marge, and was ready to bolt to safety, when the man smiled and said, 'Don't tell me! You're Florence.'

She clamped her mouth shut, eyeing him warily. How did a burglar know her name?

He smiled broadly, obviously amused at her expression, and stepped forward to walk into the office. Florence quickly retreated before him, uncertain but alert. Should she shout for Marge just in case?

'Before you call the cops, kiddo, I'd better tell you I'm Cliff.'

Florence continued to stare. The name meant nothing to her. Now she noticed he was holding several brown envelopes, the kind used for pay-packets. When he threw them onto the desk, Florence heard the chinking of coins. Was he stealing their wages after all?

'Who are you?' she demanded to know, trying to steady the tremor in her voice. If she'd caught a burglar red-handed, he'd say anything, wouldn't he, to get away? 'I warn you,' she went on, attempting to sound fierce, 'I'm not on my own here, mind. Now, what are you doing with those pay-packets?'

To her consternation, he laughed, pulling out the chair behind the desk and sitting down.

'Relax, Flo. I'm no burglar.' He smiled again. He seemed to smile a lot, Florence noticed. Quite a pleasant smile, too, though she was still suspicious of him.

'May I call you Flo, by the way?' he went on and without waiting for her answer, continued. 'I'm Tony's brother. Cliff Longford. I do the book-keeping around here and put up the wages. Anything else you'd like to know?'

Florence shook her head, her face growing warm with embarrassment. Now she felt a fool. The man would think she was mad.

'I'm sorry,' she said. 'I didn't know...'

'Of course you didn't,' Cliff said. 'Don't worry, kid. No offence taken.'

He smiled again. It *was* an engaging smile, Florence decided, and she could swear it was genuine. She resisted the urge to smile back.

Tony's smile always looked like a leer and appeared false, at least to her anyway. She'd quickly learned during this last week that Tony fooled a lot of people with that false charm. Maybe Cliff was the same? There was an intelligent look in his eyes. Perhaps he was more clever than Tony, more subtle? Florence considered that to be likely, and was on her guard again.

'Yes, well.' Florence lifted her chin. 'I'm sorry I spoke out of turn.' She suddenly felt she needed to explain her own presence there. 'I came in for Mrs Patterson's money. I'll take it to her.'

'Okay, Flo. Oh, and ask Marge to bring me in a cuppa, will you?'

Florence was glad to get back to the kitchen. Glenys had arrived, and Marge and Mrs Patterson were finishing off their cigarettes. Florence handed over the envelope.

Mrs Patterson pocketed it eagerly, but seemed settled, a bony hand still clutching her mug of tea.

'There's a man in the office,' Florence said to Marge. 'Says his name's Cliff.'

Mrs Patterson got up from the table quickly.

'I better be off, then. See you Wednesday, girls.'

Despite the frailty of her appearance, Mrs Patterson moved quite swiftly, and was gone.

'He wants some tea,' Florence said to Marge, and was relieved to see her smile.

'Take him a mug of tea, Glenys, will you?' Marge said. 'I bet he hasn't had any breakfast, either.'

161

Glenys drew back, looking startled.

'Not going anywhere near him, am I.'

'Now, Glenys, don't be *twp*, will you?' Marge said.

There was a vague warning in her voice, Florence thought, and decided she'd been right to suspect that Cliff was no more trustworthy than his brother Tony. But Marge's obvious benevolence towards Cliff surprised her. She made it so plain she despised, even hated his brother.

'Cliff Longford is a convict. He hasn't long come out of prison,' Glenys said, breathlessly. 'I'm staying well away from him. He's dangerous.' She nodded at Florence's startled look. 'Yes, in prison. And for murder, too!'

'Now, stop it, Glenys, will you!' Marge was furious for some reason. 'You keep your trap shut. Here! Give me that mug. I'll take his tea.'

In the doorway she glanced back.

'Glenys! Don't stand about gossiping. Get those clean towels out of the bags and into the cupboard. And make sure each cubicle has a supply. You'd better be quick, too, or you'll have Darlene and Tony on your back in a minute.'

Glenys pouted.

'It's not nine yet, Marge. Thought I'd have a cup of tea first.'

'I said, get cracking!' Marge snapped, and Florence stared. She'd not seen the older woman angry before. What was it all about?

Glenys reluctantly began emptying the canvas bags and stacking the towels in the cupboard. Florence helped her with the task.

'She's always sucking up to Cliff,' Glenys muttered. 'Her and Darlene, as well. Both of them fancy their chances with him, even though he's married.' She pulled a face, her lips curling back in disgust. 'A murderer, he is, mind. How could they fancy *him?* It's no wonder his wife ran off and left him. Australia, she's gone. Can't get further away than that, can she?'

'Glenys, it's not nice, making up awful stories about people,' Florence reproved.

Over the week Florence had found the younger girl to be immature with a tendency to silliness. It was no wonder Tony considered getting rid of her. Still, Florence thought charitably, perhaps it wasn't all Glenys's fault. She was an only child, and appeared to have hardly any friends.

'It's true, I tell you!' Glenys was indignant. 'You ask anybody. He killed a man in a fight and they sent him to prison.'

Florence sighed impatiently. She didn't believe a word of it.

'If it's true why wasn't he hanged, then?'

Out of her depth, Glenys pouted.

'I dunno. But he's a murderer, and murderers get a taste for blood, don't they? I'm not giving him a chance to murder me!'

CHAPTER 11

Mid-December 1948

Glenys and Marge were in the kitchen, poring over a daily paper when Florence arrived at the salon one Thursday morning breathless and shivering from the seasonal cold outside.

She glanced over their shoulders at the open paper, unwinding a woolly scarf from around her neck.

'What's all the "oohs and aahs" for, then?'

'It's this picture of the new prince with his mother. Isn't he lovely?' Glenys said, pointing to a photograph of Princess Elizabeth with her son and heir in her arms. 'Little Prince Charles. Oh, there's romantic, Flo, isn't it?'

She agreed, and looking at the photograph, the happiness on the face of the young royal mother, Florence felt a new longing in her own heart.

A child of her own to love and be loved by. It must be a wonderful feeling, Florence imagined, with a tightening of her throat; to give life to another being; someone who needs you, depends on you, and gives love unconditionally.

She wanted that, yearned for it suddenly. She'd never rest until her special dream came true, but one day, she promised herself, she'd also have a family of her own, a son perhaps, her own heir to the business she'd build up.

First, though, she reminded herself sternly, she

165

had to get established and that couldn't be done sitting around goggling at newspapers.

'It's really wonderful, but come on, Glenys,' she said, putting a hand gently but firmly on the younger girl's shoulder. 'We've got our jobs to think of. Let's get cracking.'

Florence had been at Terri's three months already, and it wasn't getting any easier either. It took more staying power than she realised she had not to break under Darlene's constant persecution, which had transferred from Glenys to her.

Sometimes she wanted to let rip at Darlene, give her a mouthful back, but Florence was too aware of Lillian's eagle eye, and wouldn't risk it. The longer she stayed here, the more she had to lose. Would she ever win Lillian's confidence? she wondered.

It was a hectic day all round. Everyone wanted their hair done for Christmas, and Hazel had booked more perms than the staff could comfortably handle; not that anyone would grumble at the volume of business. Florence and Glenys worked frantically, washing head after head, sweeping up what felt like a ton or so of hair-clippings and handing out thousands of curlers.

Florence, her feet aching, looked forward to the time when she'd help the last customer into her coat and wish her goodbye. When at last that time came, she sighed with relief. All she wanted was to get home, have a cup of tea and then go to bed. She'd had enough.

All the salon staff was gone, except Tony.

Florence helped Glenys with the last of the clearing up, and they were in the kitchen getting their coats when Tony came in.

'Flo, I want a stock-take of the storeroom tonight,' he said. 'Stay behind and do it. You'll get paid overtime.'

Florence's mouth fell open with dismay.

'Has it got to be tonight, Mr Longford? Can't Glenys and I come in early tomorrow to do it?'

He shook his head.

'We'll probably be just as busy for tomorrow and I want to make sure we don't run short of supplies before the weekend. I may have to go to the wholesalers tomorrow morning first thing, so it's got to be tonight.'

Reluctantly, Florence removed her coat. If she was getting overtime for it, how could she complain? she thought wearily. After all, it was all part and parcel of the job. Perhaps she and Glenys could make short work of it.

Glenys started to take her coat off too.

'You can go, Glenys,' Tony said quickly. 'I won't need the two of you.'

Florence stared.

'I can't do it on my own, Mr Longford.'

'You won't have to,' he answered. 'We'll do it together. It won't take all that long. Goodnight, then, Glenys.'

Florence felt the hairs on the back of her neck stand up on end as Glenys scuttled hastily out of the kitchen with a backwards, covert glance at her. Florence heard the rattle of the wooden bead curtain, and the shop door slam shut.

She was alone here with Tony Longford. The

thought made her skin prickle with apprehension. She didn't know why it should. He hadn't done or said anything out of place these last months, yet alarm bells rang in her head. Was it her imagination? She wasn't sure. She didn't want to stay around to find out, either.

'I don't think I want to work tonight, Mr Longford,' she ventured carefully.

He was watching her, his eyes narrowed.

'Why not? I said I'd pay overtime.'

'I … I just remembered I have an appointment.'

'An appointment?' He raised his eyebrows, looking at her as though he didn't believe a word she said. 'Do you mean a date?'

Florence swallowed.

'Yes, that's right, a date. I have to go now. I'm late already.'

His mouth tightened, his eyes flashing with sudden anger.

'What's more important, Flo, your job here, or a date so exciting you forgot about it?'

'That's unfair, Mr Longford!' Florence cried. 'I'm working as hard as I can. It is a bit short notice, after all. My parents'll worry if I don't get home at my usual time.'

'Oh, so you don't have a date after all, then,' he said. 'Why did you lie about it?'

'I'm not lying,' Florence protested hotly, but at the same time feeling in the wrong. She was lying, after all, but how could she explain that she didn't trust him further than she could throw the kitchen stove. 'I don't want to work tonight, that's all.'

Suddenly the anger left his face, and he smiled.

'Look, Flo, I'm not being unreasonable. We've had a busy day. Stocks might be low. We can't be careless in business. Stock-taking is a bore, but it shouldn't take long. We'll probably be finished within the hour. Your mother runs a guest house, right, so she must be on the telephone? Give her a ring. Explain you'll be late. I can't be fairer than that, can I?'

Florence swallowed hard, uncertain now. He sounded reasonable, even concerned. Perhaps she was making a mountain out of a molehill. She certainly didn't want to get on the wrong side of Tony. He was all that stood between her and Lillian. If she lost his patronage, Lillian would boot her out of the door for sure.

But Tony was such a tricky customer, a voice of caution warned her.

'You're sure it can't wait until the morning?'

He sighed heavily.

'Flo, do you want to be a hairdresser or don't you? You've got to start at the bottom, and you've got to be flexible. Now, I'm asking you to work overtime. Are you refusing? Because if you are...'

'No ... no, of course I'm not,' Florence said hastily. She wetted her lips nervously. Perhaps she was being over-cautious. They probably would've been halfway through the stock-taking by now if she hadn't held them up, arguing. 'I will telephone my mother, though, if you don't mind.'

He stepped aside for her to pass through into the salon.

'Use the telephone in reception, then come straight to the storeroom. I want to get home

169

tonight as well, mind.'

Tommy answered the telephone. His response sounded garbled, obviously eating something as usual. She wished fervently she were there, too. He took her message, but slammed the receiver down before she could say more.

She stood for a moment in reception, feeling isolated and apprehensive. She could slip back to the kitchen, get her coat and handbag, and sneak off before Tony knew she'd gone. But she wouldn't have a job to come back to tomorrow, that's for sure.

Florence squared her shoulders and lifted her chin determinedly. What could he do to her anyway? Surely she could put up with his suggestive remarks for the next hour? There'd be no one around to witness her humiliation. She'd even give him a piece of her mind if it got too much.

Shelves ran around three sides of the storeroom. The top shelves were close to the ceiling, needing a stepladder to reach them. The room was quite small, but adequate for the shop's supplies of shampoos and perming liquids. The job would take less than an hour, she was sure of it.

Tony was already marking items off on a clipboard.

'Right, Flo,' he said briskly. 'Let's start off with shampoo.'

Reassured at his businesslike tone, Florence started to count bottles.

In three-quarters of an hour they'd finished. She was still up the stepladder.

'Right, that's it,' Tony said. 'You can come down now.'

Florence glanced down to see him standing at the bottom of the steps, holding it with both hands. She tentatively stepped one rung down, then stopped. He hadn't moved away, but was smiling up at her in a way that made her heart turn over with renewed apprehension.

'You can let go the steps now, Mr Longford, I can manage,' she said firmly, trying to quell the tremor in her voice.

'I like it here,' he said, grinning up at her. 'The view's pretty good. You've got smashing legs, Flo. As good as Betty Grable's any day.'

Holding on to the steps with one hand Florence grabbed the front of her utility skirt with the other, trying to draw it closer around her legs.

'Please move aside, Mr Longford. You're in my way.'

He laughed.

'You going to stay up there all night? Come on down, kid. There's nothing to be scared of.'

Florence tossed her head, feeling annoyance at being in such a silly position.

'I'm not in the least scared, Mr Longford,' she said airily. 'I just want to get off the steps, and go home.'

'No, you don't, sweetie.'

'What?'

'You don't want to go home just yet, any more than I do, otherwise you wouldn't have agreed to stay on tonight.'

Florence stared, thoroughly alarmed.

171

'What are you talking about?' she cried. 'You demanded I stayed. You as good as threatened to give me the sack if I didn't.'

'Oh, come on, Flo! You knew I was only kidding. You stayed because you wanted to.' He leered up at her, jerking his head in an invitation. 'Come down by here, pet. Let's get to know each other better.'

Thoroughly frightened, Florence clung even more tightly to the steps. She must not panic, she told herself sternly. That was the last thing she should do.

She peered down at him.

'Why are you doing this, Mr Longford? You promised Lillian...'

'To hell with Lillian!' Tony was almost shouting. 'Come down, damn it!'

He shook the ladder violently, and Florence screamed in terror, suddenly fearful she'd be shaken free and fall. It wasn't all that far to the floor, but she didn't fancy landing in a helpless heap at Tony's feet.

'Stop it, please!' she called out, nearer to panic than was comfortable. 'All right, I'll come down. But please stand aside.'

He moved away from the ladder, and Florence breathed a little prayer of thankfulness.

She stepped down awkwardly from rung to rung, feeling her legs stiff and strained with mounting trepidation. He was standing between her and the doorway. The room was so small there wasn't enough space to dodge round him.

When she reached the floor he quickly moved forward again, and Florence hastily stepped aside, suddenly realising, too late, that she'd made a wrong move and was now in the corner of the room furthest from the door.

Trapped!

He advanced again, grinning, and Florence drew away from him, flattening herself against the only wall without shelving. She could only stare wide-eyed at him, her mind a tumbling jumble of thoughts. How could she get away? What was he going to do?

'Flo, sweetie, don't look so scared,' he said, coming so close she could feel his breath hot on her face.

'Let me go, Mr Longford, please,' she murmured, her voice shaking with fright, the like of which she'd never known before.

'Don't be silly, sweetie,' he said, with a low, husky laugh. 'And don't be coy, either. I haven't got time for it. You don't really want me to let you go, and you know it. Now, come on, pet, give, give to Tony.'

He put his hands on her shoulders, trying to draw her to him as Florence resisted, pressing herself even closer to the wall.

Her throat felt dry, scorched with a growing terror. This couldn't be happening! What did he intend to do?

Anything he wanted, a voice screamed in her head.

She was tall, but he was big and powerful. She'd never be able to fight him off. She could only reason with him, talk, persuade.

Florence swallowed hard, gathering all her remaining courage that had started to ebb away the moment he'd caught her up the ladder. She couldn't allow this to happen, whatever it was.

'Mr Longford … Tony…'

'That's better, sweetie. Now you're getting the idea. I promise you won't be sorry. After all, a kid like you, you haven't met any real men before I can teach you things, lover, you never even dreamed about…'

'Don't touch me!' Florence screamed as his hand strayed from her shoulder to her breast.

'You don't mean that, pet. I know women.' He laughed softly. 'They like to play games, play hard to get, when all the time they're as keen as mustard. But I don't mind playing your game, sugar.'

His touch on her breast became suddenly more demanding, and he leaned heavily against her, pinning her to the wall.

Terror overwhelming her, Florence screamed again, the rawness of it ripping at the membranes of her throat. She struggled violently, pounding at him with her fists. The blows she rained on his shoulders and chest made little impression. He was laughing, exerting more strength against her.

'Oh, ho! You like it rough, eh?' he sniggered. 'I'll oblige, sweetie, as rough as you like.'

His hand squeezed her breast cruelly, and Florence screamed again in pain and horror. This couldn't be happening to her!

'Stop it! Stop it! You're hurting me. Let me go, please, please!'

He laughed again. 'What? When we're having so much fun? I knew you'd be a little corker. I can always tell. I've seen the way you've looked at me

174

these last few months. You've been waiting, kid, haven't you? Waiting for an opportunity like this. Now, come here, let's make the most of it.'

Florence twisted her face away, unable to bear his closeness. His body was pressed heavily against her, the contact making her skin crawl, and nausea rose in her throat.

This is some awful nightmare, her mind kept saying over and over. It can't be real. It can't be true.

His hand released her breast to grip her lower jaw, forcing her face around to his.

'Come here!' His voice was harsh now, all pretence gone. 'Give me a kiss. Come on, you little bitch, give!'

'No! Don't! Stop it, please.'

Her words were smothered as his mouth came down on hers savagely. She couldn't breathe! She couldn't see! The nausea was swelling. She felt vomit rising. She would choke on her own vomit!

Dear God! Please help me!

No sooner was the prayer thought than she was suddenly free, the violence of her release sending her tumbling to the floor. She didn't understand why; all she could do was retch and vomit.

Her eyes were watering so badly she still couldn't see properly. She was aware, however, of tumult within the small room, of voices raised in fury, and outlined against the bright lights of the salon beyond, the figures of two men struggling in the doorway.

Florence blinked in confusion, peering helplessly at them, her mind in total confusion. What was happening? Who had saved her?

Wiping the back of her hand across her streaming eyes, she recognised the other man as Cliff. Cliff had saved her.

She pushed herself to her feet and stumbled after the men as the struggle spilled into the salon. She watched, leaning against the door jamb for support, residual fear making her legs weak and shaking.

Tony, his face dark with rage, faced Cliff. Separated now, they glared at each other like two mad dogs.

'What the bloody hell do you think you're doing?' Tony yelled at his brother. 'What business is it of yours?'

Cliff, his face suffused with blood, lifted a fist and shook it in Tony's face, his voice low and menacing.

'I'll smash you into the ground if you ever lay another finger on that girl. I mean it, Tony.'

Tony swiped the fist away.

'Oh, yes! You and whose army? What's the matter with you, mun, Cliff? She's only a bit of skirt. She's asking for it. A bit of fun, it was, that's all.'

There was a growl deep in Cliff's chest and he stepped closer to Tony, shoulders hunched. Florence stared helplessly at them both, her skin crawling with apprehension.

'*You're* bloody asking for it, mate!' Cliff snarled. 'Flo's a decent girl. Leave her alone, I said, and I'm not kidding.'

Tony's lip curled with scorn.

'You poor dope! You're a fine one to tell me what to do with a woman. Can't even keep one of

176

your own. They wipe their feet on you.'

With a roar of rage, Cliff lashed out at Tony's jeering face.

Florence heard and almost felt the sickening thud of flesh striking flesh, bone striking bone. Then Tony was sprawled on the salon floor, blood streaming from his nose and splashing onto his white shirt. There was a cut on his lip, too. His stunned look would've been comical under different circumstances, Florence thought in a daze, the nightmare still with her.

Cliff stood over his brother, daring him to get to his feet. Florence was still frightened, but this time not for herself. She didn't really care what happened to Tony, not after what he'd done to her. Cliff had saved her, but she didn't want him to go any further. It wasn't right that brother should be against brother. Cliff had drawn blood, and Tony had asked for it with his unfeeling insults, but now it mustn't go any further between them.

'Cliff!' Florence called out urgently. 'Don't!'

Cliff stepped back and Tony scrambled up, wiping the blood away on his shirt sleeve.

'I could have you for this, Cliff,' he said bitterly. 'You've just come out of clink for killing a man. I could have you charged for assault.' He pointed a finger at Florence. 'She's a witness. They'd put you away again for a long time.'

'Maybe it would be worth it,' Cliff said. 'Because I'm itching to beat you to a pulp anyway, you bastard! I hate your kind.'

'I'll speak out against *you*,' Florence glared at Tony, suddenly regaining her courage. 'I'll tell the police what you did to me.'

'Huh!' Tony threw her a scornful glance. 'Do you think they'd believe a silly bitch like you?'

'Be careful, Tony.' Cliff lifted a fist in warning, his voice harsh. 'Because I'm liable to thump you again.'

Cliff looked his brother up and down, an expression of deep contempt set hard on his face.

'You're pathetic! A low-down, womanising, slimy worm. You make me puke. It was a worthless louse like you that got me a prison sentence. But I'm not sorry I killed him. He killed my marriage, didn't he?'

'Cliff!' Florence took a tentative step forward. 'I want to go home.'

Cliff let out a long breath, and his shoulders relaxed.

'Okay, Flo. Get your things.'

'Yes, get out!' Tony said, his voice thickened with the flow of blood. 'And don't come back here, you bitch. You're finished here.'

Florence stopped for a moment, shocked at the venom in his voice, and the rage still flashing in his eyes. Of course, it was inevitable. Tony'd probably been planning this all along. He'd never seriously considered her as an apprentice.

Disappointment plunged through her like a sharp knife. To think her dream must end like this.

'Hold on a minute,' Cliff said. 'Lillian does the hiring and firing around here, remember?' He glanced at Florence. 'Do you want to go on with your apprenticeship, Flo?'

Florence swallowed, venturing a look at Tony's face.

178

'I don't know,' she answered Cliff. 'I'm very upset at the moment.'

Would she ever be able to stand the sight of Tony, let alone work with him, after what had happened?

She felt nausea rising again, remembering those awful moments in the storeroom. If she wasn't standing here this moment, watching these two men face each other in anger, she might think it *was* only a nightmare. But it was real, only too real, and now, although she was innocent, the consequences of Tony's evil doing had to be faced and borne.

But did she have to give up her dream? Did she have the guts, the determination, in the face of all that had happened to go on with it? Despite Tony Longford?

She flashed him a glance of bitterness and disgust.

'What you did to me was horrible!' she cried out. 'I ought to tell my father about you.'

She knew if she did that it would be the end. There'd be no going back then.

'I happen to know, Flo, that Lillian is changing her attitude towards you,' Cliff said. 'She thinks you're working out well. She told me herself she's beginning to believe she misjudged you. Think about that while you make up your mind.'

Florence stared. Was that true? It might make all the difference in the world.

Tony gave a scornful laugh.

'One word from me can change all that.'

Cliff lifted a finger and wagged it in Tony's face.

'One word from me and Lillian will know about

179

your little games,' he said. 'You want trouble, Tony? You'll get trouble, believe me.'

Tony looked livid, but could only grind his teeth in silence.

'What do you want to do, Flo?' Cliff asked.

'If Lillian is willing to accept me, I want to stay on.'

'It won't work,' Tony muttered tightly.

'It'd better work,' Cliff said. 'Or Lillian'll know the reason why.' He turned to Florence. 'Come on, Flo. I'll take you home.'

CHAPTER 12

Panic and dread made Florence feel sick again the next morning as she travelled up to Swansea on the Mumbles train. She'd have to be close to Tony Longford, take his orders, work with him. The thought was so unbearable it made her skin crawl.

But it was unavoidable, she told herself sternly, wrapping her scarf tighter around her neck.

She gazed through the windows of the swaying coach, as it rattled furiously along the rails that edged Swansea Bay. The tide was out, and patches of wet muddy sand reflected the gloomy December morning light, making the vast stretch of beach look bleak and cold and uninviting.

That was the way her life was at the moment, she reflected sadly, already deciding to go resolutely along her chosen path. She couldn't, *wouldn't* give up now and back down at the first unpleasantness.

Unpleasantness! Florence almost smiled at her own understatement. The way Tony had behaved was criminal, ghastly. She should've told her father everything. But it would be the same as confessing she'd made a terrible mistake. That she wasn't ready to do because she didn't believe it was true, despite what had happened.

There were plenty of men like Tony Longford about. She must learn to be wary of them, learn how to deal with them.

At least she wouldn't be totally alone with Tony today. It was Friday, market day in the town. The salon was always packed with clients on a Friday and Saturday, and the girls would be rushed off their feet.

Matrons down from the Valleys for a day's shopping. Affluent ladies preparing themselves for weekend dinner parties, rationing or no rationing. While Saturday afternoons brought shorthand typists, nurses, secretaries, the ones who could afford Terri's prices. Determined on having a good time on Saturday night, dancing down at the Pier Hotel or at the Patti Pavilion, they wanted Terri's to help them look like their favourite film star to attract the most handsome boys.

Florence envied them sometimes. They didn't seem to hanker after any dream. Fancy-free, all they looked for was a good time.

Her envy was always short-lived. There was more to her than that, much more. She had the ability to be somebody, make the most of her life. She had determination and drive. She had a dream.

Getting off the train at Rutland Street, she began her walk through the town towards High Street. Her steps were heavy today, her feet seemed to drag, and she wondered whether Tony Longford's unspeakable behaviour had drained that determination from her. He'd tried to rob her of something very precious, her wholesomeness and self-respect. Had he taken her spirit, too?

Nearing the salon doorway, she stumbled and almost fell, her trembling legs hardly able to hold her body upright. She felt that awful nausea return, souring her mouth and stomach.

How could she face him this morning or ever again? How could she even bear to look at him after what he'd tried to do to her?

She thanked her lucky stars Cliff was passing on his way to have an early pint at the Pullman. Thank heavens he'd been curious enough to investigate the light in the salon when there shouldn't have been one.

Florence felt more grateful to Cliff than she could express. He'd been so kind, so patient when she'd cried all the way to the Mumbles. Then, at a café in The Dunns, he bought her a cup of tea, which helped her compose herself, and after washing her face in the 'ladies' she felt well enough for him to take her home.

Cliff was a tower of strength, and she saw him as a knight in shining armour, saving her from the wicked Baron.

How different he was from Tony. He had none of his brother's arrogance or vanity, and was so easy to talk to, so comfortable to be with. She'd not believed the things Glenys said about him, but now she knew they were true; in part anyway.

It made no difference to the friendship she felt for him. He had killed, and admitted he wasn't sorry, yet instinct told her he wasn't an evil man. After all, many men returning from the war had killed, not once but many times, but no one blamed them for it.

For reasons she couldn't explain to herself, she

183

was ready to absolve him from any blame too. One day perhaps, when he was sure of her friendship, he'd tell her the true story.

Florence kept a mental picture of Cliff's face before her as she stepped over the threshold of Terri's, her heart in her mouth.

Nothing would ever be the same again. Was it a big mistake to carry on working here? she wondered, as she passed through the bead curtain. Would she be able to stick at it here for the rest of the day, let alone the rest of her training?

Her enthusiasm for Terri's and its reputation was tarnished by Tony's lust, dirtied by the memory of his hands raiding her body; the brutality of his mouth on hers, the feel of his hot breath on her skin, and the sweating anticipation emanating from him as he'd struggled to subdue her. She'd never forget that. Never!

If Cliff hadn't intervened, what might have happened? The unthinkable! This thought tormented her throughout the night and still filled her mind with horror. It really didn't bear thinking about, but she couldn't push it from her mind. And now she must come face to face with him again.

But the first face she saw as she passed through the bead curtain was Cliff's. He was standing just outside the office door as though waiting for her. Never was she more pleased to see anyone before in her life.

He stepped forward.

'All right, Flo, love?'

She nodded, and even managed a smile.

Cliff smiled back reassuringly. His face wasn't as even-featured as Tony's, and had more of a lived-in look about it that was altogether more pleasant and sensitive. Florence warmed to him, hoping she *could* count on him as a friend from now on.

Of course, on Fridays he always came early to put up the wages, but all the same, it was good of him to be here to greet her as a good friend would. He understood her feelings, and she liked him for it.

'I'm okay now,' she said quietly, only too aware of voices from the kitchen. 'But I'm dreading the rest of the day.'

At that moment Darlene marched out of the kitchen already in her overall. The poor man's Lana Turner, Florence thought with a twisted smile, then was ashamed of her own spite.

Darlene stopped and stared at them, looking suspiciously from one to the other, perhaps sensing she'd interrupted something private between them. That wouldn't suit Darlene, Florence knew. That young woman was always hanging around him, but as far as Florence could see, Cliff took little notice.

'What time do you call this, miss?' Darlene asked loudly, tapping the watch on her wrist.

'It's just on nine now,' Florence said defensively, still ashamed of her uncharitable feelings towards the young woman.

It was no secret that Darlene's husband had left her as soon as he'd been demobbed, going off to live in Glasgow with an ATS girl he'd met in the Forces.

Florence saw the bitterness just beyond her bold stare and the hard-hearted front she always assumed. Darlene was a chronic pain in the neck, to be sure, and she did make the trainees' lives a misery, but Florence found a spark of sympathy for her despite that. They had something in common after all. They'd both been let down by the men in their lives.

With the misery she was feeling herself, Florence didn't know if she *could* muster much sympathy this morning; not with the prospect of coping with Tony, and the way Darlene was glaring at her.

Darlene sniffed haughtily, lifting a hand to pat her bleached locks as though to reassure herself.

'Well, *I* say you're late, and what I say goes.'

She stuck her nose in the air imperiously.

'I'm in charge, see,' she went on. 'Tony's ill and won't be in till Monday. Now put your overall on sharpish, and get cracking. Won't tell you again, will I?'

'Yes, Darlene,' Florence said meekly, relief flooding through her like cool refreshing water at her unexpected reprieve.

She moved away obediently to do as she was told. But suddenly she had the silliest urge to throw her arms around Darlene and give her a great big kiss.

'I reckon Lillian ought to give us Christmas Eve off,' Glenys grumbled a week later. 'Haven't got my ma a present yet, have I, and it's Christmas Day tomorrow.'

'Get it lunchtime,' Florence suggested.

186

There hadn't been many pretty trinkets, like necklaces and earrings, in the shops over the last few years, but now things were getting more plentiful.

'I saw some lovely bead necklaces in Woolworths,' she went on. 'One and sixpence each. Now that's a bargain. I'm getting one for my sister, Amy. She's home from university today.'

Glenys looked glum. 'Only got a bob left, haven't I.'

Florence gave a resigned sigh.

'Look, I'll lend you sixpence from my lunch allowance, but I want it back next week, right?'

Glenys's face brightened. 'Oh, thanks, Flo. Hey! There's a pal you are.'

'It's only a loan, mind,' Florence warned. 'I'm not made of money.'

She was feeling generous today. It was more relief than anything. With Christmas falling on Saturday and Sunday it meant a couple of extra days off. They wouldn't have to come back to work until Wednesday. Longer away from the salon and Tony.

Looking back over the last week she wondered how she'd managed to remain here, where she'd found the courage.

Cliff had helped there. He called in the salon much more often these days, and Florence felt grateful that he was taking the trouble to keep an eye on her. She felt safer for it.

All the same, it was painful and hideous just being in the salon at the same time as Tony. Even when he was behind the curtains with a client, Florence was aware of his presence, like a bad smell or a grating sound that scratched at the nerves. She couldn't bear to rest her gaze on him, even for a moment. When she did, a terrible nauseating heat overtook her, making her tremble and shake. She'd never get over what happened, she knew. It would haunt her always.

Tony was wary of her, too, she noticed. Thankfully, she'd not been asked to assist him once. When he needed help he called on Glenys. The younger girl was delighted, of course, thinking she was finally winning his approval.

Poor Glenys! Florence was sorry for her, sorry that she was being misled. But maybe it would all work out for the best. Glenys was now being trained by a master-craftsman. Tony had a special gift and the ability to instruct.

There was no doubt that as a Paris-trained stylist, he was superb. He was a beast and she detested him, but over her months at Terri's she'd been fascinated by his skill. Often when assisting him she'd watched in admiration as an unruly head of hair had gradually been trimmed into perfect shape.

He always knew instinctively what was right for any client. Go with the bones, he'd advised her. It galled her to think that because of his philandering ways she'd lost out on the best training to be had in town.

She felt a lightening of spirit when the last client had gone and Lillian said they could leave all the clearing-up until after the holidays.

Florence wished everyone a happy Christmas, except *him,* and hurried home with her few parcels. Though money was very tight, she'd saved all she could out of her meals allowance, and had managed to get something for each of the family. The presents were more tokens than gifts, but she was sure Amy would be pleased with her necklace of blue beads, the most expensive gift of all.

As she walked up the steep hill from the village, she glimpsed the lights of the guest house through the trees. She prayed that Christmas would heal some of the damage between herself and her parents.

There were no recriminations from her mother and father now, just quiet resignation. She wouldn't go so far as to think that they'd washed their hands of her. She wouldn't believe that. She knew without question they loved her still, would support her financially; but there was a discernible separation from them, a divide, which was uncomfortable. The warm Christmas feeling that usually permeated their home would mend that, she was sure.

The family had the place to themselves, the stragglers of holidaymakers having gone at the end of October. Mam-gu and Gramps would be spending Christmas with them, and Florence was looking forward to that.

When Florence opened the back door and stepped thankfully into the big, warm kitchen, Mam-gu was already there, trying to help Edie out with preparations, but getting under her daughter's feet. Florence couldn't help smiling at the exasperated expression on Edie's face.

'Where's our Amy, then, Mam?' Florence enquired, disappointed at not seeing her sister in evidence. 'Didn't she come home after all?'

'She's gone down to Swansea to see Grandma Hilda,' Edie said distractedly, wiping the back of her hand across her brow.

It was unusual to see her mother in a sweat. Florence could guess the reason why. Edie could handle a houseful of holidaymakers practically single-handed, but her own mother was often too much for her. Their relationship had always been somewhat scratchy, and as Mam-gu got older she became more cantankerous.

'Don't know why she wants to bother,' Mam-gu said, irritably. 'Hilda's all right, but that Charlie Philpots wants shooting.'

'Now, Mam,' Edie warned sharply. 'Don't let Will hear you talk like that about his family.'

'Tsk! Credit me with a bit of sense,' Mam-gu snapped back. 'Your husband's got more gumption than you, Edie, my girl. He knows what Charlie's like, and he'd be the first to admit it.'

Looking at the set of Edie's jaw, Florence saw her mother was about to make an issue of it, but the moment was saved as the door opened and Amy swept into the room.

Florence stared, her mouth dropping open in astonishment at the way her sister looked. A girl had gone away to university, but a woman had come home, and a beautiful woman, too.

She wore a gingham dress with white-cuffed cap sleeves, tight round the bodice and waist, which showed her bust-line to full advantage, and a voluminous skirt, from under which peeped several lacy petticoats. She reminded

190

Florence of models she'd seen in glossy advertisements. She didn't seem like their Amy at all.

What interested Florence most was her sister's hair. When she'd left home it had been long. Now it was short, and styled in a halo of shiny soft curls, with kiss curls screening her forehead.

Florence's eyes were round as she stared at her sister.

'Who did your hair, then? It's gorgeous!'

Amy patted her locks, looking smug.

'A *very* high-class hairdresser in Oxford. It cost a bomb, I can tell you, but it's worth it. It's called a Gina Lollabrigida, after that new Italian actress.'

Florence curled a lip.

'A what? Never heard of it!'

Amy looked down her nose, sniffing disparagingly.

'Well, you wouldn't, would you, not down here in the back of beyond. But up London and Oxford, it's the very latest thing, I can tell you.'

Florence came closer, lifting a hand to finger Amy's hair.

'You'll have to let me look at it later, see which way it's been cut...'

'Keep your paws off!' Amy jerked her head away. 'I didn't pay through the nose just to have you mess it up.'

'How's your grandmother?' Edie asked Amy.

She frowned, looking worried.

'She's lost weight, Mam. Doesn't seem to have much go in her. She's getting to look frail and ... old. I feel quite worried about her.'

There was silence for a moment. Grandma Hilda hadn't really got over the illness she'd had in September. All the family could see she'd gone downhill. Everyone except Florence. To her lasting shame, she'd not called to see her grandmother since that awful day last September when Auntie Sybil had betrayed her. She couldn't bring herself to face her aunt or Rita.

Florence hated her own weakness in this, her lack of courage, and her grandmother was the loser. She must wonder at Florence's neglect.

But she'd make it up to her, Florence decided, smitten anew by a burst of conscience. Why should she let the spitefulness of her aunt and cousin come between her and her dear grandmother? She must go and see her, before it was too late.

'Oh, by the way,' Amy went on, suddenly regaining some of her exuberance. 'I've got some news. You'll never guess.'

'What's your Aunt Sybil up to now?' Edie asked wearily.

'It's Rita, Mam. She's engaged to be married.'

'*What?*'

Florence stared transfixed at her sister. She was on the point of pouring herself a cup of tea, and almost dropped the teapot in astonishment.

What on earth was Amy talking about? Rita was such a mouse. It couldn't be true. There'd been no hint of a boyfriend on the horizon at the time of their quarrel last September. How could she have met someone and got engaged in the matter of three months?

'I don't believe it!' she said forcefully. 'Amy! Are

you trying to get my goat, or what?'

Amy shook her head, laughing.

'It's true, Flo, honest! Auntie Sybil said Rita is getting married next March. Quick, isn't it?'

She gave Florence a nudge.

'Hey! Do you think our Rita's got a bun in the oven?'

'Amy!' Edie exploded, her expression aghast. 'Watch your tongue, please. I won't have that kind of vulgar talk in this house. I don't know what's got into you since you've been at that university.'

'Oh, Mam!' Amy tossed her head. 'There's nothing in that. If you heard how some of the students talk...'

'That's enough!' her mother retorted sharply.

'Mam's right, Amy,' Florence agreed, gazing at her sister reproachfully. 'That's an awful thing to say about Rita.'

Amy rolled her eyes towards the heavens.

'Oh, for heaven's sake, Flo!' she replied, scathingly. 'You're as bad as Mam, you are. We're nearly in the second half of the twentieth century, for goodness sake. You want to wake up to the modern age, you do. It's no wonder your boyfriend gave you the elbow.'

Florence felt her jaw drop open with shock. She flashed an accusing look at her mother.

'Mam! You told her! That was private, between you and me. You had no right to do that.'

Edie paused in her preparations, pursing her lips.

'I haven't said a word.' She sniffed loudly, and reproachfully. 'Since Amy's come home she's not stayed in one place long enough to say hello to me properly, let alone have a conversation.'

'Mam didn't tell me,' Amy said airily, ignoring her mother's rebuke. 'Auntie Sybil filled in all the details.'

'What?' Florence was furious. 'What's it got to do with her?'

Amy raised her brows in surprise.

'Well, everything, I should think, since Rita is marrying Ken in March.'

'Ken? Marrying Ken? My Ken? Don't be so daft, will you!'

Florence gave her head a little shake to clear it. She must have misheard. How could Rita be engaged to Ken? It wasn't possible.

Ken denied they'd ever considered marriage, and they'd quarrelled bitterly, but she couldn't believe he'd rush into it with someone else, especially not with soppy, namby-pamby Rita.

It wasn't true. For some reason Amy was being spiteful, teasing, trying to wind her up.

'Yes, Ken Henderson,' Amy assured her with a careless shrug. 'After all, you had your chance with him, Flo, didn't you?' she said scornfully. 'Because of some stupid ideas, you threw it all away. According to Auntie Sybil, Ken's a real catch.'

'You're saying all this to be spiteful,' Florence flared angrily, still unwilling to take her sister seriously. 'I don't believe a word of it!'

It just couldn't be true. It didn't make any sense.

'I saw the ring, a diamond cluster,' Amy insisted, with a smile. 'Not bad, either. But then

194

the Hendersons are loaded, aren't they? Rita's flashing it about like Lady Muck.'

Florence felt something catch in her throat, and was speechless with mortification. That was *her* ring Rita was sporting. Ken had bought it for her, not Rita. How could he do such a thing to her? How could Rita, who was supposed to be a friend, accept it? She must know that ring was never meant for her. How low could anyone stoop?

'You've missed the bus good and proper, haven't you?' Amy wrinkled her nose as she grinned at her sister. 'Mucked up your work prospects, landed yourself a tuppenny-ha'penny job instead, and jilted into the bargain.'

'Oh, shut up! You conceited cat!' Florence yelled at her, the pain of humiliation burning in her breast. 'You and your pompous university pals, and your silly hairdos. You don't know what life is all about, you don't. You think you're so damned clever...'

'Florence!' Edie sounded harassed and snappy. 'Don't swear, please.'

Florence felt feverish with anger and humiliation in front of her family. How could she bear to visit Grandma Hilda now? She couldn't face the triumph in Auntie Sybil's eyes.

'I'll do and say what I like!' she cried out, unrepentant at Edie's shocked expression.

'Florence!'

She turned on her heel, unable to bear it another moment, and rushed from the kitchen. She fled to her room, hot tears burning her eyes as she went.

She'd looked forward to Christmas so much, hoping against hope that feelings between her and her parents would improve. She needed their love and support more than ever before. It was all she had left.

She was prepared to stick it out at Terri's, despite Tony's abominable behaviour and the disgust and anger she felt for him. But she needed the comfort of her family; the way it used to be.

Why, oh why had things turned out so badly?

She couldn't face going down to the Christmas Eve meal the family were enjoying, despite requests from her father relayed by Tommy. How could she sit there miserable when everyone else was happy and carefree?

She didn't feel hungry anyway. She was too full of anger and even, perhaps, regret. She'd been betrayed by Ken and Rita. It was intolerable! She'd been made to look a fool – second best again – and in front of her family, too! Would she ever rise above that?

Florence lay on her bed, her face buried in the pillow as she cried. She could hardly believe how her life had changed within three months. Her plans and dreams had all gone sour. Was it her own fault?

Florence pushed herself up, and sat on the edge of the bed. From there she saw her reflection in the dressing-table mirror.

She looked awful! A complete hag! The memory of her eighteenth birthday flashed into her mind. She'd been glowing with happiness and excitement as she got herself ready to meet

Ken for the evening. She wasn't vain, she told herself, but she couldn't help but notice then how pretty she'd looked. Now she looked like an old dish rag that had seen better days.

Her hair was hanging limp and dull, and her eyes and nose were red and swollen. What had she done to herself?

Had everyone been right after all? Had she made a terrible mistake changing her life?

Florence gave a shuddering sigh as doubts assailed her. If she'd stayed at the office she'd have been gloriously happy this Christmas with Ken's engagement ring on her finger, making plans for the future.

She might've been bored to death going back to that office, but at least she wouldn't be filled with the disgust and dread she felt now. Christmas would be over in a few short days, and the misery would begin again. Tony and the crushing shame she felt because of him were inescapable.

Ken and Tony. They'd both betrayed her. She thought of Darlene alone this Christmas again because of another man's treachery. Men couldn't be trusted. There were some good ones like her father and perhaps Cliff, but as far as she could see they were few and far between.

I'll never trust another man again, she thought, dabbing at her eyes with a handkerchief. No more giving her heart like a silly schoolgirl. No more trust. From now on she'd watch every man she met very closely. No one would take advantage of her innocence and inexperience again. Of that she was determined.

Florence gulped back one last sob, and lifted

197

her chin in renewed determination, looking her reflection straight in the eyes.

You *let* them do this to you, she told her reflection, sternly. Now pick up the pieces, and get on with it!

That's what her mother would do. She'd be strong, like her mother. She'd already shown considerable strength to get this far. There was still a lot ahead of her yet. It wasn't too late. She'd learn from her mistakes.

Florence picked up a brush and pulled it through her hair in slow, easy strokes. It made her scalp tingle which made her feel better.

She wasn't finished yet. She *hadn't* made a mistake, not really. Fate had thrown a few curves her way, and she'd fumbled, but it was no good looking back. She still had her dream despite everything. She'd go on striving towards that, and no one, not Ken, or Rita, or Tony would stop her. And she'd start now.

Florence washed her face in the little handbasin in the corner of her room, changed out of her utility skirt and blouse, and slipped into a blue wool frock. It was old, pre-war, but it still fitted her well, and it made her feel good.

She pinched a bit of colour into her cheeks, set a smile on her face, and chin up, set off downstairs to the family reunion.

Who knew what the New Year would bring?

CHAPTER 13

New Year 1949

Rita was chilled as she waited opposite Terri's salon. Her stockings, already wet from the walk through the town, clung heavily around her ankles, making her feet feel like blocks of ice.

The doorway in which she sheltered was shallow. She pulled her coat more tightly around herself, pressing back against the glass pane of the door, trying to avoid the slanting rain as it gusted across the High Street.

Light from the salon shimmered in the pools of water on the road, the tyres of passing vehicles sending up spray that reached out to her, sparkling like the diamonds in her engagement ring, then falling into the darkness of the gutter.

How much longer would Flo be? Rita had been in a conciliatory mood all day, and instead of going straight home after work, she felt she had to make an effort to see Flo.

It was a funny feeling, this mood she was in, a vague feeling of being guilty of something. She'd done nothing wrong, of course, and wasn't quite sure what made her feel this way. She wanted to shrug it off, but couldn't. She felt certain a reconciliation with Flo would do it.

She had to see Flo, talk to her, get her approval. After all, Flo had always been her best friend. Well, her only friend, really. It would be nice if they made up. She needed someone, anyone but her mother, to talk about her wedding plans.

She was conscious of a lack of excitement at the prospect of marrying Ken. She was enthusiastic, but not excited, and instinctively knew there was something missing. A good old free-and-easy chat with Flo, like in the old days, would help.

She'd always been Flo's confidante, too. She wanted it to be like that again, only now their roles were reversed, weren't they? She wanted to talk, to discuss Ken, her engagement, her future plans, just as Flo used to do. There was so much she was unsure about, so much she didn't know or understand.

The truth was, and she had to admit it to herself, she'd always felt inferior to Flo. Now she felt equal. Now someone wanted to marry *her*, someone ... important.

Ken was important, or at least his family were. Ken would be important one day, too. He was so full of ambition, it was a bit overwhelming at times, Rita thought.

What did impress Rita very much was that Ken had her mother's respect. Although it was embarrassing sometimes, it gave Rita a wry pleasure to see Sybil bow and scrape before him. It gratified her no end that in Ken she'd have a husband who her mother wouldn't or couldn't bully. He'd stand between her and her mother. She'd be independent at last.

Rita held out her left hand, contemplating her engagement ring. Against the shop lights this January evening it glittered in a most satisfactory way. She was so proud of it, yet she felt surprise, even astonishment, each time she admired it. She still couldn't believe it was really true.

Engaged to be married! She'd get away from the clutches of her mother at last! Something she'd yearned for so long. Just a few more months to go. She felt exhilarated at the prospect of her promised freedom. If only she felt some excitement about Ken, too.

Nevertheless, being engaged had already given her a new status. Miss Hopkins was obviously impressed to learn that Rita was marrying into the Henderson family, and she'd been quite friendly lately, as though she and Rita now both belonged to a select club.

Brenda was green with envy and hardly spoke to her. Far from upsetting her, this attitude made Rita feel like crowing with delight and, indeed, superiority. If only Flo was there to share it.

Rita sighed, pulling her coat collar higher around her neck. She missed Flo, missed their evenings out.

She rarely went anywhere now. Ken took her to the cinema on Saturday evenings, and perhaps he'd come to tea one evening in the week. The rest of the week he was busy. Committee meetings and rallies for some political party.

She wasn't sure which one. It was all the same to her anyway, although from now on she supposed she ought to take more interest, get involved. That's what her mother said anyway.

Yes, she missed Flo no end. But perhaps they'd make up this evening? She didn't mind being the first one to offer the olive branch. She could afford to be magnanimous now she was engaged to be married.

So much had happened since last September, and she marvelled at it. She'd felt uncomfortable at first, contriving to invite Ken home to tea. She probably wouldn't have found the courage if it weren't for her mother's goading. She finally steeled herself to ask him just to get some peace, and was astonished, indeed flattered, when he'd readily accepted the invitation.

She'd never forget that first meeting between Ken and her parents, she reflected wryly. She'd been so ashamed of her mother. The silly posh accent she'd put on, her boasting, and that awful snobbery.

Rita winced as she recalled the way her mother fawned over Ken, but he'd taken it well. He'd been so polite and courteous. He even went so far as to confide in Rita afterwards that he thought her mother had done quite well, under the circumstances. Rita wasn't sure what he'd meant, but Sybil took it as a compliment when told later.

She'd been astonished, and her mother stunned, when six weeks later Ken proposed to her. Rita felt the way Cinderella must've felt when the glass slipper fitted.

Her father was quiet and subdued after her announcement. He made it plain he didn't like Ken, and begged Rita to think again. Sybil was furious with him, and gave him a tongue-lashing. Poor Da!

Although Rita couldn't make out what he had against Ken, his words did make her stop and wonder at how easy it'd been. Vague doubts circled in her head, because she valued her father's opinion, despite what her mother said about him. But she hadn't voiced them. She was afraid the fairy tale would pop into oblivion like a soap bubble. And she so wanted it to be true. It was a secret fantasy made real. She wouldn't let it slip away now.

Ken suggested an early wedding, and that was all right with her. The sooner she got away from her mother and Granddad Charlie the better. Though she was sorry for poor Da, and felt guilty at deserting him.

Rita stepped out of the doorway when she saw people leaving the salon, calling goodnight to each other. As the group parted she saw Florence hurrying down the street, head bowed against the rain. She darted across the road and hurried after her.

'Flo! Flo! Wait a minute.'

Florence stopped and turned, but only for a moment. When she saw who called her, she turned on her heel, and it seemed to Rita that she hurried away even faster.

'Florence! Wait, mun! I want to talk to you.'

Cold rain was driving into Rita's face, dripping from the rim of her hat and trickling down her neck. The loose, cracked paving stones, still not replaced since the Blitz, were treacherous underfoot, and dirty rainwater splashed her legs.

'Flo!'

Florence stopped, waiting, obviously reluctantly. She kept her face turned away, gazing through a shop window nearby.

Panting, Rita finally caught up with her.

'Why didn't you wait, Flo?'

Florence was silent, and turning, continued down the High Street, her pace so fast that Rita had to trot at her side. She began to wonder if this was such a good idea, after all.

They passed an Italian café and Rita suddenly felt very cold and hungry. A cup of tea wouldn't go amiss, she decided. She couldn't race about in the rain like this. Her coat was already soaked through, and underneath, dampness made her silk blouse cling uncomfortably to her shoulders.

'Flo, stop a minute, for goodness sake!' she said, grasping at Florence's arm.

Florence pulled her arm free, but paused in her flight.

'Why should I? Why should I give you one minute of my time?'

For a moment Rita was taken aback at the rancour in Florence's voice. Yet, she detected a tremor in it too, as though Florence might be about to burst into tears. That wasn't a bit like Flo.

'Because I want to talk to you,' she said. 'We're ... we're friends, aren't we?'

'*Friends!*' Florence gave a short bitter laugh. 'Friends? Oh, that's good, that is. Friends? You don't know what the word means.'

She turned to walk away, but Rita clutched at her arm again.

'Look, let's go in this café by here,' she suggested eagerly. 'I could do with a cuppa, couldn't you, Flo?'

Florence turned again, shielding her face from the rain. The light from the café fell directly onto

204

her face, and Rita was startled by the anger and resentment she saw there.

'You've got the cheek of hell, Rita,' Florence answered. 'Do you think I'd sit down at a table with you after what you've done?'

'What did I do?'

'You stole Ken from me!'

Rita's mouth dropped open for a moment before she could reply.

'I didn't steal him at all. You'd quarrelled. You'd finished with him, or he'd finished with you, I don't know which, but he wasn't your boyfriend anymore. Why shouldn't I go out with him?'

'My God! You jumped in quick enough, didn't you?' Florence cried out furiously. 'Talk about dead men's shoes.'

'Oh! Don't be so horrible,' Rita almost shrieked, distressed at the choice of words. Florence made her sound like some ghoulish grave robber.

'And that ring you're wearing,' Florence said belligerently. 'That's my ring, that is. Ken bought that for me.'

'No, he didn't,' Rita cried, feeling the swell of indignation rising in her breast, all idea of reconciliation dissolving.

She held out her left hand.

'I chose this ring myself. Ken did have another ring, it's true.' She lifted her chin defiantly. 'But I didn't like it. It had coloured stones. It was common.'

'Ooh!'

Florence stepped back as though Rita had slapped her, her expression one of disbelief. She stood still for a moment, her mouth working, but no words came.

'I despise you, Rita,' she gasped out at last. 'You're just like your mother. A social climber. You don't love Ken, I know you don't. You're only marrying him for his money, and to spite me. You little gold-digger!'

'How dare you say that?'

Goaded, Rita was furious; heat rising to her face, and knowing her cheeks must be reddening, she felt vague guilt resurface again.

She'd never admit to anyone there was a smallest grain of truth in Florence's accusation, but she couldn't deny to herself how her mother was impressed and perhaps motivated by the Hendersons' money and position in town. She herself didn't give a button for the money. She just wanted to be free, happy and independent.

Ken was a nice enough man; steady, dependable. Perhaps a little starchy and precise, but she didn't mind that. She could live with it. She'd certainly make him a better wife than Flo would.

'Envy doesn't become you, Florence,' Rita said, stiffly, her jaws almost rigid with anger. 'You don't want him, but you don't want anyone else to have him. Is that it?'

'I loved him!' Florence shouted back at her.

Rita gave a derisive snort of disbelief.

'Rubbish! You're too selfish to love anyone, Flo. If you'd loved Ken you'd have done what he wanted; given up that silly idea of being a hairdresser.'

'No, I wouldn't knuckle down like you. I've got more spirit.'

'Spirit!' Rita sniffed disparagingly. 'You don't look as though you've got much spirit now, or much of anything, for that matter.'

In the light from the café, she looked her former friend up and down, from head to toe. Florence looked shabby. There was no other word for it.

She remembered Florence buying that coat several winters back. It was the year the war ended. They'd saved up their coupons for the January sale in Lewis Lewis. It'd seen plenty of wear since then by the look of it. And the hat Florence was wearing. Rita was sure she'd seen Auntie Edie wearing one exactly like it.

Florence hadn't been doing very well by the looks of things, despite all her so-called dreams. She'd thrown everything away. What a waste!

'What do you know about love, anyway, Rita?' Florence was saying, her scorn persistent; as if she was still the superior one, Rita thought with irritation.

'You've never even had a proper boyfriend before,' Florence went on relentlessly. 'You're so stupid you grab the first man that asks you.'

'And you're only jealous because he prefers me,' Rita snapped. 'You were a big mistake in Ken's life. He told me he was thankful he found out in time.'

'Ken wouldn't know a mistake if he fell over it,' Florence cried, enraged. 'Which he's going to do, when he marries you.'

Rita drew in a deep breath and held it tightly, counting to ten. She felt if she didn't she'd explode with anger.

Her composure recovered, she pushed her handbag firmly under her arm. She wasn't going to stand here much longer, getting soaked to the skin just to appease her conscience. What was she blaming herself for anyway? Florence deserved everything she got.

'You've made a right mess of your life, Flo,' she said at last, lifting her chin defiantly. 'I've tried to be friends with you for old times' sake, but what thanks do I get?'

'You stab me in the back, and you want my thanks!' Florence tossed her head, and the wrinkled, rain-soaked brim of her hat sprayed out water like a miniature cascade. 'Believe me, I don't want too many friends like you.'

'Huh!' Rita looked her up and down again, this time with some disdain. 'You look as if you could do with one, anyway.'

'Oh, push off, Rita!' Florence exploded. 'Go home and count Ken's money.'

With that parting shot she turned on her heel, leaving Rita to stare open-mouthed after her.

Cold rain trickling down her neck galvanised her into action, too, and she hurried towards the bus station.

What a fool she'd been to believe she and Florence could ever be friends again. Eaten with jealousy, she was, that was the problem. Well, that's the last time, Rita decided there and then. Flo could stew in her own juice.

Rita felt a sense of relief steal over her. She'd faced Flo, she'd tried to make amends, though for what she wasn't sure. There was nothing more she could do.

From now on she'd concentrate on her future with Ken. Excitement or no excitement, it promised to be good, and after all, it was what she deserved.

That's what her mother kept telling her anyway.

CHAPTER 14

March 1949
She couldn't believe it was really happening; not to *her*, Rita Bevan, of all people. She wondered at times what she'd done to deserve such good fortune. Marrying someone like Ken. Having her own home; being her own mistress; getting away from her mother.

Sometimes she had a sense of unreality, as if she were living a dream, as now, standing in the driveway with Ken and her parents outside the detached house in Killay, bought by Bernard and Ursula Henderson for their wedding present.

It was elegant, and so much more than she'd ever dreamed of having. The house was long rather than square, gabled in the main section, with large bay windows on the ground and first floors. At the side, French windows opened out onto a lawn and flower beds. The entrance was especially impressive, with a pillared portico, reminding Rita of houses she'd seen in films.

She was thrilled with it, so thrilled she feared it might still be a dream and she'd wake up to her old life.

'Pity it's not on Gower Road,' Sybil said to her in a disappointed whisper.

It was supposed to be a confidential whisper, but it was loud enough for Ken to hear as he put the key into the lock. Rita saw the tightening of

211

his lips and felt ashamed. Trust her mother to spoil things.

'It's beautiful, perfect,' Rita said loudly, mostly for Ken's benefit. 'I wouldn't want to live anywhere else.'

Their wedding day was only three weeks away, but there was still plenty of time to buy furniture, carpets, curtains and to set the place up the way she wanted. After all, she had nothing else to think about, nothing else to do all day, now that she'd given up her job at the solicitors, as Ken had insisted.

She'd ask her mother to help her choose, knowing Sybil would be over the moon with the opportunity to spend someone else's money.

Ken had the door open and her parents were already stepping into the hall. Rita hesitated a moment. She wanted to stand back and take another look at the house, see it as others would see it.

She retreated a few steps and turned to gaze admiringly. It was then she noticed the curtains draping the windows.

Rita was taken aback. Perhaps they were only temporary, or left by the previous owners? Somehow she didn't believe it, and had an ominous feeling.

She hurriedly followed the others into the hall. This, too, was furnished. A tall hall-stand stood on one side and on the other a highly polished half-moon table was set against the wall below a large ornate mirror.

Scattered on the parquet floor were Chinese rugs. For a moment Rita felt herself back in the

Hendersons' own house in Gower Road. The furnishings were almost identical.

Disappointment descended on her like a damp blanket.

Ken was calling to her from an adjoining room, and she went in search of him, entering the large lounge with French windows.

Here too, all was furnished in Ursula Henderson's rather pompous style. There was nothing left for Rita to do, nothing of her very own to add.

Struggling up through her disappointment came a spark of annoyance.

'Ken, where did all this furniture come from?'

'Oh, the very best furnishers, Rita, I can assure you. I asked my mother to see to it. She has excellent taste, don't you agree?'

Rita had never yet had cause to disagree with Ken, to question his views or plans. She felt she must speak up now. This was to be her home. Surely she had a right to decide how it should be?

She wetted her lips, nervously.

'I'd have liked to see to the furnishings and fittings myself, Ken. I have my own ideas...'

'Don't be absurd, Rita, my dear,' he said in a dismissive tone. 'My mother's taste is impeccable.'

'But, Ken...' Rita glanced around her. The furnishings were elegant and impressive, yet they were not to her liking and she knew she'd never be comfortable with them.

The surroundings probably made Ken feel very much at home, but she could never feel like that, Rita told herself. It would never be her own place, not while it was an extension of Ursula Henderson's.

'Your mother might have asked me first what I wanted,' she ventured. 'I was looking forward to choosing everything. After all, Ken, this is *our* home, yours and mine. We're going to live in it, not your mother.'

He stared at her for a moment, then he frowned.

'Rita, you're not criticising my mother, are you?'

'Of course not...' She smiled uncertainly, hoping to lighten the moment. Ken was looking really annoyed, and suddenly her own annoyance melted away in confusion.

'I should hope not, either!'

He glanced around to confirm they were alone, but Sybil and Ronnie were already inspecting the rooms on the first floor.

'Rita, dear, your ideas would be totally out of place here,' he went on, his tone cool despite the endearment. 'I've seen your parents' home, remember.' He shook his head. 'It's hardly in the best of taste, now is it?'

Rita blinked, feeling crushed. She stared at him, unable to say a word in defence of herself or her parents.

So this is what he thought of her and her family. Why on earth then had he asked her to marry him? For the first time since their engagement, she felt real doubt. The Hendersons were out of her league. She knew it, had always known it, despite her mother's ridiculous pretensions.

Why *had* she agreed to marry Ken? She didn't

love him. She'd never even pretended to herself that she did. He was a good catch. And was it really one-upmanship on Flo?

Suddenly she remembered vividly, standing in the pouring rain facing Florence, and her accusation of being just a gold-digger. Could there be a grain of truth in it after all?

She'd always wanted to be as good as Florence, if not better; to have what Florence had, if not more. Ken had seemed so ideal, but now she looked at him with opened eyes, and a cold shiver passed over her. She didn't love him. At this moment she wasn't sure she even liked him! Why *was* she marrying him?

'This isn't a criticism of your parents, Rita,' he continued patronisingly. 'They can't help it. But you have a chance to learn about the finer things from my mother.'

Rita swallowed hard.

'I may want to change a few things…'

Ken sighed heavily, and his lips tightened with irritation.

'Don't be tiresome, Rita, dear, please.' His tone was edgy and she had the impression he was holding his feelings in rein. 'My mother has gone to a lot of trouble. This house is a very handsome wedding present. At the very least you could be grateful.'

'Well, of course I am, Ken,' she answered hastily. 'But…'

'Look,' he interrupted. 'I have to get back to the office. I've got some wholesalers to see this afternoon. Take the key and stay here a while. Look around. Make yourselves at home. I'll call

215

back for you later.'

When Ken had gone Rita went slowly upstairs to look at the bedrooms. She would've liked to choose their bedroom, but more than likely Ursula had already chosen for her. The bed, the sheets, the drapes. Everything was stamped with Ursula's personal preference.

There were four bedrooms, all quite spacious. Sybil sat on the bed in the largest bedroom at the front of the house, running an appreciative hand over the satin quilt. Her father was in the bathroom across the landing. Rita could hear the lavatory being flushed.

Rita sat on the bed next to her mother.

'What do you think, Mam?' she asked, longing to ask Sybil outright if she believed she was doing the right thing.

Sybil sniffed.

'It's not Gower Road, but it'll do, I suppose.'

It was meant to be disdainful, but Rita knew her mother well enough to know she was very impressed, maybe even a little over-awed.

'Mrs Henderson might have left it to me to fit it out though, don't you think, Mam?' Rita asked, plaintively.

She needed sympathy and support from her mother now. Could she hope for that? The house was a very fine one, she couldn't deny it, and the Hendersons had been generous. At the same time she thought she could detect a finger of interference. The last thing she wanted was Ursula Henderson running her life. That was the very thing she was trying to get away from.

'Oh, I don't know,' Sybil said, glancing around,

scrutinising the decor, the carpets and curtains. 'It's all good quality stuff.'

Rita jumped up hurriedly.

'Yes, but it's not me! I didn't have a say in it. My own home!'

Biting her lip thoughtfully, Rita walked over to the window which overlooked the driveway and the main road.

'Do you think I'm making a mistake, Mam, marrying Ken?'

Sybil rose to her feet and came to stand next to her.

'What on earth do you mean, Rita? What are you thinking?'

She turned and looked into Sybil's eyes. If only they were close as mother and daughter should be. If only she could speak her heart to her mother. Getting engaged; marrying a good-looking man from a well-to-do family; this lovely house, it was all so glamorous, the stuff of dreams. But was it right for her? Was it really what she wanted? And most important of all, would she be happy?

'Mam, I'm having second thoughts.'

Sybil laughed.

'Everybody feels like that before they get married.' She put a hand briefly on Rita's arm in an unprecedented show of warmth. 'But you've fallen on your feet here, my girl. Everything I've ever wanted for you.'

Rita bent her head, suddenly feeling ashamed.

'They despise us, you know, Mam, the Hendersons.'

'Nonsense!'

217

Sybil stepped away to view her reflection in the dressing-table mirror. It had three mirrors, so that she could see herself from all angles. Rita hated it already.

'Ken said he wouldn't let me furnish the house because he could tell from our home that my family has no taste,' she said deliberately.

Sybil was suddenly still. Rita waited for the outburst. When her mother turned to look at her, Rita could see Sybil's face was stiff and set, but there wasn't the explosion she'd expected.

Sybil lifted her chin.

'Well, it's true, isn't it?'

'*Mam!*'

'Oh, yes, it's true, all right. It takes money to develop taste. I've been denied money, thanks to your father.'

Sybil's tone was suddenly and familiarly bitter. Rita knew what was coming next, and wished she'd kept her mouth shut.

'It's all your father's fault!' Sybil burst out then. 'He ruined us. He prevented me having the life I should've had, the life I deserve. But now you, Rita, are going to have the chance that was taken from me. Don't make a mess of it like your father did, for God's sake!'

'I want to be happy more than anything else, Mam,' Rita burst out. She wanted to say, happy like Auntie Edie and Uncle William, but her courage failed her. 'I want that more than anything. I think it's the most important thing in life.'

'Happy! What's happy?' Sybil snapped angrily. 'You talk like a silly schoolgirl, Rita. I'll tell you

218

what's important. Money, that's what's important. When you've got that you've got everything. I've never had it, neither am I likely to. But you've got a chance in a lifetime, Rita.'

Sybil paused to catch her breath. She was peering at Rita so hard and defiantly, that Rita felt transfixed for a moment.

'Ken'll be an important man in this town one day,' Sybil rushed on fervently. 'He's got it in him. I can see it. And you'll be right there with him. Looked up to and respected. Somebody of consequence.'

Rita knew exactly what her mother meant, Sybil wanted to bask in that reflected glory, boast about her daughter's well-to-do husband, her daughter's elegant house, brag about her social connections. As usual it was all about what Sybil wanted. For a moment Rita was aggrieved.

'I'm not like you, Mam,' she began hotly. 'I don't want that. I just want to be loved.'

As soon as she said it she knew it was true beyond doubt. That's all she wanted. To be loved and cherished just for herself.

She certainly didn't love Ken. Did he love her? Carried away by her mother's enthusiasm and ambition, and by the glamour of it all, she'd never asked herself this before. Now it was so important.

Sybil's top lip curled scornfully at the sentiment, but she said nothing. Not for the first time Rita saw the hardness in her mother; like granite – like Granddad Charlie – and pity for her father rose up in her breast.

Her mother was always bleating about what

she'd been denied, but what about Da? He'd been denied love. She wouldn't end up like that, Rita told herself. She had to do something before it was too late.

'Mam, I don't think I can go through with it. I don't think I ought to.'

Sybil's hand clutched her arm, and this time the grasp was hard and painful.

'*Yes, you will!*' she hissed, and Rita was shocked by the passion in her voice. 'Don't be an ungrateful little fool, Rita. I've given you everything to help you get on, to have more and better than I did. You owe it to me, Rita. Owe it to me!'

She paused, and Rita felt her mother's hand shake as she held on to her arm. Sybil's beady eyes were aflame with anger and determination, and Rita felt her mother's powerful will encompassing her. She wanted to struggle against it, but as always found no strength of her own for the combat.

'You owe me everything. Don't be a failure like your father,' Sybil almost spat the words. 'Don't disappoint me like he did. I'll never forgive you if you do! Never!'

CHAPTER 15

Florence sat in the kitchen, her chair tilted against the wall, feet resting on the rim of the china sink, glad to get the weight off her legs. The salon was busy this week with her and Glenys having hardly a minute to call their own.

She'd been working with Nancy for the last few days, and she always liked that. For all her languidness, Nancy was a good instructor, patient and friendly.

Florence dreaded next week when she was to work with Darlene. She'd probably be climbing the walls by Friday! At least she'd have no time to brood over Ken and Rita and she wouldn't waste a minute thinking of them now, either.

The salon was shut for lunch. The others were spending their hour the usual way, queue-hunting. See a queue and join it, never mind what for. It could be anything from half a dozen Canadian eggs to a bar of scented soap. It didn't matter, as long as you came back with something.

No use going queue-hunting herself, Florence decided, half-heartedly munching her sandwiches. She didn't earn enough to afford such luxuries.

She glanced at Glenys sitting beside her, head down, poring over this week's *Beano*. Just *her* level, Florence thought spitefully, then instantly regretted her uncharitable thoughts. She shouldn't take her misery out on Glenys or anyone else.

The sandwich was suddenly dry and tasteless, and she thrust it back into the paper bag. She tried to direct her thoughts away from what was uppermost in her mind.

It was to be a posh wedding by all accounts. The ceremony in Clyne church would now be over, Ken and Rita were man and wife and the reception at the Mackworth Hotel, just yards away from the shop, would be in full swing. The whole family were there, including Granddad Charlie and Grandma Hilda. It salved Florence's guilty conscience to know her grandmother was sufficiently recovered in health to attend.

Her parents were there too, and so was Tommy, and she resented their readiness to join in. Didn't they appreciate how she felt? Couldn't they guess at her humiliation?

Florence was invited, too, but she wouldn't dream of going. She'd not admit that pride had anything to do with it. Ken and Rita had treated her very shabbily, particularly Ken. But apart from the principle of the thing, she couldn't afford a new outfit anyway, which was particularly galling as now that clothing coupons were abolished all the shops had been holding celebratory sales these last couple of weeks.

Of course, she didn't love Ken; she knew that now. She probably had once, she told herself defensively, but he'd killed any feelings she'd had for him. He'd humiliated her, insulted her.

On receiving her invitation she'd been moved to

tell her mother of Ken's appalling accusations.

Edie had regarded her without sympathy. 'Count your lucky stars,' was all she'd said.

Despite that sentiment, and their inexplicable dislike of Ken, the family had attended the wedding just the same. To Florence it didn't make sense.

By the time the lunch-break was over the others had returned. Darlene was in a right old temper, having queued at Chitzoy's for oranges for over half an hour to be told when her turn came that they'd sold out.

She flounced out of the kitchen ahead of the others, only to come rushing back within minutes, her face alive with excitement.

'Hey! You'll never guess what's happened,' she said.

'Tony's fallen on a pair of scissors and slit his throat?' Marge suggested, hopefully.

'Don't be sarky! This is serious, this is, Marge,' Darlene retorted, but her expression belied her words. 'It's Cliff!'

'*What!*' Marge was startled, all humour leaving her face. 'God! What's happened to him?'

'Nothing. It's his wife, isn't it? He's just been told she's dead. Died in Sydney nearly three weeks ago – knocked down by a car. He's a widower now.'

There was silence for a moment. The relief on Marge's face was very apparent to Florence, as was the anticipation on Darlene's.

'I wonder what he'll do now?' she said to no one in particular.

'Same as before,' Marge said evenly. 'It's four

223

years since Connie left him flat with those kids. Nothing's changed.'

Darlene's tongue flicked across her lips.

'Except that he can marry again.'

Muscles tightened visibly around Marge's mouth.

'He won't look at a brassy piece like *you* anyway, so don't waste your time.'

'At least I'm not ten years older than him, like you,' Darlene retorted savagely. 'You big fat lump!'

The two women glanced at each other in a moment of electrified stillness.

'Pack it in, both of you,' Nancy drawled at last. 'Don't be so indecent, will you? The woman's dead. You two squabbling over him is the last thing Cliff wants.'

Florence heartily agreed, but hesitated to voice her thoughts.

Business went on as usual in the salon in the afternoon. Florence caught sight briefly of Cliff as he left Tony and Lillian in the office.

A black patch was sewn onto his sleeve, and he looked sombre. Florence felt a wave of sympathy for him.

He'd proved a good friend to her over these last three months. Tony had kept well away, and she was certain it was because of Cliff's watchful eye.

He was a good listener, too, and already she'd confided in him about Ken's rejection, and Rita's betrayal; about her difficulties at home and about her dreams for the future. He didn't criticise or jeer; he didn't talk down to her as if she were naive and foolish.

They were good friends now. Like herself, he'd been betrayed and she felt they had a common bond. She accepted his past, but something told her he wasn't really to blame. He'd been a victim of fate and circumstances.

Even though she'd heard him say himself that he didn't regret the killing that had sent him to prison, she felt he'd been under stress when uttering those words. There was no badness in him, she was certain of it.

She didn't like the idea that he might fall victim to Darlene's cunning and blandishments. She'd much rather he had someone homely like Marge.

She didn't have a chance to offer her condolences until he came to give out the pay on Friday. He handed her the brown envelope with his usual smile.

'I'm sorry about your loss, Cliff.'

His smile faded, and he bent his head, fingers fiddling with the other pay-packets. Suddenly, he looked quite upset.

'Thanks, Florence, love.'

'If there's anything I can do...'

He looked up, a quick smile returning.

'There's nothing. Everything's over and done with. Has been for a long time.'

Florence felt a surge of warmth and sympathy.

'You've been lonely,' she said impulsively.

Even in the midst of her family, she knew about the loneliness of being on the edge of the family circle; outside her mother's sympathy, out in the cold.

It must be worse for Cliff, with two children

depending on him and no one to share worries and hopes.

'Yes, I am. A lot of people don't realise that.' His smile deepened. 'You're very understanding for your age, Flo.'

'I don't think age has anything to do with feelings.' Her tone was a bit sharp. That was the first time he'd ever said anything patronising to her, and she felt disappointed.

'I'm sorry, Flo.' He looked crestfallen. 'Daft thing to say, wasn't it? I suppose I'm embarrassed. Death is an embarrassing subject.'

Seeing his discomfort Florence relented immediately. He was under strain. She had no right to expect anything from him. Stop being so touchy, she told herself.

'Marge was right, then,' she said.

'Marge?' He looked mystified.

'She said nothing has changed for you. You'll go on as before.'

He sighed. 'She's right. The kids still miss Connie, of course. It's no life for children without a mother at their ages. I know they need a woman's touch and love, but what can I do about it?'

'Marge has got a soft spot for you, Cliff,' Florence ventured, suddenly made bold by his confidences. 'She's a very homely person, easy to talk to and get on with.'

He leaned back in the chair, gazing at her without smiling, and Florence felt her cheeks begin to burn.

'Are you trying a bit of matchmaking, Flo?'

Florence felt confused and silly. What was she

trying to do anyway? 'No, of course not.'

He smiled.

'Marge is a good soul, but not my type.'

Florence opened her mouth, then hesitated. She'd been about to ask if Darlene was his type, but stopped herself in time. She was prying, going too far. And it was hardly the time to talk about a replacement for Connie. Still, she hated to think of Cliff's loneliness. He was too good a man not to be happy in life.

CHAPTER 16

June 1949

Florence concentrated on the deft movements of Darlene's hands as they parted and divided the client's hair into precise two-inch sections, handing her the exact size roller for each section.

She knew better than to make a mistake when assisting Darlene. Her tongue could be bitter and her criticism waspish.

'That one's too tight, Darlene!' Mrs Grantham complained peevishly. 'I usually have Nancy do my hair. She's always very careful.'

'My set lasts longer,' said Darlene unfeelingly, pinning the roller into place with relentless efficiency. 'You'll thank me for it on Saturday.'

Mrs Grantham winced again.

'Where's Nancy anyway?'

Darlene fixed the next roller, pinning it just as tightly.

'On her honeymoon,' she replied. 'Have you ever heard anything so daft? She's been married two years, already. Wasting money on a honeymoon!' Her tone was scornful. 'It could've gone towards a deposit on a nice little house.'

'They couldn't afford a honeymoon when they married,' Florence ventured in defence of Nancy. 'I think it's romantic, myself.'

Darlene sniffed dismissively.

'Oh yes, you would!'

When the last roller was in place, Darlene spoke in an undertone to Florence.

'Bung Mrs G under the drier, will you? I'm going out the lav for a ciggie.'

Florence stared, her own devotion to duty giving her some courage to speak out, risking the wrath of Darlene's savage tongue.

'But what about the queue?'

'Bugger the queue!' Darlene snarled. 'Need a break, I do.'

Darlene and Marge were the only hairdressers in the salon that morning, and the waiting area was congested with clients.

Hazel, who'd failed to come in to work, had overbooked appointments again, obviously forgetting Nancy's holiday.

Tony and Lillian were later than usual, and Marge, struggling to see to clients and man the reception counter, was kept running back and forth to answer the telephone and see to clients coming in to make appointments. Florence could see it was wearing her out.

'Marge can't cope with it all,' Florence retorted heatedly. 'It's not fair, Darlene.'

'Now, listen, you!' Her face contorted in anger, and she wagged a finger in Florence's face. 'Don't you talk to *me* like that. You're nobody round here. Get it?'

She put a hand in the pocket of her overall, bringing out a packet of cigarettes, then turned to leave.

Florence's own anger flared at the injustice of it.

'You wouldn't get away with skiving off if Lillian and Tony were here,' she said loudly, not

230

caring whether the clients heard or not. 'If they come in when you're out the lav smoking don't expect me to cover for you, Darlene. I'm not going to lie for you or anyone else.'

Darlene stared at her, then scowling fiercely, thrust the cigarettes back in her pocket. 'Oh bloody hell! It's all that flaming Hazel's fault. I'd wipe the floor with her if she was here. Well! Don't stand by there gawking at me, mun.' She jerked her head angrily. 'Go and shampoo some heads.'

It was about noon when Lillian arrived, but there was no sign of Tony. Busy shampooing, Florence gave her employer only a cursory glance, then did a double-take.

Lillian looked awful. Her blonde hair was dishevelled, her eyes reddened, and she looked as though she hadn't had much sleep.

Usually she stopped at most cubicles on arrival to have a word with favourite clients, her eagle eye taking in everything going on in the salon. This morning she stared straight ahead, and hurried to the office, her face chalky white.

'Marge!' she called out as she went. 'I want to see you, now.'

Marge was in the middle of doing a set. She paused, looking flustered for a moment.

'I'll go, shall I?' Darlene called eagerly from the cubicle opposite.

Marge's uncertainty cleared immediately.

'It's the organ grinder she wants, not the monkey,' she snapped, belligerently.

Then turning to Florence she went on in an even tone:

231

'Flo! Come by here, kid. Finish off this set for me, will you?'

Florence's mouth dropped open in astonishment.

'What? Me! On my own?'

'Go on!' Marge urged encouragingly, wiping her hands. 'You must've got the hang of it by now.' She paused, giving Florence a worried look, and lowering her voice, said: 'Something's wrong. Lillian's in trouble. I can feel it in my water.'

'She does look upset,' Florence agreed.

And where was Tony? They'd probably had one of their eternal rows, only this one looked more serious than most.

Marge laid a hand on Florence's arm.

'Keep things going by here, love. Do the best you can. Lillian will be grateful.'

Florence's fingers felt clumsy as she wound hair onto rollers, trying to remember everything she'd learned over the months. When the set was completed to the best of her ability, she ushered the client to a seat under a drier.

There was no sign of Marge; the office door remained firmly closed. Florence stood for a moment, wondering what to do next.

Keep things going, Marge said. Should she tackle another set on her own? Keep things going.

'Glenys,' Florence said to the younger girl who was half-heartedly sweeping up hair-cuttings. 'Leave that. Get on with some shampooing.'

Glenys pouted.

'Who put you in charge?'

'Glenys! Do it, will you?' Florence retorted,

nervousness sharpening her voice. She was all too aware she sounded like Darlene.

It seemed hours before Marge emerged from the office, but glancing at the clock, Florence saw only thirty minutes had passed. She was just finishing off her second set as Marge made an appearance. She looked grim as she drew Florence out of earshot of the client.

'Pass the word to Darlene and Glenys, quietly mind, that Lillian wants them to stay behind after we close. She's got something to tell them.'

'Is it bad news?'

Marge's lips tightened.

'Yes. That bloody Tony...' Marge took a deep breath, controlling her outburst. 'You all better hear it from Lillian.'

She glanced at Florence's handiwork, the client sitting patiently waiting for the drier, and smiled with approval.

'You've done all right, kid. Make a first-class hairdresser, you will.'

Florence closed the salon door behind the last client, pulled down the blind and turned the key in the lock, then went back into the salon to join the others. As the day wore on, her heart grew heavier, sensing impending doom.

Something was very wrong. Lillian hadn't set foot outside the office all day, not even to have some lunch. Marge had Glenys make pot after pot of tea for their employer.

All day, Florence watched Marge closely, trying to glean some information from her face. The older woman's persistently dour expression

233

deepened her own sense of foreboding. Whatever had happened in the lives of the Longfords, it was bound to have repercussions for the staff of Terri's, and Florence wondered whether her dream had finally come to a full stop.

Darlene was sitting in one of the cubicles, feet up on the rim of a washbasin, cigarette dangling from her mouth.

'I wish Lillian would get on with it,' she remarked peevishly. 'I've got a home to go to if nobody else has. Ought to be getting overtime for this, I did.'

'Overtime!' Marge exploded. 'You'll be lucky if you've got a job tomorrow!'

'What?' Darlene sat up with a jerk. 'What're you on about?'

At that moment the office door opened and Lillian came into the salon. She stood still for a moment, looking as if she might change her mind and retreat to the office again. She stood with her arms across her chest, hands gripping each arm, as if she were cold right through.

Florence couldn't help staring at the change in her employer. Gone was the power that normally emanated from her; gone was the elegant, dominant woman who had inspired her to reach for her dream. Lillian looked exhausted, drained of all her drive and essence. Florence felt shocked to her core. What on earth had happened?

Darlene came out of the cubicle and all four of them stood waiting for Lillian to speak. She kept her gaze on the ground, obviously having difficulty looking directly at them, and again Florence was dismayed at the change in her.

'Girls, I have to tell you...' Her voice faltered, and her lips trembled. 'I have to tell...'

Lillian averted her face, putting a handkerchief to her lips.

She's not going to burst into tears right here in front of us all? Florence wondered with growing embarrassment. How humiliating for her!

Marge stepped forward to Lillian's side, and put an arm across her employer's shoulders protectively.

'It's Tony,' Marge spoke up, her face grim. 'He's buggered off.'

'He's what?' asked Darlene, disbelief in her voice.

'The bloody swine's done a bunk,' Marge said loudly. 'He's left Lil flat, and what's more he's taken money from the business. A lot of money.'

'What's going to happen to us?' Darlene asked; she sounded angry. 'Is the shop going bust? Lillian better tell us now. I don't want to be stranded without a bloody job, do I?'

Lillian straightened her shoulders, obviously making a supreme effort to get control of herself again.

'I won't lie about it. The salon's in trouble. We can't carry on business if we can't pay for supplies. As it is, I'll have to close down the work-rooms in Dillwyn Street and let the girls go.'

Florence felt a spasm pass through her. She'd be out of a job now if she'd stuck to wig-making. Looking at Lillian's devastated face, Florence realised that might still be her fate.

'What about asking wholesalers for credit?' Darlene said irritably. 'Terri's has a good reputation. Cash in on it.'

'Don't be stupid, Darlene!' Lillian retorted, her eyes flashing momentarily with some of her old spirit. 'Tony *is* ... *was* our reputation. We can't afford to let it be known he's gone. Not for a while, anyway.' She threw Marge a stubborn glance. 'That's why I won't call in the police.'

'He's banking on that, the swine!' Marge muttered through clenched teeth.

'We don't want the bad publicity,' Lillian insisted. 'Tony drew the wealthier clients. It's going to be difficult enough to keep them as it is. If it gets around we're in financial difficulties as well, that'll finish us.'

'Then what the hell are you going to do, Lillian?' Darlene demanded angrily. 'My living is on the line, here, mind? Might as well pack it in right now, as far as I can see.' She tossed her head. 'I'm looking for another job first thing tomorrow.'

Marge's eyes narrowed in fury.

'Always knew there was something ratty about you, Darlene,' she shouted savagely. 'Leave the sinking ship; go on! Never mind about anybody else.'

'Well, what do you expect?' Darlene retorted, her face flushed. 'On my own, I am, mind. Haven't got a husband to keep me, have I?'

'Well, welcome to the bloody club!' Marge screeched furiously. 'You selfish bitch! We've got to stand by Lillian.'

'What about us?' Florence asked, swallowing hard and staring desperately from one woman to the other.

She and Glenys drew together, the younger girl clutching at Florence's arm. She could guess how Glenys felt. She felt the same. Their whole future was tumbling down around their ears.

Lillian shook her head.

'I can't pay back the premiums now, so you both might as well stay.'

'Is there any future for us, though?' Florence insisted.

She didn't want to be disloyal to Lillian, but there was a lot of truth in what Darlene said, thought Florence. She and Glenys needed to know their apprenticeships were safe, that there was a future for them.

'Look,' said Lillian. 'I'll do as much as possible to keep the salon going. I'll look for a partner. Someone who'll invest in the business. I've been making contacts all day.'

'Huh!' Darlene threw up a hand in disgust. 'The country's bankrupt, on the bone of its arse, and you're looking for an investor? Fat chance!'

'There's plenty of money about,' Lillian cried. 'We see it every day.'

'Yeah, but who'd be daft enough to invest in a business that's just lost its main asset? Tony's Paris training *was* Terri's, like you said,' Darlene turned away despondently. 'So, what's the point of going on?'

'Well, get out, then!' Marge shouted at her furiously. 'Push off! Go on. We'd be better off without *you* anyway. I'm sticking by Lillian, and so will Nancy.'

Darlene whirled around, her eyes flashing with malice.

237

'Best of luck, then, because you'll need it.'

Darlene didn't turn up for work the next day. Florence saw no one else was very much surprised, but she was dismayed at Darlene's lack of loyalty and faith. The shop was in a bad situation, perhaps worse than Lillian was letting on, but Darlene's selfishness made it even more so. By deserting them she put all their futures at risk.

As Marge said that morning, they must pick up the pieces and fight on. Florence was all for that. She felt determination stir her blood and set herself to working as hard and as efficiently as she could, encouraging Glenys to do the same.

'Pity Nancy isn't back until next week,' Marge said quietly as Florence was liberally dabbing a client's head with perming lotion. 'Hey! And go easy with that stuff, will you, kid? We don't want to run short.'

'Sorry, Marge, I forgot.'

Though she hadn't forgotten. How could she? She'd spent a sleepless night wondering where it could all lead. She'd said nothing at home, less out of caution for the reputation of the shop than avoiding the told-you-so looks from her family.

This was *her* life now, and her worries. She'd have to deal with disappointments herself. She'd no intention of crying on anyone's shoulder.

Strangely though, she felt easier and less tense now that Tony was gone for good. Only now did she realise how much she hated and despised him and everything he stood for.

Lillian was bitter and unhappy at his desertion,

but Florence couldn't help feeling her employer was better off without him. She'd build a new life, a better life.

Florence wondered how Cliff was feeling. He might not even know since he was often away for days, driving for a long-distance haulage firm, and that's why he'd not been in the salon yet. She was certain of his loyalty. His was a strong arm that Lillian could lean on. Florence had no doubt he'd be ashamed of his brother.

She was deeply sorry for Lillian. Tony's disappearance had hit her harder than she was letting on, but she couldn't really hide the physical effects of her pain, and Florence couldn't help staring.

Her employer looked even more haggard this morning than yesterday. The overall she wore looked strange on her, out of place. She was doing a set, her long fingers handling the rollers awkwardly.

She must feel awful, Florence thought with growing sympathy; deserted and humiliated by her no-good husband whom she'd obviously trusted too much. Her livelihood brought to the point of ruin because of his treachery; she was reduced to working in the salon along with everyone else. It was a comedown, and Florence imagined the shame she must feel.

'I didn't realise Lillian was a trained hairdresser,' Florence remarked to Marge as they worked.

'Oh aye,' she replied sadly. 'She was good in her day, the best. She's out of practice now, mind. Bloody Tony! I'd swear he planned it like this,' she went on. 'I blame Lillian, as well. Too soft with him, she was. Letting him have things his way. Now look at her!'

'How long can we go on, Marge?' Florence asked. She dreaded the answer, but it had to be faced.

The older woman shook her head, her face grim.

'I dunno, love. Tsk! And that Darlene's really left us up the river without a paddle, hasn't she? Never mind, kid. We're not finished yet, are we?'

By Wednesday things were settling down a bit, Florence saw. They were managing. Everyone was pulling their weight, and even Glenys entered into the spirit, getting things right for once. But there was no doubt they missed Darlene. As Marge pointed out, she might be a chronic pain in the neck, but she was a good worker.

There'd been some awkward moments, too, when some of Tony's regulars kicked up a fuss because he wasn't there to dress their hair and generally fawn over them. Lillian managed to smooth things over without revealing that Tony was gone for good, although Florence could see she was very close to tears at times.

It was mid-morning when Marge gave Florence a quick dig in the ribs.

'Ho-ho! Look what the cat's dragged in.'

Florence glanced up and was startled to see Darlene standing in the salon. For once she looked uncertain, and just a bit down in the mouth.

Had she come to beg for her job back? Florence wondered with mixed feelings. Darlene was difficult, a bully, but there was no doubt the shop was in desperate need of another pair of skilled hands. But would Lillian be prepared to take her back? What choice did she have, though?

Lillian was just putting a client under the drier. She took her time before even acknowledging Darlene was there. Florence paused in fixing the next roller, waiting to see what would happen, aware of a sudden tension.

'Hello, Darlene,' Lillian said at last. Some of her old spirit was back in her voice, though Florence suspected her employer was forcing it. 'What do you want?'

Darlene looked uncomfortable. She fiddled with the belt of her dress as though it was suddenly too tight. Her complexion, usually sallow, was tinged with pink around her cheekbones. If it had been anyone else Florence would've felt sympathy. But she couldn't feel sorry for a traitor.

'Can we go in the office, Lil?'

'No, we can't!' Lillian snapped loudly. For once she didn't seem to care that clients were listening. 'Speak up. What is it? Come on, we're busy here. Left short-handed, aren't we?'

Darlene tried to rally, flicking back her hair, attempting to look unperturbed, but Florence could see that the pink spots had turned dull red. Florence couldn't decide whether it was stubbornness or embarrassment. Whatever it was, Darlene was getting a taste of her own medicine, and Florence felt a spark of malicious

241

delight in her discomfort.

'I … I never gave in my notice, mind, Lillian,' Darlene blurted.

'You walked out.'

Darlene shook her head emphatically.

'No, no, it was a protest, that's all.'

Lillian stood with her hands on her hips, looking down her nose.

'Protest, my foot! What's the matter? Couldn't get another job, is it?'

Darlene's shoulders drooped.

'All right! I'm sorry I was awkward. I was worried sick.' Her voice took on a high, whining tone, which grated on Florence's nerves. 'I can't afford to be out of work, Lillian.'

'Tsk!' Lillian jerked her chin as though amazed at her own softness. 'I want my head examined, taking you back.'

She stared hard at Darlene, who nervously shifted her weight from one foot to another, as she awaited Lillian's pronouncement.

'Oh, go on, then!' she said at last. 'Get your overall on and get cracking. But you watch your step, Darlene. I'm not in the mood for any funny buggers. Get it?'

The day hadn't finished surprising them. After lunch, Florence was in the reception area answering the telephone. She'd just finished booking another appointment when the salon door opened and a thin young woman came in carrying a baby, wrapped in a shawl Welsh fashion, and dragging a toddler behind her. The child was grizzling and wiping his running nose on the sleeve of his none-too-clean jumper.

Florence stared. The woman didn't look like a client. Her dark greasy hair was scraped back and tied with a piece of old ribbon. Her print dress, too, looked well overdue for a date with the wash tub.

Yet there was something oddly familiar about her – the bold expression in her eyes – which gave Florence a queasy feeling in the pit of her stomach, and her intuition warned her that something unpleasant was going to happen.

'Can I help you?' she asked, her nose twitching at the smell of neglect exuding from the woman and children, and she was left in no doubt of the baby's urgent need of a nappy change.

The woman's insolent stare fixed on Florence.

'Where's our Hazel?'

'Pardon?' Florence was momentarily perplexed at the question.

Then suddenly the sense of familiarity was explained. The young woman looked like Hazel, the receptionist, but older, careworn.

Florence had never taken to Hazel, and in fact, despised her, but at least the girl was clean and quite smart in appearance. How could she be connected to this slovenly woman?

'Our Hazel,' the woman repeated, belligerently this time. 'Our mam wants to know where she is.'

'She's not here,' Florence assured her hastily.

She edged around the counter, planting herself in front of the bead curtain. The musty smell of dirty clothes and unwashed bodies began to fill the reception area. Florence had visions of the woman pushing her way into the salon. That was the last thing they needed.

243

'You'd better go,' she insisted. 'Hazel isn't here, I tell you.'

The salon door opened again and one of their regular clients came in, a doctor's wife.

Florence was immediately ashamed when she saw the client stare in astonishment at the visitors, her nose wrinkling in distaste. Florence waited until the client had passed through the bead curtain before she spoke again.

'You'd better leave,' Florence said.

The woman sniffed.

'I'm not budging from by here till I know where our Hazel's gone to,' she answered truculently. 'Mam wants the rent money, don't she?'

'Look, Hazel's off sick as far as Mrs Longford knows. She's at home.'

'No, she isn't. I bloody-well ought to know. I'm Angela, Hazel's sister. She went off to work last Friday morning and we haven't seen her since.'

Despite herself Florence was suddenly concerned. Hazel was missing; perhaps something had happened to her. Florence had no liking for her, yet she wouldn't want to see her come to harm.

'Have you told the police?' Florence asked.

'Police?' Angela looked appalled at the suggestion. 'We don't have nothing to do with them. Them buggers put my man in clink, didn't they?' She sniffed again. 'In any case they won't do nothing because Hazel took a suitcase with her and all her best clothes.'

'What?'

Florence felt her jaw drop open, surprised at a new and awful thought. Tony and Hazel? Had

244

they gone off together? Florence remembered things Hazel had said and done. Now it all made sense.

Immediately, Florence's thoughts were for Lillian. Tony and Hazel must've been carrying on right under Lillian's nose. She'd have to be told, but Florence knew she'd never be able to do it. It might be easier coming from Marge, Lillian's oldest friend. It would be an added blow, and Florence felt deeply sorry.

She was conscious that Angela was staring at her with curiosity, and hastily recomposed her expression.

'If Hazel's gone it's nothing to do with Terri's,' she said as firmly as she could. She opened the salon door and gestured Angela towards it. 'That'll be all, thank you!'

'Hey! You can't shove us off like that. What about Hazel's pay...'

'Listen!' Florence snapped, losing patience. 'I'll call a policeman if you don't leave right now.'

With a ferocious scowl Angela went, dragging the squalling child behind her.

'And don't come back, either!' Florence shouted after them.

She closed the door firmly, then with distaste, sniffed the tainted air left in their wake, reflecting that treachery had its own stench.

CHAPTER 17

Florence tried not to let herself dwell on the uncertainty of Lillian being able to pay her way, but despite that, worried all through the week about her wages. Would she get any pay on Friday? Surely her premium was safe? She was afraid to ask, not wanting to appear mercenary, like Darlene. Her wages were small enough, and she'd never been able to save anything, barely managing from week to week. Now Friday was here, and she lived in hope.

Florence was just putting the telephone receiver down in reception when Cliff breezed in through the door. He was grinning from ear to ear, looking pleased with himself about something, Florence thought. He appeared happier than he'd done for some time, and she was momentarily shocked.

'Hello, Flower,' he greeted. 'How's everything?'

Florence continued to stare at him in dismay, her shock turning to apprehension in the pit of her stomach. Obviously, he knew nothing of what had happened. Why on earth hadn't Lillian told him? Florence wondered.

'Cliff! Have you been away or something?' she hedged, realising she must be the one to tell him before he breezed in on Lillian and upset her unintentionally. She couldn't keep the tension under control, and her voice sounded tremulous.

Cliff picked it up immediately, his smile disappearing.

'Been away three days earlier in the week,' he said, his tone serious now. 'Took a load up to Glasgow. What's the matter, Flo? Why are you looking like that?'

Florence bit her lip, wondering how she should break the news. All she could do was say it straight out.

'It's Tony...'

Cliff's lips drew back from his teeth in what looked like a snarl. He reached across the counter and tightly grasped Florence's wrist.

'Has he touched you? Has he hurt you?'

Florence, shocked again at the intensity of Cliff's anger, shook her head, pulling her arm away sharply.

'No! Not that.'

She was about to say it was something much worse. Tony's attack on her had been horrendous, terrifying and disgusting, and they'd never forget it. She'd not told anyone else what Tony had done to her that evening in the stockroom, not even Marge. She'd been too ashamed. But perhaps what he'd done to Lillian *was* worse. Tony's new villainy was hurting them all.

'It's awful, Cliff. Tony's left Lillian and he's taken money from the business, as well. The salon's in serious trouble, Cliff, from what Lillian says.'

Cliff's face paled visibly, and Florence saw he was stunned.

'He's absconded? Oh, my God!'

'And that's not all of it,' Florence rushed on, eager now to reveal the full extent of Tony's treachery. 'Hazel's missing, too. We think they've gone off together.'

Cliff slammed his clenched fist down on the counter, making Florence almost jump out of her skin.

'The bloody fool!'

She stared as his face darkened with fury. He looked wild for a moment as he had that evening in the storeroom when his fist had pounded Tony's face.

'We're all worried sick for our jobs,' she went on, a sudden hope in her heart that he might rescue them somehow as he'd rescued her that other time.

Cliff turned his head away, his face shuttered for a moment.

'What'll happen now, Cliff?' Florence spoke after a moment's uncertainty. 'Do you think Lillian can find someone to invest?'

Cliff shook his head, blowing out breath between his lips in a gesture of doubt.

'One look at those books, kid, and any astute businessman would give it the thumbs down. I *might* have a solution, though. Better have a talk with Lillian. See what can be done. It depends on her.'

Florence followed Cliff into the salon. Despite it being market day in the town, there weren't so many clients this morning, and they'd had one or two cancellations. Obviously, news of Tony's absence had got around, although Lillian was making the excuse that he was ill whenever a client questioned. How long they could keep up the pretence, Florence couldn't guess.

Lillian glanced up from rolling perm curlers when Cliff came in. Florence thought she'd be glad to see him, but instead a look of hatred flashed onto her face. Florence was shocked at it, and she could see by Cliff's face that he was also taken aback at her unconcealed animosity.

'Lillian, we've got to talk,' he said.

She didn't look at him again and didn't pause in her task, applying more of the perming lotion and reaching for another curler.

'I've nothing to say to you.' Her voice was as hard as granite, more like the old Lillian. 'You've got no business here anymore, Cliff, so get out.'

Florence gasped, feeling affronted for him. Why was her employer behaving like this? It wasn't Cliff's fault Tony had absconded. She was being totally unfair.

Florence wished she could speak out, shout at Lillian the way she had when her employer had accused her of being Tony's latest piece of skirt. She'd had nothing to lose then. Now nine months later, she had so much time and money invested in Terri's, she knew she dare not jeopardise all this by being too outspoken.

Cliff glanced around briefly, obviously embarrassed at her words and tone. Most of the clients were under the driers so would be deaf to what was said, but some of the others were looking alert and curious.

Florence felt a great sympathy for Cliff at that moment. If there was anyone whom fate had treated unfairly it was Cliff.

'Lillian, please!'

She turned her face to him, her mouth a hard line.

'Haven't you and your brother done enough?'

Florence couldn't stand it another minute and threw caution and sense to the winds.

'That's unfair, Lillian,' she cried out heatedly. 'It's Tony who's the villain here, not Cliff. He can help you. Don't be a silly fool. Listen to him!'

Lillian looked furious, her mouth working in rage. She glanced around the salon, obviously embarrassed.

Marge darted from a cubicle nearby and tugged a warning on Florence's arm, and Florence stared at her employer appalled, knowing she'd gone too far.

'Lil!' Marge said loudly, giving a meaningful glance around the salon. 'Not by here, mun, Lil.' She jerked her head towards the office door.

'Oh, all right!' Lillian said angrily. 'Carry on with this perm, then, Marge.'

With that Lillian marched into the office. With one glance at Florence, Cliff followed. The door was closed firmly, and Florence was eaten up with curiosity as to what they might say to each other.

Before long nobody in the salon was left in any doubt, as Lillian's voice was raised in anger, carrying through the closed door, berating Cliff as though he were the cause of her trouble. The awful silence in the salon underlined the quarrelling voices in the office, and Florence felt her skin crawl with embarrassment.

Marge must've felt the same for suddenly she

251

left her client and rushed to the office door, barging in on the quarrelling couple. Lillian's ringing tones cut through the silence like a sharp blade through butter.

'Get out! Get out, Marge, damn you!'

And Marge got out, her face crumpling. She stared around at them all, glancing towards the kitchen, obviously longing to escape there. Instead, she squared her large shoulders, pulling herself together and returned to her client who was looking startled and bewildered.

Florence saw it took great effort for Marge to remain in the salon with everyone staring, seeing her humiliation, and she felt deeply for her. She had the same urge to go in and defend Cliff herself. What Lillian was doing was unfair, and not only that, stupid. If anyone could help her it was Cliff, Florence was certain of it.

He'd said that it would probably be difficult for Lillian to find an investor. Florence's stomach turned over at the thought. The business would sink without trace, and with it her premium and her future career.

Nancy and Darlene would find work elsewhere, and Marge too, probably. But what about Glenys and herself? With their premiums eaten up by a failing business they'd have no further chance. How was she to tell her father that his one hundred and fifty pounds was lost for good? How could she face the humiliation of having her mother proved right? No! She wouldn't let it happen!

Florence ground her teeth in sudden anger with her employer, glaring at the closed office door, hearing the angry voices. Lillian was throwing away *Florence's* money and with it, *her* chances.

She stepped forward bravely. She'd faced Lillian down before. She could do it now. Her future was threatened again, and this time the stakes were even higher, too high to allow her to stand back and do nothing. A wave of dogged determination coursed through her. Her mother had been a fighter all her life, and Florence knew she had the same strength of purpose.

Feeling that power surge through her veins, Florence opened the door and strode into the office without bothering to knock first. There was silence for a moment as both Cliff and Lillian paused in their argument to turn and stare at her. Then Lillian shouted, her expression thunderous.

'Get out, girl!'

'I won't!' Florence cried defiantly, trying to make her voice as strong as possible, though her heart was thumping like a drum in her chest. 'I've got a right to be here.'

Mindful of the clients listening in the salon, she kicked backwards against the door, slamming it shut. She was shaking like a leaf from head to foot and wished she had something to hold on to. Seeing the glare of rage in Lillian's eyes she felt she was facing a tiger in a small cage.

'This is none of your business!' Lillian screamed furiously.

'It *is* my business,' Florence said loudly, gathering her courage about her. 'You've got my money and you can't pay me back. That gives me a say in what happens next. Me and Glenys have

253

a right to protect our premiums.'

'You little bitch!' Lillian snarled. 'I knew you were trouble the minute I set eyes on you.'

Florence was enraged.

'How dare you say that to me!' she shouted as remembered humiliation caused hot blood to rise up, burning her face. 'After what your beast of a husband did to...'

'Flo!' Cliff's voice cut into Florence's fury. For a brief moment, in her anger, she'd forgotten he was there. 'That'll get us nowhere,' he said, a warning look in his eyes.

Florence drew in a deep breath to steady herself, but she couldn't help continuing to glare at Lillian. All her hatred and resentment for Tony, his awful attack on her, had flared up at Lillian's unfair words, but Cliff was right. Nothing would be gained by harping on that now. Keeping the business afloat was all that mattered.

'I don't want *your* damn sympathy, Cliff,' Lillian said bitterly. 'You and your bloody brother have done enough damage. I want you out of here, and I don't want you near the salon again.'

'That's unfair, Lillian,' Florence butted in again, feeling she had to defend him. 'It's no good blaming Cliff. You knew what Tony was capable of. I bet you even suspected what he was up to with Hazel. Well, didn't you?'

Lillian's eyes widened as she stared at Florence, and for a moment looked as though she would burst into tears.

'You were too cowardly to challenge him,' Florence went on ruthlessly. 'So if anyone's to blame, you are.'

'Flo!' Cliff said quickly. 'Take it easy, will you, mun.'

'Why should I?' Florence snapped, suddenly irritated at his careful attitude towards his sister-in-law. 'My whole future is at stake here, mind. And I don't know why you're defending her. She's willing to condemn you for nothing, isn't she?'

'You don't understand, kid.'

'Yes, I do, Cliff,' Florence retorted angrily. 'You're feeling guilty at what Tony's done. You're letting her walk all over you.'

Florence paused as a grim expression darkened his face, and she suddenly remembered Tony taunting him with something similar. She felt deeply ashamed then. Hurting Cliff was the last thing she wanted to do.

'I'm sorry, Cliff,' she blurted. 'I didn't mean that the way it sounded. But she *is* being unfair to you. And you don't deserve it.'

She went to him and laid a hand on his arm, feeling relief as his expression relaxed.

'Listen,' she went on eagerly. 'You said you had an idea how the business could be saved. Lillian must listen to you.'

Lillian's features were stony and stubborn, her mouth a straight line. Obviously she was determined not to be influenced by anything her brother-in-law said. Looking at her, Florence felt her heart sink, thinking that her employer's perversity would ruin them yet.

Cliff regarded her with uncertainty, too, Florence saw.

'I've a little money saved,' he said cautiously.

255

'It's not much, mind, but I think it's enough to get the business back on its feet. Would you consider me as a partner, Lil?'

She jumped to her feet, eyes flashing angrily.

'No, I bloody won't! I'm finished with the Longfords for good. Neither of you is any good, and I certainly don't want an ex-gaol-bird for a partner, thanks very much!'

'Lil!' Cliff's voice echoed his obvious pain at her blunt words.

'For heaven's sake!' Florence burst out angrily. 'He's trying to help you, help us all. Are you going to let everything go to pot just because your husband has done the dirty on you?' she demanded passionately. 'You owe it to the rest of us to accept Cliff's offer.'

'Shut your mouth, you interfering little hussy!' Lillian stormed at her. 'You know nothing about me or my life.'

'You're being stupid, Lillian,' Florence shouted back, thoroughly enraged. 'You're giving Tony the last laugh.'

She was so upset her legs were trembling like reeds in the wind.

'Take Cliff's offer. You may not get another one.'

'Cliff can get out now,' Lillian cried. 'I won't have a Longford near me or the salon. Get out, Cliff. Get out and don't come back!'

'Don't be such a stubborn fool, Lillian, will you!' Angry at the older woman's obtuse attitude, Florence stamped her foot so hard shock waves ran up her leg.

'And you can get out, as well,' Lillian rounded

on her, eyes flashing. 'I've had enough of *your* lip.'

'You can't sack me,' Florence stormed, almost beside herself with fury. 'You owe me money, and I'll have the law on you.'

Cliff lifted both hands in despair.

'Lil! Flo! For God's sake, stop this cat fight.' He turned towards the door. 'I'll go, Lil. I don't bear you any hard feelings. Tony's a swine and he doesn't deserve you. My offer remains open if you change your mind.'

'Don't hold your breath because I won't!'

He stared at her for a moment longer, then without another word left the office, closing the door quietly behind him.

Florence glared at Lillian in despair, her mouth set in a thin line. Something told her Lillian had thrown away the only chance they'd have to get back on their feet. Everything thrown away because of pride, and, Florence suspected, revenge. Tony would be laughing up his sleeve if he knew about it.

At that thought a wave of intense anger engulfed her, and she wanted to hurt Lillian.

'I hope you're satisfied, Lillian,' Florence said through clenched teeth. 'You've just scuttled the salon good and proper.'

Without waiting for Lillian's retort, Florence hurried from the office, hoping to catch Cliff before he left. He was still in the reception area when she brushed through the bead curtain.

'Cliff! I'm so sorry.'

His answering smile was strained.

'It's all right, kid.' He grasped her hand. 'Don't be hard on Lil, mun. She's suffering badly. She still loves Tony, that's the trouble.'

'After what he's done to her?' Florence was astonished.

Her mind darted to Ken and his betrayal. She felt nothing but resentment and anger against him now. How could Lillian go on loving a man who did that? Florence found it difficult to understand.

'Keep an eye on things for me, will you?' he asked. 'Let me know if she has any luck finding a prospective partner.' He sighed, shaking his head. 'I'll give her time to cool off. Maybe she'll accept my offer when she gets desperate.'

Lillian was desperate already, Florence thought, but she wouldn't accept it. She squeezed his hand.

'Cliff, be honest,' she asked, biting her lip in vexation because she felt she knew what his answer would be, 'how much longer can the salon stay open?'

'It's obvious you're losing clients now that Tony's gone. It can only get worse,' he said quietly. 'In a month supplies will dry up because there'll be no more money to pay the wholesalers.' He pressed her hand. 'I'm sorry, Flo. I know how much your career means to you.'

He left the salon then, and Florence's heart sank at the sight of his retreating figure. He'd been her last hope.

She felt like giving way and having a good cry there and then. It was all coming to an end, everything she'd struggled for, fought her family for, fizzling out like a damp squib. For once there wasn't a thing she could do about it.

CHAPTER 18

In the little Italian café in Union Street Florence pulled forward a bentwood chair and flopped down onto it. The warmth of the day was still oppressive even though it was early evening. Her cotton dress stuck to her back as she leaned her elbows on the table.

The aromas of freshly brewed coffee and hot meat pies usually made her mouth water, but today she felt too tired to be hungry. Her tiredness wasn't due to overwork. She only wished it was. The number of clients at the shop had noticeably dwindled over the four weeks since Lillian had refused Cliff's offer of help. Florence was worn out with worrying and fretting about her future, so much so that she felt the last four weeks had been the hardest of her life so far.

She looked across at the counter where Cliff stood waiting to be served. She was meeting him regularly in the café each week now to report on the situation at the shop.

Since she hadn't yet dared tell her family what was going on, talking to Cliff was the sole relief she had from her nagging worry. He was the only one who understood, the only one who offered sympathy.

He was served at last and came across to the table, putting a glass of sparkling lemonade before her. He set down his own cup of coffee on the table and took a seat opposite.

'Sure you wouldn't like a meat pie, Flo?'

'No thanks, Cliff, really.'

'Any news? How's Lil?'

Florence gave a deep sigh. She couldn't hide the depression she felt, not in front of him. She didn't have to pretend with him, didn't have to save face. With him she could be herself, without the need to smother her feelings.

'Things are really bad, Cliff. Lillian came back from the wholesalers empty-handed today. They wouldn't even give her credit, mind. Isn't it awful?'

'Rumours get about in business, Flo,' Cliff said. 'Times are hard for everyone. You can't blame people for not wanting to take a chance.'

'But it's so unfair!' Florence cried out, unable to control the misery she felt. 'I could kill that Tony myself. Look what he's done to us all.'

Cliff reached across and placed a comforting hand on her own.

'Something will turn up, kid, I'm sure of it. When Lil realises the truth I'm sure she'll take up my offer.'

Florence bent her head over her glass. Having to listen to Lillian berate the Longfords almost daily, she had small hope of that. Everything was so hopeless.

'Cliff, listen.' She looked up at him. 'You know lots of people. Isn't there anyone who'd be interested in the business? I mean, just a year ago it was thriving. Women were clamouring to get their hair done with us, even from as far afield as the Valleys.'

Cliff shook his head.

'When Tony buggered off he took more than money,' he said bitterly. 'In a way he took the business, too.'

Florence straightened her spine and lifted her chin defiantly.

'I can't believe that. We've still got Nancy and Darlene. They're London-trained, and they're good, too, really good.'

Darlene was a troublemaker and a pain in the neck, but at least she was a craftswoman in her way. She had flair, as had Nancy, and Florence knew, given time, she herself would acquire their skills in hairdressing. Now it looked like she'd never get her chance.

Cliff smiled.

'You're a loyal kid, Flo, and I like that very much. I wonder if Lillian knows how lucky she is to have you on her side?'

Florence shook her head.

'It's not only loyalty, though, Cliff, is it? A selfish interest I've got, too, mind. I don't want to lose my premium. I want to go on learning my trade. I want that more than anything else on earth. It makes my blood boil to think my chances are smashed because of a womanising louse like Tony.' She gave him an apologetic glance. 'I know he's your brother, and all, Cliff, but I can't help hating him.'

He grinned.

'Don't mind me, kid.'

Florence felt her shoulders droop.

'So, Cliff, in your opinion, Lillian hasn't got a hope, then?'

His grin turned to a weak smile.

'All she's got is me.'

When Florence went into the salon kitchen the next morning to hang up her coat and put on her overall, she found Marge and Glenys already there. The younger girl was sitting at the table, head in her hands, crying.

Florence stared, feeling dread like a lump of lead in the pit of her stomach.

'What's happened?'

'Sit down, kid,' Marge said. 'Have a cup of tea.'

'Marge!' Florence couldn't help snapping. Her nerves were strung as tight as violin strings. They'd come to the end of the road. She could see it in the older woman's eyes. She really didn't need to ask. 'What's wrong?'

'I was over Lil's last night. She told me she's closing the salon at the end of this month. We'll all be out of a job.'

'She can't do that!' Florence cried out.

'She can, love,' Marge said evenly. 'It's her business, after all.'

'But what about us? Me and Glenys? Has she got our money for us?'

Marge didn't answer, but lowered her gaze, her finger absent-mindedly circling the edge of her cup.

Florence felt her anger mounting.

'I'll have the law on her,' she threatened, but even as she spoke she knew it was an empty threat.

'Well, what good would that be?' Marge asked tartly. 'When she hasn't got a blooming penny to scratch her bum with? Talk sense, Flo!'

Florence flopped onto a chair, forgetting to take off her coat and head scarf. It couldn't be happening! Her dream, her life's ambition was draining away, like dirty washing-up water down the plug hole.

'What am I going to do?'

Glenys looked up, giving a big sniff of misery.

'It's all right for you, Flo. You've still got your shorthand and typing. I've got nothing. I expect I'll end up in some grocer's shop, weighing out dirty potatoes.'

'Well, I'd rather do that than be chained to a typewriter,' Florence declared defiantly.

'Who'll take *me* on at my age?' Marge asked disconsolately.

'Lillian should come straight out and tell us to our faces,' Florence said angrily. 'Instead of getting you to do her dirty work.'

'She'll announce it on Friday,' Marge told her.

'But it doesn't have to happen.' Florence sat up straight, suddenly hopeful again. 'Cliff will lend her the money. She's *got* to accept it.'

'Do you think I haven't tried to persuade her?' Marge asked sharply. 'She doesn't trust him. She won't trust a Longford again, ever.'

Glenys burst out with fresh grizzling, and Florence sympathised, being near to tears herself. But it was no good giving way to disappointment and misery. It was finished. Kaput! Yet she could hardly believe it. And at the moment she had no idea what she'd do next. Her future seemed a total blank.

'Oh, if only I had the money!' Marge cried out.

'I'd buy into the business myself.'

'Me, too!' Florence muttered.

As soon as the words were spoken, her shoulders straightened, and she stared at Marge for a moment, suddenly stilled. All at once her head was buzzing as a brand-new notion began to form.

Why on earth hadn't she thought of it before? Her parents were business people. Her father was part owner of a flourishing market garden as well as a builders' merchant business. Her mother owned the guest house, a café in Plymouth Street, and a ladies' outfitters in the Mumbles.

They were always on the lookout for good investments. Florence was sure they'd jump at the chance of a partnership in Terri's.

Suddenly she began to glow with new hope. Her parents would save them, save them all. It would be wonderful! It would be like owning part of the salon herself.

She opened her mouth to tell Marge her new idea, then stopped. No, she must do things right. She'd speak to Lillian first, who would surely consider the idea eagerly. Then tonight Florence would approach her parents with the proposition.

She considered carefully how she'd go about this. She'd talk to her father first, she decided; get him on her side, then together they'd tackle her mother.

In a much happier frame of mind Florence jumped up to take off her coat and scarf and put on her overall to start work. She wouldn't say anything to the others just yet. But she felt like hugging herself with joy and excitement at the

264

prospect of a brand-new and secure future. Everything was going to be all right after all. She just knew in her heart.

That evening, Florence waited until after supper to talk to her parents, though how she contained herself she didn't know. Instinct told her not to rush at it. This was business and a serious matter. She must show her parents she understood this principle. She wouldn't dash into it like a silly young girl might, like she might have done a year ago. She had to be patient and pick the right moment.

Florence thought back to earlier in the day when she'd gone hesitantly into the office to speak with Lillian. For once her employer had listened to her patiently. She'd asked a lot of questions about the Philpots' various businesses, and then agreed she was interested in any offer they might make.

'I expect they'll want to see the books, though,' Lillian said rather sadly.

'I expect so,' Florence agreed, suddenly realising how ignorant she was in business matters.

She knew only too well that the state of the books was a stumbling block to prospective partners, but she was certain her parents, being farsighted people, would look beyond that to see the real worth of the business. They'd see the salon did have a future; her future.

Her father was down in the gardens after supper, turning up some potatoes for the following day. Tommy was with him, reluctantly giving a hand.

Although the vast market gardens some three miles to the west of Swansea supplied all the vegetables they could possibly need at the guest house, William insisted on cultivating fruit and vegetables for the family's consumption in the guest house grounds. With food shortages continuing to be a big problem, the 'dig for victory' ethic was still strong.

Florence watched her father for a few moments from the path as he placed the fork in the ground, forcing it down into the earth with the sole of his boot, then lifting and turning, the rich soil yielding its fruits; in this case, large, healthy-looking potatoes. He bent to shake the tubers, pulling the potatoes free and throwing them into a bucket nearby.

He handled the soil lovingly, Florence thought, watching him fondly, knowing that here her father was in his element, at his happiest, dealing with growing things.

'Dad?'

He looked up. So did Tommy. At the sight of Florence he threw down his fork.

'Got to go, Dad,' he said quickly. 'Scouts tonight.'

'All right, son,' William said indulgently. He squinted at Florence as Tommy sped away.

'Pass me that other bucket by there, Flo,' he said. 'This one's full nearly.'

She fetched the bucket, feeling a spurt of annoyance that Tommy had used her appearance to skive off.

'Dad, can I talk to you a minute?' she asked as she came to where he stood on the dark earth recently turned.

She could smell it, rich and strong. She didn't know whether she liked the smell or not, then decided she couldn't share his love of the earth. It was somehow alien to her. She wasn't as much of a one for the great outdoors as he was.

'All right, Flo, love,' he said absent-mindedly. 'Get the other fork, will you, and give me a hand by here to lift some more spuds?'

'Er ... no, Dad, I won't if you don't mind. It's my hands, you see. I can't be doing people's hair with dirt under my fingernails, now can I?'

He squinted at her again in the mellowing evening sunlight, a slight sweat on his face from his exertions, his spectacles balancing precariously on the end of his nose. He pushed them back into position with an earth-encrusted finger.

'No, I suppose not, *cariad*,' he agreed.

He forced the fork into the earth again.

'Dad, could you stop a minute and listen?' she asked quickly. 'I want to talk seriously.'

He paused to lean heavily on the fork handle, wiping the back of his hand across his forehead.

'A break might be a good idea,' he agreed.

He looked more closely at her then, his brown eyes intent on her face.

'What's the matter, Flo? There's serious you're looking.'

Florence chewed her bottom lip, her mind working furiously, trying to find the right words to start.

'It's about Terri's, Dad. The business is in trouble...'

She stopped, confused at her own carelessness.

Those were the wrong words.

William straightened, staring at her.

'What?'

'I haven't told you before,' Florence rushed on, hoping to repair the damage. 'Tony Longford has pushed off, left his wife, and taken money as well. Now Lillian can't pay her way, and the salon will close at the end of this month unless she can find a partner to put up some money.'

'Tsk! There's bad luck, isn't it? I suppose your premium has gone down the pan as well, has it?'

He didn't sound too surprised, and for a moment Florence felt vexed at his calm acceptance of the salon's fate, as though he'd expected it; as though anything *she* was connected with must fail.

She swallowed hard, forcing down her vexation. She couldn't afford to be oversensitive now, or show anger. She needed his help.

'Yes, Dad, and that's why we can't let it happen.'

'We?' He frowned at her, pushing his spectacles to the bridge of his nose again. 'How d'you mean?'

'Lillian Longford is looking for a business partner. It's a good investment, Dad. Terri's was booming before...'

She was going to say, before Tony left, but hesitated. Perhaps Cliff was right? Tony had been the salon's only asset. She didn't want to believe that. She didn't want her parents to believe it, either.

'Terri's has a good reputation in town, Dad. You ask anybody. Eight hundred pounds, that's all Lillian needs.'

William stared at her, his mouth slightly open.

'Eight hundred quid?' he said at last. *'Duw annwyl!'* He gave a chuckle. 'She don't want much, does she?'

'I'm telling you, it's worth it, Dad,' said Florence, straining to keep the desperation out of her voice. But perhaps her father knew her too well not to see it. 'Apart from the good return on your money, you'd be saving our jobs, too.'

William looked at her in silence for a moment, then put the fork into the ground again.

'You could buy the top end of the High Street for that kind of money,' he said dryly, stamping several times on the fork to drive it into the ground.

This wasn't going at all well, Florence realised. She was failing to sell him the idea. If she wanted to go into business herself, she'd have to do better than this.

'Well, make Lillian an offer, then,' she suggested in desperation.

'Flo, love!' William leaned on the fork again. 'It's out of the question, mun. My businesses are doing all right,' he went on more gently. 'But I haven't much loose capital. These days you've got to plough everything back.'

'But, Dad!'

'Look!' he exclaimed. 'Your mother didn't approve of giving you the money for the premium. I gave it because I love you, Flo, and want you to be happy. But your mother didn't believe it would do you any good to encourage ... well, your silly dream, as she put it. She was convinced it would fail, and she was right, wasn't she?'

'*I have not failed!*' stormed Florence, stamping her foot in the soft earth, thoroughly angry. 'It's not my fault that blasted Tony Longford robbed the business, is it?'

'Well.' William looked grim. 'Lost my hundred and fifty pounds, haven't I?' He shook his head. 'It's a lot of money, Flo. You don't seem to realise that.'

'I do, Dad! And you haven't lost it yet,' Florence rallied eagerly. 'Make Lillian an offer. I'm sure she'll be reasonable. You won't regret it, Dad, I promise you.'

'Hardly in a position to promise anything, are you, *cariad?*'

There was tenderness in his eyes, and perhaps pity, too, Florence saw with a jolt, and felt a great hurt around her heart. She didn't want pity. She wanted faith and support.

'If it were Amy or Tommy asking, you'd do it like a shot,' she accused, lifting her chin defiantly, at the same time, feeling tears sting the backs of her eyes. With determination she fought them off. 'But I'm ignored, I am. My family don't care about me.'

'Now, that's unfair, Flo!' William objected loudly. He wrenched the fork out of the ground and threw it down.

Florence stared at him. It was rare her father showed anger. She was feeling sorry for herself, but had she gone too far?

'We don't treat you any different from the others, as well you know,' he went on forcefully, his lips thinned in indignation. 'You've got a lot to learn, you have, my girl.'

Florence turned her head away stubbornly. She wouldn't say she was sorry, because she wasn't. They did treat her differently, and she'd proved it, even if they couldn't see it.

Look how her father was treating her now. Even a criminal had a fair trial, but he was dismissing her as a failure without even bothering to listen, let alone help.

There was silence between them for a moment, while Florence looked out across the gardens to the road that sloped down to the village. Her parents had all this and more, and still they couldn't spare her a measly few hundred. It just wasn't fair.

She heard her father throw the rest of the potatoes into the bucket and turned to look at him. His features were relaxed again, his anger gone quickly.

She loved him, loved him dearly. There wasn't a better father anywhere. If only he would try to understand her, stand by her.

He picked up both buckets and turned to go up to the house. Florence's shoulders drooped with despair. So that was that! She'd failed to win him over. There was little point now in approaching her mother with the idea.

After a moment's hesitation, Florence followed in his footsteps, dragging her feet. He climbed the steps towards the back door, then waited at the top for her.

'Tell you what, Flo. I'll look at the salon's books...'

'Oh, Dad! Oh, Dad!'

He'd look at the books! Florence swallowed her

excitement with difficulty, hardly able to believe it.

'Hold on, now! Hold on!' he warned her as she raced up the few remaining steps to throw her arms around him. 'Not promising anything, am I? I haven't much margin for outside investments, and I don't think your mother is faring any better.'

'She finds enough to buy property, doesn't she?' Florence asked pertly.

Edie believed in property, having lived in rooms most of her life. Her favourite investment was buying up houses in the village, renovating them and letting them out at reasonable rents. This gave her a small, steady and safe income.

'Only now and then, Flo,' William said firmly. 'When something reasonable comes up for sale.' He shook his head. 'I don't think your mother and me can come up with the kind of money Mrs Longford wants.'

'Make her an offer, Dad. Any offer!'

Lillian was probably desperate enough to take anything.

He sighed. 'Your mother'll have something to say about this, mind.'

'Does she have to know? It can be between you and me, Dad. I'm sure you could come up with some spare capital if you tried.'

He shook his head, looking solemn.

'I don't have secrets from your mother, Flo,' he said reproachfully. 'Never have, never will. Remember that, my girl, if you meet a bloke and get married. Secrets can kill love quicker than anything else.'

Her mother was in the kitchen, just saying goodnight to Vera when Florence and William went in. Florence decided to beat a hasty retreat to her bedroom while her father did the groundwork in introducing Edie to the new idea.

She didn't have to wait long for a result, and knew there was going to be trouble as soon as her mother marched in without knocking.

'Of all your nonsensical ideas, Florence,' Edie exclaimed, as soon as the bedroom door was shut. 'This takes the biscuit!'

Florence had a sudden and sickening sense of history repeating itself. The last time she'd battled with her mother in this room, she'd considered herself the victor. Now she had a premonition of disaster and her courage ebbed.

'You haven't even thought about it, have you?' Florence accused. 'You're prejudiced against me, that's what you are, Mam, and I'm fed up with it.'

'Don't you speak to me like that!' Edie said. 'I'll get your father to take a slipper to you, my girl, big as you are.'

Florence nearly burst out laughing at the notion, but managed to keep herself in check. Her father had never laid a hand on her in anger in her life. He'd hardly start now she was eighteen going on nineteen. The idea was ludicrous.

'And don't you talk to me as if I were a child,' Florence retorted. 'Treat me with a bit of respect, Mam, for goodness sake.'

'Respect! Huh! I will when you deserve it.' Edie was scornful. 'Indulged you, your father has. I

273

was against giving you the premium, for a start. A waste of good money. And now look what's happened. It's gone. Tsk! I feel very angry with you, Florence, very angry.'

'It wasn't *my* fault,' Florence exclaimed loudly. 'I didn't do anything wrong.'

'It's been wrong from the start. But you'll have to come to your senses now. And don't make a face like that, Florence. You *have* to be sensible. You can't live in a dream for the rest of your life.'

Florence shook her head angrily. What was the good? Her mother didn't even want to meet her halfway.

'I can't talk to you anymore, Mam. We don't speak the same language, apparently.'

'Don't be impertinent!'

'I'm trying to save my job,' Florence explained crossly. 'And other people's, too. I'm trying to save Terri's. If you'd only stop being prejudiced against me and open your eyes you'd see what a wonderful chance it is. Terri's, Mam!' Florence exclaimed again with added emphasis. 'Think about it. Among the top hairdressers in town. It could be a gold mine.'

'Gold mine, my foot!' Edie sniffed. 'It's too much of a gamble. I don't need to look at the books to know that. Throwing good money after bad, even if we could afford it.'

'You don't want to help *me*, that's the truth,' Florence said sullenly. 'You could afford it if you tried.'

'Oh! That's typical of you, Florence, that is,' Edie nodded her head sagely. 'Have you any idea how much eight hundred pounds is? No! Of

274

course you haven't. You've got no idea about money at all. That's because you've never been without like your father and me. Struggling to make ends meet. Working our fingers to the bone...'

'Oh, for goodness sake, Mam, don't go on,' Florence interrupted savagely. 'I'm sick to death of hearing about how you struggled to live. That was years ago. You're not short of a bob or two now, I know you're not.'

Edie drew in her chin, reproachfully.

'I don't throw it away, investing in any kettle of fish offered me. I've had to learn the hard way. And so must you.'

Florence stared.

'What do you mean?'

Edie's mouth tightened.

'Start looking for a proper job in the morning, a sensible job, one you've been trained for. Your father will speak for you.'

'I don't want him to speak for me, Mam,' Florence flared, resentment burning in her breast. 'You don't know how humiliating that is. As if I'm not capable of getting a job on my own merit.'

'Well, that's up to you, then, isn't it?'

'Yes, it is, as a matter of fact,' Florence agreed, tossing her head energetically. 'I've got a job, Mam. I'm a hairdresser, well a trainee anyway. And I love the work. Yes, I do! I've got no intention of giving it up.'

Edie gave a bitter laugh.

'It's given *you* up by all accounts, hasn't it?'

A pang of despair struck through Florence's

heart at her mother's words. Things had changed between them, and she didn't know how or why it'd happened.

But she wouldn't let anything undermine her resolve. Staring at her mother's bleak expression, Florence felt the despair undergo a rebellious change. How much more of this treatment could she put up with? And why should she have to? Edie was behaving as though she owned Florence's life, and that was wrong.

Her spirits rallied in a quick burst of defiance; enough for her to throw off despair altogether. She'd fight back, and it wasn't over yet.

'Dad has promised to look at Lillian's books,' she said loudly and defiantly. 'He promised me! Is he going to break his word, then? You can't *make* him do that.'

Edie's expression faltered, and she looked uncertain for a moment. But the moment passed quickly, and she sniffed disparagingly before answering the charge.

'Well, he can look all he wants,' she said stiffly. 'But I'll never agree to the investment. Never! And he can't do it without *my* help.'

She turned on her heels and walked to the door. Florence viewed her mother's straight back with growing dismay and disappointment. She'd played her last card and still her mother had won, yet again. It just wasn't fair!

Edie paused in the doorway, glancing over her shoulder, her expression tight and withdrawn.

'The *Evening Post* is in the sitting-room,' she said. 'I suggest you study the situations vacant, my girl.'

CHAPTER 19

Florence could hardly wait to get to the café to see Cliff a few evenings later. So far, it was one of the most miserable and disappointing weeks of her life. She felt so unhappy. None of her family seemed to care or even try to understand what she was going through.

She felt rejected and belittled at her parents' unyielding attitude and what she saw as their callousness. At least she had Cliff to talk to, and she suddenly realised how much she'd come to depend on him.

The café in Union Street was packed with people, mostly mums sipping their well-earned cups of tea, and kids, fresh from sand and sea, scooping up mouthfuls of ice-cream, giggling, arguing, yelling at the tops of their voices and generally having a good time.

Florence looked eagerly for Cliff amongst the crowded tables but he wasn't there. Usually, he was waiting for her, and her spirits sagged further. Surely Cliff hadn't deserted her, too?

The girl behind the counter eyed her speculatively, waiting for her order. Florence managed an apologetic smile.

'A glass of lemonade, please.'

'And a cup of coffee, miss. I'm paying,' said a familiar voice at her elbow.

Cliff! Florence turned eagerly with a greeting

smile, so glad to see him. He hadn't let her down. She shouldn't have doubted him.

Served with their order, they turned to find a place to sit. Luckily at that moment one of the noisier families vacated a table next to the window.

'What a racket!' Cliff said cheerfully, sitting down and looking around the room with a bemused expression on his face. 'Most of these kids should be in bed by half-six.'

But Florence was in no mood for small talk. Filled to the brim with despondency and hopelessness, she wanted to talk about her problems to relieve the strain. Often, when she shared them with Cliff, she felt eased. Of course, there was nothing to be done about her present situation, she knew that. It was all over. A shoulder she needed now, to cry on.

'It's the end, Cliff,' she said miserably. 'It's been all for nothing.'

She wanted to burst into tears, but held herself in check. If she did cry she'd do it in private. She didn't want to embarrass Cliff, or herself for that matter. There'd be plenty of time for tears later when her dream was just a sad memory.

'So, your parents aren't interested?' He looked at her with sympathy. 'I'm not surprised, kid.'

Florence sniffed back the tears that still threatened to shame her.

'My father did look at the books as he promised.' She shook her head sadly. 'He told Lillian straight away it was out of the question.'

Florence choked up again, remembering the look on her father's face as he told her the news.

It was a half-impatient look, as though she were asking too much of him.

'Oh, Cliff,' she cried out. 'He could've taken it up for *my* sake, don't you think? I am his daughter, after all. He could've taken the chance to help *me*.'

'That's a bit unfair, Flo, love,' Cliff said gently. 'Your father's a businessman. He can't afford to take chances, especially not these days. No one can.'

Florence pressed her lips together tightly, still struggling not to cry. It was hard trying to keep control when her heart was breaking with despair and unhappiness. There was no one she could turn to for solace except Cliff. He was the best friend she'd ever had.

'They've turned their backs on me, Cliff,' she said miserably. 'Dismissed me as unimportant, their own daughter. Not worth taking a chance for. It's unbearable!'

Cliff reached across the table and covered her hand with his own. Florence felt the warmth of his skin on hers, and was comforted by his gesture. He was showing her more feeling and understanding than either of her parents.

'These days,' she went on, 'I dread going home after work. My mother keeps telling me I should look for proper work. Why won't she understand how important this is for me? Can't she see how much I'm hurting?'

'Listen, kid,' Cliff said, squeezing her hand. 'I hate to see you miserable like this. I've got an idea how I can help. I'll lend you the money myself. How's that?'

279

Florence stared at him open-mouthed, hardly believing what she was hearing.

At that moment at the next table, two small children, obviously brother and sister, began a high-pitched argument over the possession of a bucket and spade. Their mother, having a smoke and deep in conversation with a woman at another table was taking no notice.

'What did you say, Cliff?' Florence asked, wide-eyed. 'Lend me the money?' She spread her hand against her breast in disbelief. *Me?*

Cliff glanced impatiently at the squabbling children, then gazed at her, his expression serious, yet perhaps uncertain, too.

'We can't discuss it properly here, Flo. Look, will you come to my house now, right away? You don't feel like going home, you said. Have a bit of tea with me and the kids. Then we'll talk about the loan. What do you say?'

Cliff was willing to lend her the money! She felt breathless at the prospect. *She* could save Terri's, save her job, save her dream. It seemed like a miracle, but did he really mean it?

Suddenly she was anxious to know if he did, and to get on with the discussion that might mean her salvation. She picked up her glass of lemonade, drank it up thirstily, then stood up ready to leave, eager to learn more.

'Let's go, then,' she urged excitedly.

She accompanied Cliff to a narrow two-up-two-down terraced house in Catherine Street, near the hospital, where the front door stood open. She followed him inside and down a short passage to a living-room at the back.

As they walked into the room a fair-haired boy of about ten or eleven years jumped up from a leather sofa, where he'd been reading a comic. Florence eyed him curiously. He didn't look a bit like his father.

'Dada! What's for tea, Dada! Can I have it now?'

'In a minute, Pete,' Cliff said calmly. He glanced around. 'Where is she?'

Pete looked scornful.

'Hiding in the pantry again.'

Cliff jerked his head towards the scullery.

'Go and fetch her. I want you both to meet someone.'

With a perfunctory glance at Florence, the boy darted off, returning in a moment or two, dragging a little girl by the hand. She looked to be about eight years old, dark and small. She didn't look up at Cliff or Florence but kept her eyes downcast.

Pete was gazing up at his father, his expression expectant and impatient, too.

'Can I have bread and jam for tea, Dada? I'll have to have it soon 'cos me and Billy are going down the park on our bikes.'

Cliff turned to Florence, taking her arm and bringing her forward.

'This is Florence, Pete. She's a friend of mine so be nice to her. We'll be seeing a lot of her in future.' He looked at Florence and smiled quickly. 'At least, I hope so.'

Peter gave Florence a cursory glance, obviously dismissing her as of little interest.

'I wants thruppence, as well,' he said single-mindedly. 'Billy and me wants some ice-cream in Joe's.'

Cliff gave a resigned sigh, jerking his head towards the scullery.

'Go and lay the table, then, you mercenary little pest,' he said, his tone warm and loving despite the choice of words.

Florence sat on her heels before the girl, who stood with her head bent and hands behind her back. Her hair, falling around her shoulders, was silky chestnut brown with a slight natural wave. She was a pretty little thing who ought to be running around, lively and full of fun. Florence remembered the noisy, rumbustious children in the café, and couldn't help noting the difference.

'Who's this then, Cliff?' she asked, trying to peek at the child's face to catch her eye.

'That's Tansy.'

His tone was flat, with no sign of the warmth or love that had been in his voice a moment ago when speaking to his son. Florence glanced up at him in sharp surprise, taken aback at the sudden change, but he turned away to follow Pete to the scullery.

Florence straightened up, wondering at the strangeness of it. But she hadn't come here to pry into Cliff's family life, she reminded herself sharply. It was none of her business. Nevertheless, filled with curiosity and concern, she glanced down at the child, standing there so still; so small and quiet and so different from the demanding Pete.

'Tansy,' she said encouragingly. 'That's a pretty name. And you're a pretty girl, too.'

282

Slowly Tansy lifted her face and looked up at Florence, who smiled at her, but there was no answering smile. The child just stared solemnly.

Florence found the look disturbing and she longed to gather the child up in her arms to comfort her.

Suddenly she felt very uncomfortable. Cliff's talk of a loan had gone to her head, and although she did want it desperately, was it a good idea to be here in his home? He was her friend, and she valued that more than she understood. But Cliff's family was his own concern. She had no business to be curious about it, let alone interfere.

Cliff came back into the room, smiling at her.

'Sit down, Flo, for goodness sake,' he said. 'Tansy, go and get a cushion from the front room for Auntie Flo's chair.'

Tansy moved off immediately to do as she was asked, returning in a moment with the cushion. She placed it behind Florence's back as she sat, readjusting it several times until Florence had to laugh.

'That's very comfortable. Thank you, Tansy.'

Tansy sat on the mat near Florence's chair and stared steadily at her. Looking at her, Florence realised the child had not yet spoken one word.

'She misses her mother,' Cliff said, as if he thought an explanation was needed.

After tea, when Cliff had cleared away, they sat at the table in the living-room. Pete went out on his bike. Tansy silently deserted them, too.

Cliff was sorting through some papers on the table, and Florence was curious to know what they were.

'Thinking about this for weeks, I've been,' he said. 'And I've worked out a few details.'

'You really mean it?' Florence stared at him, a bemused smile on her lips, afraid to believe it was true.

He looked up, his expression serious and curiously tense.

'Oh, yes, I mean it, Flo. There's no other way. I mean … you need me.'

Florence put her elbows on the table, and placed her chin in her hands, smiling at him.

'Yes, I do. You know, Cliff, you're the best friend I've ever had.'

His smile was uncertain as he looked back at her.

'Friend? Yes, of course I am, and soon we'll be partners, too. Secret partners, though, mind,' he warned. 'Lil mustn't know I'm involved.'

Florence straightened up, bewildered.

'But how will we manage that?'

'First things first,' Cliff said in a businesslike tone. 'I can manage five hundred pounds, Flo. That's more than enough to get the business back on its feet.'

Florence glowed with excitement, then a sobering thought struck her.

'Cliff! It's such a lot of money,' she cried. 'It must be your life's savings!'

His smile was slow.

'Yes, kid, it is.'

She felt a pang of uncertainty strike at her enthusiasm, and her heart, riding so high a moment ago, sank.

'You can't risk it on me,' she exclaimed, aghast.

'I can't let you do it.'

'I believe in you, Flo,' he said. His voice was soft, and almost tender, Florence thought with surprise, and was confused for a moment.

Then with more energy, he went on: 'And I believe in Terri's. It always was top-notch and will be again.'

Florence felt a lump in her throat. He was a comparative stranger, yet he believed in her so thoroughly, where her family had no faith. She felt indebted to him.

'How am I going to thank you, Cliff?'

He lowered his gaze to the papers again, flicking through them.

'I've drawn up a few simple documents. A receipt for the money, and an agreement on the terms of our partnership, both of which you can sign, but only if you still want to after we've talked some more.'

Florence laughed, delighted that he had everything so well organised, and thrilled at his confidence in her and her dream.

'So, what's to talk about?'

He was silent, arms folded. He rested them on the table, his wide shoulders hunched, his dark curly head held low.

'Cliff?'

'You've got a right to know about me, Flo; my past.'

Florence put a hand on his arm as it rested on the table and he looked up quickly.

'Cliff, I know you've been in prison. Marge told me.' She shook her head. 'It makes no difference. I trust you.'

'I want you to know the truth, everything,' he said, straightening up to look directly at her. 'It's only right if we're to be partners.'

He glanced down at his hands resting on the table, obviously reluctant to begin.

'I'd just qualified as an accountant when I married Connie,' he said at last, then shrugged. 'The usual tale and I'm not proud of it. I got her into trouble and did the "right" thing. I married her.'

He paused, his mouth tightening.

'Only it wasn't right, was it? Wrong time, wrong reasons, wrong woman. She was no good. Knew it from the beginning, I suppose. Should've known she wouldn't change.'

Florence shifted uncomfortably on her chair. Once more she was glimpsing into the privacy of his life, this time by invitation, yet she felt the same sense of prying. Was all this heart-searching necessary? She'd be his business partner, not his life's companion.

'This isn't necessary, Cliff.'

He looked at her earnestly.

'Yes, it is, Flo. I need to be honest with you.'

Florence nodded her head, lowering her gaze. If he needed to unburden himself, she owed it to him to listen as a friend.

'Despite everything,' he went on, 'I was delighted when Pete was born. It made up for a lot.'

He was silent for a moment, perhaps remembering those early years of being a new father, savouring them, Florence thought. The years when his wife was alive and his family complete.

'I was twenty-three when the war broke out,' he went on, coming out of his reverie. 'It wasn't long before I was called up.'

He looked at Florence, his eyes shimmering with unshed tears.

'When a man is away, risking everything for his country, his family are all he has to cling to for sanity, for comfort. I came home on leave in forty-one after being away for over a year. We'd been having difficulties, Connie and me, before I was called up. I thought, hoped, the separation would help bring us together again.'

He shrugged again, and a self-mocking smile played around his mouth.

'How naive can you get? I came home to find Connie in the family way. There were plenty of well-meaning friends with tales to tell. Tony among them,' he added bitterly.

He reached across and took her hand in his, his look appealing, as though desperately hoping she understood. Florence smiled encouragingly. There was nothing she feared to hear. She had faith in him; faith that he was a good man at heart.

'I was bitter, Flo, betrayed. I no longer felt anything for Connie, but my honour had been dirtied, so I believed, and I wanted revenge.' He shook his head in disbelief. 'God! What a young fool I was.'

Florence saw that this remembering, reliving those bitter years, was tearing him apart. She felt helpless to comfort him except to urge him to forget.

There'd been no real tragedy in her young life,

yet instinctively she knew it was worse than useless to let past mistakes fester. There was no way back to put things right, so forward was the only course open.

'Cliff, there's no need to go on with this explanation for my sake,' she urged. 'That's all behind you. You must forget now.'

'I don't think it'll ever be behind me, Flo, love. It goes too deep. I took a life. I can hardly believe it, even now.'

'Oh, Cliff!'

'It wasn't murder, Flo. I swear it.'

His gaze desperately searched her features for some sign of disapproval or revulsion. Florence pressed his hand. He'd been a friend to her, saving her from Tony. She'd be his friend now. She wouldn't turn away from him, desert him.

'Go on, then, Cliff. Tell it if you must,' she said quietly. 'Get rid of it once and for all.'

He seemed to have difficulty in swallowing for a moment. Then he squared his shoulders, pulling himself together.

'I went in search of the man. I found him in a pub in the High Street. Give him a beating, that's all I intended. Almost blind with rage, I was. I hit him hard. He fell ... smashed his head against the corner of a table ... an unlucky blow!'

Cliff swallowed hard again. Perspiration glistened on his brow. His hands, resting on the table, were trembling and restless. He drew a long harsh breath as if about to suffocate.

'Manslaughter they called it. It cost me five years of my life. Five wasted years.'

He gave a jagged sigh, his gaze slipping past

her; looking back to that awful time, Florence surmised, and was silent, afraid to speak.

He glanced up at her then, his expression changing.

'The war was over by the time I got out,' he said, his voice stronger and more confident. He managed a weak grin. 'They say there's no ill wind, don't they?'

'Cliff, I'm sorry.'

She did feel deeply sorry that such a thing had happened to him. It shouldn't have. Not to Cliff. It made her angry to think that fate spared the likes of Tony, amoral and selfish. He seemed to get away with anything, unscathed. Cliff, basically a decent man, must suffer.

'Of course, I found my career in accountancy was finished,' he went on in a matter-of-fact tone, though Florence saw bitter regret in his eyes. 'So I took a job as a long-distance lorry driver.'

'It's unfair, Cliff.' She couldn't think of any comforting words.

He smiled. 'It suits me. After five years locked up I like to be on the move. It gives a sense of freedom.'

'What happened to Connie while you were in prison?' Florence asked tentatively.

Cliff's expression darkened.

'She was up to her old tricks. Had a man living here, in *my* house, with *my* son looking on, for God's sake!'

He clasped his hands together until the knuckles were white.

'Just before I came out of prison in forty-six she pushed off to Australia with him. Left the

289

children with a neighbour. I suppose she was afraid of me.'

Without even knowing, Florence despised Connie for deserting her children. Now Connie was dead, and Tansy was without her mother, and that was sad.

'You may think less of me for this, Flo,' Cliff said in a subdued tone. 'But I have to be honest with you. I just can't ... love Tansy.'

Florence thought of Tansy and the steady gaze of those solemn, sad eyes. Not love the child? Florence found this hard to believe. Yet she thought she understood him.

'She never speaks to me, you know,' he went on. 'She behaves normally in school, so I understand, and she talks to Pete. But she never speaks to me. It's as if she knows I ... killed her father.'

'Oh, Cliff! Don't say that.' Florence was appalled at the idea. 'She couldn't possibly understand something that happened before she was born.'

Cliff bent his head.

'Perhaps you're right,' he murmured. 'What she *does* know is that her mother left her here alone, and a strange man, me, came in her mother's place. I provide for her, but I just *can't* treat her like a daughter, Flo.'

Florence felt her heart ache at the thought of Tansy's lonely existence. In a way she really couldn't *blame* Cliff for his lack of feeling for the child. Tansy was a constant reminder of his wife's betrayal. There were too many bitter memories. It was hard for a man alone.

'Hasn't Connie got any relatives?' she asked.

'No, she had no one, not around here anyway.'

'But there must be *someone* who could take Tansy,' Florence insisted, perhaps a little too quickly. 'Someone who'd give her a proper life.'

An expression of anger flashed across his face for a moment.

'A proper life?'

Florence lifted her chin in defiance. Cliff wanted to be frank and open with her, and she would do the same.

'Don't pretend, Cliff,' she said sharply. 'All children need love, and you have none to give her, have you? She needs someone to love her, Cliff.'

His shoulders sagged wearily.

'You're right, Flo. I knew you'd understand.'

But Florence didn't understand what he meant. She shifted uneasily in her chair. Their conversation was getting too involved, far too personal.

'Cliff, to get back to our partnership,' she began hurriedly. 'I'm ready to sign any papers you want.'

He looked at her, a new eagerness in his eyes.

'You're sure, Flo?'

She smiled at him warmly.

'I've never been more sure of anything, Cliff, except my dream, of course.'

He held out a hand, grinning broadly at her.

'Shake, partner!'

They shook hands enthusiastically. Florence was tempted to plant a kiss on his cheek, but, shy for once, thought better of it.

Signing the papers made her feel really grown-up and responsible. At that moment she knew she'd taken an important step into the rest of her life. Success was assured because she'd taken her future into her own hands. It was up to her to work hard and build on what she had. It was good to know that Cliff would be at her side, supporting and advising. How could she go wrong?

'I'll have the cash ready for you next Tuesday,' he said, gathering up the signed papers. 'So come here in the evening to pick it up. Then you can present your offer to Lil on Wednesday.'

'Cash?'

'It has to be cash, Flo. Lil's ready to cut off her nose to spite her face, so she mustn't know where the money has come from,' he warned. 'If she suspects I'm involved in any way she'll refuse to listen to reason.'

Florence was dubious, her doubts showing on her face.

'You do understand, Flo? She mustn't know. It has to be this way.'

He was looking at her so earnestly. Florence shrugged, throwing off her doubts. Cliff was right. Lillian had refused Cliff's help when accepting would have saved the business.

'I suppose so,' she was forced to agree. 'But how am I to explain the money, Cliff? She knows I haven't got it.'

'Tell Lil your parents changed their minds. They don't want to invest themselves but they've agreed to lend you the money. You'll be Lil's partner.'

Florence drew in a sharp, excited breath at the thought of it. A partner in Terri's High-class Hairdressers! She let her mind drift for a moment, daydreaming, picturing how it would be. She'd be Lillian's equal; well almost. She'd introduce new, exciting ideas to the business. Clients would flock in. It will be like in the old days only better.

A shadow passed over the daydream, making Florence uneasy. She stared at Cliff, disturbed again.

'I can't tell a deliberate, outright lie to Lillian, Cliff. It isn't right.'

Deceit was no basis for a partnership, which depended on trust to be successful at all. Lying was foreign to her. She might've been guilty of omission in the past, but had never resorted to fabrication. She didn't want to start now, not when she was on the brink of the beginning of a wonderful future.

'There must be some other way, Cliff. I don't want to lie.'

'It's a white lie, Flo, love,' he said persuasively, taking her hand and squeezing it. 'You're doing it for Lil's sake, remember, and for the sake of Terri's. How can it be wrong?'

'Suppose she finds out?'

He shook his head, smiling encouragingly.

'How can she? Only you and I know the truth, and we're not going to tell her, are we?' He patted her hand reassuringly. 'It's going to be all right, kid. More than all right! You'll be Lil's partner. In business for yourself.' He laughed out loud. 'Even Darlene will have to take orders from *you!*'

The picture that conjured up made her laugh out loud, too. She couldn't wait to see Darlene's face when she learned Florence was her new boss. That might be *worth* telling a white lie for.

She took in a deep breath, feeling excitement bubbling up. Tonight, in her room, she'd start planning how she could make Terri's first-class again. She'd persuade Lillian to take on another hairdresser; a fashionable cutter from London, a presentable young man perhaps, who'd draw in the fashion-conscious women. Terri's will be the talk of the town again, Florence vowed to herself.

But first she must do something she hated, something that went right against the grain. She'd have to lie to Lillian. Florence placed a hand against her breast in apprehension as a sudden chill raced up her spine.

Please, God, don't let me regret it!

CHAPTER 20

Lillian came out of the office at last, rolling up the sleeves of her overall. Florence thought the older woman looked tired, even haggard. Her make-up, applied thickly as usual, stood out on her skin, white and powdery.

'Listen, everybody,' Lillian called loudly, rapping her scissors on the nearest chrome curtain support when no one took notice. 'Listen, will you!'

The doors weren't opened yet, so there were no clients in the salon. Most of the staff were standing around listlessly, waiting for Doomsday.

Everyone except Florence, who tried not to appear too animated in the face of everyone else's misery. She felt hot with suppressed excitement, knowing *she* was the one to save the salon and their jobs.

'Listen,' Lillian went on. 'As you all know, this week is the last week for the salon. I hope you've all been busy looking for other jobs. If you haven't that's your lookout.'

She paused as a squeak of despair came from Glenys. Lillian looked at her with contempt and irritation as the girl began to snivel.

'Put a sock in it, Glenys!'

Annoyed at her brusque and callous manner, Florence felt compelled to speak up.

'Have you got the balance of our premiums to

give us?' she demanded to know. 'You owe us that money, mind?'

Lillian's mouth, with its overemphasis of bright red lipstick, drew back from her teeth in a silent snarl. Her eyes glittered as they glared at Florence.

'You know damn well I haven't. You'll get your money when I sell the business. You'll have to wait.'

'That doesn't help Glenys get another apprenticeship, does it?' Florence persisted stubbornly.

She was asking herself why was she taking Lillian on like this, making her angry? It would be no advantage to her when she made the offer. Why make things harder for herself?

'Oh, bugger this!' Lillian exploded, her patience snapping. 'Do you think I like what's happening? My business, the business my father built up from scratch, the business I've worked in since I left school is going down the pan. I'm losing more than any of you.'

'Don't upset yourself, Lil, love,' Marge said soothingly, coming forward, and giving Florence a dark look. 'These youngsters don't know nothing about anything.'

She stood at Lillian's side, a comforting hand on her arm.

'Flo, go and open the door and man the reception, will you?' she went on firmly.

'But I want to talk to Lillian,' Florence protested strongly, annoyed at being dismissed. After all, she was practically a partner now. 'It's important!'

'Flo! Stop blooming arguing, will you?' Marge

snapped back, really cross for once and showing it. 'You've said enough already.'

Florence stalked off to reception, fuming. By mid-morning she'd bitten her thumb-nail almost down to the quick, thinking of the five hundred pounds in her handbag in the kitchen. She must speak with Lillian soon. She couldn't take the money home with her again.

Last night was a nightmare. Feeling so guilty and deceitful at having such a large sum secretly in her bag, she'd changed the hiding place several times during the evening, terrified her mother would stumble across it. The money had spent the night under her pillow but she'd hardly got a wink of sleep. Any further delay and her nerves would be in tatters. The sooner she made her deal with Lillian the better, then the money could be safely stowed in the office safe.

In the midst of her brooding, Glenys came into reception.

'Hey, Flo! Marge said go and have a quick cup of tea,' she said. 'I'll wait by here.'

Florence saw a comic book pushed down the front of Glenys's overall. Well, why not? It was unlikely any prospective clients would disturb her reading.

Where was Lillian? was Florence's first thought. The salon was unnaturally quiet for this time of day. The 'perm' was sitting patiently reading *Woman's Weekly*, her head covered in rollers plugged into the electrical appliance suspended from the ceiling. Nancy and Darlene were dealing with a shampoo and set each. Lillian and Marge were nowhere in sight, but the office door was open.

Florence made straight for it. This was the moment, the perfect moment. It was now or never.

Lillian was sitting reading a copy of *Vogue*, a cigarette held loosely between her fingers and a cup of tea on the desk before her. Marge sat, too. They'd obviously been commiserating with each other by their expressions.

They both glanced up when Florence came barging in, and Lillian's features hardened.

'Don't want to hear no more about your bloody premium,' she exclaimed loudly.

'I'm not here about that,' Florence said breathlessly. One glance at Lillian's stony face had taken the breath out of her. 'Can I talk to you in private?'

Marge started to rise from her chair, but Lillian waved her down again.

'Anything you want to say to me you can say in front of Marge, or else hop it!'

Florence bit down on her resentment, and took a deep breath. Perhaps it was just as well Marge was here anyway. They'd all know soon enough.

'My parents have changed their minds.'

'*What?*'

Both women spoke at the same time, and Lillian sat forward with such a jerk that the ash dropped from her cigarette into her teacup, forming a grey froth for a split second before being dissolved.

She sounded overawed. 'You mean they're going to invest after all?'

Both women were staring at her transfixed, and

Florence swallowed hard on her lie, finding it stuck in her throat for a moment.

'Well … not exactly.'

She was squirming now, and Lillian's eyes narrowed suspiciously.

'What the hell are you playing at, Flo? This isn't funny, you know. Now then, are your parents investing or not?'

Florence tried a weak smile, knowing she was making a mess of it. Her legs were trembling uncontrollably and she longed to sit down, but there wasn't another chair.

'It's like this,' she said, gathering up her courage and willing herself to be calm and not flush, betraying her duplicity. 'My parents don't want to invest themselves, but they've lent me some money to do with as I see fit, and I want to invest in the salon myself.'

Lillian stared at her for a moment.

'You?'

Marge burst out laughing.

'Oh, yeah! Very funny, kid.'

Florence jerked up her head, her mouth tightening at their dismissive tone. Wouldn't anyone ever take her seriously?

'Yes, me. Why not?'

Lillian gave a derisive guffaw, echoed by Marge.

'You're just a kid, that's why not. What do you know about business? Besides, you're an apprentice. You haven't been here five minutes yet.'

'But I've got the money, Lillian,' Florence cried out, disappointed at Lillian's attitude. 'And that's what you need, isn't it?'

'Good God, girl! Money isn't the whole story.' She shook her head. 'I need a partner. Somebody I can rely on, who'll share the burden like Tony used to.'

Florence was contemptuous.

'Tony!' she exclaimed sharply. 'Tony! Oh, yes! He was a big help, wasn't he?' Florence nodded vigorously to emphasise what she felt for him. 'He cut the ground from under your feet, that's all. Huh! The last thing you need is another Tony.'

Lillian looked furious.

'Don't you speak to me like that!'

'Yeah! Steady on!' Marge added brusquely.

Florence swallowed her anger, running her tongue over her lips nervously.

'I'm sorry, Lillian.'

Florence could've kicked herself for her outspokenness. It was getting her nowhere fast. She stepped nearer to the desk, earnestly wanting to make amends.

'I want to save the salon. I've got five hundred pounds, cash.'

Lillian's expression was still scathing.

'Five hundred. Don't be daft, will you? That's not near enough.'

Florence was annoyed again despite resolving not to be provoked.

'Well, my father told me five hundred was a more sensible figure than eight.' She tossed her head, impatient that Lillian disparaged the only offer she'd had. 'He's a good businessman. He knows what's what.'

'It's out of the question.' Lillian's tone was

belittling. 'You're a kid, barely out of your nappies.' She gave a harsh laugh, and glanced at Marge. 'I'd want my head read even to think about it.'

Marge nodded vigorously in agreement.

'You'd be a laughing stock, Lil.'

'Listen!' Florence glared from one woman to the other, seething with indignation. 'Do you want to save the business or don't you?'

'Don't be impertinent!'

'For heaven's sake, Lillian!' Florence snapped back, unable to control her impatience any longer. 'This is the only offer you're going to get, and you know it. You owe me money, Glenys, the wholesalers, and God knows who else. Even if you manage to sell the business, which is doubtful under the circumstances, you'll be in debt up to your ears. I'm offering five hundred pounds! Cash!'

Marge tut-tutted, while Lillian's eyes flashed angrily at Florence.

'You little schemer!' she said. 'Planning how you can get your hands on what's mine, is it?'

Florence's mouth fell open in utter disbelief at the accusation.

'That's not true!' she said furiously. 'I'm throwing you a life belt. Are you too thick to see that?'

There was a sudden silence, and Florence felt as stunned as Lillian looked. Marge was glaring furiously at her, and Florence knew she'd gone too far.

'Lillian, I apologise,' she said quietly. 'I'm sorry I spoke to you like that. You're right. I'm young and I've a lot to learn. But you could teach me, Lillian, couldn't you? The salon needs the money I have to offer. I ... we can make a go of it, I know we can. Save your livelihood, Marge's, mine and the others. Take my offer. I'll learn, I promise, and I'll work hard. Please, Lillian. Please give me a chance.'

Lillian looked at her for a silent moment, then shook her head, breathing out a long and disbelieving sigh.

'Like I said, I need my head read.' She paused, staring at Florence again, then sat up straight with a jerk. 'Oh, all right, then! Let's save the salon by all means.'

Marge rose to her feet, looking astonished.

'I don't believe it!' she burst out, staring at Lillian as if her friend had two heads. 'She's an apprentice, Lil, for God's sake. What the hell are you thinking of?'

Lillian looked suddenly desperate and vulnerable.

'She's got the money, Marge. I can't lose the business. I just can't!'

Marge turned her gaze on Florence.

'I don't know what to say. I'm bloody flummoxed.' She shook her head. 'I don't know what the others will say, either.'

'I've got to take the offer, kid,' Lillian said earnestly to her friend. 'But!' She wagged an index finger at Florence. 'I want to talk to your parents first before anything is signed.'

Florence was suddenly filled with panic.

'No, no! That won't be necessary.' She felt her cheeks flush uncomfortably. 'They are leaving

302

everything to me. I'm the one you deal with. I shall be your partner.'

'Partner!' Marge squeaked. 'Oh my God!'

'An apprentice for a partner!' Lillian looked bemused now, and disbelieving. 'Am I going senile at thirty-eight?'

Florence had to smile.

'Lillian, this partnership will be the making of Terri's, I'm telling you. I've got so many ideas, so many plans...'

'Hold on!' Lillian warned. 'Don't go getting too uppity. I'm still the senior partner, mind? Your five hundred is just a drop in the ocean.'

'That's right, Lil,' Marge interposed. 'You tell her! Partner, my bum!'

Florence lifted her chin, ignoring Marge's remark.

'It's an awful lot of money, Lillian, and you know it,' she said, trying hard to keep her tone reasonable. 'And it cuts me a good slice of the business.'

'Oh, Lil! I hope you're not going to regret this,' Marge wailed.

'She'd regret it a damned sight more if she lost the business,' Florence snapped back at her, then checked her outburst.

She'd try not to be impertinent or insult Lillian from now on, but at the same time, she didn't intend to be stepped on or pushed aside. She had ever intention of standing up for herself and fighting for Terri's survival with every ounce of her strength.

And right now, with a partnership in her pocket, she felt as strong as ten men. There was nothing she couldn't achieve.

She couldn't resist a proprietary glance around the small office, at the same time visualising the salon filled with clients as she was convinced it would be in a few months' time. This was just the beginning. From now on everything would be just rosy in her life.

CHAPTER 21

Lillian agreed to make the momentous announcement about the new partnership and the salon's survival after the lunch hour. Florence could hardly wait. She sat in the kitchen nibbling at her tomato sandwiches but was too over-wrought with excitement to swallow properly, while Lillian and a disapproving Marge remained closeted in the office.

Covertly, Florence watched the others as they ate and gossiped, wondering what they'd say when they found out she was their new boss.

She was their boss! She was her own boss! She almost choked on a piece of bread at the astounding thought. No one took any notice of her. All unaware, they kept on talking, mostly about finding other jobs.

She glanced at Nancy, whose violet eyes were more pensive than usual. Glenys's eyes and nose were red from crying. They all looked miserable, even Darlene, though as usual, she had the most to say and none of it helpful.

Florence felt she'd burst with enthusiasm and excitement if she didn't tell them soon. She longed to impart the good news, put them out of their misery, but still held her tongue. It was Lillian's place and her privilege to do that.

How would they take it? she wondered again, practically vibrating with anticipation. They'd be very relieved, she was sure, but would they be pleased? Well, they should, after all; she'd saved their jobs.

The meal-break over, they all trooped back to the salon. Florence couldn't stop quivering with renewed anticipation. The moment had finally come.

There were only three clients booked for the afternoon, the first one not due until a quarter past two. The doors would remain closed until Lillian said her piece.

'Pay attention, everybody, please,' Lillian exclaimed loudly as everyone shuffled back to the cubicles. She gave a cough and cleared her throat, seeming to hesitate before speaking again.

Darlene groaned loudly.

'Oh God! Not more blooming bad news, is it? Don't tell me! We won't get paid Friday.'

'Darlene, belt up!' Lillian snapped. 'If you'll shut your big mouth for a minute you might hear something to your advantage.'

That got everyone's attention.

Florence sidled closer to Lillian, feeling she was taking her rightful place. Her mouth was dry and her skin was hot and prickly with suppressed expectation. She'd be the heroine of the day. She'd saved them all.

She ignored Marge's sour glances.

'It's good news, as a matter of fact,' Lillian went on, but her manner was hesitant and Florence glanced sharply at her, wondering why she didn't get on with it.

'The salon won't be closing next week after all.'

'*What?*'

Everyone spoke at once, an excited babble, and everyone was looking at Lillian expectantly, hopefully.

She lifted a hand for silence.

'The fact is, I've found a partner,' she said. 'The investment isn't as much as I'd hoped, but it's enough to carry on trading.'

'Who is it?' someone asked.

Lillian's gaze swept around them all, but didn't look Florence's way, not even the merest glance, and Florence was momentarily flummoxed.

'I'm ... I'm not at liberty to say yet,' Lillian said.

Florence's jaw dropped open in astonishment and keen disappointment cut through her like a knife.

'They ... we ought to be told now,' she said, her voice trembling. 'They have a right. And so do I.'

Lillian looked at her then, her mouth in a hard line.

'Shut up, Flo! This is still *my* salon.'

Florence felt it like a slap in the face. She watched helplessly as the older woman turned and strode off into the office without another word.

The whole atmosphere of the salon had changed suddenly. Florence felt stunned at Lillian's denial, yet even she could feel the change.

Fury burst through her disappointment. How dare Lillian do that to her? It was outrageous.

It burst into her thoughts that Lillian might be trying to do something underhand. Florence had handed over the five hundred pounds earlier and watched Lillian lock it in the safe until she could go to the bank. Why had she refused to acknowledge Florence as her new partner? She had to find out now.

Glancing around at the others she saw no one was taking any notice of her, except Marge who was eyeing her with a tight little smile. The others were chattering excitedly, and Glenys was bouncing up and down on her toes, looking as if she might turn somersaults any minute.

Making the most of their preoccupation, Florence hurried after Lillian and striding into the office, closed the door firmly behind her.

The older woman was sitting behind the desk, the account books spread out before her, the inevitable cigarette held in her fingers.

'What do you think you're playing at, Lillian?' Florence exploded.

She found she was shaking from head to foot, and knew her feeling was one of dread that the older woman was trying to do her down. She'd not considered Lillian in any way dishonest before, but how well did she know her really? She hadn't even thought of asking for a receipt for her money.

'I'm not ready to tell them yet,' Lillian said in sulky defiance, the corners of her red mouth turned down belligerently.

It was a familiar expression, and Florence saw immediately that Lillian was now ready to meet her eye. It was a steady gaze, not at all sheepish or guilty, and with a burst of relief, her dread subsided.

She'd seen that look before when Lillian was

dealing with Tony. It might have worked with him once, but Florence was a different kettle of fish and Lillian would find that out, and soon.

'Why not, may I ask?' Florence rapped out, aware that she was on the verge of losing her temper completely.

That wouldn't help, not where Lillian was concerned. She had to try to control herself, she realised, though her new partner was making it extremely difficult for her.

Lillian jumped to her feet, her expression furious.

'Don't you question me, miss. Who do you think you are?'

'Your flaming partner!' Florence yelled at the top of her voice, losing control despite herself. 'That's who I am, and you'd better not forget it.'

She didn't care whether the others could hear her from the salon. Marge was probably telling them everything anyway.

But she didn't like this hole in the corner game Lillian was playing. She was straightforward herself, and expected others to be the same. Yet she was convinced now Lillian was not being underhand, but there was something she was hiding.

'You've taken my money!' Florence shouted again. 'I demand to know what's going on.'

Lillian looked taken aback at Florence's fury. Then, recovering, she said angrily:

'All right! Marge is right, isn't she? I *am* afraid of looking like a bloody fool, taking an apprentice for a partner! Laughing stock of the town, that's what I'll be when it gets out.'

'You should have thought of that before you took the money, then,' Florence spluttered in indignation. 'And you took it quick enough, didn't you?'

She ground her teeth in rage as it dawned on her what Lillian was really up to. She wanted Florence to be a silent partner only, to stay in the background. Well, that wasn't on!

'We're partners, Lillian, like it or not,' she said hotly. 'I've no intention of taking a back seat. I'll run this salon on equal footing or the deal's off.'

Florence stood up straight and held out the palm of her hand.

'If your pride can't cope with that, then I'll take my money back – now.'

Lillian sat down again.

'You know nothing about business,' she complained, her tone bitter. 'Or the hairdressing trade.'

She looked so deeply concerned that Florence's anger was suddenly cooled. She couldn't deny what Lillian said was true, and felt ashamed of her thoughtlessness. She was being arrogant, acting like a spoilt child, trying to run before she could walk; the very attitudes her parents deplored in her.

Humbled, Florence wanted to make amends.

'Well, that's why I'm here, isn't it,' she said, more gently. 'I'll learn all there is to know, and you'll teach me. I've got ideas and plans, Lillian. The salon will thrive, because I'll *make* it happen.'

Lillian looked scornful.

'Talk is cheap. You've got a hell of a lot to learn.'

Florence lifted her chin, taking in a deep breath.

'Yes, I know Lillian,' she said, firmly, 'but don't mistake youth for stupidity. I know what I want and how to get it.'

Lillian was silent, glaring at her, obviously furious again, but acknowledging that for the moment Florence had the upper hand.

She had been standing; now she drew the other chair towards her and placing it at the side of the desk, sat down. While she was determined to curb her headstrong attitude towards Lillian, she still needed to protect her rights.

'You must inform the rest of the staff right now.'

Lillian still hesitated, saying nothing.

'Well, if you don't, I will!' Florence exclaimed determinedly.

She half rose in her chair when the door was flung open and Darlene burst in. Marge edged up behind her, the others crowding round the open door.

'Lillian! It isn't true what Marge says, is it?' Darlene asked loudly, shaking her head vigorously and looking ready to explode. 'You haven't agreed to a partnership with that little jumped-up pip-squeak, Flo?'

'I had to!' Lillian's face reddened as though someone had accused her of a shameful act. 'I didn't have a choice.'

Florence didn't like Lillian's deep tone of regret, and despite her resolve to be reasonable, felt a new annoyance. She expected Lillian to stand by her from now on.

'You don't have to make excuses to *her*,' Florence exclaimed with energy. 'She's lucky she's got a job to come to next week.'

Darlene rounded on her, seething.

'Shut up, you conniving little bitch!' she stormed, so angry that spittle foamed at the corners of her mouth. 'I'm talking to the organ-grinder not the bloody monkey.'

She turned back to Lillian, leaning forward, both palms flat on the desk.

'I'm senior stylist here after Tony, and I want what's due to me, see. I'm not having *her* queening it over me in the salon.'

'That's not going to happen,' Florence assured her, stepping behind Lillian's chair to face Darlene. 'Nothing will change in the salon. I'll go on with my apprenticeship as normal. Everything will be as before, except that I'll have a say in management decisions.'

Darlene glared steadily at Lillian.

'Tell her to shut up, Lil, will you? I don't talk to any lackey.'

Florence was outraged.

'You'd better learn to talk to me, Darlene, if you want to keep your job,' she blurted angrily. 'We're getting a fashionable cutter down from London, so you won't be missed.'

'What?' Lillian almost jumped out of her chair, turning her head to stare up at Florence with consternation. 'What did you say?'

'We *have* to, Lillian!'

Florence came round the side of the desk then to face her partner. She felt a spurt of guilt that she'd sprung this on Lillian without discussing it

312

first. But it couldn't be helped. It was what she honestly believed to be essential for the future of the business.

'We need a young chap from London,' she went on, deliberately avoiding Darlene's furious stare. 'Somebody attractive and fashionable to draw in the women.'

'Here! I'm not bloody having this!' Darlene stormed.

Florence was very conscious that everyone, except Darlene, was staring at her with mouths open, as though stunned. Florence lifted her chin and stared back at them all, her mouth set firmly.

'We've got to replace Tony, don't you see?' she said with quiet determination, realising at the same time that she was probably hurting Lillian's feelings about him.

'Are you daft, or what?' Lillian cried out.

'She's more than daft,' Darlene yelled furiously. 'She's dangerous!'

Florence was relieved that Lillian didn't sound hurt, just angry again.

'We're on the brink of bankruptcy,' Lillian rushed on. 'And you want to take on more staff, and from London at that. Have you any idea what that'll cost us?'

'Lillian, don't be so short-sighted,' Florence exclaimed with irritation. 'We've got to be realistic. Terri's was once considered among the best in town. Right now we're only second-rate.'

Darlene started to splutter incoherently.

'Yes, second-rate is what I said, Darlene!' Florence went on again. 'We need class, and a

313

fashionable cutter from London will build that for us.'

'She may be right, Lil,' Marge said, quietly pensive, taking Florence completely by surprise.

'*What?*' Darlene stared aghast from Marge to Lillian, her mouth open as Marge's words sank in. 'You're all going barmy listening to this little jumped-up...'

'Shut up, Darlene.' Lillian said almost absent-mindedly, as she stared at the suddenness of Marge's turnabout, yet Florence could have kissed Marge for it.

'We lost business when we lost Tony,' Marge rushed on hastily as though afraid Lillian might think she was being a traitor. 'Damn him to hell and back!' She paused, looking pleadingly at Lillian. 'You know your way around the salons up the Smoke. Go up there, Lil. Find us somebody special. You can do it if anybody can.'

'This is madness!' Lillian shook her head in bewilderment, looking askance at her old friend.

'I'm willing to stay on apprenticeship wages to help towards the cost,' Florence said eagerly. 'We've got to make sacrifices, Lillian, for the sake of the salon.'

'You dirty turncoat, Marge!' Darlene exclaimed angrily. 'I can't believe you're siding with this toffee-nosed bit of flotsam, by here. After all Lil's done for you.'

'Leave Marge alone,' Florence flared. 'I'm getting fed up to the back teeth with your attitude, Darlene. For two pins I'd give you your cards right now.'

'Shut your mouth!' Darlene yelled back.

Florence was affronted.

'She can't talk to me like that,' she insisted. 'It's uncalled for. After all I am a partner...'

'Keep quiet, Flo, will you?' Lillian raised her voice. 'If you say that one more time I'll scream.'

Florence stared dumbfounded. It wasn't supposed to be like this. She'd made a mess of it. Was her mother right in her assessment of her capabilities? Doubts crowded her mind. Had she made a mistake? Perhaps a partnership at Terri's was beyond her? She'd failed her dream, and it was disintegrating before her eyes. And all because she'd been rash and self-conceited.

Florence hid her dismay and disappointment as best she could.

'Perhaps we'd better call it a day, Lillian,' she said evenly, trying to disguise the tremor in her voice. She wouldn't show weakness or doubt in front of Darlene. 'Maybe we'd better forget about a partnership. Pack it in before any legal papers are signed. I'll have my money back.'

'Huh!' Darlene's lip curled in scorn. 'That's the most sensible thing you've ever said. Go on, Lil. Tell her we don't need her. Tell her to get lost.'

'You button your lip as well, Darlene,' Lillian barked, her eyes blazing. 'I'm not letting this salon go. The partnership stands, see. Flo has given us a reprieve. This salon opens next week as usual, and we're going on from there.'

Florence's spirits were uplifted at Lillian's words and positive tone. Someone *did* believe in her after all. There was still hope.

Darlene's mouth tightened.

'Let's get one thing straight, Lillian,' she said

315

belligerently. 'I'm not taking orders from *her.*'

'Then you can get out now.' Lillian glared at her. 'The other girls support me in this.'

She turned her gaze to Nancy and Glenys at the door, but they stared back stonily.

'Don't be too sure!' Darlene retorted, her eyes sparking spite and malice.

'What do you mean?'

Darlene flashed a nasty little smile around at them.

'We're coming out on strike, as from now!' She glanced back at the others in the doorway. 'Right, girls?'

'What are you talking about? You can't do that!'

'If the miners can do it, so can we.' She looked triumphant. 'Me and the girls won't have this...' She wagged a forefinger in Florence's direction. 'This scheming little bitch bossing us about. We'll be out on strike for as long as it takes.'

She took up a stance, arms folded across her chest.

'So, Lillian. It's either her or us. Take your pick.'

CHAPTER 22

To Florence's intense relief, Darlene's frantic efforts to whip up animosity amongst the other girls and draw them out on strike that afternoon, failed, and failed miserably. Her years of bullying hadn't helped at all.

Nobody liked her or even had sympathy for her, Florence saw, as she listened to the older girl storm and rage in the salon to no avail.

For once it was Darlene who was humiliated, but Florence couldn't feel sorry for her. Darlene's hasty threat had always been an idle one, Florence realised. There was no union support, and none of them could afford to take even a few days off without pay.

Florence's change of role bewildered the other girls at first. She couldn't expect anything less. But when they were assured that nothing would really alter, they settled down to business as usual, and she and Lillian breathed freely again.

Darlene was sullen, but obviously not beaten. There were dark looks, grumblings and a great deal of gossiping from her. Florence decided she had to live with that for the moment, and tried to make the best of things, though there were times when Darlene's undisguised antagonism got up her nose, and she had to hold herself in check from making a fuss.

She waited eagerly for the day when they all

317

welcomed the stylist from London. Darlene would have to watch herself then.

It was more than clear that she was Florence's enemy now. She was a good stylist and a good worker, but her hostility and short temper were bad for general morale, and Florence didn't need Darlene constantly undermining her authority. She had no intention of throwing her weight about. That had got her nowhere previously. At the same time she wanted the other girls to remember that, apprentice or not, she was their boss.

Darlene's days at Terri's were numbered, if Florence had anything to do with it.

Within a fortnight all papers had been signed and sealed, and Florence was officially a partner in Terri's High-class Hairdressers.

It was wonderful!

A day didn't go by when she didn't congratulate herself on her good fortune, and at the same time, feel gratitude to Cliff for his generosity and faith in her.

She had to confess to him that she'd foregone her partner's salary, remaining on apprenticeship wages to help finance the new cutter from London. Cliff approved her move, and insisted he did not expect a return on his money for some time, not until the business was showing a substantial profit.

There was only one fly in the ointment. Lillian was dragging her heels with regard to visiting London to look for a new cutter. She gave Florence one excuse after another as to why she wasn't able to go just yet.

Florence was beginning to lose patience. Business at the salon had picked up a little, but they were never as busy as in Tony's day. She could hardly wait for the tide of business to turn in their favour again. A new and fashionable face was the only way to do it.

Florence was determined that Lillian would keep her word, and she wished that she could openly convey Cliff's support for the scheme, but dared not mention his name.

One morning in September, just after Florence's nineteenth birthday, she looked up from shampooing a client's head, as another client walked into the salon, and her heart took an awful jolt.

Auntie Sybil!

Goose-pimples of fright rose on Florence's upper arms and she began to quake, as her aunt stood looking around the salon with open curiosity.

Auntie Sybil hadn't had her hair done at Terri's for months, not since the Town Clerk's wife had stopped patronising them. So, why had she suddenly turned up? She'd heard something, and was nosing about, as usual.

Florence had a sudden and dreadful foreboding that her aunt's visit meant big trouble for her. No one at home knew anything of her new status at Terri's. She hated having secrets from her parents and deceiving them, but knew they would never approve, not after their decision that the investment was a bad one.

Florence knew they were looking at it from the wrong angle. They didn't have her faith and trust, her belief that Terri's could be great again. Only Cliff shared that with her. Her parents wouldn't approve of him, either.

Now Auntie Sybil was here and Florence felt instinctively that the apple cart was about to be upset good and proper.

She drew the cubicle curtains a little closer together in an effort to hide herself. She felt cowardly doing that, but nothing could induce her to face her aunt at this moment, not with the staff and other clients looking on. Her aunt's tongue was caustic. She'd make a fool of Florence in no time.

Through a gap in the curtains she watched Glenys greet Auntie Sybil.

'Is Mrs Longford here?' her aunt demanded to know.

'She's at the wholesalers, madam,' Glenys replied.

'Very well. Darlene will do my hair, then,' Auntie Sybil's ringing tones filled the salon.

In response, Glenys escorted her to the cubicle right next door to where Florence was hiding. She felt all her muscles stiffen, and for a moment was afraid to take a breath, until she glimpsed the face of her own client through the mirror, regarding her statue-like pose with obvious irritation.

'I need a dry towel, miss. This one is soaking. I'll catch my death in a minute!' the woman pointed out peevishly. 'Will Nancy be long?'

Florence replied in an undertone, afraid Auntie

Sybil would hear her voice and call her to her side.

Thankfully Nancy came at that moment. Florence thought it might be a good time to sneak off, perhaps hide in the office until her aunt had gone. She didn't normally take advantage of her position, but today was an emergency.

'Go and fetch my roller trolley, please,' Nancy asked her, forestalling her escape.

Florence couldn't refuse. She'd told the staff to treat her as they would any other trainee. She couldn't keep changing the rules to suit herself. They'd stop trusting her, and she needed that trust.

'Go on, then,' Nancy said mildly. 'And I'll need some help by here, as well.' She smiled serenely into the mirror. 'Sorry to keep you waiting, Mrs Gibbins? Setting lotion?'

Florence did as she was told and was sorting rollers for Nancy when she heard Darlene enter the next cubicle and speak to her aunt.

'Oh, there's nice to see you here again, Mrs Bevan,' Darlene began in oily tones. 'We've missed you, mind. Shampoo and set, is it? Or would you like a nice permanent wave?'

'Just a set,' Sybil replied, then asked archly: 'Is my niece about?'

Listening on the other side of the curtain, Florence's blood ran cold, and she froze, holding her breath, waiting. She almost dropped the roller she was handing to Nancy, who frowned at her.

'Niece?' Darlene repeated.

321

'Florence Philpots.'

'Oh, her!' Darlene burst out, a sting in her voice. 'Jumped-up little... Oh! Sorry! She's your niece. Shouldn't say anything, should I?'

'Go on! Go on!' Sybil urged eagerly.

'Well!' Darlene obviously needed no further prompting. 'She's just bought herself a partnership in Terri's. An apprentice, mind you, that's all she is. A blooming trainee!'

'Preposterous!' Sybil sounded excited, as though she'd struck gold.

'Throwing her weight about, too,' Darlene went on spitefully, a distinct whine in her voice. 'Got no flair, she hasn't. Hasn't got a clue. Had to *buy* herself into the business, didn't she? Never do it any other way.'

Florence's lips compressed in indignation. Darlene made no attempt to modulate her voice. She didn't care who heard her. In fact it was obvious she wanted Florence to hear, and be embarrassed, and she was succeeding, too.

'Thinks she knows it all,' Darlene went on relentlessly. 'But she's pig-ignorant where hair-dressing is concerned. Pig-ignorant!'

Florence felt hot blood rise in her neck to flood her cheeks. Suddenly, the heat in the salon was overwhelming. She had the urge to rush out onto the street into the cool air, but held her ground. Darlene would really enjoy that!

Florence met Nancy's startled eyes over the top of Mrs Gibbins's head. She nodded towards the next cubicle, obviously urging her to intervene, but Florence shook her head, turning her gaze away in all self-conscious distress, still fighting the urge to retreat.

They say eavesdroppers never hear anything good about themselves, but she was prepared to take the risk. She already knew the extent of Darlene's disloyalty, yet wanted to learn how far she was prepared to go in her vendetta, and how much her aunt knew.

'I'd heard rumours,' Sybil said, her tone encouraging further confidences. 'Where did she get the money I'd like to know.'

'Her father, apparently,' Darlene said. The envy in her voice was unmistakable.

'Well, I've never heard the like! My brother wants his head seen to,' Sybil remarked vehemently. 'Throwing money away on the whim of a girl like that. It's that scheming mother of hers behind this. Grasping woman! Always has been.'

Florence felt a surge of guilt. She ought to rush in there and defend her mother against such slander, but she quaked at facing her aunt. It would only make things worse. A vulgar scene was the last thing the salon needed just now.

'Spoilt, Florence is, spoilt,' Sybil went on spitefully. 'And it won't do her any good in the end. She hasn't got the brains for business.'

Finally, it was too much for Florence. She couldn't even meet Nancy's gaze, but ducked out through the curtains as silently and as quickly as she could, making for the sanctuary of the kitchen, feeling all eyes on her as she went.

Darlene had gone too far this time! Betrayed her to her most powerful enemy, Auntie Sybil. Her aunt was always on the lookout to make trouble in the Philpots' household, and she could cause family strife so easily with what she'd learned from Darlene. The only comfort Florence had was that Auntie Sybil had no idea of the real explosive nature of her information.

Florence was deceiving her parents. It gave her pain to think about it. The pain was even more intense, she had to admit, at the thought that they would find out from her aunt. That would be utterly damning in their eyes.

Florence went into the outside lavatory to think without being disturbed. She couldn't face the other girls yet, anyway, and she also had to decide what she would do about Darlene. She was a rotten apple! A troublemaker, her undisputed skills not worth the persecution of her spite and enmity.

But first, there were her parents to think of. Auntie Sybil could spill the beans at any time with just one word.

Florence had been trying to work herself up to confessing to her parents, but the moment never seemed right. Now Darlene had forced her hand. She would have to tell them this very evening. There would be trouble, perhaps big trouble for her, but not the bitter strife that her aunt could cause. Why had she let herself be pushed into this position once again? But it was by her own cowardice, she told herself sternly. She could blame no one else.

When she felt sufficiently calmed and was sure Auntie Sybil was gone from the salon, Florence emerged, still feeling embarrassed, dreading having to face the others, especially Darlene.

Lillian had returned from the wholesalers, and

Florence sought her out in the office.

'That Darlene has to go!' she said as soon as she saw Lillian at the desk, poring over invoices.

'What now?' Lillian sounded as irritable as Florence felt.

'She's been slandering me and my family in front of the clients,' she said tensely. 'And I won't have it, Lillian. She's not doing the image of this salon any good. She's poisonous!'

Lillian looked up with a sigh.

'Tsk! You're overreacting, Flo.'

Florence was furious. Now it *was* time to assert herself, she decided. Darlene's behaviour was unforgivable.

'I'm not! How would *you* like it if she was tearing your reputation to shreds?' she asked heatedly, jutting out her chin in determination. 'I'm telling you she's got to go!'

'I'm still senior partner around here, Flo,' Lillian said evenly. 'If you can't handle Darlene then maybe you don't belong here after all.'

'Don't take that line with me,' Florence snapped, outraged again. 'I'm not a child. Darlene goes as soon as we get that new cutter from London. You'd better see about it straight away, Lillian, because I'm not giving in till you do.'

It was after supper when Florence ventured into the back sitting-room. She rarely went in there these days, finding small talk difficult with her parents. No matter what she talked about she was always conscious of her mother's disapproval.

Edie was sitting in front of the fireplace where, despite a shortage of fuel, a small spluttering log fed the first fire of the autumn.

Her mother was knitting a pullover for Tommy, her strong face composed.

Her father looked up from reading the *Evening Post*.

'Sit down by here, Flo, *bach*. Put your feet on the fender for a warm,' he said gently.

Florence glanced at her mother, wondering if the warm welcome came from her, too, but Edie's gaze was on her knitting.

Disappointed, Florence sat on the edge of the sofa, next to her father. He folded the newspaper and put it to one side. His brown eyes were smiling behind his spectacles, as warm as ever.

'How are things going at the shop, Flo, love?'

Florence glanced at him, pleased at his genuine interest and the opening he'd given her.

'Salon, Dad. It's a salon.'

She loved him, loved him dearly, and if ever she was in real trouble he'd be there for her, she knew that without a doubt. But would he stand by her now, when he heard what she'd done?

'Things are going very well, Dad, thanks.'

He frowned, puzzled. 'Thought the salon was due to close? Has anything happened?'

'Lillian has found a partner,' Florence blurted.

'Oh!' Her father looked genuinely surprised. 'Well, that's good. Who is he?'

Florence took a deep breath, gathering up her courage to speak out the truth. This was it! The moment she'd been dreading for weeks. But it couldn't be postponed any longer. She prayed her parents wouldn't be too angry.

Glancing at Edie, Florence saw that the speed of the knitting needles had slowed, and knew her mother was listening carefully for her answer. Florence ran her tongue nervously over her lips before continuing.

'It's not a he. Actually ... well ... it's me.'

'What?'

Florence felt her throat go dry, unable to find enough moisture to even swallow. Edie was motionless, staring at her open-mouthed, a stitch half-formed on the needles.

William sat forward, half turning towards her, staring at her incredulously.

'What did you say, Flo?'

'I'm Lillian's new partner,' Florence muttered, her teeth chattering all of a sudden.

Edie suddenly came alive, her knitting dropping into her lap.

'But how can you be?' she demanded, her features animated. 'Eight hundred pounds! I mean, where could *you* get money like that?'

'Lillian settled for five hundred,' Florence went on hurriedly. 'I borrowed it.'

'Borrowed!' Edie looked astounded.

'But, Flo, love,' her father said, and she could hear the deep perplexity in his voice. 'What bank or building society would lend you money? You've got no property or security, and you're under age. I mean, five hundred pounds would buy a nice little house. It's a lot of money.'

Florence shifted uncomfortably on the sofa.

'It was a private loan,' she said. 'From a friend.'

Her parents exchanged a special glance,

327

reading each other's minds. It was always like that between them; private, meaningful looks that excluded everyone else.

'Who is this very generous friend?' Edie asked evenly. 'Is it Rita?'

Florence was annoyed at the idea.

'Rita! Why mention her, Mam?'

She wouldn't take a sip of water from her cousin, even if she were dying of thirst in the Sahara desert.

'Well.' Edie gave a shrug. 'She's married into the Hendersons, now. Plenty of money there, like. I thought you two had made up...'

'Never!' Florence exclaimed. 'I said a friend, Mam. I meant a real friend, not a two-timing little ... witch, like Rita.'

'Well, who then?' her father asked, frowning.

'Cliff Longford,' Florence said, a hint of defiance in her tone.

Edie looked puzzled. 'Who?'

'Cliff. Tony's brother. I told you about him, Mam, remember?'

Edie's puzzlement remained for a moment, then her eyes were round as she looked at Florence.

'Not that ex-convict chap?' she cried out. 'Someone said he actually *killed* a man. Florence! How could you associate with such a person, let alone take money from him?'

Florence was angry at the prejudice in Edie's voice. The only excuse she could make for her mother was that she didn't know Cliff; didn't know the kind of man he really was.

'He's a real friend to me, Cliff is,' Florence

exclaimed. 'He's the only person who takes the trouble to understand me.'

Florence glanced from her father to Edie, wondering if her parents fully appreciated her last remark. It was a shame she had to go outside the family for any sympathy.

'Cliff knows how much I want to be a hairdresser,' she went on determinedly. 'He knows how much I dream of success. He loaned me the money willingly.'

She intercepted another glance between her parents, and had no difficulty in reading their thoughts.

'And no strings attached either, if that's what you're thinking, Mam.'

'Flo!' Her father sounded upset, and disappointed, too. 'You've done a very foolish thing.'

'Dad, listen!'

'Be quiet, Flo!' His tone was sharp for once, and she was taken aback at the reproach in his voice. 'You've got yourself into the debt of a man we know nothing about. And I don't care what you say, Flo, his background is very shady.'

'It's not, Dad!' Florence cried out passionately. 'You're condemning him and you don't even know him.'

'I've lived longer than you, miss,' William said brusquely. 'And I know men. You've taken on a debt you've little hope of repaying, and also a commitment that's beyond you. Damn it, Flo!' He sounded really cross. 'You're barely nineteen.'

'I know what I'm doing, Dad!' Florence burst out, agitated at his tone, which wasn't like him at all. 'I'm *not* a child.'

His undisguised anger with her made her smart. She just wasn't used to it, and expected any berating to come from Edie not her father. She counted on him.

Strangely disturbed by Edie's sudden silence, Florence glanced across at her mother, her thoughts returning to the acrimonious row they'd had back in the summer. Her mother had said such hurtful things to her then. She'd expected something similar now.

Edie's silence was unnerving. Florence would prefer her mother to go for her, hammer and tongs, then she could answer back; give as good as she got. Had Edie given up on her altogether? Florence's heart felt sore at the thought.

'Mam, you're not saying a word.'

'What's the point?' Edie picked up her knitting, the needles flying furiously in her fingers. 'You take no notice. You'll do whatever you want, I see that now. I'm sick to death of worrying about you.'

'You've no need to worry, Mam.'

Edie paused in her knitting to stare at Florence, her lips tight.

'Oh, of course not! My youngest daughter is only consorting with a criminal...'

'He's not!'

'A *criminal*,' Edie repeated, emphasising the word. 'It's obvious the Longford brothers are no good, either of them. You accept money from Cliff Longford, a small fortune at that; taking on business responsibilities, when you haven't...'

'Got the brains for it?' Florence cried, stung to the core of her being by Edie's disparaging tone.

330

'That's what you were going to say, wasn't it? Well, that's one thing you and Auntie Sybil can agree on.'

'What do you mean?'

'Oh, never mind!' Florence exclaimed. 'I'm fed up with being second best in this family...'

'Don't start that childish nonsense again,' Edie snapped. 'You make that an excuse for all kinds of stupid behaviour. And *I'm* fed up with *that.*'

William sat forward on the sofa, elbows on knees, one hand clasping his jaw thoughtfully.

'We'll have to find some way to buy you out of this debt, Flo,' he said. 'I can't manage the whole five hundred.' He glanced across at Edie. 'Perhaps your mother can help out with, say, half?'

'But, Dad...!'

'I'm sorry, Will,' Edie interrupted swiftly. 'I've just bought that cottage up the top of Newton. A sensible investment! I've got no spare capital now, especially not for bailing wayward children out of scrapes.'

She threw a challenging glance at Florence.

'You've made your bed, Florence, now you can lie in it. Your father and I have done all we can. This latest featherbrained scheme is the last straw.'

Seething, Florence jumped to her feet.

'I'm not asking for help from either of you,' she stormed. 'I don't want it, or need it. It's a bit too late for that, anyway.'

Turning on her heel she marched to the door, then glared back at them.

'I'll show you both what brains I've got. I'll

331

make Terri's High-class Hairdressing *the* most fashionable salon in town. A year from now I'll be riding high. I'll show everybody what I'm made of. You just wait and see!'

CHAPTER 23

December 1949

Florence rose to her feet as the organist began to play the last hymn. For once she was glad to see the Sunday morning service end. It was colder inside the church than outside. She longed for a cup of tea and to warm her feet on the fender.

She paused in her singing, her gaze leaving the page of the hymn book to slant sideways at her sister standing beside her, and in particular at Amy's new coat.

In cherry-red wool, it was double-breasted, with a nipped-in waist, peplum and full skirt. Apart from being the height of fashion, it looked warm and snug, too. And Florence was envious.

She hadn't been able to afford a new coat, not for ages. Clothing coupons might be a thing of the past, but price rises were still with them. There wasn't much she *could* afford on apprentice's wages.

For a moment she regretted her rash offer to Lillian to forego a partnership salary to finance the new cutter. Lillian had still not done anything about that matter, and Florence was beginning to feel she'd made a foolish bargain.

Amy's coat was, of course, a family buy. Being at university she wasn't able to keep herself, which Florence appreciated. She didn't begrudge her sister, yet she felt hard done by. Florence's one coat had seen better days, yet her mother hadn't offered to fit her out with a new one. One of the penalties of being independent.

Amy turned her head to catch her eye, and smiled. Florence smiled back. Amy was home for Christmas, and Florence was glad to see her. They'd been close at one time. But now her sister was like a friend with whom she'd lost touch. They had little in common anymore.

Florence had to admit she was a bit piqued at the fuss her mother was making at Amy's homecoming, as if she'd been away years in some distant land, instead of just a few months. She tried to tell herself it wasn't jealousy. It just struck her as being unfair.

The hymn was over and they sat down. Out of the corner of her eye Florence saw Edie lean forward to look along the pew at Amy, her features soft with affection.

Florence bent her head to the last prayer. *She* never got such looks these days. What had she done that was so terrible for her mother to pass her over? All she was guilty of was trying to make something of herself; to be her own person and to do things her way. Was that so awful?

Finally the service was over and the congregation began to leave the pews and straggle out of the church door. Florence followed behind her family, having to pause now and then as old friends and acquaintances greeted Amy, asking how she was, how she was getting on, complimenting her on her healthy looks. And Edie fussing every other moment.

They left the church, and began the walk home.

Her mother and father strolled arm in arm, as usual. Tommy ran on ahead to meet some pals.

Amy fell into step beside her. Florence noted her sister did look extremely well. Glowing, in fact. To complement the new coat, a small black fur pillbox hat with a narrow veil perched on the side of her head. It was classy and fashionable, and did give her an air of sophistication.

'I've been hearing things about you,' Amy said.

'What things?'

'Mam says you've got yourself into a bit of a mess.'

'No such thing!' Florence was furious. 'I've bought myself a partnership in a thriving business, well ... it will be thriving before much longer.'

'It was a daft thing to do, though, wasn't it?' Amy persisted.

'Daft? Buying a future for myself?' Florence flung a punishing look at her sister, who seemed unaffected by it. 'You're taking care of your future at university. I'm doing the same.'

'Borrowing a large sum of money *is* daft, Flo,' Amy insisted. 'It's a millstone around your neck. What rate of interest are you paying?'

Florence felt confused for a moment.

'I'm not paying interest. It's not that kind of a loan.'

Amy came to a stop, standing looking at Florence, her head tilted to one side, quizzically.

'No interest? Do you mean to say this bloke, who's been in prison, has loaned you five hundred pounds, and asks no return on his money?' She shook her head, her eyes glinting.

'He's after something, Flo, my girl, and it ain't hay! He's after your body.'

'Amy!' Florence was appalled. 'That's a disgusting thing to say!' She stared at her sister, shocked at the suggestion. 'You've got it all wrong. Mam's been feeding you a lot of bunkum about Cliff. He's not like that.'

Amy sniffed knowledgeably.

'All men are like that.'

'Well, Cliff isn't,' Florence retorted angrily. 'And I'll thank you to mind your own business, too.'

'I'm giving you a bit of advice as an older sister, that's all.'

'I don't want your advice, Amy. I can manage my life myself.'

Florence strode off. She heard Amy's high heels on the pavement behind her, running to catch up.

'And another thing,' Florence went on as her sister fell in step again. 'Mam shouldn't be discussing my affairs with you. I've a right to some privacy, but I'm treated like a child at home, and I'm fed up with it.'

Amy stuck her nose in the air.

'Don't behave like a child, then,' she returned haughtily. 'You're making a pig's ear out of everything, Flo. You gave up a good job, and lost Ken Henderson in the process.'

She gave a disdainful glance at Florence's hat and coat.

'You're obviously living from hand to mouth by the look of you, and now you're in debt up to your neck. All in the space of a year. Good going,

I don't think!'

Mam-gu and Gramps came for Sunday lunch. Florence's grandparents were obviously pleased to see Amy, too. As the afternoon wore on, Florence felt less and less a part of the family circle, uncomfortably conscious that it would go on being warm and loving even if she weren't here.

Then Gramps winked at her, calling her over to his side.

'How are things going with you, Flo? I hear you're a businesswoman now. I always knew you had it in you.'

'Oh, Gramps!'

She hugged him and planted a kiss on his cheek, remembering fondly her childhood and the many times he'd carried her on his shoulders around the park to see the monkeys.

'I wish Mam felt the same, Gramps.'

Gramps glanced across the room at Edie.

'Give her time, Flo. Try to be patient.'

Gramps was right. She was pushing too hard, the wrong tactic with her mother. Edie accused her of stubbornness, yet, if it were true, it was something Florence had inherited.

She was being too sensitive, she told herself firmly. Her independence at such an early age must be difficult for them to accept. She must try to see it from Mam and Dad's point of view, then perhaps, they could reach an understanding.

But her new resolve to be less touchy and sensitive was difficult to maintain.

In the evening, after her grandparents had gone

home, the family gathered in the cosy back sitting-room. To Florence's disgust, Amy's studying at Oxford seemed to be the sole topic of conversation; what area of medicine did she intend to specialise in when she'd got her degree? In which London hospital would she do her training?

Florence, watching and listening, noted Edie's attitude to Amy was one of an equal. Her sister wasn't talked down to, and with a pang, Florence realised her parents had deep respect for her sister and her opinions.

To Florence, this was a blatant example of their partiality. How could her mother go on denying it?

It was when her father and Amy got into a deep discussion about the prospect and implications of the Government implementing Emergency Powers, calling in troops to operate the electricity stations in London in the face of the present strike by power workers, that Florence lost the last vestige of patience, and abandoned her resolve.

Seething, she watched father and daughter, equals it seemed, deeply intent on their arguments for and against.

Amy was poised and confident, her father seemed to hang on her every word, agreeing, discussing, taking his eldest daughter's opinions very seriously.

Florence was aggrieved. One might believe she had no place here anymore, she thought resentfully, that they were deliberately blocking her out.

She, too, had an opinion about the power strikes, as she'd had about the dock strike earlier in the year, but her father never discussed such things with her. Obviously, he thought these matters were above her head.

Well, she wouldn't say where she wasn't appreciated!

The new idea jolted her. Was she really thinking about leaving home? Could she afford to, and where would she go? She'd have to find rooms somewhere.

She felt a quivering in the pit of her stomach at the idea. Excitement mixed with apprehension. Living on her own would be total independence. Living alone? Could she bear it?

Florence looked around the sitting-room at her family. Never had she felt more lonely than she did at this minute.

There was a lull in the general buzz of conversation, when Edie, getting to her feet, announced:

'I'll get us a bit of supper.'

On impulse, Florence jumped to her feet, too. Now was the opportunity to drop her bombshell. She hoped it was a bombshell!

'Mam! Dad! I've got something to say.' She paused, taking a deep breath. 'I'm leaving home.'

Her announcement didn't have the devastating effect she'd hoped for. Edie looked merely impatient and William bemused. Amy had a disbelieving smirk twisting her lips.

'It's true!' Florence cried, almost stamping her foot. 'I'm renting...' She was at a loss for a moment, then the idea flashed into her mind.

'I'm renting the flat above the salon.'

She was astounded at her own invention. She had no idea where the idea came from.

There *was* an empty flat above the salon. It hadn't been occupied for years, not since the time of the Blitz. She didn't even know if it was habitable, let alone whether Lillian would be willing to rent it to her. But now she'd burned her boats, hadn't she?

'Rent a flat?' asked Edie, incredulous now. 'What with?'

'You're forgetting I'm a partner now, Mam,' Florence said defiantly, lifting her chin. 'And I'm in the way here, aren't I?'

'Flo!' Her father stood up, his expression pained. 'Don't say that. It's not true. Your mother and I don't want you to go.'

Florence flashed a glance at her mother. Edie was looking impatient again.

'Of course you can't go. It's absurd,' she said firmly. 'Your place is here, my girl. How would you manage on your own, anyway? It's as much as you can do to boil an egg.'

Florence was indignant. That was it! The last straw. She'd leave now if it killed her.

'It's all fixed up with Lillian,' Florence lied, swallowing down her guilt. 'I'll be going before Christmas.'

'What?' Now her mother was shocked and looked distraught. 'Not before Christmas, Florence! Mam-gu and Gramps will be here. Everybody! I want all my family around me, like always.'

'You won't miss *me*,' Florence said with a pout.

'Of course I'll miss you,' Edie cried, agitated, clasping her hands in front of her as though saying a prayer. 'You're my youngest daughter. I love you. I worry about you every minute.'

For a moment Florence was mollified and encouraged. Of course her parents would miss her about the house. She'd never been parted from them before. It wasn't their love and concern she doubted. It was their faith and esteem she lacked and longed for. She didn't have them, and Christmas at home wouldn't change that.

And, she thought contrarily, perhaps missing her, worrying about her would bring it home to them.

'I can't change my plans now,' she said stubbornly. 'It's all fixed.'

'William! Do something!' Edie pleaded. 'Don't let her go. She can't go before Christmas. It's a time for families to be together.'

Her father came to her side, putting an arm around her shoulders, hugging her to him.

'Flo, love. Don't do this to your mother, mun. We don't want you to leave home at all. Please stay here, where you belong.'

He looked so solemn, so upset, that Florence felt she might burst into tears herself. The last thing she wanted was to hurt him or Mam. She loved them both, despite everything.

But she had no choice. She couldn't, wouldn't remain here, second best to Amy. Because, no matter what her mother might think and say now, nothing would change if she remained. She had to go.

She put a hand on her father's chest, and reaching up, kissed his cheek. Then stretched out a hand to her mother, who came forward quickly and grasped it.

'Florence, lovey, listen…'

'I'll miss you, Mam, too,' Florence interrupted quickly. 'And you, Dad. I'll miss everyone. It's something I have to do. It's for the best.'

Edie was visibly shaken. Her hand was trembling as it grasped Florence's tightly. Her father looked forlorn. His tone was edged with pain and regret.

'We don't understand, my girl…'

'Exactly, Dad!'

'Florence!' Edie exclaimed, distressed. 'Don't speak to your father like that. After all he's done for you, too.'

Florence felt deeply ashamed then. She was trying to be clever at her father's expense, and that wasn't fair. She did owe Mam and Dad so much; she couldn't deny it. But she didn't fit in anymore, and she was saddened at the thought.

'I'm sorry. I didn't mean to be insolent. Dad knows that.'

She was profoundly sorry, but in her present frame of mind it was better that she left.

She lifted her chin, her self-assurance reasserting itself.

'But don't you see?' She went on regretfully. 'I'm not happy at home anymore.'

Her father gave a little groan of distress, while Edie stared at her in open-mouthed concern. Amy rose to her feet, coming forward looking astonished.

It was ironic, Florence thought bitterly as she glanced at each face in turn. Now she was on the point of moving out she'd got their attention. But it was too late. Her mind was made up. Perhaps renting Lillian's flat wouldn't be possible, but she'd find somewhere to go, Florence decided resolutely.

The New Year, a new decade, was almost upon them. She'd begin it in complete independence.

Lillian's face was a picture.

'Upstairs? You want to live upstairs?'

'Why not?' Florence went on doggedly. 'It's ideal.'

Lillian laughed.

'I don't know about ideal. No one's lived there for years, not since forty-one. It'll need cleaning, redecorating.' She looked dubious. 'I don't want to spend money right now.'

'You won't have to. I'll do it myself,' Florence volunteered eagerly.

She'd never painted or wallpapered a room before, but she'd watched her father many times. It would be fun!

'Please, Lillian,' she pleaded. 'I'll pay rent, of course, like any other tenant. Why waste the flat, when it could be used? Please!'

Lillian looked bemused.

'Well, all right, then.' She leaned over and opened the top drawer of the desk, rummaging about inside. 'I suppose you want to look at it now?'

Florence nodded eagerly, swallowing hard in relief.

'I'd like to move in before Christmas.'

Lillian looked up, startled.

'Before Christmas?' Her eyes narrowed. 'Flo, what's going on?'

'Nothing.'

Florence tried to look composed, though she was suddenly fearful. How could she explain her parents' anger with her over the partnership when they were the ones who'd supposedly loaned her the money? She'd have to tread warily, be very careful what she said to Lillian.

'I'm nineteen,' she went on, feeling obliged to offer a reason after all. 'I want a life of my own.'

Lillian sniffed, and brought a small bunch of keys out of the drawer.

'Young people today,' she said. 'Too much freedom.'

Lillian led Florence through a door leading off the reception area. Behind it was a flight of dusty stairs without covering. There was little light.

'Mind how you go,' Lillian said. 'The electric's on, but the bulb's gone.'

The stairs gave onto a narrow landing with a small window, which was thoroughly grimy.

'Don't expect Buckingham Palace,' Lillian commented unnecessarily, as she unlocked the door. 'My father lived here until he died. After that I rented it out until the Blitz.'

She let them into a small square lobby. The only other door led to a front room, where faded flower-patterned linoleum covered the floor.

'This is the living-room,' Lillian explained, waving a hand around a long, and to Florence,

344

vast room. 'Besides this there's a bedroom, a small box-room and a kitchen.'

The living-room was empty of furniture except for an old-fashioned sideboard against one wall and an ancient gate-legged table against another, next to a fireplace. At the far end, a wide, uncurtained window overlooked the High Street.

'It's a big room, isn't it?' Florence said in awe, trying to keep disappointment out of her voice.

It was chilly, too. Even in her coat, she shivered in the cold. This room would be the very devil to keep warm, but she wouldn't let that put her off, she told herself sternly. There were ways and means, and she'd find them.

'It's a bit of a barn,' Lillian agreed. 'Perhaps you've changed your mind. You don't want to see the rest of the place?'

'Oh, yes, I do,' declared Florence quickly. There was no going back now.

The place was dusty and neglected, but she couldn't smell dampness, and was immensely relieved. Dust and dirt could soon be despatched with a bit of determination and a dab of elbow grease.

The other door in the living-room led into a dark passage. Lillian flipped a switch and a yellowed light showed other doors.

'That's the bedroom,' Lillian volunteered, pointing.

Florence popped her head around the bedroom door. It was a decent size, but not too big. She'd be comfortable there. There was even a small grate.

'That's the box room,' Lillian told her, pointing

345

again. 'Might be a few bits and pieces of furniture there you can use.'

She opened the last door.

'This is the kitchen.'

Linoleum again, very well worn, but it would clean up, and Florence itched to begin.

'The bath's here, look,' Lillian said, pointing to the far end of the kitchen. 'Under that wooden board. The geyser is still working, I think.'

Florence gazed around.

'Where's the cooker?'

'Ah! There isn't one. Just the gas ring on the table by there. The gas is off. You'll have to ask the Gas Board to reconnect it.'

'Oh!'

Lillian smiled knowingly.

'Yes, it's primitive, Flo. Not what you're used to, is it?'

Florence smiled.

'I'll manage. I'm not helpless, mind.'

'There's worse to come,' Lillian went on.

'What?'

'You'll have to use the salon lavatory down in the back yard. It's hell on cold winter nights.'

That was a blow, but Florence took a grip on herself. She wanted independence, freedom. A little discomfort was a small price to pay. She'd get used to it. Others had to.

'If it was good enough for your father, Lillian, it's good enough for me.'

Lillian stared at her for a moment, then laughed out loud.

'My old man was a tough old boot!' she said. 'But I'm beginning to see you're a tough little

346

beggar yourself.'

'Well, thank you, Lillian,' Florence grinned. 'That's the nicest thing you've ever said to me.'

Lillian chuckled good-naturedly, and for the first time in their acquaintance, Florence warmed towards her. Lillian was tough too, and it was hard getting close to her. Perhaps from now on they might see things eye to eye.

'So you want the place, then?'

Florence nodded, and Lillian dropped the bunch of keys into her open hand.

'You agree with the rent I want?' she asked.

Florence nodded again, happily. A place of her own! Her mind was filled with all the things she could do to make it comfortable. She wouldn't be able to get everything at once, of course. But there was plenty of second-hand stuff about. A bed was the biggest headache.

'I'll be here every evening this week, cleaning up,' Florence said. 'And I'll be moving in at the end of the week.'

'What?' Lillian looked astonished. 'You're spending Christmas here – alone?'

'Yes.' Florence straightened up. 'I have my reasons, Lillian.'

'Now, hold on a minute!' Lillian wagged a finger, looking suddenly cross. 'There isn't a bloke involved in this, is there? I'm not having this flat turned into a love nest.'

Florence gasped, shocked to the core at the disgraceful suggestion that she was carrying on.

'Lillian! How could you even think such a thing?'

Lillian sniffed, unaffected.

347

'Like I said, young people, girls, have too much freedom these days. There are things going on today that were unheard of in my time.'

Lillian looked at her speculatively.

'Look at you for example. Your parents letting you buy a partnership, and you only in your teens. And now you're setting up house on your own.' She shook her head. 'Too much latitude.'

'I'm nineteen,' Florence retorted. 'And if the war were still on I'd probably be away from home in the Forces.'

Lillian nodded sagely.

'Yes, and that's the answer, isn't it? The war. It's changed everything, everybody. Values are slipping. Look at the divorce rate. Scandalous!'

'Well, it hasn't changed me,' Florence asserted strongly. 'I don't have a bloke, and I'm not likely to for a long time yet. I've … we've got a business to build up.'

Lillian smiled, her features relaxing.

'All right, Flo. I expect I'm jealous.' She looked wistful. 'I wish I were nineteen now.'

Florence spent her evenings after work rubbing and scrubbing. She was delighted when Marge offered to give her a hand on a couple of occasions.

Darlene was even more sullen when she learned Florence was to move in upstairs, and had little to say. That suited Florence very well. She had no energy to waste on scrapping.

Her parents were dismayed when she announced on Thursday that she'd be moving out the following Saturday. Her mother's eyes were red-rimmed from crying, and her father's pleasant face was wreathed with worry.

Florence felt deep regret that she was causing either of them pain, and almost burst into tears herself when her mother told her she might take her bed with her.

'I'm against you going, Florence, but I can see your mind's made up. We're sorry that you're...' Edie stumbled over the words, 'unhappy here. Take your bed, at least, and any other bits and pieces you need.'

She knew she'd be eternally grateful for that kindness. She could manage without other amenities, but a bed was essential, and she offered a little prayer of thankfulness.

On Saturday afternoon, to her immense surprise, her father insisted on helping her to move in.

He stood in the centre of the flat's empty living-room, his expression grave and concerned.

'Flo, love! It's a mausoleum.'

'Oh, Dad! It's not that bad,' Florence said, trying for lightness of tone. 'I won't use this room, not until I can afford to heat and furnish it anyway. I'll live and sleep in the bedroom. It's got a fireplace. I'm going to redecorate right through, bit by bit. I'll be comfortable, Dad. Don't worry.'

'Come home for Christmas, Flo, love,' he pleaded. 'Your mother's awful cut up, you know. She was crying again this morning.'

He looked unhappy, and Florence's heart ached for the pain she was causing. But she wasn't a child anymore. She had her own life and it was time she lived it.

Florence tried to laugh lightly, again, but it sounded more like a whimper.

'We've got my bed on the van downstairs, Dad.'

'You could use a spare guest room. Christmas won't be the same without you. You're still my baby daughter, Flo.'

Florence went to his side, lifting a hand to touch his face.

'I'm a woman. I'm sorry, Dad. I know you think I'm an awkward cuss, and perhaps spoilt, but I'm just struggling to be me, to be my own woman. I had to leave home some time. Look at Amy. She's left home.'

He shook his head.

'Somehow that's different. She's...'

Florence was suddenly offended.

'She's capable and I'm not! That's what you were going to say, isn't it, Dad? That's exactly *why* I'm leaving home.'

Her father put his arm around her, drawing her close.

'No, I didn't mean that, mun. What's happening, Flo? We used to be such pals, didn't we?'

Florence wasn't mollified. She stood stiffly in his embrace.

'That was when I was a child. Now I'm all grown-up.'

Florence's offended mood eased as they brought her few bits and pieces into the flat. In the box-room William found a rolled-up rug which wasn't in too bad condition. There was also an old hide armchair.

These things Florence arranged in the

350

bedroom. She made a fire in the small grate with twisted spills of newspapers and pieces of coal she'd brought from home.

The Gas Board man had been so they were able to put the kettle on the ring and have a cup of tea, William sitting on the one kitchen chair, Florence perched on the board covering the bath.

'You'll catch pneumonia here, Flo,' he warned, with a shiver.

'There's plenty of coal in the coal house in the yard,' she assured him. 'I've checked. I think it's been there for ages. You know, stock piled. I'm lucky!'

William's expression remained glum. Obviously, he couldn't share her enthusiasm.

She met Cliff in the Italian café in Union Street as usual on Thursday in the week before Christmas. He was already at a table, looking uncertain.

'Sorry I'm late,' Florence gasped. She'd been hurrying, and it was so cold.

He looked on the verge of annoyance.

'At least you turned up, this time.'

Florence touched his hand as it rested on the table.

'I'm sorry about last week, Cliff. I was so busy preparing the flat. I couldn't get word to you in time.'

'Flat?'

Florence grinned at his puzzlement, and told him her news. He looked astonished, and then pleased.

'Well, we won't be meeting here from now on then, will we?' he said.

'What?'

'We'll meet at the flat from now on. Much more private, Flo.'

Florence was disconcerted for a moment. She hadn't considered inviting him there. Not right under Lillian's nose.

'Is that wise, Cliff?'

He grinned. 'I think it's perfect.'

Florence was silent, still uncertain. If Lillian discovered Cliff was a visitor at the flat, what would she do?

'So,' Cliff said, interrupting her disagreeable speculations. 'You're moving in after Christmas.'

'I'm already installed,' she said. 'Christmas on my own for the first time ever.'

She didn't mean the words to sound so pathetic. She saw the change in his expression and knew exactly what he intended to say next.

'Oh, Flo, we can't have that.' He took her hand in his. 'Look, kid, come to us. Have Christmas dinner with me and the kids. A pal of mine is getting me a chicken, a plump one, I hope. Stay for the afternoon.'

Florence thought of the cold flat, the loneliness. Yes, she'd been lonely since she'd moved in only days before. Maybe Christmas Day on her own was going too far.

She looked into Cliff's eager face and knew she'd accept his offer, and gladly. It would be a family Christmas after all.

CHAPTER 24

Christmas Day 1949

Alone in the small scullery at Cliff's house in Catherine Street, Florence wiped the dishes they'd used for tea. She went at the task slowly, reluctantly to finish. Soon now she'd have to leave, returning to the empty flat to spend the rest of the holiday alone. That prospect wasn't very appealing, not on Christmas night.

It had been a strange Christmas Day, the strangest she'd ever known. Cliff made her very welcome, and the children seemed pleased to see her there, too. She was glad of some family warmth, even if it wasn't her own family.

She could easily have gone home. They'd have welcomed her, but she knew she wouldn't really enjoy Christmas there. For one thing, it would be like surrendering, and that she wouldn't do, no matter how miserable she felt.

Another reason was that her feelings of isolation at home were too painful to bear. Rivalry with Amy, real or imagined, would plague her throughout the weekend. It was better to be here with comparative strangers, where, ironically, she could be herself.

But she couldn't spend the whole of Christmas sheltered here. Already she felt she was taking advantage of Cliff's generosity.

You've made your bed, now you must lie in it.

Those were her mother's words. And, of course, Edie was right. Florence did want to go her own way; lead her own life; make her own decisions.

It was inevitable she'd make mistakes, but she'd learn to live with them, and wouldn't let her present loneliness, and yes, homesickness, deter her from pursuing her dream. With a partnership settled, that dream was coming true, giving her everything she'd ever wanted. She wouldn't let go, no matter how bad things got.

But she wouldn't use others either, nor take advantage. Cliff had got her over the worse of it, and she was so grateful to him; owing him so much, more than could be repaid.

Finishing the washing-up at last, she could delay no longer. It was time to go.

In the living-room the children were sitting on the mat in front of the fire reading comics, but Tansy was yawning widely.

'They'll be going to bed soon,' Florence said quietly. She should go before that.

'Pete's pleaded for extra time,' Cliff grinned. 'I'll let them have an extra hour, because it's Christmas. Thanks for doing the dishes. It wasn't necessary, you know.'

He patted the cushion beside him on the settee.

'Sit down, Flo, love. I know you said you don't drink, but have a glass of sherry anyway. It'll do you good.'

Florence shook her head, making no move to sit.

'Thanks, Cliff, but I think I'd better be going.'

He jumped to his feet, looking disappointed.

'What? So soon?' He glanced at the clock on

the mantelpiece. 'It's only just gone seven. We've got the whole evening before us.'

For the first time since knowing Cliff, Florence felt a little uneasy. When the children finally went to bed, she and Cliff would be alone. The idea had never disturbed her before. Now she felt an awkwardness and didn't understand why.

Perhaps it had to do with the festive season, she thought in a rising panic, her loneliness and the cosiness of the little house in Catherine Street.

Did it also have something to do with Amy's outrageous suggestion that Cliff had an ulterior motive? Angry with herself, Florence dismissed that thought as quickly as it came into her head.

Cliff wasn't like that, and there had never been anything even mildly suggesting an intimacy in their relationship. Did they have a relationship? No, they were friends.

'Do you have to go, kid?'

He looked glum. He must get lonely, Florence thought. And when the children went to bed he'd be sitting here on his own, too. It was silly for them both to be alone, when they could have each other's company, as friends.

But the disquiet within her wouldn't go away. Instinct told her that if she remained their friendship would change, and she didn't want that. That was the unknown, and it frightened her.

Florence smiled up at him weakly.

'Yes, Cliff, I think it's best.'

'Best?'

Florence foundered for a moment, even more embarrassed. She couldn't explain this strange feeling.

'I must get used to being at the flat,' she blurted, unable to think of another explanation.

'I'll walk you home.'

'No need,' Florence said.

'I know, but I want to,' he said firmly. He turned to his son. 'Pete! I'll be gone a while. No mischief, mind,' he warned, as he placed the fire guard around the grate. 'Otherwise you'll get a walloping, Christmas or no Christmas.'

As they walked up through the town, the empty streets made it like a ghost town, and for all her protests, Florence was glad of his company. The street lights lit their way, the vast dark areas of cleared bomb sites on either side, were eerie and somehow frightening.

It was a little livelier in the High Street. Opposite the salon, lights blazed from a pub, where raucous singing could be heard.

Cliff took the key from her and opened the salon door and they went inside. Florence hesitated, embarrassed, in the reception area. She didn't open the door to the stairs, not wanting to invite him up.

'Will you be all right, Flo?' He sounded concerned. 'Is there anything I can do for you before I go?'

Florence bit her lip. There was something. It was silly, but she dreaded doing it at night.

'Well, there is the coal,' she said. 'I could do with another bucket of coal from out the back yard.'

She wanted to keep the fire going in the bedroom for as long as possible. Tonight, sleep would be a long time coming to her.

'Say no more, kid,' Cliff replied cheerfully. 'I'll get it.' He sounded very happy to be able to do it for her.

It meant, of course, that he had to come up to the flat for the coal bucket. She watched his face as she switched on the light in the vast living-room.

'I've never been in this flat before,' he said. 'God! What a mausoleum.'

Florence laughed, feeling a little more relaxed now.

'That's what my father said.'

Cliff looked at her, concern in his eyes again.

'Is this a good idea, Flo? You can't be comfortable here.'

'I live in the bedroom,' she explained. 'I'm okay.'

'Hate to think of you all alone here, Flo. It isn't right.'

Cliff stood regarding her speculatively, thumb rubbing at his jaw.

'Look, kid, don't take this the wrong way, but I've got a spare room at our house. You're welcome to it. I mean, you could pay me rent if you wanted to, if it made you feel better.'

Florence was taken aback, and stared in surprise.

'This is kind of you, Cliff.'

She didn't know quite what to say. It was out of the question. She recalled the awkwardness she'd felt earlier. Living in the same house? No, it wouldn't do, but she appreciated the offer, because she knew it was prompted by kindness, nothing else.

'It's very kind,' she repeated for want of something to say. 'But I'm all right here, honestly.'

He brought the coal up and put the bucket in the bedroom while Florence waited in the living-room, shivering, hesitating to follow him.

'The fire's still going in there,' he said as he came into the room. 'I've put more coal on, and banked it up with some small. It should last most of the night.'

Florence smiled.

'Thanks, Cliff. Thanks for everything. You're a real friend.'

His answering smile was a little awry.

'Friend, yes,' he repeated thoughtfully, then grinned. 'Well, you've made my Christmas, kid,' he said. 'Usually I spend the day playing games with the kids or listening to the wireless.' He paused. 'What'll you do tomorrow?'

Florence turned her gaze away.

'I'll probably go down the Mumbles to my mother's,' she lied.

'The buses aren't running,' he reminded her.

'I'll ring my father,' Florence said hastily. 'He'll come and fetch me.'

'We'd be glad to see you again at our house,' he said hopefully.

'Thanks, Cliff. But I'll probably go home.' Lying wasn't getting any easier.

'I understand, kid.' Cliff grasped her hands, and held them tightly. 'Thank you so much for your company, Flo.'

She was embarrassed again, but her embarrassment turned to confusion when he leaned down and planted a brief kiss on her cheek.

'Goodnight, Flo, love, and God bless.'

Florence let out the long breath that she'd been holding.

'Goodnight, Cliff, and thank you once again.'

Florence locked the salon door after him, turned out the lights and returned upstairs. In the big empty living-room she looked down from the window on to the High Street. She could still hear the singing faintly from the pub opposite, and found it strangely comforting. She wasn't alone in the world.

Florence undressed immediately and climbed into bed. The sheets felt quite warm, really, and she thought the room was cosy, considering the bleakness of the flat in general.

Lying there, she couldn't help thinking of her family gathered together at home. They'd all be there, listening to the wireless or the gramophone, playing games and chatting. They'd be together, enjoying the warmth and love that only a family can give at such a time of the year.

She was outside that, and it was her own fault. Tears filled her eyes as she remembered Christmas times in the past. Her parents had bought her a present, she was sure, but she hadn't given them a chance to give it to her. She'd turned her back on them, that was the truth.

Florence dabbed at her tears with the edge of the bed sheet. Grow up! You got what you wanted, she scolded herself; independence; success. These things don't come free.

Florence buried her face in the pillow as fresh tears flooded her eyes.

The price of success, the price of her dreams was higher than she'd ever anticipated. Right at this moment, here alone, she wondered whether it was all worthwhile?

CHAPTER 25

March 1950

Florence was busy cleaning the window on the landing outside the flat when she heard someone tapping the glass of the salon door below. With a sigh of irritation she went down, wiping her wet hands on her apron.

Clients weren't yet used to the new half-day closing on Monday afternoons, and she'd forgotten to hang up the 'closed' sign.

Coming into the reception area she was surprised to see Marge grinning and waving at her through the window. She unlocked the door immediately and let her in.

'Marge, this is a nice surprise,' Florence greeted, delighted at the prospect of a visitor.

Marge continued to grin.

'You sound as if you haven't seen me for a year instead of only a couple of hours ago,' she said, stepping over the threshold.

Florence smiled back.

'Well, you haven't visited the flat before.'

The fact was, no one visited her except Cliff. She wondered for a brief moment how it was she'd wound up without a real friend. She had to admit she was often lonely, and was very glad to see Marge.

'Come on upstairs,' Florence went on eagerly. 'I'm about to make a pot of tea.'

'Something smells delicious,' Marge remarked as she climbed the stairs.

'I've just taken some scones out of the oven,' Florence said. 'My dad got me a second-hand stove. It's old, but it cooks a treat.'

Marge sat at the kitchen table while Florence poured the tea.

'You've got it cosy in by here,' Marge said. 'Fair dues to you.'

Florence was pleased.

Marge had taken her new status at the salon more philosophically than the others, with the exception of Nancy, perhaps. Marge wasn't rebellious like Darlene continued to be, or sullen like Glenys.

But even so, Florence was always aware that Marge was Lillian's ally, and didn't expect any support from her that would be against Lillian's interests. Lillian had a good friend in Marge, and Florence wished she had someone like her.

'Have another scone,' Florence suggested, slicing one through and applying a thin layer of blended butter and margarine, regretting that rationing prevented her being more generous to her visitor.

'Don't mind if I do.'

'So,' Florence began, sipping her tea. 'Lillian caught the two-ten to Paddington, then? I can hardly believe she's really gone up the Smoke to look for a new stylist at long last.'

'Saw her off, myself. She won't be back till some time next week. You know, kid,' Marge chuckled. 'She's still grumbling about our Monday half-days off.'

Florence tossed her head.

'She'll have to get used to it, won't she,' she said firmly. 'It's only right we should have a half-day like everyone else. This is the second half of the twentieth century, for heaven's sake, not Victorian times.'

Marge laughed and nodded enthusiastically.

'Sitting by here having tea and scones, I can't think of a better way to spend my half-day, either.'

Florence thoughtfully traced a pattern in the tablecloth with the handle of a teaspoon.

'I can't help feeling I should have gone with her, though, to make sure she goes through with it,' she said. 'But I couldn't afford to.'

'You can trust Lil,' Marge said immediately, an edge to her voice. 'She'd promised she'll find a good cutter for us and she will. She never goes back on her word.'

Florence sighed.

'I can't wait! What I'm looking forward to is telling Darlene to sling her hook. I'll be glad to see the back of *her!*'

She expected a hearty agreement from Marge and looked up in surprise when the older woman was silent. She was even more surprised to see Marge looking troubled.

'What's up?'

Marge shrugged.

'Darlene and me could never be friends. Often she gives me the screaming abb-dabs, but you got to feel sorry for her, deep down, like.'

Florence laughed outright.

'You've changed your tune, Marge.'

363

'Yes ... well...' Marge's expression showed sympathy. 'Darlene's on her own, mun, like I am. No kids, see, like me.'

Florence put a comforting hand on her arm. 'You'd have made a good mother, Marge.'

Florence suddenly felt overcome. She hadn't seen Edie since before last Christmas, and her heart ached in missing her mother. It was all very well being independent, but being cut off from family, from those she loved the most, even if it was for a principle, was hard to bear. The image of her own mother's face was suddenly clear in her mind. The warmth and love she'd known at home was still dear to her. She should turn back to that warmth while there was still time.

'What's the matter, kid?' Marge asked.

'It's my mother's birthday next Sunday,' Florence said, feeling choked up. 'I was thinking of going to see her; take her a little present, you know.'

'Oh, I would!' Marge urged.

'Mam and I haven't been the best of pals for a while,' Florence said. 'Not since I bought into the business and left home.'

She spoke without thinking, then glanced at Marge fearfully. She was as sharp as a tack, was Marge. She'd spot an inconsistency in a flash. But Marge was gazing at her with concern in her eyes.

'Go and see your mam, kid. Smooth things over. It's good to have your family behind you. You never know when you'll need their support.'

Florence straightened up, smiling broadly.

'I will go and see her, Marge. Thanks a lot. I've

got no one to talk things over with these days.'

Marge put her head on one side, pursing her lips. Her bright glance at Florence was knowing, and with a flash of insight, she realised the older woman was more aware of how things really were with her than she would've guessed.

'I'm not your only visitor, though, am I?' Marge said confidently. 'I've seen Cliff knocking at the door here on a few Thursday evenings when I've been on my way to the pictures at the Elysium.'

Florence stared at her open-mouthed, lost for words again. Marge's eyes turned brighter, and Florence didn't like what she read there.

'It's not what you're thinking, Marge,' she blurted in her haste to explain. 'It's quite innocent. Really, it is!'

Marge's smile was sardonic.

'Well, I can't blame Cliff, like, can I? You're young and pretty. Of course he'd fall for you.' She sighed. 'I know I never stood a chance with him but...'

'Marge!' Florence jumped to her feet. 'You've got it wrong, I tell you. Cliff and I are business partners, that's all.'

Marge wrinkled her nose, looking mystified.

'Business partners? How'd you mean, kid?'

Florence sat down again with a bump. Her face was growing hot and she saw Marge studying her flushed cheeks speculatively.

She'd have to explain it all now, tell the truth. She couldn't let Marge go on believing that she and Cliff were ... well ... carrying on. The very idea made her skin prickle with embarrassment.

'The truth is, Marge,' she rushed on. 'Cliff

loaned me the money to buy into the business. My parents had nothing to do with it. That's why things are cool between us.'

Marge looked incredulous.

'Cliff loaned you five hundred pounds? Just like that!'

She was looking at Florence with the same expression of disbelief that she'd seen on Amy's face, even the brief knowing smirk.

'He calls in every week for a report,' Florence went on defensively. 'That's all!'

Marge's lip curled. 'A report?'

Florence felt confused. She was explaining this badly.

'He wants to know how his investment is going.'

'But, kid, the investment is in your name, isn't it?'

Florence's shoulders sagged. She betrayed both herself and Cliff for the sake of pride. No, she corrected herself sternly. It wasn't pride, it was self-esteem, and that was different. Her self-esteem was all she had, really; that and her reputation. She wouldn't have those sullied.

But, nevertheless, she'd landed herself and Cliff in a mess of trouble, because Marge wouldn't keep quiet. She was too loyal to Lillian.

'Lillian wouldn't accept Cliff's money, would she?' Florence said quietly, though still on the defensive. 'I was desperate for the salon to stay open.' She lifted her hands in despair, her voice rising to a wail. 'For all our sakes, Marge.'

'So the pair of you put one over on Lillian. Very nice!'

'You make it sound despicable,' Florence said defensively.

She was feeling very edgy now. What had they done that was so wrong? They'd saved everyone's jobs. The salon was well on the way to getting back on its feet. Everything had turned out well. Well, almost everything.

'Well, it is deceitful, Flo,' Marge said, her voice low. 'Poor Lillian.'

Florence felt like wringing her hands in desperation. There was no going back now. She'd really done for herself. What would her partner say and do when Marge told her? Florence cringed at the thought.

'I suppose you're going to tell Lillian as soon as she gets back?' Florence said, trying to hold down the sob of hopelessness in her voice.

Marge sat back in her chair, reached into her handbag nearby and took out a packet of Woodbines.

'Got a match, kid?'

Florence leaned across to the gas stove and retrieved a box of matches, handing it silently to her companion.

Marge lit up and drew deeply on the cigarette.

'No, Flo, I'm not going to tell her. You'll do it yourself, in your own time, I hope. Lillian's my friend, and she's been hit hard by that swine, Tony. But, she's been happier these last few months than she has for a long time. I don't want to give her any more misery.'

'Oh, Marge,' Florence stood up, wanting to reach over and give the older woman a big kiss of gratitude. 'Thanks so much!'

Marge took another long drag on the cigarette, her expression detached. There wasn't even a glimmer of humour in her face now.

'Oh, don't thank me,' she said, letting the smoke rise from her lips, curling in rings and swirls like some secret writing. 'I'm not doing you any favour.'

She paused a moment, studying Florence keenly.

'Don't leave it too long before … confessing, though,' she said at last. 'Because if Lillian finds out Cliff is involved in any way, all hell will break loose. Do yourself a favour, Flo. Come clean.'

By teatime Marge had long gone, but Florence still sensed her presence in the flat. Or was it her own guilt at betraying Cliff? She'd wrecked everything. Marge promised not to tell, but Florence couldn't believe she'd keep quiet for long.

Florence dreaded facing Cliff, and wouldn't blame him if he was angry. Well, if he was, that was just too bad. She'd had to explain, unable to bear the idea that people were willing to believe the worst of her.

First it had been Lillian, accusing her of being Tony's bit-on-the-side, a disgusting idea that revolted her. Then her own sister suspected her of having an affair with Cliff; and now Marge.

She reflected on something her mother often said. War brought out the worst in people in more ways than one, and the effects were lasting. Suddenly, she felt even more anxious to see her mother.

A sound disturbed her morbid reflections. Someone was knocking and rattling the salon door again. Had Marge returned? Or was it Cliff?

Florence sat still, alarmed. She didn't want to see either of them. She'd remain quiet, pretend she was out. Abruptly, a new thought struck her. It might be someone she did want to see, her father for instance. Reluctantly she went downstairs.

A woman stood on the pavement, her back to the door, perhaps on the point of moving away. She was smartly dressed in one of the very latest swing-back coats in Prince of Wales check, and a fashionable black felt hat with a curled brim.

Merely a client. Someone who didn't know they closed on a Monday afternoon. Florence felt relief flood through her.

She tapped briefly on the glass to attract the woman's attention to the closed sign. The woman turned and Florence got a shock.

Rita!

Florence stared for a moment longer, astonished, then hastily unlocked the salon door.

'Rita! You're the last person I expected to see.'

Rita hesitated on the threshold as though unsure of her welcome.

'Can I come in, Flo?'

Florence opened the door wider.

'Of course you can.'

She was conscious of rising excitement and curiosity, and recognised immediately that the enmity she'd felt against Rita a year ago had completely disappeared. And as for Ken, she

369

hadn't given *him* a passing thought for many months, and couldn't even remember what she'd felt for him. Whatever it was, it hadn't been real. That much was obvious now.

'You know I've taken the flat upstairs?' she said, relocking the salon door.

'Yes, my mother told me,' Rita replied.

Auntie Sybil! Florence might have guessed her aunt would be keeping a close watch on her, aided and abetted by Darlene, no doubt.

Still, in this instance Florence was glad. Rita was her cousin as well as being a one-time friend. There was still much between them, despite their quarrel, and Florence was suddenly keen to learn all about Rita's new life.

'Let me take your coat, Rita,' she suggested when they were in the flat. 'I use only the bedroom and the kitchen. I'm not posh like...'

Florence bit back the words. She had been about to say something childish and spiteful, but checked herself. Perhaps she and Rita could be friends again? She wouldn't appear envious, because she wasn't. So much had happened since Rita's wedding last March; so much that Florence had to be thankful for. She'd achieved a lot, and by her own efforts, too. She had nothing to be envious about.

'I'm just about to have something to eat,' Florence went on, as she poured Rita a cup of tea. 'A boiled egg. Would you like one, too?'

Rita looked up from her cup. There was something disturbing in her gaze. She looked different somehow.

'I can't take your ration,' she said.

'I insist,' Florence said, overly cheerful to dispel the unease. 'A boiled egg and a slice of bread and scrape will go down nicely.'

She sat down at the kitchen table, waiting for the eggs to boil.

'Well, how's life treating you, Rita? No sign of a family starting, then?'

Rita took a sip of tea, her eyes downcast, and was strangely silent. Florence studied her cousin, still disturbed by Rita's appearance.

She'd lost weight. The skin under her eyes had dark smudges and she looked tired and ill. Her cup rattled on the saucer slightly, uncontrolled by her trembling hand.

'No, no family.'

Her tone was expressionless. Perhaps she thinks I'm still angry with her, Florence thought, and on impulse reached out a hand to touch Rita's arm in reassurance.

'I'm sorry for the things I said and the way I behaved last year, Rita. It was so childish of me!'

Rita sipped her tea, not saying a word; her eyes still downcast.

'I ought to thank you, Rita,' Florence went on hurriedly, not understanding her friend's silence.

Rita was always timid, scared of her own shadow really. Florence thought marriage would have brought her out of her shell, yet she seemed even more unsure of herself.

'I thought I was in love with Ken,' Florence went on, then gave a chuckle. 'So infantile! And do you know, I think I'd have been daft enough to marry him if he'd asked me. I don't think it would have worked, somehow.'

Florence paused, waiting for a response, but there was none. Perplexed and uneasy, she jumped up to see to the eggs, which were boiling furiously, and was annoyed to see the shells had cracked, letting out some of the egg-white to form white clouds in the water.

Oh, drat! She hated it when that happened.

Turning down the gas a little, she looked back at Rita. Her cousin had turned her face away slightly, and Florence studied her more closely.

Yes, she'd lost a lot of weight. The two-piece suit she wore was beautifully tailored, expensive-looking, yet it seemed to hang on her.

'So things turned out for the best, Rita, didn't they? I'd have probably landed myself with an unhappy marriage if it hadn't been for you. You saved me from it.'

Rita looked up sharply.

'I saved you from much worse than that!'

Rita was staring at her wide-eyed. For one awful second Florence saw fear and repugnance in Rita's eyes before her cup and saucer rattled down onto the table and she burst into tears.

'Rita!'

Thoroughly alarmed, Florence stepped quickly to her cousin's side, putting an arm around her shoulders. To her surprise, Rita stood up immediately and clung to her, sobbing uncontrollably.

'Rita, kid! Whatever is the matter?'

'Oh, Flo!' Rita choked through her tears and sobs. 'I've made a terrible mistake. I don't know which way to turn.'

'Tell me about it. Tell me!' Florence said

urgently, hugging her cousin closer, feeling her body tremble.

'I don't know how to,' Rita sobbed. 'It's so awful, Flo; so shameful.'

'Look, come into the bedroom,' Florence suggested quickly. 'It's more comfortable. I think a drop of gin and hot water would do you good right this minute. Come on.'

Florence led her into the bedroom. The fire in the small grate glowed, making the room pleasantly warm. Her bed and a few bits and pieces of furniture filled up the space.

The armchair her father had found in the spare room was drawn up to the fire. It was deep, roomy and comfortable and Florence was fond of it.

'Sit by here, Rita, love,' Florence said kindly, leading her to the chair. 'I'll get you that drop of gin and you tell me everything.'

Florence drew up an old leather-covered stool to the side of the chair and sat watching Rita sip the warm spirits.

The smell of the liquor made Florence feel a bit queasy because of her empty stomach, but Rita's distress put thoughts of food out of her head. Something was very wrong, and it was plain Rita needed help.

'Rita, kid, you must tell me what's wrong.'

Rita clamped her lips together, obviously striving not to burst into tears again.

'Is it ... is it Ken?' Florence persisted.

Rita nodded sadly and her eyes, full of pain and misery, stared into Florence's.

'He...' Suddenly she hid her face in her hands.

373

'Flo, I don't know how to tell you. It's something decent people don't talk about. I feel so ashamed, humiliated.'

Florence kindly but firmly pulled Rita's hands away from her face, and putting a finger under her chin, lifted her head.

'This is me, your cousin, Flo, remember?' Florence said encouragingly. 'We can talk about anything. Come on, Rita, love. Get it off your chest. You'll feel better.'

Rita stared at her silently, eyes brimming with tears.

Florence took the plunge.

'Is Ken a wife-beater, or what?'

'Oh, Flo!' Rita was biting her lip so hard, Florence expected to see blood. 'Ken's a brute! A sickening beast and a...'

She choked on the words. With hands shaking, she untied the chiffon scarf she wore around her neck and unwound it, undid the buttons of her jacket and pulled aside the neckline of her blouse.

Florence stared in horror at the variety of shades of the bruises, violet and purple, staining the skin on Rita's neck and upper chest. The fresh bruises stood out, but Florence's horrified gaze detected the shadows of old ones, too.

'Rita! My God, this is awful!'

Rita's face puckered in misery.

Florence put a hand on her arm in sympathy.

'How long has this been going on, for heaven's sake?'

'Since our honeymoon.'

Florence was appalled. 'What?'

'Not a week goes by. Every time he ... he touches me ... you know what I mean, Flo. Every time, he punishes me.'

'But why? Why?'

'I think it's because he's frustrated. He hates me. He tells me so frequently.'

'This is terrible!'

Florence was shocked. She could hardly believe it, yet the evidence was indisputable. Starchy, straight-laced Ken a wife-beater? Who would credit it? She felt sorry for her cousin. Poor Rita!

'Have you told your mother?'

Rita shook her head, bowing it.

'No. You see, Flo, there's much worse to tell. I don't know how to begin...'

'What can be worse than this?'

Rita looked up at her then, and Florence was shocked again. This time it was the look in Rita's eyes. The girl she used to be was gone. A woman looked out at Florence, a woman with knowledge of a world of which Florence had little inkling.

'There is worse, Flo, much, much worse. Ken is ... he's not...' Rita bit her lip again in confusion.

Florence tried to help her.

'Ken's not what?'

'He's ... not natural,' Rita burst out with a rush. 'Do you understand me, Flo?'

Rita sounded desperate now, clearly longing for Florence to read her thoughts so that she wouldn't have to voice the words that needed to be said. But Florence was silent, not understanding.

'He has unnatural appetites...' An expression of revulsion passed across Rita's face. 'Sexual

375

appetites,' she murmured, then shook her head in despair. 'Oh God! This is so difficult, so shaming. You're the first person I've talked to like this, Flo. The first one I've told.'

'Go on, Rita, love,' Florence urged apprehensively. Her instinct told her this was something she didn't want to hear.

'Ken doesn't like women. He prefers men ... boys.' Rita looked appealingly at Florence. 'Please understand what I'm talking about, Flo.'

Florence swallowed with difficulty, her understanding growing into horror.

'I think I do. I've heard the girls in the salon, Darlene and Marge, making jokes about such men...'

She didn't understand the jokes but pretended she did. She didn't believe some of the things Darlene said either, and was shocked at the older girl's crudity at times.

But here was Rita, her friend, in terrible distress, saying something similar; but this was no joke. Florence felt an icy chill spread through her veins. That such ugliness should come into Rita's life; Rita of all people!

'Sometimes,' Rita went on, 'Ken brings young men to the house.'

'Who are they?'

Rita shrugged, indifferently.

'Complete strangers, as far as I know.'

'That's terrible!'

'No! No! I'm glad when he does bring them.' Repugnance marred her features again. 'Because it means he'll stay away from me for a day or two.'

She looked at Florence, cold dread in her eyes.

'You see, Flo, it's not only the beatings, though they're bad enough; it's...' She paused then rushed on, 'He doesn't treat me like a woman.' Rita wrung her hands. 'You couldn't possibly know what I'm talking about! He's unnatural, disgusting and I'm terrified of him!'

Rita threw herself back in the chair and covered her face again, her sobs of wretchedness shaking her body.

Florence could only stare at her, profoundly appalled; coldness of unimagined horror chilled her very bones.

She was remembering the day at Ken's home when he'd thrown her out. She remembered the photographs on the table, and the way he'd gathered them up; guiltily, she thought with hindsight. He'd flown into such a rage.

'You must leave him,' Florence said firmly, at last. 'Tell your mother and father.'

Rita sat forward.

'I couldn't possibly!' she cried out, her voice shaking in trepidation. 'It was hard enough telling you. I can't talk about ... sex with them, Flo.'

She looked down at her trembling hands.

'Besides,' she went on. 'I dread to think what my father might do. He's a quiet man, Flo, gentle and kind. He puts up with a lot from my mother. But, if he found out about Ken...' She swallowed hard. 'When the quiet ones lose control, Flo, anything can happen. I don't want my father to get into trouble over Ken. He isn't worth it.'

'But you can't go on living like this,' Florence persisted.

Rita pushed herself to her feet.

'I must go.'

Florence jumped to her feet, too.

'Rita, please! We can't leave it like this,' she cried. 'Look! Leave Ken. Come and stay with me until we can sort out something.'

Rita shook her head, fear in her eyes again.

'Ken's warned me if I try to leave him, he'll come after me. I'm afraid of him, Flo. He's a violent brute, and his family protect him.'

Florence's mouth dropped open in astonishment.

'You mean his parents know!'

'They know all right.' Rita's tone was bitter. 'They're all afraid in their hearts that I'm going to tell. Ken could end up in prison. Imagine the scandal for their precious family?'

'Prison's where he belongs after making your life a misery,' Florence said harshly. 'Why did he marry you, Rita, if he's…?'

'Camouflage,' Rita said apathetically. She looked into Florence's eyes. 'He decided on you first, Flo.' She managed a weak, wry smile, though her tone was bitter. 'But you proved unmanageable. I went like a lamb to the slaughter.'

Florence clasped Rita's hands tightly, feeling tears sting her eyes.

'Rita, love, we *must* do something,' she said urgently. 'You can't live like this.'

Rita's shoulders drooped.

'It's no good, Flo. I can't see any way out. My only hope is he'll grow tired of humiliating me.'

'Oh, Rita!'

When Rita had gone, Florence sat for a long time before the fire, brooding on what her cousin had revealed. Despite everything Rita had told her, she couldn't really imagine what her friend was going through, but that didn't stop Florence feeling some of the horror.

The belief that she must do something was strong in her. If Rita couldn't bring herself to tell, then Florence must do it for her.

Florence thought about her mother. She'd been longing to visit Edie on her birthday, and was still making up her mind whether to go or not. Now she knew she must. She'd see her mother, take her a little gift for her birthday, and then talk to her about Rita.

It wouldn't be easy. Florence and her mother had never ever discussed the 'facts of life'. What knowledge she had, she'd gleaned from other girls' gossip or jokes. It was imperfect knowledge, she knew that. But she needn't be shy or embarrassed about discussing it, though her mother might be. After all, this was the second half of the twentieth century.

Florence rose at last, deciding she needed a cup of tea. It was then she remembered the eggs boiling away on the stove.

With a screech of dismay she rushed down the passage. The air in the kitchen was heavy with the stink of burning egg shells and scorched metal. She almost made the painful mistake of grabbing at the saucepan handle straight away, but seized a tea-towel first.

The eggs were just two dark brown mounds

stuck to the bottom of the saucepan, which was black inside. Ruined!

Florence stared at it for a moment before turning away and throwing the whole thing into the dustbin in disgust. The mess reminded her of Rita's life.

Sunday was a nice day. There was a definite tang of spring in the air. Florence caught an early bus to the Mumbles. It was a bit of a cheek, but she hoped to be asked to Sunday lunch. It would be like old times; that is, if her mother was pleased to see her.

The walk up the hill from the village was pleasant and she savoured it. The guest house stood on the brow of the hill, peaceful amidst its gardens in the March sunlight.

Florence wasn't too sure what kind of a reception she'd get, but coming back to the house and home she loved was a joy in itself.

Deciding it wouldn't be a good idea to barge through the back door into the big kitchen unannounced, she chose the front entrance used by guests.

There was no one behind the reception desk and Florence judged that at this time of year there weren't many guests; probably just a few salesmen on business.

Unchallenged, she made her way through to the back staircase and up to her parents' private sitting-room at the back of the house. Opening the door, she went straight in.

Edie was sitting in an armchair, legs outstretched on a foot stool. She still wore her cotton wrap-around pinny, so had just finished breakfasts for the guests.

'Happy birthday, Mam.'

Edie sat up with a jerk, staring.

'Florence!' She jumped to her feet and came rushing towards Florence to engulf her daughter in that longed-for embrace. 'Oh, Florence, lovely. There's lovely to see you, chick. How are you?'

'I'm fine, Mam.'

Clutched in her mother's arms, Florence wanted to burst into tears. Her greeting was just what she'd hoped for. She valued her independence more than ever, yet homesickness was never far beneath the surface. She missed her mother and the comfortable home she'd always known.

Edie held her at arm's-length, her gaze, suspiciously shiny, inspecting Florence's face and figure.

'You're looking well, lovey, I must say. I expected to see you half-starved.'

Florence laughed, despite the implied doubt of her ability to survive outside the family home. Her mother would never change.

'I'm teaching myself to cook, Mam, and I'm pretty good at it, even if I say so myself. You must come up to the flat one day and try a dish of my vegetable stew and suet dumplings.'

Edie's eyes widened in surprise.

'Yes, lovey, perhaps I will.'

'And how about you, Mam. How are you these days?' Florence searched her mother's face. 'You're looking tired. Don't you think you ought to retire from the guest house business now?'

Edie tossed her head.

'Stuff and nonsense! I'm only forty-seven I'll have you know! I'm not doddering yet.'

They went into the family's small kitchen adjacent to the sitting-room, where Edie made a pot of tea. When they sat down to drink it, Florence opened her handbag and took out a parcel wrapped in fancy paper.

'I'm sorry I rushed off Christmas time without giving you a present, Mam,' she said. 'That was mean of me. This is just a little something to make up for it.'

She'd been filled with righteous indignation, then, she conceded, full of her own needs and ambitions, careless of everyone else's feelings. She wanted to make up for it all. She wanted her family back.

Edie accepted the parcel, opened it, and took out a pretty silk paisley-patterned shawl, fringed with white. Her face lit up with obvious pleasure. It was a look that warmed Florence's heart.

'Oh, Florence, lovey. There's beautiful! But you shouldn't have. It looks too expensive.'

'I'm doing all right, Mam,' Florence reassured her. 'Business at the salon has improved. If Dad inspected the books now he'd see a different picture, I can assure you.'

Edie carefully folded the shawl, her gaze downcast.

'I hear that man has finished with the business,' she said. 'That Cliff Longford. Auntie Sybil told your father that Lillian Longford threw him out. Can't say I'm surprised.'

Florence bit back a retort, mentally counting to

ten. Darlene had been busy with her mouth again, like a fifth-columnist, spreading rumour and gossip in an effort to undermine everything. Florence decided she wouldn't rise to the bait. There was no need any longer. She had made her point.

'Lillian's gone up to London,' she said lightly. 'We're hoping to find a young, fashionable stylist.'

'Your father and I were relieved to hear Cliff Longford has gone,' Edie persisted. 'But we're still worried at you owing him money. It gives him a ... hold over you.'

'How's Mam-gu and Gramps?' Florence asked brightly, determined that the pleasure of her visit home should not be soured.

'Mam-gu's leg is playing her up,' Edie said. 'But otherwise they're both all right.'

She rose from her chair.

'I've got a present for you, too, Florence lovey,' she said, a touch of excitement in her voice. 'A belated Christmas present.' She paused. 'I should've sent it up with your father, but I was hoping to give it to you myself.' She smiled happily. 'Now I can.'

She left the room, returned shortly with a large brown paper package tied up with string, and handed it to Florence.

'There you are, chick,' Edie said. 'With all our love.'

With shaking fingers Florence undid the string and folded back the paper. When she saw what was inside she gave a squeal of pleasure, jumping to her feet.

It was a wool coat in peacock blue, full skirted and double-breasted, with a nipped-in waist. Florence held it against herself admiringly, running appreciative fingers over the blue velvet collar, and the velvet-trimmed peplum.

It was just like Amy's, and what Florence had longed for.

'Oh, Mam! It's beautiful. Oh, thank you, thank you! You and Dad.'

She hadn't been forgotten after all! Putting the coat on the chair she rushed at her mother, hugging her tightly, and kissing her cheek.

'Mam, I'm so sorry I hurt you at Christmas,' Florence murmured. 'Can you forgive me?'

'Oh, Florence, lovey,' Edie said, hugging her back. 'You're my youngest daughter, and I love you very much. So does your father. We'll always be proud of you, whether you're a success or not.'

'I know, Mam.'

That was almost a recognition of her progress, Florence thought fondly, and philosophically. It would take a while for them to come round to her way of thinking, but she felt certain they would eventually. Everything was going swimmingly at the salon; if one ignored Darlene, and that Florence was determined to do.

They chatted for a while, Edie furnishing Florence with all the gossip of the village; who'd died, who'd given birth, and sadly, which husband had left which wife.

'I don't know what the world's coming to,' Edie said. 'Where are the values people used to have?'

The time had come to talk about Rita's predicament, Florence realised, and felt nauseated at the thought. She'd been putting it off moment to moment. But how to begin such a delicate subject? She didn't know the right words to describe Ken. There were derogatory names Darlene and Marge used to make fun of such men, but she couldn't bring herself to utter them herself, especially not to her mother.

'Rita came to see me last Monday,' Florence started, fighting the rise of shame and nausea.

Edie looked surprised.

'I thought you two had quarrelled.'

'That was my fault,' Florence admitted. 'Now I'm sorry.'

'Well, I'm glad you're friends again,' Edie said, with satisfaction. 'It doesn't do for relatives to be at odds. How is she? Any signs of a family?'

Florence took a deep breath. 'No.'

She'd been hoping her mother would ask that very question, but now she found she couldn't take advantage of the opening it provided. Everything Rita had told her was so horrible and disgusting, she was unable to utter a word about it. It wasn't as if her cousin had asked her to reveal her plight to the family; indeed, quite the opposite. Rita didn't want her father in trouble for taking revenge on Ken, as he very well might. She knew her own father would.

But how could she let Rita go on suffering? It was awful!

'I don't think she's very happy,' Florence went on lamely.

'Oh?' Edie gave a questioning look.

'Ken's ... difficult...'

Her mother was frowning now.

385

'What's the matter, Florence? Your face has gone very red.'

Florence swallowed hard. She should be able to tell her mother anything, but they'd never talked about sex. Besides, what she'd learned about Ken Henderson was too shocking and obscene for her to speak openly about it to anyone. She just didn't have the courage.

'I'm getting a cold in the head, I think,' she said evasively, and mentally berated herself for her cowardice.

She'd help Rita some other way.

CHAPTER 26

The following Tuesday evening, Florence was surprised to see Cliff outside the salon waiting for her to let him in.

'This is a surprise,' Florence said, wondering why he'd called so early in the week.

Cliff removed his trilby as he came through the door.

'Can't come Thursday. I'll be on a long haul up to Newcastle,' he explained.

She was pleased to see him. She'd been thinking about Rita too much these last few days, and was glad of the diversion. The thought of her cousin having to bear Ken's violent abuse for one more day, let alone weeks, plagued Florence's mind. She felt she'd betrayed Rita in a most lily-livered manner in not speaking up, and was racking her brain to find another way to help her, to no avail.

But Cliff was here now, and for the moment she'd find some distraction.

Florence made some tea, and Cliff settled on a kitchen chair, making himself at home as usual.

'How's the kids?' Florence asked, taking some biscuits out of a tin and putting them on a plate. 'You could've brought them with you.'

'They're okay.' He grinned, reaching for a biscuit. 'And enough's enough.'

He helped himself to a small spoonful of sugar

and stirred the tea.

'Heard from Lil?'

'Not a word,' Florence said with a sigh of resignation. 'You know, I think she's up there enjoying herself instead of seeing to salon business.'

Florence was about to refill his teacup when she heard the door of the flat slam shut, and the echoing sound of high-heel shoes clicking across the linoleum in the big living-room.

Florence and Cliff stared at each other in dismay.

'What the hell!' Cliff uttered in a hoarse whisper. 'Who's that?'

Florence felt the hairs on the back of her neck stand on end as a voice called her name; the unmistakable voice of Lillian.

'Flo! Where are you? I'm back.'

Before either of them could move, the kitchen door was jerked open and Lillian breezed in. She stopped in her tracks and the wide smile on her face froze as Cliff jumped guiltily to his feet.

Florence rose, too, her mouth going suddenly dry with embarrassment. They'd been caught out!

'What's this?' Lillian stormed, her expression furious.

'I wasn't expecting you,' Florence said lamely.

'Obviously!'

'I'd better go,' Cliff said, reaching for his trilby nearby.

'No, wait, Cliff!' Florence said defiantly. 'I pay rent on this flat. I can invite who I like here.' She turned her indignant gaze on Lillian. 'How did you get in here, Lillian?'

'My own key,' she snapped back, glaring at Cliff with visible hatred. 'This is my property, after all.'

'And my tenancy,' Florence answered wrathfully. 'You've got no business using your key without my permission. I didn't invite you in. It's an invasion of privacy, that's what it is.'

'Privacy!' Lillian's eyes glittered. 'I can see why you need privacy, you little slut! You've been carrying on with *him* behind my back.'

'*What?*'

Florence felt hot blood of fury rise up her neck into her cheeks. She was appalled at Lillian's accusation and embarrassed, too, in front of Cliff.

'You've got the wrong idea, Lillian,' Florence said defensively, feeling the heat of embarrassment grow.

'Oh yeah!' Lillian sneered. 'I was right about you from the start. You couldn't get Tony so you latched on to his brother. You scheming tart, you!'

'Ooh!'

Florence stared wide-eyed at her opponent for a few seconds, speechless with indignation. There had been some accord between them over these last months. Now it was suddenly wiped away as though it had never been. Lillian was showing her true colours.

Florence managed to find her tongue at last.

'How dare you call me names, you old hag,' she shouted, enraged.

Lillian's eyes opened wide with shock and she remained silent, obviously stuck for words, and

Florence felt marginally better. Lillian was attacking them without giving them a chance to explain, and that was very unfair, Florence thought. But, she too, could exchange insult for insult.

She flung Lillian another challenging look to show she meant business.

'Your husband put you on the bread line, Lillian, don't forget that. You'd still be there if it wasn't for me.'

'Stop it! Both of you,' Cliff intervened, raising a hand for silence.

Florence flicked a look at him before turning her blazing glance back to Lillian. Trembling with fury, she had the urge to lunge at Lillian and scratch her eyes out.

'Lil, listen a minute,' Cliff said in a reasonable tone. 'There's no need for all this squabbling...'

'Don't speak to me, you rat!' Lillian spluttered, incensed. 'And clear off, now!'

'That's it!' Florence yelled, lifting an arm and waving it threateningly. 'You've gone too far. Get out yourself, Lillian. You're trespassing.'

Lillian bristled visibly.

'You can't order me out. I won't have it.'

'I've got my rights,' Florence said. 'You may be the landlady, but you can't come into my flat and insult me and my friends like this.'

'*Your flat!*' Spittle foamed at the corners of Lillian's mouth.

'It is, while I pay the rent,' Florence insisted defiantly, 'and who visits me is my business, not yours, and I'll thank you to keep your long nose out.'

Lillian's mouth worked furiously, but no words were emitted for a few seconds, as she struggled to regain composure.

Florence felt triumphant for a moment, then suddenly apprehensive. She'd gone too far. Her relationship with Lillian would never be the same again after this battle. Suddenly the future of their partnership looked more than a bit murky.

Lillian found her voice at last.

'I should've seen your dirty little game before,' she muttered, her face ashen. 'You persuaded me to let you have this place so you could carry on with him. But no more! I want you out of here, Florence. Out! As soon as you like.'

Florence was aghast, remembering suddenly that Lillian hadn't yet given her a rent book, and without that she didn't have a legal leg to stand on. She was angry with herself then, for having let Lillian get away with it.

'You can't do that,' she protested weakly.

'Oh, yes I can.' Lillian gave a crooked little smile of malice, clearly delighted that she'd scored a bull's eye. 'You don't have a rent book, right? So, you're evicted as from today. Pack your things and go. No one does the dirty on me and gets away with it.'

'No one except Tony,' Florence flared furiously, her hand itching to smack Lillian's face. 'You're not a very good judge of character, are you?'

'Shut up! Leave Tony out of this.'

'Oh, no I won't,' Florence snapped, outraged at the turn of events. 'It's all his fault. Talk about a rat!'

'I said, shut up!' Lillian stormed.

'You insult Cliff,' Florence pressed on determinedly. 'But it was him that really saved the business. We wouldn't be standing here now if it weren't for him.'

Lillian took a step back, looking momentarily uncertain.

'What do you mean?'

Florence swallowed hard. She had to tell now. It was only right that Lillian should know the truth for Cliff's sake, and for Florence's reputation, too. It wouldn't make any difference to the partnership now.

Too much had been said that couldn't be taken back, too much that couldn't be forgiven, at least, not by herself. Lillian's appalling insult had cut her to the quick, and she'd never be able to forgive the older woman.

'My parents didn't lend me the money to buy the partnership,' Florence said, her voice calmer now. 'They wouldn't have touched it with a barge pole! No! It was Cliff who saved *our* bacon, Lillian. He used his life-savings. I borrowed the money from him. That's why he's here. I'm bringing him up to date on his investment.'

Lillian stared from one to the other, thunderstruck. Then her eyes narrowed and she glared at Florence.

'You tricked me, you little crook! Paid me off with my own money!'

'Tony stole your money, not Cliff,' Florence shouted. 'You stupid fool of a woman!'

Lillian looked venomous.

'You knew I wanted nothing to do with the Longfords,' she hissed. 'You did this deliberately.

You're a scheming little fraud. But I've found out in time. You're out of this flat, and you're out of the business, too. Our partnership is dissolved. I always knew it would never work.'

Florence took a step forward. She was trembling from head to foot, not only from intense anger, but from consternation, too.

The thought that her hard-won dream could be snatched from her unfairly, shocked her. She wouldn't let it happen.

'Now, just one minute!' she said tensely. 'You can turn me out of the flat since you cleverly avoided giving me a rent book, but I'm staying in the business. You'd have to *buy* me out, and you haven't got the money, remember?'

Lillian's face was still chalky white. She stared at Florence in dismay, then her face hardened.

'I'll find a way.'

Florence tossed her head in triumph.

'Until you do, I'm still a partner in Terri's, and I'll have my say.'

Lillian looked grim.

'You're my enemy. I know that, now,' she grated. 'And none of the girls will take orders from you. I'll see to it. And don't forget–' Lillian's eyes gleamed with spite–'you haven't finished your apprenticeship, yet. Still got a year and a half to go. It won't be easy, I can guarantee.'

'You spiteful old witch!' Florence howled. 'I'm sorry I ever set foot inside Terri's...'

Florence paused at her own words. Yes, it was true in a way. She'd thought it the best in town. She couldn't have been more wrong.

'I didn't know Terri's had a rotten core, like

393

Tony,' she blurted. 'If it hadn't been for Cliff, saving me from him...'

'Flo!' Cliff intervened sharply. 'That's enough!'

Florence closed her mouth firmly, but fumed inside. Why shouldn't she tell Lillian the truth about her no-good husband? Why shouldn't she know the depths of his rottenness?

'What's she accusing Tony of?' Lillian demanded, eyes flashing.

'She's upset, Lil.'

'Huh!' Lillian's lip curled in disdain. 'Her kind don't get upset. Look at her! Only nineteen, and as hard as bloody nails. She's an alley cat, that's what she is.'

'Get out of this flat!' Florence exploded. 'I've paid my rent until the end of the week, and I've got some rights. Stop slandering me or I'll ... I'll have a solicitor on you.'

Lillian was scornful.

'Shameless hussy!'

With that parting shot she turned on her heels and left.

Listening to the sound of her steps hurrying across the linoleum in the big empty living-room, Florence felt a succession of chills pass through her.

She had to get out of the flat at the end of the week, and had nowhere to go. She couldn't go home, but would have to look for rooms. There wasn't much time to pick and choose, so she'd have to take the first thing that came along. It wasn't a very pleasant prospect.

Florence flopped down on a chair, her shoulders drooping in despair, tears ready to flow, but she got a grip on her feelings, not wanting to cry in front of Cliff.

Would her struggle to settle and find happiness never end?

She dreaded to think what the coming weeks, months, would be like, working alongside Lillian. Florence could picture Darlene's triumphant face, too.

Florence straightened up determinedly. She wouldn't let anything get her down. She'd fight on, because despite everything, somewhere along the way, she'd achieve all she ever dreamed about.

'Flo, I'm sorry,' Cliff said, standing near and placing a comforting hand on her shoulder. 'That's the last thing I wanted to happen.'

Florence stood up, lifting her chin in defiance.

'It's not your fault, Cliff,' she said, controlling her voice. 'Lillian had to know some time. I'll get over it.'

She regretted leaving the flat, though. She'd grown used to the place and felt comfortable, and yes, safe, here. Heaven only knew where she'd end up next.

'Remember my spare room?' Cliff asked lightly, as though reading her thoughts. 'The offer still stands to rent, kid.'

Florence glanced up at him, uncertain.

'Only temporary,' he said hastily, sitting down at the table again. 'Until you find something better. And you can have the run of the house.'

Florence felt a little embarrassed. How could she refuse without hurting him?

'What about the children?' she asked.

She knew they quite liked her, but how would they feel if she moved in?

'They'd love it,' Cliff assured her.

But Florence wasn't so sure. She shook her head, smiling at him gratefully.

'That's very kind of you,' she said. 'I do appreciate the offer, but…' She put a hand on his arm, smiling into his face. 'You're the kindest man, Cliff. Are you sure Tony's your brother?'

He laughed, then looked serious.

'What do you say, Flo?'

Florence bit her lip before answering.

'I don't think it would be … practical, Cliff. You know how tongues would wag. But thanks all the same.'

Florence rose from sleep the next morning with a heaviness about her. She always looked forward to her work in the salon, despite Darlene's antagonism, confident she could rise above it, with strength and steel in her backbone, like her mother.

But today, that inner strength had waned and she carried a ton of misery on her shoulders. There was no way she could lay down this burden, short of giving up, and she wouldn't do that. She must go on and on carrying it, and hope and pray somehow to find relief.

Lillian was already in the office at nine o'clock, much to Florence's dismay and astonishment, and had obviously been busy with her tongue.

Florence didn't bother to speak to her, but went straight into the kitchen, more concerned with her reception from the girls. Marge didn't look up or answer when Florence came in voicing her good morning greeting. Glenys's eyes were like saucers as they regarded her, an embarrassed flush tingeing her cheeks.

'Where's Nancy?' Florence asked in a determined voice.

She was still a boss here, and she would throw her weight about if necessary. Lillian wouldn't get the better of her.

No one answered, which made Florence's cheeks burn with fury.

'Do you believe everything Lillian tells you, Marge?' she demanded to know angrily.

'Why should *she* lie?' Marge muttered darkly. Her eyes narrowed. 'I *knew* there was something between you and Cliff.'

'You don't understand,' Florence insisted. 'He did lend me the money for the partnership, yes, but he's my business partner, that's all.'

At that moment, Darlene came through the back door from the lavatory in the yard.

'Sleeping partners, more like,' she said truculently, her eyes gleaming with enmity. 'You're a sly cat, aren't you? Making up to Cliff behind our backs.'

'It's not true!' Florence exclaimed.

'Don't give me that!' Darlene's face darkened in a scowl. 'Lillian said she caught you both in the act.'

Glenys gave a shocked gasp, staring at Florence in fascination.

'That's a dirty lie!' Florence shouted angrily, feeling her cheeks flush with embarrassment and humiliation. 'Cliff and I are business partners, I tell you! If Lillian is saying anything else, I'll … I'll have her for slander.'

Darlene's lip curled disdainfully at the weak threat, and Florence could still see antagonism in the older girl's eyes, and jealousy, too.

'I've had enough of this!' Florence said loudly. 'I'm going to have it out with Lillian now.'

Lillian had gone too far, telling such awful lies about her. Florence could guess at her motive, though. Her partner would try to force her out, if she could.

Well! We'll see who is the stronger, Florence thought in anger. She'd not let anyone take away what she'd achieved.

Lillian was still in the office, the accounts books open in front of her.

'Listen here, Lillian,' Florence began, barging into the room.

Lillian didn't look up, but her shoulders stiffened visibly. Florence was angered even more. She wouldn't be ignored like she was the office cat.

With a quick flick of the wrist, Florence reached forward and slammed shut the accounts book right under Lillian's nose. She sat back startled, glaring up at Florence, belligerence in every line of her face.

'You'd better listen to me, Lillian,' Florence wagged a finger at her. 'I've had just about enough of you and your dirty lies. I won't have it, see!'

'Bugger off, then!' Lillian answered savagely. 'Nobody wants you here. You're finished!'

'Like hell, I am!'

Florence was astonished and startled at her own strong language. But she realised it was necessary. It was the only language the likes of Lillian and Darlene understood. She'd fight fire with fire; meet them on their own terms.

'I'll see *you* out of here first,' Florence declared aggressively. 'I've got a stake in the place and I'm not budging.'

'It's Cliff that got the stake,' Lillian reminded her spitefully. 'You're just his mouthpiece. I don't even know whether the partnership is legal now.'

'Don't kid yourself, Lillian.' It was Florence's turn to be scornful. 'It's as legal as if I'd borrowed the money from a bank. I'm your partner and it'll stay that way. Make up your mind to it.'

Lillian was silent, glaring furiously.

Florence looked her partner steadfastly in the eyes.

'For a start,' she said determinedly. 'I want to know when we can expect the new stylist from London?'

'There isn't going to be a new stylist,' Lillian announced, with a smile of malicious satisfaction. 'From London or anywhere else.'

'What?' Florence was taken aback. 'You mean you couldn't get anyone to take the job?'

Lillian's smile was scornful.

'I mean, I didn't even try. Never intended to. It was a daft idea from the start. We can't afford it. And besides...' A strange look passed across her face. 'No one can replace Tony.'

Florence was speechless for a moment. She felt so angry she thought her head would explode from the pressure.

'Do you know what you've done?' Florence was beside herself with disappointment. 'You've thrown away our one chance to get back on top.'

'We're doing all right as we are.' Lillian was defensive.

'We could do better, much better,' Florence said fervently. 'Flaming Tony!' She glared at Lillian. 'You've set us back years. Years!'

Florence heard the salon door open and knew the clients had started to arrive for their appointments.

She looked at Lillian, her mouth set.

'I want my back pay in a lump sum.'

'What?'

'You heard me, Lillian,' Florence said in a hard voice. 'I sacrificed my full partners' salary to pay for a new stylist. If we're not getting one then I'm entitled to my back pay, and I want it in full. Pronto!'

She turned to leave the office, then paused, looking back at her partner.

'You won't get rid of me, Lillian. I'll fight you all the way, and any way I can, so be warned.'

For all her staunch words and her determination, Florence found it hard going. Nancy was the only one who'd co-operate with her.

Tired and fed up, she felt very miserable alone in the flat that evening. Lillian would never soften, that was obvious. She'd continue to hold a grudge, and would try to stir up the others against Florence whenever possible.

She felt very much alone. It struck her that she didn't have a real friend, someone she could turn to who would sympathise, except, perhaps, Cliff.

She thought about him; his support, and the warmth of his home. Was she being silly in refusing his offer of a room to rent? Why was she so reluctant?

She had to admit she felt awkward about it. People would talk; a widower and a girl living in the same house. But people were talking already, thanks to Lillian's lies, she reminded herself. Did it really matter what people thought? She needed somewhere to live, and she needed a friend.

Florence decided there and then she'd take Cliff up on his offer. She'd let him know first thing tomorrow. He'd take care of everything for her.

Although she didn't feel happy, Florence did have a sense of relief. War might rage between Lillian and herself from now on, but at least she'd have a safe haven each evening with Cliff.

CHAPTER 27

'You're looking really smart, Rita,' Sybil said with satisfaction. 'That's a lovely outfit you're wearing. Looks expensive, too.'

Rita didn't answer, but sat in an armchair, taking off her kid gloves and putting them with her crocodile-skin handbag at the side of the chair.

Her mind was in turmoil. It had taken all her courage to call on her mother today. Florence was right. She had to speak out against Ken, and must do it now, before it was too late. She was growing more and more afraid of him, and couldn't go on much longer like this.

But how could she find the words to explain her terrible plight; make her mother understand?

'Were any of the neighbours outside in the street when you came along?' Sybil asked, gloating. 'You put their noses out of joint, I bet. It's time you joined the WI, too. Your expensive outfits will give Mrs Prosser-Rees something to think about.'

'Where's Da?'

'Tsk! Father, Rita, Father! It's common to say Da.' Sybil sniffed disapproval. 'Anyway, he's up the shed, tinkering with that blood ... that blinking wireless set. I won't have it in the house now. The screeching drives me mad. He can go and sit up the shed if he wants to mess with it.'

Rita felt relief. She could never say what she had to in front of her father. It would be hard enough telling her mother.

'Is he likely to come in, Mother?'

'Not until teatime.' Sybil sat on the settee, and crossed her legs. 'Now, then, Rita,' she said with obvious relish. 'Tell me, are you and Ken planning to go abroad for your summer holidays? I was telling Mrs Prosser-Rees that my daughter, Mrs Kenneth Henderson, of Henderson's Stores, Sketty, will probably be taking a holiday in the South of France this year.'

Rita clenched her teeth in misery. Sybil could have no idea of the kind of world her daughter had entered, and the fear and revulsion she felt for her husband.

'There won't be any holiday, Mam.'

Sybil sat forward, looking piqued.

'Why ever not?'

Rita swallowed hard.

'Because ... because I'm leaving Ken.'

'*What?*' Sybil jumped to her feet as though shot from a cannon. 'What did you say?'

'I'm leaving him. I want to come home, Mam. I've made a terrible mistake.'

Sybil sank back onto the settee.

'Oh, nonsense!'

She gave Rita a knowing look.

'It's ... bed, isn't it? We've all had to put up with it, Rita. It's the price we women have to pay for having the security of marriage. Ken'll get tired of you... What I mean is, in time they're less demanding.'

'Mam, you don't understand.'

'Of course I do.' Sybil pulled in her chin, looking smug. 'Your father was full of himself when we were first married, but I soon put a stop to that. You've got to be firm, Rita. Tell him you've got a headache or something...'

'Mam! Don't be so damned stupid, will you,' Rita cried out desperately, jumping to her feet. 'I have a serious problem, and it won't go away by pretending it's not there. My marriage is a sham, a pitiful, shameful fraud!'

Sybil stared.

'What are you talking about, Rita?'

She bit hard on her bottom lip, struggling to find the right words; words her mother could understand. She must start with the less shameful aspect of her marriage.

'Ken beats me, Mam.'

'What?' Sybil gave a short, disbelieving laugh. 'I don't believe it! Ken's a gentleman. You've only got to look at him to see that.'

'Ken is a beast! A disgusting beast.'

Rita sank back into the armchair and after a moment's hesitation, unbuttoned her jacket and her blouse, pulling the garments down over her shoulders.

Her recent bruises were still dark and angry-looking, the oldest yellowing her skin. She couldn't bear to look at them anymore; the pain she'd suffered was sharp in her memory. She looked pleadingly at her mother in silence, praying for deliverance.

Sybil looked visibly concerned at the sight of Rita's arms and shoulders, and the purple stains on her chest, which her slip couldn't quite hide.

But after a moment, Sybil's face relaxed, her concern dissipating. She peered at Rita suspiciously.

'Why haven't you mentioned this before?'

'I was ashamed.'

'Your trouble is you're too timid, Rita; weakwilled,' Sybil said dismissively. 'I've said it before. You've got to stand up for yourself, my girl. Ken loses patience with you. That's what it is. He's got a position to keep up. He can't be bothered with a namby-pamby wife who's afraid of her own shadow.'

Rita couldn't believe her ears. She stared at Sybil in dismay. Did her mother have no feeling, no understanding?

'Mam! Are you really saying that it's my own fault that Ken beats me? Do you think it's right that he should do it?'

'Well! Of course not!' Sybil tossed her head. 'But that's the way men are, isn't it?'

'Da has never laid a hand on you, Mam.'

There was a faint sneer on Sybil's face which roused Rita's anger, and she knew what her mother was about to say. She'd heard it all before.

'That's different,' Sybil said. 'Your father's weak, too. Always has been.'

'You ignorant, cruel woman,' Rita burst out. 'You don't deserve a man like Da. You don't know what life's all about. Da is the salt of the earth; a *real* man, not like Ken.'

Sybil stood up abruptly.

'Don't you speak to me like that. I'm your mother.'

Rita's lip curled with contempt.

'Mother! You haven't got the foggiest idea how to be a mother. You're selfish and grasping...'

'Ooh!' Sybil's eyes were almost popping with indignation.

But Rita wouldn't stop now. She'd been longing to say these things for years. It occurred to her, for just a brief moment, that she was scuttling any chance of coming home. But that didn't seem to matter, not in the rush of exhilaration at finally telling her mother off.

'Auntie Edie is what I call a good mother,' Rita went on ruthlessly. 'You've always been jealous of her, haven't you, Mam? Because you *know* she's better than you.'

Sybil drew in a deep breath, her bosom swelling with fury, and she glared at her daughter.

'How dare you, Rita! This is outrageous, this is. After all I've done for you.'

Rita glared, anger bitter in her mouth. She wanted to pay her mother back for all the repression she'd suffered; for all the abuse and neglect Sybil had meted out to Ronnie Bevan over the years because he couldn't get her all the things she clamoured for and coveted.

'What you did for me? Oh, yes,' Rita said. 'I want to pay you back for that. It was you that made me marry Ken Henderson, simply because he has money. I'm paying for your greed.'

'A few bruises?' Sybil drew in her chin con-temptuously. 'You'll live! You're on your high horse now, but you'll thank me later.'

For a moment Rita was speechless at her mother's gall and her lack of humanity.

'Bruises are the least of my suffering,' she said quietly. 'Ken Henderson is ... I don't know the proper word for the kind of man he is, but ... sexually...'

Rita paused as her mother visibly cringed at her use of the word, then repeated herself deliberately.

'Sexually, he prefers men, young men, to women. He hates me, hates all women, so he tells me, and I believe him!'

Sybil stood silently, her mouth dropped open, her face white with shock.

'His hatred doesn't stop him coming to my bed, though, to abuse me,' Rita went on miserably.

The exhilaration of a moment ago was leaving her, and she felt washed out and drained of all spirit.

'He enjoys the violence, you see,' she said listlessly. 'And my humiliation. He treats me as he would any young man he picks up. He brings them to the house. Oh, yes!' she went on as her mother stared anew. 'Disgusting, isn't it? And this is my life, Mam.'

Sybil flopped onto the settee. Colour was coming back into her cheeks. By the sharp movement of her eyes, Rita knew her mother's brain was working at full speed. The intense expression on her face was familiar, too. She was scheming, weighing up the damage to herself.

Rita felt a great weight of despair on her shoulders. It was plain her mother wouldn't help her leave Ken. All Sybil thought about was her own image.

'Does anyone know about Ken?' Sybil asked. There was furtiveness in her glance at Rita.

'Ken's very careful. He could go to prison. I've told Florence. I had to tell someone.'

Sybil was agitated and angry. Her cheeks flushed bright red.

'That was really stupid, Rita! She'll blab to everyone. I'll … we'll be a laughing stock.' She placed both hands dramatically on her breast, and closed her eyes. 'Oh! The scandal.'

'What about the hell I'm going through, Mam?' Rita cried out desperately. 'Physically as well as emotionally. I have to leave Ken; get away from him. But he's threatened me, Mam, if I do. I need protection.'

Sybil squared her shoulders and lifted her chin.

'You mustn't leave him,' she declared firmly. 'You must hang on to everything you've got.'

Rita stared at her mother aghast.

'Think, Rita! Think!' Sybil cried out impatiently at the expression on her daughter's face. 'You have all the money you could possibly need or want. And you can demand more from him. Use him! Have a bit of gumption for once.'

'Do you know what you're saying, Mam? I can't stand any more of him. I'd … I'd rather kill myself…'

'Oh, don't be so melodramatic,' Sybil exclaimed in a bullying tone. 'If you had a bit of backbone you'd control him.'

'I'm afraid of him, Mam. He goes mad, sometimes. The look in his eyes when he's punching me; forcing me…' Rita buried her face in her hands. 'He enjoys every moment, every blow. I'm terrified. Don't you understand?'

'Huh! Pull yourself together, Rita, for heaven's sake!' Sybil's tone was contemptuous, and Rita knew her visit today had been useless. Her mother had no intention of protecting her or helping her. The realisation rallied her spirit.

'I'm leaving him, Mam,' she exclaimed defiantly. 'I'm divorcing him, and I don't care what you say. I want to come home straight away.'

Sybil's nostrils flared with anger.

'You'll do no such thing. Divorce will bring the whole thing out in public. I'll be shamed if Mrs Prosser-Rees gets to know.'

She shook her head emphatically.

'I tell you, Rita, I'd never get over it. It would kill me!' Her mouth took on a hard line. 'If you bring scandal to me, Rita, then you're no daughter of mine. I'll want nothing more to do with you.'

'Mam!'

'Your grandfather would have a fit,' Sybil went on relentlessly. 'We've always been a respectable family. It's your duty to us, Rita, to keep Ken's … problem a secret. And no more talking about your business to that Florence, either. All I hope is the little minx keeps her mouth shut.'

CHAPTER 28

Florence moved into Cliff's house in Catherine Street on the following Saturday. He took care of everything; even found a burly friend to help manhandle the bed and cooker down the stairs to the removal van.

The front bedroom at Catherine Street was quite adequate for Florence's needs. Cliff guaranteed her utmost privacy, and at the same time, assured her she had the run of the house.

The children were shy of her at first but within days Florence had them eating out of her hand. She didn't make too much of a fuss over them, however, very conscious that this accommodation was only temporary, and she didn't want to complicate their young lives too much.

The following weeks at the salon seemed to pass slowly, with her working life much more difficult than she'd imagined. She was bitterly disappointed that there was to be no new stylist, and felt they would regret Lillian's selfish and short-sighted attitude in the future.

There *was* one good aspect, however. She demanded and got a full partnership salary, and felt more affluent than she had for a long time. She wanted to start repaying Cliff, so that he should at last see a return on his money. But he insisted that he could wait a little longer. Wait, he said, until the business was really back on its feet.

Florence wondered, somewhat gloomily, when that might be. Working at the salon was uncomfortable, even more so than the time when Tony was there. She was glad when leaving work at the close of business each night to have a place where she could find peace, relaxation and friendship.

But even that posed a problem. Florence told no one at the salon about renting a room with Cliff, but somehow, Darlene got wind of it, and had been vile, raking up malicious gossip about them again, openly insulting Florence to her face in front of the others, and even the clients.

There was little Florence could do about it without Lillian's support. Obviously her partner saw Florence's move as confirmation of what she'd already asserted, and far from supporting her, she seemed to encourage Darlene.

More tactics to oust her, Florence thought, feeling the pressure build. Darlene's malignant gossip wounded her, and caused her painful embarrassment. But that pain made her even more determined, and she knew she'd have to thicken her skin to survive.

With well over a year of her apprenticeship still to run, she was anxious that there would be no interruption of her training. Lillian was cold, and ignored her for the most part. Expecting and receiving no civility or co-operation from Darlene, Florence relied on a neutral Nancy, and sometimes Marge for training. Florence was determined to see the year through to qualification, come what may.

After the term of apprenticeship, her future was

vague in her imagination. She'd thought that a partnership in Terri's was the be-all and end-all; her dream come true. Now she was realising, more and more each day, that this was a false dream. She wanted to own her own hairdressing business outright, with no awkward partners getting in her way, holding her back on the climb to success and recognition.

Setting her face firmly against opposition and hostility at the salon, Florence was determined to battle on. She would come out on top, despite them all.

She'd been at Catherine Street three weeks, when one Sunday morning she had a caller, and was astonished to find her father standing on the doorstep.

'Dad!'

Florence recovered from her surprise quickly. She opened the door wider.

'There's nice to see you, Dad. Come on in.'

There seemed to be reluctance in the way he stepped over the threshold and hesitated in the passage.

Florence smiled encouragement.

'The living-room is at the end of the passage, Dad. Here, let me take your overcoat.'

There was another split second of hesitation before he let Florence help him out of the coat. And she noticed that so far he hadn't said one word.

'Is Mr Longford here, Flo?'

'Who? Oh, you mean Cliff?' Florence shook her head, laughing. 'No. He's on a haulage job to Scotland. He won't be back until Tuesday. We've got the place to ourselves, except for the children, of course. I'm just preparing some vegetables for dinner.'

Her father relaxed a little and followed her more readily into the living-room. The two children were sitting on the mat in front of the fire, each with a comic book. They looked up silently at William.

'This is my dad,' Florence felt obliged to explain.

She was still conscious of their territorial rights, and was careful not to take advantage.

In the past, Cliff had enlisted the help of neighbours to tend the children's needs while he was away on short hauls. Now that Florence was there constantly as a lodger, he was able to take more lucrative longer hauls, knowing she would look after the children. And she was glad to do it.

The children's interest in William was short-lived and they returned to their reading.

'Sit down, Dad.'

'Want to talk to you, I do, Flo,' her father said quietly. 'In private, like.'

Florence sat beside him on the sofa.

'Oh, don't mind them, Dad,' she said, indicating the children.

William looked uncomfortable despite her reassurance. He adjusted his spectacles, fidgeted with his tie, took a pipe out of his jacket pocket, pressed the blackened tobacco in the bowl with a thumb, then put the pipe back in his pocket.

'What I've come to say is ... delicate...'

'I don't understand, Dad. Is everything all right at home? Is Mam ill?'

'Everything's fine, but, Flo, we're very concerned that you've taken this serious step.'

'What are you talking about?'

'Your Auntie Sybil told me that you've taken up with this Cliff Longford; that you're living with him in...' William gulped, embarrassed, '...in sin.'

'*What?*'

'Flo, this is the worst thing you've ever done,' William rushed on. 'Your mother and I are ashamed of you, and for you. We want you to end this now. Come home. Try to get back some self-respect.'

'*What?*'

Florence jumped to her feet.

'How can you believe that evil-tongued, poisonous, malicious woman? Oh, I know she's your sister, Dad, but that woman is a viper.'

William got to his feet, too, staring in astonishment at her outburst.

'Flo!'

Florence was shaking with fury. She wanted to hit out at something. If Auntie Sybil were here now, Florence knew she'd be hard-pressed not to strike her aunt.

Why was it that people, even her own family, thought the worst of her; thought her capable of loose behaviour? Was it because she had chosen to live her own life, establish an independence? She refused to knuckle down like other girls. Did that make her hard, worldly and immoral? It seemed most people thought so, even her own father.

'I know since the war, people of all ages have

lowered their standards, but I'm not one of them,' Florence cried out, with energy. 'And if you are willing to think the worst of me, Dad, then we've nothing more to say to each other.'

William reached out a hand to her.

'Flo! Please! Don't be like that.'

'No, Dad.' Florence wrapped her arms around herself. She was trembling so much, suddenly cold right through. 'You believe Auntie Sybil. Nothing ever changes, does it? You've never believed in me, never had faith in me. In your eyes I was a failure from the time I was born...'

'Flo, now you're going too far, being unfair...'

'Unfair!' Florence cried. 'After all I've achieved you still doubt me. Today there aren't many girls my age who have got the gumption, nerve and backbone to do what I've done.'

She took a deep breath before rushing on.

'I'm a partner in business, with all the privileges that brings. In many ways I'm your equal, Dad; yours and Mam's. I've done in a short time what it took you and Mam years to achieve. And you still refuse to recognise it.'

'Flo, I'm sorry, *cariad.*'

Florence took in another gulp of air, trying to steady her heart which was racing away like a steam engine. Her father's accusation of immorality was the last straw.

'Sorry isn't enough, Dad. I'm a lodger in this house. Cliff respects me and I respect him.'

'People gossip...' William ventured.

'Evil people, like Auntie Sybil,' Florence said. 'She's got her own skeleton in the closet. This gossip about me is a smoke screen.'

William looked puzzled again.

'I don't understand.'

She couldn't possibly explain.

'Ask Auntie Sybil.'

She lifted her chin, struggling not to burst into tears.

'Now, Dad, I'll be glad if you'll excuse me. I have things to do.'

Florence's resentment lasted throughout the day. It was only when she was sitting alone before the fire, the children in bed, that she began to regret her sharp words to her father, and couldn't control her tears.

He just didn't deserve it. He was a good and loving father. It was Auntie Sybil who was to blame, and once again she'd successfully caused strife in her brother's family.

Florence dabbed at her brimming eyes, wishing Cliff was here to talk it over. For the first time she realised she was missing him, and wondered at it. It seemed a long time until Tuesday.

CHAPTER 29

July 1950

Peter and Tansy scrambled down from the table and ran into the front room to play. Florence got up, too, and began collecting the dishes they'd used for tea, feeling heavy and listless.

She'd spent a most horrible day at the salon, ending up quarrelling savagely again with Lillian. These constant battles were taking it out of her, and she wondered for the umpteenth time this week how much more she could stand, and was it all worth it?

She sighed heavily as she turned towards the kitchenette.

'Flo? Leave the dishes, kid,' Cliff said as he got to his feet. 'I'll do them later. Come and sit down. You look washed out. I think you need to talk, don't you?'

There was such sympathy and understanding in his voice that Florence felt like bursting into tears, but struggled to retain her composure, realising that feeling sorry for herself and giving way wouldn't help her situation at all.

Cliff was the only one she could turn to these days. She hadn't seen or heard anything from her family since that Sunday in late March when she'd dismissed her father so curtly and resentfully. She bitterly regretted that. She had been hurt, but she'd also been unforgivably rude to him. What must he think of her now?

Cliff sat on the sofa and patted the place next to him.

'Come by here, Flo, love.'

Although they'd agreed that her stay at Catherine Street was only temporary, Florence had made little or no effort to find other lodgings. She knew how much she'd miss Cliff's company, and the children's, too, and dreaded the prospect of being alone again. She wondered if Cliff thought she was imposing, but couldn't bring herself to ask.

Florence sat down beside him now, leaning back thankfully against the sofa.

'Now pour it all out,' Cliff advised kindly. 'That's the best way.'

Florence shook her head.

'Where to begin?' she asked helplessly. 'Basically, Cliff, I'm at rock-bottom at the salon. I'm ready to quit. Yes, I am!'

'Then do it!' he said. 'Nothing's worth unhappiness.'

Florence sighed, managing a rueful smile.

'I *must* keep going though, mustn't I?' she said wistfully. 'My apprenticeship doesn't finish until September next year. But trying to get my training is like trying to get blood out of a stone. Lillian and that blasted Darlene try to sink me at every turn. They're real...'

Florence glanced at Cliff, embarrassed.

He grinned. 'Go on, say it!' he urged. 'It'll make you feel better.'

Florence clenched her fists, her cheeks flushed.

'They're real bitches!' she burst out.

Surprisingly, she did feel better for giving vent to her feelings in strong language. It had its uses.

'The other thing is, business is good, really good,' Florence went on after a moment, feeling calmer. 'The salon is almost back where it was before Tony left. And there's your investment to think of, Cliff. Lillian is so tricky. You might lose your money if I just up and go.'

'Don't worry about that,' Cliff said reassuringly. 'What's best for you, that's what's important ... to me.'

Florence leaned forward, hands clasped in front of her.

'Besides, I'm not a quitter!' she declared with energy. 'I'd hate myself later if I did.'

She straightened up, rallying her strength. It was kind of Cliff to be sympathetic, and she was grateful, but if she gave up now she'd be admitting that everything her parents thought about her ability, or lack of it, was true. The fight must go on to the bitter end, because any other course of action was unthinkable in her philosophy.

'How long before Lil can buy you out, do you think?' Cliff asked.

Florence looked quickly at him. He *was* anxious about his investment. He was probably sorry he'd become involved. Well, she couldn't blame him.

'Another year, perhaps,' she replied listlessly, looking down at her hands. 'It hasn't been very profitable for you, Cliff, has it?'

'I'm not interested in profit, Flo. I'm interested in you.'

'You're a good friend...'

421

He rose abruptly from the sofa to stand near the mantelpiece. His movement was so sudden and sharp that Florence wondered if she'd said or done something to offend him, and was immediately concerned. She'd hate to do that because he was so kind, and generous, too.

She looked up to see he was watching her in the small ornamental mirror hanging over the fireplace. His expression was strange, and for a moment her concern turned to puzzlement.

'The ideal thing for you, Flo, would be your own business,' he said at last, and Florence was startled at his insight.

She laughed. 'You're a mind-reader.'

'No, Flo,' he answered with a crooked little smile. 'I know you so well. If Lil bought you out, you could do that. Nothing very glitzy, but it'd be your own.'

Florence lowered her gaze.

'I can't forget it's your money we're talking about, Cliff. Any business would never be really be mine, would it?'

'Yes, it could!'

He strode quickly back to the sofa, sat down and took hold of her hand.

'Flo, listen!' There was urgency in his voice that made her stare. 'I've got something to ask you.'

He drew in a very deep breath. Florence saw that strange look on his face again, and wondered what was coming next. His expression was very serious and strained, and for some reason the skin on the back of her neck began to prickle, and heat rose to her face. She almost snatched her hand away, but caught the impulse in time.

'Don't be frightened or upset, Flo...'

'Cliff?'

In one swift movement he was down on one knee before her, still holding her hand. Florence's mouth dropped open and she could only stare at him in astonishment for a moment before finding her tongue.

'What *are* you doing, Cliff?'

'Proposing marriage,' he said breathlessly, his face turning pale, and with a worried look around his eyes. 'Now, don't be frightened...'

'I'm not the one who's frightened, Cliff,' she said.

And she wasn't. She was just astounded, taken completely by surprise.

He looked hurt, and reminded her of the way his son Peter looked sometimes.

'Don't laugh at me, Flo, please.'

Florence was aghast at the idea.

'Cliff! I wouldn't do that...'

'I love you, Flo,' he burst out earnestly. 'I've loved you for a long time. Will you marry me?'

He was gripping her hand so tightly now, and looking at her so gravely, as though her answer was the only thing in the world that mattered to him.

Perhaps it was! The thought really frightened her then. Not that she was afraid of him, but afraid *for* him. If her answer was no. If...?

Even as she stared at him she realised part of her mind was considering it seriously, not dismissing the idea outright. That surprised her.

'I'd no idea you felt like this,' she answered lamely, out of her depth. 'Marriage?' she went on.

423

'That's a big step... I don't know...'

A flash of relief passed across his features.

'You haven't said no, Flo. Maybe there's a hope for me?'

She was about to say that this was such a surprise, but checked herself. That was so hackneyed, and he might think she was mocking him again. But his feelings for her *were* a surprise, and she didn't know how to answer.

Why had she never suspected? Was she so wrapped up in herself that other people's feelings were invisible to her? That aspect of herself wasn't very appealing.

'I need time, Cliff.' It was all she could say at the moment.

'Of course you do, Flo.' But he continued to kneel.

She pulled at his hand.

'Get up, Cliff, please,' she said, troubled by what she saw as a demeaning position for a man like him. 'There's no need to kneel.'

He seemed relieved to sit on the sofa again, but perched right on the edge, appearing uncertain.

'I want to do things right.'

Florence gave a nervous laugh.

'To do things right you'd have to ask my father's permission, and I don't recommend that.'

Florence was immediately sorry she'd said that. Cliff couldn't know how much her parents disapproved of him, but he could probably guess.

'Oh!' Cliff stared at her, obviously disconcerted. 'Yes, of course. There's the age difference, and I've been in prison.' He looked crestfallen. 'I suppose I should've spoken with your father first.'

Florence shook her head, emphatically.

'It's not necessary, Cliff,' she reassured him. 'I'll be twenty this year, and I'll marry who I please.'

'Is that an answer?' He looked eager, and so hopeful it wrenched at her heart. 'You mean the age difference and prison don't matter to you?'

'I'm not giving my answer yet.' Florence wetted her lips nervously. Something prevented her saying no straight away, and she wanted to think it through. 'But I will give it thought.'

That sounded so cold and calculating. Maybe she had her answer there? She looked up at him, feeling shy for the first time in their friendship.

'Before I say yes or no, Cliff, I should make *my* feelings clear. I like you. Yes, I'm even fond of you, but I can't pretend I love you. I've never thought of you in that way. You've always been my friend.'

He leaned forward eagerly, his eyes shining.

'You'll come to love me, Flo, I know you will, once we're married.' He hesitated, then rushed on ardently, pressing her hand. 'I want you, Flo, I want you, badly.'

He drew back at Florence's startled look.

'Please,' he pleaded, obviously concerned that he'd scared her away. 'Don't be alarmed. I'm not like Tony. I'm a patient man. I really love you, Flo, and I'd never hurt you, force you...' He gave a deep sigh. 'I can wait for your love, wait until you're ready.'

She had no doubt he meant it. She took a

moment to look at him properly, seeing aspects of him for the first time.

Cliff was a good-looking man, no doubt about that. His dark, curly hair was glossy and plentiful; falling over his forehead, it lapped his shirt collar. Florence smiled. He needed a haircut.

He had a good build, tall and broad-shouldered. Many women, Darlene, for instance, would give all they owned for the love of such a man. He was kind, considerate. He'd be a gentle lover, Florence thought, then blushed at the new notion.

Cliff spotted the change in her complexion straight away.

'What?' he asked. 'What are you thinking?'

She couldn't possibly tell him. She gently withdrew her hand from his.

'My mind's in turmoil,' she replied. 'I must sort things out.'

She meant her own emotions, but she couldn't explain. Her thoughts were jumbled, and she didn't understand her reluctance to refuse him outright. Did her feelings go deeper than she realised?

'You'll want to ask your parents, I expect?'

'No!' Florence was definite about that. 'It's *my* life and none of their concern, really.'

She rose from the sofa, and he stood, obviously anxious.

'I'll go to my room now, Cliff,' she said firmly. 'I want to be on my own. I'll ... I'll let you have an answer tomorrow. I promise.'

Florence went to bed early, knowing she

wouldn't sleep. Alone now and able to think more clearly, she could hardly believe Cliff had asked her to be his wife.

One thing struck her immediately. If she refused him she'd have to leave the comfort and security of her lodgings in Catherine Street. She'd have to stop seeing him. Feeling the way he did, he couldn't be her friend anymore, and that made her very sad.

It dawned on her then how alone she was. But she was a loner, though. She went to the pictures now and then, but always alone. She wasn't interested in going out dancing, to parties, having a good time, trying to meet boys, like many girls of her age. Perhaps she was too ambitious?

She always thought she'd marry one day; one day in the distant future. There was plenty of time. She'd meet someone, someday. But would he love her as much as Cliff did?

Ken briefly came to mind. She'd fancied herself in love with him, and he with her. She hadn't been very perceptive to recognise him as a sham.

What did she know about love, anyway? For all she knew she did love Cliff and didn't realise it.

If she married him, his loan to her would be finished, because she'd be his wife. Florence gave this thought only fleeting consideration, but at the same time, she had a strong sense of obligation.

She did owe Cliff so much: he'd saved her from Tony, saved the business, and he gave freely of his friendship and support. She trusted him, and perhaps most important of all, he really loved her.

She could do much worse than marry him. She thought of poor Rita, and the mistake she'd made. At least Florence knew Cliff thoroughly. They could be happy together. They got on so well.

Lying there in the darkness, Florence began to visualise what her life would be like in future. She'd have a steady man in Cliff, someone she was sure of. She'd be taking on the responsibility of the children, of course, but that didn't bother her. She enjoyed looking after them.

What about children of her own?

Florence felt a sense of excitement at this idea. She was ambitious and determined to be a success in business, yet having her own family was also vitally important. Could she be a successful businesswoman and a successful mother? Well, why not?

Married to Cliff, starting her own family, she wouldn't be alone anymore. It sounded good. She was convinced it would be. Her future looked very inviting after all.

With Cliff, she'd finally learn what love is.

'A special licence, Flo, love!' Cliff beamed at her across the breakfast table. 'I'll see about it this morning.'

Florence laughed, feeling genuinely happy. It'd been a long time since she'd felt so light-hearted.

'You're in a hurry!' she teased. 'Afraid I'll change my mind?'

'You'll break my heart, kid, if you do.'

His breakfast of spam fritters neglected, he put both elbows on the table, chin on hands, gazing at her.

'I do love you, Flo. I'll never hurt you, I promise. Everything I work for will be for us and the kids.' He gave a little shake of his head. 'I can't believe it's true!'

His eyes looked moist, and yet he looked so ecstatic with happiness, that Florence was moved beyond words.

She felt very proud, yet overawed, that she could inspire such deep feelings in anyone. Perhaps one day she'd feel the same about him. How could she fail to be happy in her new life with such devotion all for her alone?

A special licence would be just right. She didn't want her family to get wind of the marriage beforehand. A quiet and private ceremony, and the sooner the better. This was an important step in her life and no acrimony must spoil it.

Sipping her tea and taking another bite of toast, she wondered how Lillian and Darlene would react when they discovered she was Cliff's wife, and laughed outright.

'What's tickled you, love?' Cliff asked eagerly, fork halfway to his mouth.

'Darlene will be livid!' Florence said. 'She fancies you like mad, you know, Cliff?'

He was dismissive. 'She never stood a chance, I can tell you that!'

A new notion struck Florence.

'Oh, my goodness!' She stared at Cliff aghast. 'Do you realise that Lillian will be my sister-in-law?'

Cliff grinned. 'There's always a fly in the ointment.'

CHAPTER 30

February 1951

It was raining yet again! Florence felt the dampness seep right through her Burberry and cardigan as she stood in the bus queue outside the hospital on St Helens Road. Two double-deckers, packed with wet passengers, had already splashed past them without stopping.

The waiting seemed endless, but a bus came eventually. It was crowded too. Florence climbed up to the top deck. It was hot and muggy up on top. Everyone's clothes seemed to be steaming, fogging up the windows. Would it ever stop raining?

The bleakness of the weather was echoed in her thoughts. She'd been worried all the week; worried because she'd missed a period. The prospect of pregnancy filled her with something like panic. It was too soon.

Business at the salon was really booming, but Florence felt her hold on the partnership was tenuous. She'd hung on despite every dirty trick Lillian had pulled to get rid of her over these last twelve months. Having a baby would really sink her, she knew. She'd been too confident in thinking that business and motherhood could be balanced. They couldn't, not in her present precarious position, not if both were to be successful. She wanted children, but later, not

431

yet. After all, she was still only twenty. There was plenty of time.

Florence hadn't told Cliff about her suspicions, not wanting to see the excitement in his eyes. She couldn't match it, couldn't be as enthusiastic, and that would hurt him. She wouldn't do that – not intentionally.

He'd been so good to her, patient and understanding. A week after the wedding ceremony she accepted she could no longer deny him, yet she'd never be ardent either.

Cliff said he had enough love for both of them, but over these last months Florence became less and less sure. She tried hard to return his love, but couldn't. Without love there was no excitement.

He was her husband and she didn't want to hurt him, yet instinctively she knew she was missing out on one of the most important things in life: returning love, sharing love with someone very dear.

She got off the bus at the station and walked back down High Street, past the Mackworth Hotel. The rain bounced off the pavements, soaking her stockings and shoes. She hated having wet feet. Her mother always warned her about that. If only she had time to put her feet in a bowl of hot water and mustard, just to be on the safe side, but there was no hope of that. Several clients were booked for perms first thing, so she'd have to stand around all morning with her shoes and stockings drying on her feet. Ugh!

Florence ran the last few yards to the salon door, feeling her shoes squelch unpleasantly. She was a few minutes late and expected to see the reception area festooned with wet umbrellas and rain-soaked clients, but there was no one there. In the lobby beyond the bead curtain there was just one umbrella, tall with an elegant handle, undoubtedly Lillian's.

Puzzled, she walked straight into the salon and was startled to find her way barred by a police constable in uniform.

'Sorry, madam. The place is closed for now.'

'What's happened?'

'Sorry, madam, I can't...'

'Look!' Florence said crossly, the cold wetness of her feet making her short-tempered. 'I demand to know what's going on.'

She tried to push past the constable, but he clasped her arm, restraining her. Florence struggled.

'Let go, will you!'

At that moment a tall man in a thoroughly wet trench coat and trilby came out of the kitchen. He glanced at both of them, then spoke to the constable.

'Evans, I told you not to let anyone in.'

'Now look here!' Florence cried, wrenching her arm free. 'I work here, and I demand to know what's happening. Where's Mrs Longford?'

The man came forward.

'I'm Detective Constable Lloyd,' he said. 'And you are...?'

'Florence Longford.'

'Ah! Lillian Longford's partner.'

'Where *is* Lillian?'

'In the kitchen having a cup of hot sweet tea,'

433

he said. 'There's been a burglary. They've forced the safe, and did a lot of senseless damage.'

He swept an arm around. Then Florence saw the state the salon was in, and stared in consternation.

Cubicle curtains were torn down; three of the washbasins were completely smashed, and all the mirrors broken. The floor underfoot was wet.

'Taps were deliberately left on,' DC Lloyd explained. 'We've turned the water off.'

'Ooh!' Florence felt sick at the sight of the destruction.

The detective caught at her arm as though he thought she was about to collapse.

'You'd better have a cup of tea, too,' he said kindly.

Florence looked up at him, touched by the sympathy in his voice, something she didn't associate with a policeman.

He was very tall and very wet. The brim of his brown trilby was sodden and crinkled. He took it off self-consciously, running his fingers through his dark hair.

Florence looked into his face, into vivid blue eyes ringed with long dark lashes, and for a moment her wet, cold feet and the damaged salon were forgotten. Those eyes looked so very familiar, as if she'd once known them well, a long time ago, but she and DC Lloyd had never met before.

Florence swallowed hard, embarrassed at being so affected by the eyes of a stranger. He still held her arm and, tongue-tied, Florence felt herself blush scarlet. A married woman blushing! It was ridiculous.

'You'd better come into the kitchen,' he said. 'It's a bit of a shock, isn't it?'

He escorted her into the kitchen, still holding on to her arm, and Florence had the silly and exciting notion that she might be under arrest.

Unable to resist, she looked up at him as they walked. She liked his strong straight nose, and his square jaw with a dimple in it. He must have sensed her observation because he glanced down at her, smiling.

'A cup of tea will put you right, Miss Longford.'

Florence swallowed.

'*Mrs* Longford.' Why did it hurt to say it?

In the kitchen Lillian sat at the table. She glanced up briefly when Florence and DC Lloyd came in. She looked white and shaken; her bright blonde hair usually in a crisp marcel wave, hung damp and limp, obscuring one eye.

Florence felt awkward, not the least because DC Lloyd was standing by listening. She and Lillian had been at each other's throats for months on end; the bitterness between them steadily gathering momentum since she'd married Cliff. It was difficult now to speak reasonably to her, yet they were both victims, and yes, needed each other's support.

'Lillian,' Florence began tentatively. 'What a mess.'

Lillian's face crumpled for a moment as if about to burst into tears, but she quickly regained her composure, though her face remained very strained.

'Lucky there was only the till float in the safe,

435

wasn't it?' Florence went on. 'I expect that's why they did so much damage.'

Lillian didn't answer, but gave Florence a guilty glance.

'Lillian?' Florence felt her heart turn over. 'There wasn't much money in the safe, was there?'

Lillian seemed to have difficulty swallowing. She ran her tongue over her lips nervously before replying.

'Last week's takings.'

'*What?*' Florence stared aghast. 'But how can that be? You always deposit the day's takings into the bank's night safe every evening after closing. Why didn't you do it, for heaven's sake?'

'We've been so busy.' Lillian's voice was a shrill whine. 'I've been too tired of an evening to go all the way down to Wind Street.'

'Leaving a whole week's takings in the office safe over the weekend!' Florence was shouting now. She couldn't stop herself. 'That's the most stupid thing I've ever heard. If it was too much trouble, why didn't you ask me to do it?'

Lillian looked at her, her face hardening.

'We haven't been doing many favours for each other lately, have we?'

Florence's lips tightened.

'Yes, you've been too busy spiting me to see to important business, haven't you?'

She tried to check herself, remembering they were being closely observed by DC Lloyd. What must he think of her, ranting like that? But she felt too angry with Lillian to calm down.

'We're hundreds of pounds out of pocket

because of you, Lillian,' she went on tensely. She waved an arm towards the salon. 'And all that damage to repair. God! That's going to cost a pretty penny, too. We'll have to make an insurance claim straight away.'

Lillian's expression was sheepish.

'No!' Florence burst out. 'Don't tell me! We haven't got any insurance, have we?'

'We didn't have money for premiums, did we?' Lillian bleated. 'I had to let it go.'

Florence was speechless with fury for a moment, her mind a complete blank.

'What'll we do, Lillian?' she muttered at last.

Lillian turned from Florence's angry gaze to flash an irritated glance at DC Lloyd.

'You're not likely to catch the buggers standing about by here, are you?' she said to him. 'What are *you* doing about it?'

'Fingerprints,' he replied easily, obviously not the least offended by Lillian's attitude. 'Somebody'll be along soon to do it. We'll have to take prints from you both for elimination purposes. The rest of the staff, as well.'

'Where are the staff?' Florence asked, looking up shamefaced into the blue eyes.

Her outburst of temper towards Lillian must seem unpardonable to him. Though why she should care what DC Lloyd thought about her, she didn't know. Yet she did care, suddenly quite a lot, and felt uneasy about it.

'Having a cuppa in some café,' he said. 'They'll be back when the fingerprint bloke's ready for them.'

'How did the burglar get in?'

'Forced the back door,' DC Lloyd said, looking intently at Florence. 'Probably crossed the bomb site at the back from Orchard Street, then over the back wall. Piece of cake!'

Florence wished he didn't sound so cheerful about it, but of course, it was just another job to him.

'How soon can we get back in business?'

He scratched his ear.

'Once the fingerprinting is done, you can start clearing up. Any time after that.'

'What are the chances of getting our money back?'

'Slim, I'm afraid. We might get lucky with a print or two.' He inclined his head, regarding her closely. 'But … er … I'll pop in now and then to keep you informed on progress, if you like?'

Florence smiled up at him, feeling her heart swell with excitement. He seemed to be speaking to her alone. She tried to quell a huge sigh.

Those eyes were awfully blue!

Lillian and Florence both agreed that they couldn't work with half the equipment smashed. They'd lose too much business, so all the damage must be repaired immediately. It meant the salon must remain closed for a few days until the work was finished.

By Thursday they were back in business, much to Florence's relief, with more clients and bookings than they could comfortably handle. Curiosity about their awful experience was high, and there was a good deal of eager chatter amongst the clientele, fuelled by the staff.

'*I'll* deal with the takings from now on,' Florence firmly informed a much subdued Lillian, who obviously wasn't yet over the shock of it all.

Since the burglary Lillian had been quiet, even compliant, and Florence suspected she was riddled with guilt over the loss of so much money. Florence decided she must use this time to gain more control and strengthen her position of authority with the staff.

She tried to fill her mind with these thoughts in an effort to blot out others. Speculations about DC Lloyd came unbidden to her mind time and time again, and try as she may she couldn't stop thinking about him.

It was so silly! She'd met the man briefly and would probably never see him again. Yet one part of her mind said she would. There had been something more than a casual remark behind those extraordinary eyes when he'd said he'd keep her informed. It was more like a kind of promise. It excited her, yet made her very uneasy.

She shouldn't even be thinking about him at all, she reprimanded herself sternly. It wasn't right. She was married, and probably expecting Cliff's baby. No doubt DC Lloyd was married, too, and with a couple of kids, more than likely!

But there's no sin in *thinking*, surely?

Yes, there is, her conscience told her, when these kinds of thoughts make a person even more dissatisfied with their lot.

Am I dissatisfied with my lot? she probed her conscience. It was disconcerting that there was no reply.

Florence comforted herself with the thought that within a few busy days she'd forget the young policeman who interested her so much. Her conscience continued to tell her she should forget, but her heart persisted in believing she wouldn't.

There were other things to think about, however. She had to make plans, scheme how she could maintain a firm grip on the business and function as a mother at the same time. While it was too early yet to know if she were really in the family way, intuitively she knew there was a difference in her being.

On Saturday, with just half an hour to closing, Glenys came to tell her a man wanted to see her in reception.

'It's that policeman again,' Glenys said. 'I don't like him. He's got funny eyes.'

Florence's heart did a double somersault, then raced like an Olympic sprinter. Heat seared her cheeks and she knew she'd gone scarlet by the curious look Glenys was giving her.

Florence handed a comb to her.

'Finish off here, please, Glenys,' she said as calmly as she could. 'Perhaps it's good news about the money.'

Florence felt foolish, guilty, ashamed, yet very breathless as she parted the bead curtain and stepped into reception. DC Lloyd was thumbing through a magazine, still wearing the trench coat and brown trilby. He dropped the magazine and whipped off his hat at the sight of her.

'Ah! Mrs ... er...'

Florence wetted her lips nervously.

'Florence Longford,' she said, taking tighter control of herself. Don't let him see or suspect, for goodness' sake, she scolded herself. 'Have you any news?'

He scratched his ear.

'Well ... er ... no.'

He inclined his head – nervously, Florence thought with a little catch of her breath – and just stared at her, fingering the brim of his hat, turning it round and round.

'Oh!' Florence tried to sound disappointed, but she was far from it. He'd come to see *her* for no apparent reason, except that ... maybe...

He shuffled his feet.

'We've got a good print and a name, but we can't lay our hands on the little bu ... on the culprit.'

They stared at each other for a moment longer. Florence felt her lips trembling and pressed them together to hide it.

'Well...' he said with a shrug. 'That's all really. But I thought you'd like to know what progress we're making.'

'Yes, oh, yes,' Florence said eagerly. 'I want to know everything about the case, everything.'

'Yes, well...' He glanced towards the door. 'I suppose I'd better go.' He sounded reluctant.

Florence stepped forward quickly, reaching out a hand.

'Well, thank you ... Mr Lloyd.'

He grasped her hand eagerly, shaking it enthusiastically, his blue eyes fastening on her, sharp and clear. And utterly compelling,

Florence thought, with a smothered sigh.

'Greg,' he said. 'My name's Greg Lloyd.'

Florence lowered her gaze, smiling; her heart hammered away in her breast. His clasp was strong, and something like electricity passed between them.

'Thank you, Greg,' Florence said breathlessly, looking up at him again. 'I'm very grateful to you.'

He held on to her hand.

'It's just my job,' he said.

'You will keep me informed, won't you, Greg?'

He took a deep breath.

'I certainly will ... Florence.'

Florence felt heady and light-hearted as she walked up to the station to catch the bus home later. But the closer the bus took her to Catherine Street the more ashamed she felt. She was a married woman who had no right to feel excited and light-headed because some man she found attractive smiled at her and held on to her hand a moment longer than he should have. For all she knew, Greg Lloyd was a womaniser, like Tony.

No, she wouldn't believe it!

But, a persistent little voice of common sense told her, Greg knows you're married, yet he came to see you on the flimsy excuse of bringing you up to date on the burglary. He knows you belong to another man, yet he held on to your hand and he smiled and smiled with those incredible eyes.

And, the obstinate little voice went on, you're pregnant!

Greg called at the salon again the following Wednesday. Darlene was in reception at the time and though Florence was certain he'd asked for her personally, Darlene called Lillian to speak with him.

Eaten up with curiosity and a need to see him again, Florence followed Lillian and Darlene into reception, just in time to hear Lillian's reprimand.

'It's not good enough, Constable,' Lillian complained loudly to him, to Florence's consternation. 'I pay my rates, I expect something better than this.'

Greg was almost standing to attention, his eyes focusing on Florence as she appeared through the bead curtain. He switched his glance quickly to Lillian.

'I assure you, madam,' Greg said in a very official-sounding voice. 'Everything possible is being done.'

'Huh!' Lillian was impatient. 'Waste of time! Don't bother to come back again unless you've made some real progress,' she snapped, turning abruptly to disappear through the bead curtain.

Greg hovered uncertainly for a moment, glancing from Flo to Darlene and back again. Florence cursed the older girl's presence. She wanted to apologise to him for Lillian's rudeness.

While she dithered, trying to think of something to say, he turned on his heels to leave and Florence stepped forward quickly.

'Thank you, Greg – em – Mr Lloyd.'

Then he was gone, and Florence's heart sank. Well, that was that. He wouldn't be back. Her conscience told her it was for the best, that she'd been living in a fantasy world these last few days. The quicker she returned to reality the better.

She followed Darlene through the bead curtain, and was startled to find her waiting in the small lobby.

Darlene had a malicious smile on her face, and Florence felt the hairs on the back of her neck rise.

'Oh, so it's Greg now, is it?' she said, with a sneer. 'You're very pally with the constabulary all of a sudden, aren't you? Fast work!'

Florence flicked her tongue over dry lips.

'I don't know what you mean.'

'That copper asked for you, personally.' Her voice was thick with suspicion, 'Now why do you think that is?'

Florence's lips tightened, though she felt more frightened than angry. She'd done nothing wrong, yet Darlene's words made her feel so guilty and even ashamed. She had no right to feel these hankerings for a man she hardly knew, for any man other than her husband.

For the first time she was afraid of Darlene, knowing her own face was probably giving away too much of what was on her mind.

'I've no idea,' Florence replied haughtily. 'Now get back to the salon, Darlene. You've got clients waiting. Or perhaps you're not interested in hanging on to your job here.'

'Don't you threaten me,' Darlene said. Her eyes narrowed and her mouth was distorted with spite. 'I'm on to you, missus.'

Shocked at the naked malice in Darlene's eyes,

Florence felt a shiver go through her, touching her soul. Lillian was her foe, but Darlene was her real enemy, Florence realised. The older girl's bitterness towards her had increased since she'd married Cliff, and Florence knew Darlene was eaten alive with jealousy.

She'd have to be very, very careful from now on. With an aching heart she realised it was just as well she'd never see Greg Lloyd again.

On Saturday evening Florence was the last to leave. She locked the salon door, thankful that the busy week was over. The day's takings weighed heavy in her handbag, and she wasn't relishing the long walk down to the bank's night safe in Wind Street.

As she turned to walk down High Street she noticed a man standing in the doorway of the Red Cow opposite. In the light from a street lamp nearby she recognised Greg Lloyd, and an excited shock surged through her.

She pretended not to see him. It wasn't safe. For days Darlene had been watching her like a hawk. She could be hanging around anywhere this very minute, watching, spying. Florence wouldn't put anything past her.

Out of the corner of her eye, Florence saw Greg leave the entrance to the pub and walk down on the opposite side, keeping abreast of her. He was following her!

She quickened her step, keeping her gaze averted, though it took all her willpower not to glance across at him. She hadn't gone further than the King's Head pub when he crossed the road and intercepted her.

'Hello, Florence.'

She stopped, pretending to be surprised.

'Oh! Hello, Greg. What are you doing here at this time? Are you on duty?'

'No.' He shook his head. 'I thought I might catch you.' He shrugged. 'Bring you up to date on what's happening about the burglary.'

It was a pretty thin excuse and Florence felt her heart skip a beat with excitement, despite her attempts to remain calm.

'Why didn't you come into the salon?'

Greg smiled ruefully, pushing his hat further back on his head.

'That partner of yours is a formidable woman, isn't she?'

Florence looked up through her lashes at him.

'I get the distinct impression that doesn't bother you too much,' she said, trying not to laugh.

He grinned. 'You're not just a pretty face, are you?'

They were silent for a moment. The light from the shop window behind her fell directly onto his face. She was struck again by his strong features and the brilliance of his eyes, which sparked with an emotion she didn't quite understand. Or did she?

Thank goodness her own features were in shadow. If he could see her clearly, her expression would give her away.

He let out a deep sigh.

'Look, Florence, why don't we have a cup of tea somewhere?' he suggested casually. 'We can go in Eynon's, down by there.'

Florence swallowed hard before attempting to reply, trying to steady her voice. Her pulses beat like tom-toms, their frantic rhythm a warning to her to be sensible and honest.

'Eynon's are closed at this time of evening,' she reminded him. 'Besides...' She started to walk away. 'I'm on my way to the night safe in Wind Street.'

'I'll walk with you,' he said firmly, falling into step beside her. 'You should have an escort, anyway, carrying that money.'

'Nonsense!' Florence felt panic. 'I didn't know the police force could afford to provide guard dogs.'

'Ouch!' He laughed. 'All right! I asked for that. But, really, I'm off duty. I want to talk to you.'

'About what?'

'Well ... anything.' He grasped her arm, bringing her to a stop. 'Florence, listen. I ... er ... I just want to get to know you better. You like me,' he said. 'I know you do. Why can't we be friends?'

'Friends?' She stared at him for a moment. 'Greg, it won't do.'

'Why not?'

Florence suddenly felt impatient with him. Her hankerings and attraction to him were stronger than she'd realised, and now she felt wretched. She was kidding herself, and misleading him if she let him think there could be anything, even friendship, between them.

'Why? Because I'm married, of course,' she said, bluntly. 'And you're probably married, too.'

'I'm not!' he said quickly. 'I swear I'm not,

447

Florence.' He glanced around. 'Let's go and have a coffee somewhere. We can't talk properly standing here.'

'No! Greg. It's no good! We mustn't be seen together. I'm married, I tell you. I...' She almost told him she was probably expecting a baby, too, but held back. She didn't want anyone to know that yet. 'Please don't try to see me again.'

'But, Florence!'

Florence lifted a hand in warning. She felt like bursting into tears at turning him away, dismissing him, but she *must*. She didn't really understand why, but it felt like throwing away happiness.

'No! Look, I'm sorry if I gave you the wrong impression, Greg. I didn't mean to. I'm married and I intend to remain faithful to my husband. Please don't make trouble for me.'

He looked aghast.

'I'd never make trouble for you, Florence.'

'Then stay away from me, Greg,' Florence cried out fervently. 'For God's sake!'

With one last desperate glance at him, Florence turned and ran.

CHAPTER 31

May 1951

Florence humped the bucket of precious coal in from the coal house, placing it on the living-room hearth. It was heavy. She really should've asked Cliff to bring in some coal before he left on his latest long-distance trip.

With wonder she thought about the new life growing inside her. Early morning sickness almost every day for the last two weeks had left her in no doubt about her condition, and she knew she must take no more chances carrying heavy loads. She must keep her unborn baby safe.

She'd managed to hide it from Cliff, not really sure why she was reluctant to tell him.

She'd not seen Greg for weeks, and tried hard to put him out of her mind, but to her shame, he was forever in her thoughts. Time and again she tried to dismiss her feelings for him as a sudden and unaccountable attraction, one doomed to come to naught in her present circumstances.

But, if only she'd waited a little longer before agreeing to marry Cliff. If only she'd waited for her heart to find love. By committing herself to him she had forfeited her chance at real happiness. Now she mourned her loss.

If her mother were here now, telling her she'd been rash and foolhardy in marrying Cliff, she'd have to agree. She'd miscalculated badly. Still, she regretted nothing else in her life. Going her own way *had* been the right thing to do.

But, she commanded herself firmly, things must now be accepted as they are. There's no turning back; the deed couldn't be undone.

Despite her acceptance, Florence ached in her heart, and knew the unpleasant taste in her mouth was bitter regret.

How many times since meeting Greg had she wished fervently she was free, free to love whoever she wanted. But she wasn't free and it did no good wishing otherwise.

Florence picked up the tongs and placed a few lumps on the fire, then flopped down in an armchair. The children were in bed at last. Tired after being on her feet all day, she just wanted to sit and watch the images in the flames.

When the knock came at the front door she was tempted to ignore it, then thought it might be Peggy Rees, next door. Peggy could never manage her rations properly and was always wanting to borrow sugar or something. She was so helpful with the children while Cliff and Florence were at work that Florence didn't mind lending. So, she went to answer the door.

She got such a shock seeing Greg standing at the door that her legs almost gave way under her.

'Greg!'

Her heart leapt with joy at the very sight of him, and she chided herself for being weak and susceptible. Hadn't she just this minute decided he could have no place in her life?

He didn't smile.

'Can I come in, Florence?'

Her mouth going dry as conflicting emotions fought a battle in her mind, Florence came out onto the doorstep, pulling the door to behind her. She felt confused as joy and fear fought for supremacy. Fear finally won.

'You can't come in the house, Greg! Why are you here?'

'I have to see you, Florence, talk to you.' His voice was raw with emotion, earnest petition in his eyes. 'For pity's sake let me in.'

'This is Cliff's house,' Florence reminded him in a hushed, shocked voice. 'His children are in bed upstairs. I can't let you in. It isn't right.'

'Florence, for God's sake, what are you doing to us?'

The anguished appeal in his voice tore at her very heart, and she swallowed hard against the constriction in her throat.

She shared his anguish. Just gazing at him, being this close to him made her heart race with longing. She was astonished at the intensity of her emotion. Never before had she experienced anything like this. Was it really wrong to feel this way?

'There is no us, Greg,' she said in a whisper, knowing she had no answer to her own question. 'There can't be.'

'I won't accept that, Florence.'

He took off his hat, and held it before him. She could see his hands were shaking.

'You know in your heart something is happening between us,' he said desperately. 'From the first moment we met we both felt it.

451

You can't deny it, Florence, and neither can I.'

'Please!' Florence whispered, looking up and down the street fearfully. 'Be careful what you say!'

'Then let me in.'

Greg stepped forward, his hand pushing open the door behind her, and Florence was forced back into the narrow passage. He came in and closed the door.

Overwhelmed at his presence, Florence retreated down the passage to the living-room. Greg followed, unstoppable.

'This is all useless,' Florence said in a low voice, thinking of the children upstairs. 'I'm not free, Greg.'

'God! Don't I know it!' He threw his hat on a chair nearby. 'My job on the Force means everything to me ... at least it did until I met you. Now I'm playing Russian Roulette with it.'

Florence wrung her hands.

'What do you want from me, Greg?'

'I want *you,* Florence.'

She put hands over her ears, shaking her head.

'I shouldn't listen to this. You shouldn't be saying these things. You must go now, Greg.'

'I've tried to keep away as you asked me, Florence, but I can't. Thinking of you every minute is driving me crazy!'

He drew a deep breath to get control of himself, and spoke again in a quieter tone.

'I know it's madness, but I can't help it. Can you really turn me away again? Be honest with yourself ... and me.'

His words and the depth of feeling in his voice

tore at her. Fate was playing a cruel trick on both of them. But she must stick to her resolve.

'You *must* go,' she answered. 'Cliff'll be here any minute.'

'No he won't,' Greg said soberly. 'He's gone on a long haul to Glasgow. Won't be back until the end of the week.'

Florence stared.

'How do you know all this?'

He stared back, the vividness of his eyes making her head swim.

'I keep tabs,' he admitted, then smiled ruefully. 'I *am* a detective.'

Florence turned away. She was being weak, she told herself desperately. She should be ordering him out of the house. This was Cliff's home, and she and Greg had no right to sully it.

She suddenly thought of Connie, Greg's first wife. She had cheated on him just like this. And that had led to a terrible tragedy.

Now Florence felt real terror. Suppose Cliff found out Greg had been here?

Florence turned to him in panic.

'Greg, there's something you should know about Cliff. He...'

'I know everything about him,' he answered swiftly. 'About his being in prison and why.' He shook his head, solemnly. 'What I don't know and can't understand is why you ever married him, Florence. Why?'

She shrugged, despondently, wrapping her arms around herself, feeling suddenly chilled.

'It seemed right at the time,' she murmured. 'He'd been good to me. Paid for my partnership at Terri's. I felt ... obliged.'

'You don't love him.'

It wasn't a question, Florence realised, it was a statement as if Greg knew and understood her every thought.

She shook her head.

'No, I don't love him. Cliff knows that. He's accepted it. I thought I could accept it, too.' She looked up into Greg's eyes. 'It's good to be loved, but if you can't give love back, it's empty and meaningless.' She shook her head miserably. 'Oh, why didn't I understand that before?'

Greg took a tentative step forward to comfort her, Florence sensed, and tensed, believing he was about to embrace her. She stared up at him, wide-eyed and trembling.

'I love you, Florence. I've never felt like this before. Believe me.'

His voice was sincere and the look in his eyes told her more than words ever could. Florence covered her mouth with a trembling hand for a moment, holding back a sob. This was the love she'd always longed for in her heart, and now she was denying it.

A great battle raged in her between love and rightness, and she wavered. It *was* all right to feel this new and wonderful love, her heart tried to persuade her. But her conscience told her she had no right to it. As a married woman she mustn't take Greg's love. She must resist.

'How can you say that so easily?' she asked quietly. 'You don't know me.'

He smiled sadly.

'I feel I've known you all my life, even before

my life began.'

Florence gazed up at him, wondering what he meant.

'That first day I saw you in the salon,' he went on earnestly. 'You were so familiar to me, like I'd known you before. You're the one I've been waiting for, Florence. The only one!'

Florence blinked in awe. She'd felt that, too, remembering how familiar his eyes were. She knew exactly what he meant.

'I can't get you out of my mind since that time.' He smiled. 'And I've tried, believe me, I've told myself how hopeless it is; telling myself that my association with a married woman could scuttle my promotional chances on the Force.'

His features tensed, and his voice rose.

'But I don't care about that anymore. You're too important to me, Florence. I love you and I need you. We could give ourselves a chance, at least.'

'A chance?'

'At happiness. You've just admitted your marriage to Cliff is meaningless to you, empty.'

Florence lifted her chin, struggling to resist the urge to surrender.

'What about my marriage vows, Greg? And what about loyalty? Doesn't Cliff deserve that, at least?'

What kind of a woman would she be, she asked herself, if she betrayed him so easily, as Connie had done?

Greg stared at her, his face ashen, and suddenly he looked distraught.

'Please, Florence! Don't turn me away again.

You'll spoil both our lives. Think!' He cried out. 'Think what you're doing.'

'Hush! The children!'

Florence turned away abruptly to stare into the fire, not wanting to hear the persuasive desperation in his voice. She could so easily give in, so easily.

There was a long silence, then Greg said quietly:

'Florence, do you want to live the rest of your life with a man you don't love? Can you? It'll be joyless, purposeless.'

Florence turned to look at him, afraid to answer.

Greg took her hand and held it firmly, yet gently.

'You're young, and you married Cliff for all the wrong reasons.' He shook his head, his expression grave. 'Don't make another mistake.'

Florence felt the warmth of his hand seep through her. She felt the glow of need for him, yet held herself in check.

She sensed there was another mistake waiting to be made, but she didn't know what it was; she didn't know which way to turn.

Should she stick to convention, be true to Cliff and never know what it was to love someone deeply? Or should she throw aside all she'd ever believed in, and take a chance with Greg? She knew hardly anything about him, yet her emotions were strong in her heart. Nothing in her life so far had made her feel quite like this, not even her ambitions, her longing for success or for her family's esteem.

She suddenly realised that this glorious feeling might never come to her again if she denied it now.

Cliff was good to her, but could she go on being grateful for the rest of her life? How would she feel ten years from now?

She swallowed hard.

'Greg, I'm afraid.'

'No, don't be, darling.' His voice and words were tender. He continued to hold her hand, but made no move to initiate a more intimate contact. 'We won't rush things.'

He sighed, letting out a long breath, releasing pent-up tension.

'For the time being,' he said. 'Until you're certain how you feel, perhaps we could meet, talk, get to know each other better. Sort ourselves out ... plan.'

'How? When?'

'I'll wait for you tomorrow after you close the salon,' he suggested. 'We'll have coffee somewhere and talk.' He squeezed her hand. 'We need to talk this through, Florence. We must.'

'Yes.' She had to agree at last. Her feelings were too powerful to be ignored.

She suddenly thought of Darlene and the suspicion and malice in her eyes.

'But wait for me in Wind Street, near the Post Office,' Florence said. 'We mustn't be seen together.'

'I understand.'

'Now you *must* go,' she said pleadingly.

Reluctantly, he let go her hand, and they stood gazing at each other silently. There was no need for words; she read the longing in his eyes. He turned quickly away to hurry down the passage to the front door.

When he was gone, she stood for a moment with her back against the closed door, listening to the silence of the house; Cliff's house. It felt empty and lifeless and cold. Cliff loved her, but that knowledge didn't warm her. It had never warmed her, she realised.

And in that innermost sanctum of her heart she knew with certainty that even if she must deny Greg and his love and send him away, her marriage to Cliff was finished. She could no longer be his wife. She could no longer live a lie.

Greg was waiting for her the following evening. After she'd finished with the night safe they went to an Italian café nearby. Greg talked about himself. His mood was easy, and Florence felt no pressure.

She discovered he was only five years older than herself, and so the war had been over within six months of his being called up, and Florence was thankful. He told her about his burning ambitions for his career in the police force and about his widowed mother with whom he lived at the top end of Cradock Street.

Florence talked about herself, first shyly, then with more confidence as Greg encouraged her, eagerly hanging on her every word. She talked of her family and her need for their esteem; her determination to be independent and her work. But she didn't tell him about the new and wonderful addition to her life. Her unborn baby must remain her secret.

Florence stayed longer with Greg than she'd intended that evening, enthralled at being with him, getting to know and understand him. She knew Peggy next door would take good care of Cliff's children, as she had long before Florence came on the scene.

When they were parting Greg suggested they meet again the following evening, and Florence needed no persuasion. She felt they were doing no wrong in meeting and talking. They might be just friends. She hadn't committed herself, not really. There was still time to draw back.

So their meetings went on until the end of the week, when Cliff returned home.

When Cliff came home, Florence refused out of principle to meet Greg, but he was in her thoughts constantly.

Although she needed time to consider how she would or could tell Cliff that she could no longer be a wife to him, she knew he must be told immediately. She owed it to him to be honest and open.

On Cliff's first night back Florence went to bed early to think. She had to be clear in her mind exactly what the end of her marriage meant. She could no longer live at Catherine Street. That thought frightened her. She was safe here and protected, but she couldn't expect to share Cliff's home and accept his protection while denying him. She'd have to face up to the reality of what she was planning. She'd get rooms somewhere.

Then there was her partnership at Terri's, purchased with Cliff's money. Must she sacrifice that? Her conscience said she must, however heartbreaking and disappointing that prospect was. She realised with a jolt that she had come a complete circle. Again she was about to change her life irrevocably, as she had at eighteen. She prayed she would not repeat her mistakes.

Terri's was her only livelihood. How would she live? How could she provide for herself and her precious baby?

A chill went through Florence at a new and frightening thought. Could Cliff take her baby –his child – from her if she left him? She couldn't imagine his being that vindictive, yet he'd killed a man once because of betrayal.

Florence set her jaw firmly. She wouldn't be afraid. She didn't know the law, but she did know she'd fight tooth and nail for her child.

An hour after she'd gone to bed she heard Cliff's slow tread on the stairs. He must be weary, she thought. He'd arrived home mid-morning, after driving through the night. He'd probably fall asleep immediately, so she wouldn't tell him tonight. It could wait until morning.

Cliff quietly opened the bedroom door, but didn't switch on the light. Florence lay with her face turned away, pretending to be asleep. She heard the rustle of his clothes as he undressed, and felt the disturbance of the bed as he climbed in.

'Flo?'

She didn't respond to her whispered name, but lay still, praying that he'd fall asleep. She heard him breathing quietly, and relaxed.

Then suddenly she felt his arm slide around her

460

waist as he tried to draw her body closer to him. Florence instinctively resisted, straining her muscles to prevent contact.

'Flo, love?'

Florence didn't trust herself to speak for a moment, but continued to resist. There could be no more intimacy between them. It was meaningless for her now, and she knew she could no longer live the sham she'd helped create. The hour of reckoning had come.

'Flo, what's wrong?'

Florence wrestled herself from his hold, struggled to sit up and pulled the light cord which hung over the head of the bed.

'I thought you were tired,' she said lamely, not looking at him.

'I am,' he said. There was warmth in his voice. 'But I've missed you so much this week,' he went on, reaching out a hand to touch her breast. 'You're so beautiful, Flo. I'm a lucky so-and-so.'

Florence couldn't help shrinking away, and to avoid his touch she pulled the bedclothes up around her breasts. The action was defensive, and was not lost on Cliff.

The smile left his face.

'There *is* something wrong,' he asserted. 'You've never turned from me before, Flo.'

'I'm tired, myself,' she answered defensively. 'I've had a miserable day again.'

It was true. Worrying how she would break her devastating news to Cliff, and the constant battle to maintain an upper hand at the salon had worn her out. And she'd missed being with Greg more than she could've imagined. He filled her

461

thoughts and mind every living moment as her husband never did.

Cliff's fingers stroked her arm persuasively. 'Then let me comfort you, Flo, love.'

He reached for her again, but Florence pushed his arms away, feeling something like panic start. 'No, Cliff!' She swallowed hard, trying to calm down. 'You promised me you'd never force me.'

He sank back against the pillow.

'No, I never will,' he said, his tone flat.

He lay staring up at the ceiling, silent.

After a moment, Florence reached for the light cord again, but Cliff's voice stayed her hand.

'I met Darlene this morning,' he said in too casual a tone that didn't fool Florence. 'She was coming out of the wholesalers in Lower Oxford Street as I was walking home from the depot.'

Lillian *had* sent Darlene to the wholesalers this morning, Florence remembered. Her heart skipped a beat as she wondered what lies her enemy had told Cliff.

'She saw you and a man sitting in a café in Wind Street one night in the week.'

Florence was dismayed. Darlene had been spying on her! She'd felt the older girl's hatred for some time, and her vindictiveness wasn't all that much of a surprise. But to sink so low as to spy! It was beyond anything Darlene had done or said to her before.

But the damage was done now, and Florence knew she had to face the consequences. She decided to stick as close to the truth as possible.

'I go to the night safe every evening after work, as you well know,' Florence said defensively. 'The

462

man Darlene saw is the policeman who's investigating the burglary. We had a cup of coffee together. He brought me up to date on the progress the police are making.'

Cliff sat up abruptly, swung his legs off the bed, then stood up, reaching for a dressing gown. His back was turned to her, but she could tell he was angry by the hunched stiffness of his shoulders.

'I know he's a policeman,' he said. 'Darlene recognised him.' There was a cutting edge to his voice. 'Is it necessary to meet him in cafés at night to discuss the burglary?'

'I bumped into him!' Florence lied without thinking.

He turned to stare intently at her. Already she could read accusation in his eyes.

'What night was it, exactly?'

Florence swallowed, wetting her lips nervously. Something in his voice warned her this was a trick question.

'It might have been Wednesday evening ... or maybe Thursday,' she said. 'I can't remember, exactly. Does it matter?'

'Darlene saw you with this man on three consecutive evenings,' Cliff said tensely. 'I didn't believe her, Flo, but now you've made me wonder.'

'Cliff!' Florence cried out. 'Did you set her to spy on me while you were away?' She was appalled at the idea.

He shook his head vehemently.

'Of course not! Why should I?'

Just the same his glance held suspicion and doubt. A moment before she'd felt pity for him,

463

but now she was angry. She pulled the bedclothes aside and jumped out of bed to face him.

'Just what are you accusing me of, Cliff?' she asked, her shoulders tense with strain.

A showdown was about to erupt. She could feel the tension bouncing off the walls of their bedroom.

'I've made no accusation.'

'Haven't you?' Florence tossed her head angrily. 'Then why question me like this? I've done nothing wrong, but you're ready to believe anything Darlene says about me.'

'Are you saying she's lying, Flo?'

She was silent for a moment, trembling with indignation, yet unwilling to answer his question. But why should she feel guilty? she asked herself. She'd done nothing shameful or wrong.

She stalked to the dressing table, picked up a brush and began brushing her hair furiously, while trying to marshal her thoughts.

They'd never quarrelled before, perhaps because there was no real passion between them. She wanted to tell him it was over, but not this way. She wanted to tell him gently, reasonably, with no anger involved. Now Darlene's spying made every aspect sordid.

Feeling steadier, Florence put the brush down, looking at Cliff through the mirror.

'Darlene sees only what she wants to see,' she said dispiritedly.

'You were with the same man on more than one occasion,' Cliff persisted angrily. 'Are you denying that?'

Perhaps it was only too natural that he should

be suspicious after what Connie had done to him. It must seem like history repeating itself. Florence clutched at the front of her nightdress, feeling suddenly chilled and very tired.

'Cliff, I have never been unfaithful to you,' she said earnestly.

That was true. She was attracted to someone else, but she'd never gone in search of anyone. It happened suddenly, catching her by surprise, off-guard. It wasn't her fault that she didn't love Cliff. Why should she be made to feel ashamed?

'What does this man mean to you, Flo? Tell me the truth.'

The truth? She didn't really know it herself. There was a feverishness in her feelings for Greg, and a heady excitement when she was with him. She wanted him, yes, wanted his lovemaking with a power that astonished her. But instinctively, she realised these aching longings were separate from love. The fire she and Greg shared had flared into life almost instantly when they met. It could die just as quickly. It wasn't love – not yet.

'I don't know, Cliff.' That much was true.

'You're lying!'

'No!' Florence whirled around to face him, her cheeks hot with fury. 'The only thing I know for sure is that I don't love you, Cliff. And I can't go on in this marriage. It's a sham.'

'*What?*'

'I should never have agreed to it. Never!' Florence cried out. 'I felt grateful to you, obligated. It was wrong from the start.'

'Who has turned you against me?' he thundered. 'That bloody policeman?'

465

'No one has turned me against you,' Florence answered sadly. 'Can't you see it wasn't meant to be? It's our fault ... no, my fault,' she corrected herself. 'My fault.' She held up a hand towards him. She didn't want hostility between them. 'I should never have agreed to marry you.'

He ignored her gesture, staring at her stonily. A pulse was beating at his temple. She had never seen him angrier.

'I'm so much younger than you,' she went on. It was no use trying to be gentle now. 'I told you I didn't love you. I can never love you.' She shook her head. 'I can't be what you want me to be, Cliff.'

They stared at each other for a moment. Then Cliff sat on the bed, putting his face in his hands. Florence felt pity again, yet she knew this moment would have come eventually some time in their future, with or without Greg and Darlene.

'What do you propose to do?' he asked, his tone cold.

It was a good question. She really hadn't thought that far ahead. Thanks to Darlene's interference she was now faced with a dilemma. But she'd better solve it quickly.

'I shall leave Catherine Street. I'll find rooms elsewhere.'

He looked up at her quickly, his face set and hard.

'I suppose you fondly think you can continue at Terri's, benefiting from my investment?'

She lifted her chin, proudly.

'I'm not a money-grabbing fool, Cliff,' she said

disdainfully, hurt that he should even think it. 'I know that's over. And it's a pity, too, because I worked hard there, rebuilding what your brother destroyed.'

'So, you're leaving me. And what then? Divorce?'

Florence flashed him a look of defiance.

'Probably.'

His jaw tightened.

'No,' he said bitterly. 'No. I've given you no grounds. I love you and I've been faithful. I've never hurt you. You know it's true, Flo.'

She had to nod an agreement. Cliff was a good husband. But she didn't love him. She was beginning to understand that to know true happiness two people must share their love. She wanted that happiness more than anything else, except perhaps her baby.

'So, it's no use you seeing a solicitor as you're unable to prove grounds,' Cliff went on. 'And, I warn you, Flo, I'll *never* agree to divorce. You're *my* wife, and you'll *stay* my wife, even if it's in name only.'

CHAPTER 32

Even though her body was wracked with stiffness after having spent the remainder of the night sleeping on the sofa downstairs, Florence awoke the next morning, her spirits borne on high by an uplifting sense of freedom, of being back on the right track.

Once again she was ready to find the courage to make a new and revolutionary change in her life. There was a difference, though. She was deciding the life of her child, too, and she was very conscious of her new responsibility.

Drawing back the living-room curtains, blinking in the bright glow of the early-morning sun, Florence made a sacred resolution that her child would not be the loser for the change. She'd work the skin off her fingers for him. She was convinced the child would be a boy. He'd want for nothing.

She was giving up security for happiness, and knew she was right, although many would criticise and condemn her. She didn't care.

Florence stretched again, trying to ease her muscles. In all fairness, Cliff had offered her the bed, but she'd refused adamantly. She didn't want to quarrel. She simply wanted nothing more from him. Their relationship was at an end in all respects.

Except, of course, she warned herself, she was

469

carrying Cliff's child, and he did have some rights. But that was in the future, and she'd deal with the problem when it arose.

Putting the kettle on the gas ring to boil, Florence found the previous night's evening paper and searched for the column of rooms to let.

An advert for two rooms in nearby Westbury Street caught her eye, and she decided immediately that she'd see them that morning. Now she'd made up her mind, she couldn't leave Catherine Street soon enough.

She made breakfast for Peter and Tansy as usual, and felt sorry that she was leaving them. She wasn't sure they were fond of her, but they had accepted her and would probably miss her for a while.

Cliff remained in bed, whether to avoid her or because he was tired she didn't know. She was glad. Last night's confrontation had been a great strain, and the less she saw of him from now on until she left, the better.

He was badly hurt, angry and bitter now, but soon he'd be prepared to forgive her. She knew he was that kind of man despite his history. She didn't want to see pleading in his eyes; she couldn't bear to see him hurt further and didn't want to feel pity again.

Not that his pain would or could make her change her mind. She had a right to know love and happiness herself. She might find it with Greg; perhaps not. But it was out there somewhere and she'd find it.

Mrs Percival, the woman letting the two rooms in Westbury Street, seemed very nice. She was trim and clean-looking. The house smelt of polish and carbolic soap, and reminded Florence of childhood visits to the home of her grandmother, Mam-gu.

Mrs Percival showed Florence the two rooms, a large back bedroom and a smaller middle living-room, with the use of the kitchen. She was favourably impressed. Everything looked clean, and there were no obvious signs that the rooms were bug-infested.

They came to an amicable agreement over the rent.

'It'll be you and your husband, I expect?' Mrs Percival asked.

Quickly summing up her prospective landlady, Florence felt instinctively that Mrs Percival was someone of strong principles, who would frown on a woman planning to leave her husband.

'I'm a widow.' Florence managed the lie without stumbling over the words.

'Oh! My dear! I'm so sorry.'

Her genuine sympathy made Florence feel ashamed, not only of her lie but also of the ease with which she had spoken it.

But, still, she had to tread carefully. Although the breakdown of marriages was becoming more common since the war, most people still found it scandalous and unacceptable. Florence wanted no gossip. Now that she was forced to relinquish her partnership at Terri's, she needed to find other work. Keeping her good character was important.

'I'm not very comfortable where I am at present,' Florence said. 'May I move in as soon as possible?'

'Too many memories, I expect,' Mrs Percival replied, touching her arm in sympathy. 'I understand, my dear. I'm a widow myself.'

'Tomorrow?' Florence asked hopefully.

Mrs Percival's face clouded, shaking her head solemnly.

'Not on the Sabbath day, my dear.'

Florence moved into the rooms in Westbury Street early on Monday, having made arrangements with a removal firm on Saturday morning. She had few possessions, her own single bed which had been stored at Catherine Street, but little else.

On Saturday she had also called at a second-hand furniture shop on St Helens Road and bought a kitchen table and two chairs in very good condition, a small chest of drawers, and a cheerful kitchen cabinet yellow and red, which looked almost new. All were to be delivered to her new home on Monday.

Cliff stood in the living-room at Catherine Street watching silently as the removal men manhandled the bed downstairs. By his expression she knew he was thinking back to the time he'd helped her move from High Street.

'Flo ... listen, love,' he began despondently. 'You don't have to go like this.'

He'd obviously had time to reconsider, and was perhaps even prepared to forgive her, wanting things to be the way they were, at any cost.

'I don't want you to go. If only you'd stop and think about what you're doing, I know we can work this out.'

Florence shook her head.

'No, Cliff, we can't. Our marriage has no foundation other than obligation and debt. Is that a sound basis for any relationship? Be honest.'

'I love you, Flo.'

Florence caught her top lip between her teeth as a spark of conscience ignited.

'I know,' she said regretfully after a moment. 'I know, and I'm sorry.'

If he was trying to make her feel guilty again, he was succeeding.

'We're ready now, missus,' the van driver called. 'If you want a lift with us.'

With a sigh of relief, Florence shrugged into her coat, looking at Cliff.

'Goodbye, Cliff,' she said simply.

Now the moment had come, she didn't know how she felt.

'I'm sorry things have turned out this way. You've been good to me, and I didn't want to hurt or disappoint you.'

He gave a bitter laugh, his glance disdainful now that his pleading had failed.

'But you have, Flo. You don't know how much.'

Florence lifted her chin. He was blaming her for all of it, and that wasn't fair. After all, he'd manoeuvred her into the marriage very cleverly.

'We were good friends, Cliff. We should have stayed that way.'

Within a few days Florence felt settled in Westbury Street. It was a relief to be alone again, and her sense of freedom was still strong. It felt good.

One morning in the week, Florence was taken by surprise when Mrs Percival knocked on her living-room door to tell her she had a visitor.

'It's your brother, Mrs Longford.'

Tommy? Florence couldn't believe it, and stared guiltily when Greg appeared.

'My brother!' Florence whispered after Mrs Percival was gone, feeling a little annoyed with him.

The deception, once started, went on, growing more and more complicated. Florence didn't like it. Lying and deceit went right against the grain.

'Couldn't tell the old biddy the truth, could I?' Greg grinned mischievously. 'I can tell she's a staunch chapel-goer.'

Florence sniffed, feigning ignorance now, and trying to hide her real pleasure at seeing him again.

'Mrs Percival is not a biddy, and she's not old, either. How did you know I was here? No, don't tell me! You *are* a detective.'

He smiled, the blue of his eyes raising goose-bumps on the tops of her arms.

'This is the first time we've ever been alone, Florence,' he said softly. He stepped closer. 'Are you glad to see me?'

Florence avoided contact, stepping aside to close the door.

'I don't know yet,' she said pertly, teasing him. 'Time will tell.'

That was the truth. She was attracted to him, powerfully so. But perhaps that's all it was. Only time would tell whether she really loved him. She longed to be in love now, really in love and have all that love could bring.

'Is there a cup of tea going?' he asked casually, taking off his hat and coat and sitting on one of the kitchen chairs she'd recently bought.

'So you've taken the plunge and left your husband, then,' Greg said later, as they sat at the table while Florence poured the tea.

He heaped three spoonfuls of sugar into his tea, stirring vigorously, while Florence sadly contemplated her depleting sugar ration for the week.

'Was it because of me, Florence?'

She made a face at him.

'Not entirely, so don't get too conceited.' She smiled. 'Meeting you made me realise my mistake.'

He looked disappointed for a moment.

'Is that all, Florence?'

She gazed across the table at him, feeling a great tenderness in her heart. She couldn't deny to herself she wanted him, very badly. It was an exciting, heady feeling, making her want to throw caution to the winds. But common sense warned her to be sure of her true feelings before committing herself a second time. Too often in the past she had rushed headlong into things, only to have them turn sour.

'You played a very big part in my decision, Greg.'

She put an elbow on the table and placed her

chin in her hand, gazing at him.

'Thinking of you keeps me awake at night, you big handsome brute!'

'Oh! Just give me the chance!'

Eyes alight with excitement, he reached across and grasped her hand tightly, half rising to his feet.

'Slow down!' Florence laughed, detaching her hand with difficulty. 'I'm still a married woman.'

'I love you, Florence,' he said, subsiding onto the chair. 'I know you want me, too. Why must we wait?'

'Because I don't want a sordid, hole-in-the-corner relationship,' Florence retorted, sharper than she intended. 'I expected you'd feel the same.'

He was silent for a moment, looking down into his cup of tea, now gone cold.

'You've given up Terri's,' he said at last.

'Had to, didn't I?' Florence said bleakly.

It was a blow. She hadn't anticipated just how much it would hurt. Her dream had come crashing down, and now lay in ruins. What a careless fool she'd been!

But she refused to forget her dream. There was still time to build it up again, and she would! She was still young and determined.

Florence checked herself. Those plans were for the future. Right now she had to prepare for her baby, and that meant finding the means just to live.

'I've got to find a job,' she said. 'But as a typist, not as a hairdresser.'

It was galling. She'd have finished her

apprenticeship in a matter of four months' time if she'd stayed at Terri's. Without her indentures she couldn't hope to get a hairdressing job, not at a good establishment, anyway.

'I might be able to help,' Greg said eagerly. 'I know a bloke who has an electrical wholesale business in Lower Oxford Street. He's looking for a clerk-typist. I reckon I could get that job for you.'

'Oh! Greg, could you?' Florence grabbed his hand, excited at the prospect. 'I'd be ever so grateful.'

He put a hand over hers. It was warm and strong, and his touch had her breathing a little faster.

'Would you, darling?' he asked huskily. 'How much?'

He was gazing at her ardently again. The warmth in his eyes stirred her, making her feel dizzy. It would be so easy to give in to him, give in to her own longings. Would it matter so much? After all, she was no inexperienced, innocent girl.

Confused by the tumult of her own senses, Florence withdrew her hand gently. Things were moving too fast, and she was still unsure what she really felt for him.

She'd submitted to her husband dutifully, but with no ardour of her own. The feelings Greg aroused in her just by touching her hand astounded her, and she began to realise what she had almost thrown away in readily marrying a man she didn't love.

There could be no more mistakes or regrets.

'You'd better behave.' She smiled, her cheeks

flaming. 'Or I'll ask you to go.'

He leaned forward, elbows on the table.

'Seriously, though, Florence,' he said. 'I'm crazy in love with you. You're free now. There's no reason why we shouldn't enjoy...'

'Greg!' Florence interrupted quickly, suddenly afraid of her own powerful feelings; he'd say too much when she wasn't ready to hear it. 'I'm not ready to start another ... serious relationship yet. And I'm not free. I won't be until I'm divorced.'

Despite Cliff's assertion that he wouldn't consent to a divorce, she knew that was what she wanted and was determined to have.

Her body, mind and soul yearned for Greg as passionately as he craved her, but she didn't want their relationship to be cheapened from the start. She had to be really free. She had her pride and her principles still.

Gratification was easy to come by, she knew from other girls' talk and gossip. The hardest commodity to find was love; a shared love that was as real as life itself. And she was more than ever determined that from now on she wouldn't settle for less.

Greg was as good as his word about the job, fixing an appointment for Florence to go for an interview at the wholesalers. Florence wore a dark utility skirt and white blouse, trying to look as businesslike as possible.

She was interviewed by the proprietor, Barry Davies, a short, rotund man with a bald head and restless, shrewd eyes.

'So you're a friend of Greg's, then?' Barry

asked, eyeing her up and down.

She saw his gaze linger on her hand, and the wedding ring she wore. She could almost hear his mind jumping to conclusions.

'Acquaintance,' she said firmly. 'Mr Lloyd is an acquaintance.'

'Yes, well, Mrs...'

'Longford,' she volunteered.

'I don't usually take on married women. Always taking time off,' Barry Davies said carefully, eyes narrowing as he looked her up and down again.

'I'm a widow.' Going on with the same lie seemed the safest thing.

'Oh! I see.' Thoughtfully, he pinched his nose between finger and thumb. 'Greg never mentioned that. Got any children?'

'No.'

'Good. Well,' he said, shuffling the papers on his desk. 'I understand you were a typist in a solicitor's office. Why did you leave?'

'I got married.'

It was stretching the truth out of all proportion, and it was worrying that lying was getting easier. But she wanted this job badly. It was ideal. She could walk to work from Westbury Street, so there'd be no bus fares out of her pay.

Barry Davies nodded, seeming satisfied with her answer.

'I can do shorthand, too,' she said helpfully. 'One hundred words a minute.'

She was badly out of practice, but would soon get her speed back.

'My wife acts as my secretary,' he said, smiling for the first time. 'What I need here in the office is a woman with a bit of gumption; an invoice-clerk-cum-typist, who can answer the telephone and hold an intelligent conversation with customers.' He tapped his teeth with a pencil. 'You look as though you might be the one, Mrs Longford. You know the wages. When can you start?'

It felt good to be working again. Florence threw herself into her new job with enthusiasm, despite her natural hatred of typewriters. She worked alone in the small, untidy office; the duties were varied and not in the least boring. The best thing was that Barry left her to manage the office work without interfering.

It was a thriving business, Florence could see, and promised to keep growing. The range of goods in the warehouse astonished her; radios, toasters, electric washing tubs, and more exotic wares like the new television sets.

When Barry demonstrated a television set for her, Florence regarded almost suspiciously the small grainy black and white moving image of a man playing a cello, and could see nothing terribly wonderful in it. It could not compete with a visit to the cinema, but these sets were appearing more frequently in shop windows, and she wondered how anyone could tolerate such an intrusive thing in their living-rooms.

Barry laughingly assured her that this was the future. Florence wasn't so sure. But one thing was clear to her as paperwork on her desk piled up each day; people were somehow finding money for such outrageously expensive goods, despite the so-called recession.

As one week stretched into two and three she found Barry leaving things more and more to her initiative. After three weeks Florence pointed out that she really needed someone to help, but Barry dismissed the idea, saying he was confident she could cope.

She said no more, afraid he might change his mind about her, decide she wasn't the person for the job after all, and so struggled on under the workload.

Florence rushed into Greg's arms as soon as he appeared, hardly before the door was closed properly. With a small grunt of pleasure he clasped her to him tightly.

Her arms circling his neck, Florence lifted her face eagerly, searching for his kiss. His mouth, warm and firm on hers, was like honey to her.

'I've missed you, Greg,' she murmured, after a long moment lost in the kiss.

She rubbed her cheek against his, breathing in the scent of him; a scent that made her head spin and her heart thump.

His embrace was strong and possessive, and she loved it.

'It was only yesterday,' he said softly, kissing her throat.

She was breathless at the sensations his lips were creating.

'Seems like eternity,' she gasped.

A month had gone by so quickly, and now it was early June. Greg called on her every evening, unless he was on duty. At first Florence was afraid Mrs Percival would suspect he wasn't her brother, but the landlady never questioned his visits, and in time Florence felt easier.

In his arms, Florence knew she truly loved him. And he loved her with equal intensity. Their finding each other was the most wonderful thing of all. Often she pondered on the pure chance of their meeting. But was it chance? Wasn't fate working for her this time?

She was sure of him now; all her doubts were gone. There wasn't an area of his life that he hadn't told her about. She'd been equally frank about her life, and her family and her resentment at their lack of confidence in her.

One secret she still kept. She didn't tell him about the baby she carried; Cliff's baby. She was sure Greg loved her, but how would he feel about another man's child? There was no way she could test his attitude without giving herself away. Greg, born to be a policeman, was far too shrewd.

'Your pal Barry Davies is a slave-driver,' Florence teased later as she poured Greg another cup of tea. 'No wonder he's not been able to keep a clerk for more than two months. I'm doing the job of two in that office, you know.'

'Straight as a die, Barry is,' Greg declared confidently. 'Or he wouldn't be a pal of mine.'

Florence reached across and took his hand.

'I'm going to ask him for an hour off tomorrow, Greg. I'm going to see a solicitor about divorcing Cliff. I know he said he wouldn't agree to a divorce, but there must be some way I can get my freedom.'

He grasped her hand tightly, his eyes shining.

'You'll marry me then, won't you, Florence? Please say yes, darling.'

Florence gazed at him, her heart swelling with love and need.

'You know I will, and I promise, Greg, I'll make you happy.'

He smiled.

'We'll make each other happy, darling. I've found you at last. I waited so long. If only we'd met sooner...'

Florence sighed deeply, her heart aching at his words and the tenderness in his eyes. She knew exactly how he felt. But they must not begin their lives together with regret.

'It's no good dwelling on what might have been,' she said staunchly. 'We're together now. We'll make it come right, you just wait and see.'

He looked at her solemnly.

'It's not going to be so easy, Florence, darling. From what you've told me your husband hasn't given you grounds for divorce, has he? Are you sure there was no other woman? I could make some enquiries...'

Florence shook her head vehemently. 'No!'

She couldn't subject Cliff to that. It wasn't fair. Although he denied her a divorce she didn't feel vindictive towards him. And she must be careful not to anger him further. In time he might change his mind.

But how much time? How long would Greg wait for her?

'Cliff was faithful to me,' she said. 'He always treated me well ... and with love,' she added.

Greg shrugged, looking dispirited.

'Then what can you tell the solicitor?'

Florence bent her head, suddenly despondent herself.

'I don't know.'

She looked up at him, tears swelling in her eyes.

'Oh, Greg! I desperately want my freedom to love you. Somehow, I *must* get my life back.'

CHAPTER 33

June 1951

Florence spent most Saturday afternoons giving her rooms a thorough clean. There was a good picture showing at the Plaza tonight, and she and Greg planned to go, unless duty intervened.

Tomorrow she'd concentrate on making Sunday dinner for them. Greg would share the meal tomorrow for the first time, and she hoped to impress him with her cooking, even though her ration of meat this week was minuscule. Never mind! She'd make a nice Yorkshire pudding to go with it.

She'd taken the living-room mats out to the clothes line in the small back yard and was beating them vigorously when Mrs Percival called her indoors.

'There's a lady called to see you,' Mrs Percival said. 'Your sister, perhaps?'

Florence looked closely at her landlady, wondering if there wasn't a sarcastic edge to her voice, but decided Mrs Percival wasn't up to sarcasm. She followed her into the house puzzling who her visitor might be.

Florence stared in surprise when she saw Rita standing in the passageway. She hadn't seen her cousin for over a year. Sharp guilt suddenly pierced her, as she remembered her cowardice in not revealing Rita's terrible predicament to the family. There'd been too much upheaval in her own life recently to puzzle over a solution to her cousin's woes, though Rita was always in her prayers.

Florence drew Rita into the living-room away from Mrs Percival's curious gaze. Despite her unhappiness, her cousin looked extremely smart and well-turned out, Florence considered. She wore a beautifully tailored two-piece suit in royal blue wool, and a frothy little hat with a veil. Black patent leather shoes and handbag complemented the elegant outfit.

Feeling guilt even more sharply, Florence gave Rita a warm hug, and was concerned when her cousin winced at her touch.

'Rita! I'm sorry!' Florence was confused for a moment, staring. 'How are you?' she managed to ask at last.

Without answering, Rita lifted the small veil on her hat, and with horror Florence saw why the veil was necessary. Rita's left temple and cheek-bone were badly bruised.

'Oh, Rita!'

'As you can see, Flo,' Rita said quietly. 'Nothing has changed. In fact, it's worse.' She shook her head. 'And I've had enough!'

Florence noticed then that Rita's wedding ring was missing from her finger. So, at last, Rita meant to do something drastic about her plight, and Florence knew she must help her cousin if she could.

She was suddenly conscious of the state of the room. No mats on the floor, and the chairs stacked on the table while she'd been washing the linoleum. She hastily put things straight, bringing forward a kitchen chair for Rita to sit.

'Sit down, Rita, love,' she said, sitting herself. 'Sorry I haven't an armchair to offer you.' She smiled quickly. 'I'm saving for one.'

Rita sat down, glanced around, then looked at Florence, her eyes suspiciously bright.

'A place to yourself,' she murmured wistfully. 'It looks like heaven.'

'Yes, it is,' Florence agreed thoughtfully.

What she had wasn't very much, but it did amount to independence and a kind of freedom.

'I envy you, Flo,' Rita said sincerely. 'And I admire you, too, for the way you're dealing with your life. I used to think you were wrong, impetuous. Now I understand you were struggling to be yourself, your own woman. If only I'd had the gumption to follow your example. But it's not too late, is it?'

'Not too late for what?'

There were dark shadows under Rita's eyes, and for all her elegance she looked tired and worn. Yet, there was something else too, something new. Rita's gaze was steady, and even determined as she looked at Florence.

'When I heard recently that you'd left your husband, Flo, I knew I'd been a coward for too long.'

Florence was startled, and her heart lurched in her breast.

'Does my mother know about me?'

It was too much to hope that her family would be unaware of what was happening; not with the likes of Darlene ready to pass on any gossip, true or untrue. Florence dreaded Edie knowing her marriage to Cliff was over and that she'd failed at Terri's. It would support everything her mother had said about her.

Rita's mouth tightened.

'Oh, yes,' she said, her tone bitter. 'My mother saw to that.' She clasped her hands in her lap, her fingers twisting together in anguish. 'I hate my mother, Flo.'

'Oh, Rita! Don't say that.'

Rita glanced at Florence, her nostrils flaring in anger.

'It's true! I hate her! She has no feeling for anyone; like Granddad Charlie. She's horrible to my da. She's greedy and heartless, and I despise her.'

Florence shook her head.

'You don't mean it.'

Rita lifted her chin, though her lips quivered and her eyes were shiny with unshed tears.

'You don't know what she did or said to me.' Rita swallowed, struggling hard to regain composure.

She looked far older, somehow, than when last they talked, Florence thought with concern and pity. She was only twenty-one, yet it seemed her youth had already left her.

'Just before I married Ken I had doubts, real doubts,' Rita went on. 'But she persuaded, no, bullied, me to go ahead. Then, later, when I told her the awful truth about him, do you know what she said?'

Rita's gaze was bright and fierce, and Florence fancied she could see the hatred in her eyes.

'Put up with it! That's what she said, mind. Put up with it! She didn't care that I am being beaten and abused. All she cares about is herself. She said she'd disown me if I tell, if I bring scandal on her. My own mother said that!'

Florence jumped up from her chair to go to Rita's side, putting an arm around her shoulders and giving her a hug in sympathy.

'I'm so sorry, Rita.' It was all she could think of to say. Her own problems shrank in comparison. Poor Rita!

Rita reached up eagerly to grasp her hand, obviously eager for comfort and understanding.

'But I'm going to pay her back, Flo,' she said tensely. 'I'm going to leave Ken.'

Florence felt an overwhelming sense of relief. A weight was lifted from her shoulders. She didn't have to feel guilty any longer because Rita had found her own solution.

'I'm so glad you've found the courage, Rita, love,' Florence said.

'I *have* to, Flo. I dare not take any more beatings because...'

She gripped Florence's hand even more tightly, looking wide-eyed at her, obviously scared of what she was about to reveal.

'Promise you won't tell, Flo. Promise!'

'What is it?'

Rita took a deep breath.

'I'm going to have a baby, Flo.' A look of deep joy settled on her face as she said it.

Florence was flabbergasted, and flopped back onto the chair.

'But I thought Ken...'

'Oh, it isn't his, of course not!' Rita hesitated again, biting her lip. She lowered her gaze before saying more. 'It's Malcolm's.'

Profoundly shocked, Florence's mouth dropped open and she could only gape for a moment before speaking.

'Malcolm?' she cried incredulously. 'Ken's brother? Oh, Rita!'

Rita's glance was defiant.

'Malcolm was the only one who offered any sympathy and comfort,' Rita said defensively. 'He knows what Ken is.'

Florence shook her head in bewilderment at what she could only see as Rita's foolhardiness. Rita, always so prim and proper and conventional, indulging in an affair that could only lead to more trouble and discord for her? Florence could hardly believe it.

'Malcolm was there for me, don't you understand, Flo?' Rita blurted out, clearly reading Florence's thoughts. 'He said he loved me, and I think he did ... for a while. I was fond of him and it seemed the right thing. I needed someone...'

Florence could only gaze helplessly at her cousin.

Why do we go on making a mess of our lives? She wondered. She married Cliff because she felt obligated to him. Rita had been forced into a disastrous marriage because of the greed of her mother and her own weakness of character. Would either of them find happiness eventually? Did they deserve to?

'When I told Malcolm about the baby,' Rita

490

went on, 'he panicked and denied it was his.' Her tone was matter-of-fact as if Malcolm's betrayal didn't matter.

'The rat!' Florence exclaimed, outraged.

She gazed puzzled at the smile on Rita's face.

'Rita, aren't you angry with him?'

'No. Malcolm's given me something precious. My own child. He's also given me a reason, and the courage, to stand up for myself at last. I'm leaving Ken and I intend to divorce him. I'll take him to the cleaners!'

There was a sharp gleam in Rita's eye, and for a moment Florence was reminded of Auntie Sybil.

'I'm not interested in the money, Flo,' she said quickly. 'Though, it'll come in handy for the baby. It's revenge I'm after, against Ken and my mother. I'll make them squirm!'

Rita took in a deep breath, probably already savouring victory.

'You see, Malcolm's not very smart,' she said. 'He wrote me some letters, mentioning his brother and his ... predilections.' She glanced at Florence, the gleam still in her eyes. 'Ken's big on the Town Council now, and I know he's looking to go higher. I can stop him dead in his tracks, because I'm prepared to go public with Malcolm's letters if Ken doesn't give me what I want.'

'Flipping heck!'

Florence stared at her cousin in awe. The worm, when it turned, was as savage as the wolf.

'You've got to help me, Flo.'

'Me?' Florence was startled. 'What can I do? It

491

sounds like you've already got everything sown up tight.'

Rita smiled. She looked less tense now. Revealing her plans to someone at last had obviously eased her. Florence wondered what *she* could possibly do for her cousin.

'I need a friend I can trust,' Rita declared. 'I need a job, and place to live. My mother wouldn't give me house-room. Can I stay with you, Flo? I'll pay my way.'

'Well…' Florence hesitated, her thoughts going to Greg.

These two rooms were the only privacy they had, a haven for both of them. How would he react to Florence taking a lodger? And there was Mrs Percival to consider, too.

'Ken is going away tomorrow on a business trip to Birmingham,' Rita smiled broadly. 'I intend to do a flit. Ken gave me a bank account, a substantial one, to buy clothes and such.' She gave a bitter laugh. 'Ken Henderson's wife mustn't look a frump, even if she is black and blue underneath her pure silk underwear.'

Her face crumpled for a moment, perhaps with remembered pain, Florence surmised, and felt pity.

'I'm going to clean out that account,' Rita went on, rallying. 'Every penny. I'll take all my clothes and jewellery, too. But I must have somewhere to flit to.'

She leaned forward, her eyes pleading as she looked at Florence.

'I promise I won't be in the way, Flo. I'll even buy us a couple of armchairs!'

Florence laughed. How could she refuse Rita's desperate request after the way she'd failed her? Rita was afraid for her unborn child, and Florence could identify with that readily enough. Perhaps it would only be temporary, until Rita found a decent life.

'It's all right with me, kid,' she agreed. 'I think I can square it with Mrs Percival, my landlady. But we'll have to make up a story about you. For goodness sake don't tell her you're leaving your husband. She's a bit old-fashioned.'

Florence made tea, and put a plate of freshly made scones on the table.

'Sorry I haven't any butter,' she said. 'There is a little margarine left.'

Rita didn't seem to mind.

'I was surprised to hear you'd married Cliff Longford,' she said, helping herself to a scone. 'I've heard terrible things about him. My mother said he's a common criminal.' There was a touch of open curiosity in her voice. 'What went wrong, Flo? Was he violent towards you?'

Florence shook her head sadly.

'No. He was generous, gentle and kind to me; perhaps more than I deserved. I don't blame him for what happened, really. I didn't love him. I should never have married him.'

Florence stirred her tea thoughtfully, before saying more. She was the guilty party in this dispute and she couldn't deny it.

'The marriage blew up in my face when I met Greg,' she went on, 'and fell in love. I haven't any grounds for divorce, unfortunately. It looks pretty hopeless.'

Rita cut the scone in half and spread margarine thinly.

'Love?' She shook her head. 'I don't think I believe in it any more. I'll make a home for myself and my child. I don't need anyone else.' She gave a sniff. 'I'm finished with men. I mean it, Flo!'

Rita was very bitter, but Florence didn't blame her. She'd had a terrible experience, and Florence hoped it was over for her.

'I'm expecting, too,' she said quietly, though her heart pounded a little at finally revealing her precious secret.

Rita looked up, astonished.

'Flo! Oh, how wonderful! Who's the ... I mean...'

'It's Cliff's child,' she replied. 'He's refused me a divorce. I'm hoping he'll change his mind soon, but if he finds out about the baby I know he'll *never* agree.'

Before Rita was ready to go, Florence spoke to Mrs Percival.

'My cousin, Miss Bevan, needs lodgings,' Florence said boldly. 'I'd like her to share my rooms, Mrs Percival. Would an extra ten shillings on the rent suit you?'

Mrs Percival's expression quickly changed from doubt to delight. And so it was settled. Rita was to move in within a few days, and Florence didn't doubt she'd done the right thing by her cousin. But she worried how Greg would take it.

When he came that evening Florence knew she must tell him straight away, though she decided there was no need for him to know all Rita's history; suffice to say that her marriage had broken down, and she needed a roof over her head.

She waited until Greg was seated at the table for a meal, his coat and tie removed, his shirt sleeves rolled up, before telling her news.

He looked at her in dismay, putting down his knife and fork with a clatter. She could see he was really upset. For weeks he'd begged her to sleep with him, and although she wanted to desperately, she'd steadfastly refused because of the moral principles she held fast to.

Greg wasn't resentful, but he'd begun to question her love for him, and that was hurtful. Anxiously, she realised Rita's moving in now must appear to him to be a wedge between them; that she engineered it deliberately to avoid committing herself totally to him.

'Florence, what about us?' he demanded. 'We hardly see enough of each other as it is, without having a stranger here.'

'Rita's not a stranger, Greg,' Florence said, biting her lip with concern.

'She is to me!' he exclaimed angrily.

He took a deep breath to control himself, and was silent for a moment looking steadily at her, his blue eyes solemn.

'Florence, you know all I want is for us to live as man and wife. We love each other. You haven't a snowball's chance in hell of getting a divorce, so why wait any longer? Why waste our lives?'

Florence sat down, putting an elbow on the table, and covering her mouth with her hand to hold back a sob.

For the first time she heard bitterness in his voice, and was suddenly afraid. Was he tired of waiting? Was she being unfair, putting her principles before their love?

At the back of her mind she wondered what her family would think. Her parents would be scandalised and ashamed of her. And she'd worked so hard these last few years to make them proud of her.

What was more important? she asked herself. The love that she and Greg shared, or that elusive success and esteem she was always chasing? For all she'd been through and all her hard work, she was no nearer achieving her dream. It remained as far off as a forgotten melody.

Greg reached forward and gently took her hand away from her face, to hold it tightly in his. The pressure and warmth of his hand set her trembling with longing. She loved him so much. Why did she go on denying him?

'Florence, darling, I love you,' he murmured simply. 'Nothing will ever change that, but I can't go on like this. It's more than a man can stand.'

He stood up, drawing her to her feet, too, and enfolded her in his embrace. Florence clung to him eagerly, feeling warm and safe in his arms. She couldn't lose him now. She couldn't!

He held her close and spoke quietly, his lips against her cheek.

'I was planning to tell you this evening,' he began. 'I've made arrangements for a mortgage. I'm buying a house.'

Florence pulled away from him to stare up into his face, her mouth opening in amazement.

'*Buying* a house?'

He smiled down at her.

'Yes, a house for us. We'll live there together, and to hell with the rest of the world!'

'Greg, what about your job? Living openly with a married woman? You could easily spoil your chances of promotion.'

He kissed her lips gently.

'You're more important to me, darling. Nothing matters but you and me.'

'Oh, Greg!'

Florence clung to him again, wanting to cry with happiness. He was willing to sacrifice ambition and his good name for her. Could she do less for him? Her heart told her that Greg was all she'd ever want or need.

'Will you, Florence?' He held her at arm's length, smiling. 'Will you live with me?'

Florence gazed back at him, her mouth suddenly going dry. The moment had come to tell him about Cliff's baby. She began trembling at the thought of Greg turning away from her when he knew the truth.

She swallowed hard, trying to summon the words. How should she begin?

'Yes, Greg. I want to live with you, and I will,' she said soberly. 'But there's something I have to tell you. You may change your mind when you know.'

He smiled, disbelieving.

'Couldn't happen!'

Florence ran her tongue over her dry lips,

497

nervously, watching his face.

'I'm expecting Cliff's child in November.'

His arms dropped from her shoulders, and he took a slow step back, his expression blank.

'I was afraid to tell you before, Greg,' Florence cried. 'Don't look at me like that! Please say something.'

'What do you want me to say, Florence?'

'Tell me it doesn't matter.'

He let out a harsh breath, glancing away, but was silent.

Florence reached out for him, desperate to feel the loving comfort of his arms again.

'Greg!' she cried out again. 'You said a moment ago that nothing else mattered but you and me. Didn't you really mean it? Greg! Isn't that still true? Tell me!'

He wouldn't look at her, but turned away to sit at the table.

Seeing his stillness, Florence felt suddenly cold. Was his love only on the surface, then? Had fate betrayed her again?

'Greg, I've done nothing wrong,' she said tremulously. 'Does it make all that much difference?'

His head jerked round to stare at her.

'Of course it matters, Florence,' he uttered harshly. 'Take on another man's child?' He shook his head, bewildered. 'I don't know whether I'm ready for *that*.'

Florence put her knuckles to her mouth, biting hard on them, not trusting herself to speak at that moment. She felt sharp pain in her heart and knew it was bitter regret. If only she could go back in time to undo it all.

'Does he know?' Greg asked gruffly.

'No!' Florence rapped out. 'And I don't want him to. He'd try to get me to go back to him. There'd be more strife.'

Greg put his hands to his face.

'God! What a mess!'

Suddenly, Florence was angry.

'So much for your love, Greg!' she cried out bitterly. 'Your undying love! Huh! It was all smooth talk, wasn't it, just to get me into bed?'

He lifted his head to gaze at her, and she saw shock in his eyes.

'That isn't true, Florence! I do love you, deeply. But be fair! You throw this bombshell at me and expect me to take it in my stride?' He shook his head. 'I'm only human, Florence.'

'Well, so am I!'

Florence flopped on a chair and burst into tears. It was too much to bear! Her life was going horribly wrong again.

Her dream of success and recognition was already smashed in pieces. She'd gathered the pieces and kept them in a small corner of her heart, hoping that one day her dream would rise again like the Phoenix. She'd almost given up all hope of that.

Now the love she'd given to Greg was being thrown back at her for something that wasn't her fault. Why was it nothing ever went right for her?

She felt Greg's arm around her shoulders. He drew her up, and held her against him, the way she longed for.

'Florence, darling, don't cry.' He kissed her

cheek tenderly, and wiped a tear away. 'We'll work it out. It's a disappointment, that's all. I was thinking of the children we might have together.'

Florence looked up at him, half ashamed. She must look awful with red eyes and an even redder nose.

'It's a little, innocent baby, Greg,' she whispered. 'I already love him beyond reason, even though he's not born yet. There'll be time for us, Greg, time for us to have our own.'

'You're right, darling,' he said softly. 'Look!' he went on lifting an arm as though waving a hurrah. 'I'm used to the idea already.'

Rita moved in with her belongings a couple of days later. They put another single bed in the bedroom and there was still plenty of space.

Florence decided to tell Rita straight away about her plans to move in with Greg when the purchase of his house in Sketty was complete, although it wouldn't be for a month or two yet.

Rita could remain at Westbury Street and have the rooms to herself, at least until her baby was born.

Rita didn't seem surprised at Florence's decision to live in sin – as Auntie Sybil would probably describe it. Rita's life with Ken had evidently knocked all the naiveté out of her.

'Ken won't know I've gone until next week,' Rita said with obvious satisfaction, as they sat having tea that first evening. 'He'll never find me here.'

Florence felt alarmed.

'Will he come looking?'

The thought of Ken Henderson revolted her now she knew the truth about him. She didn't want to meet him face to face.

'He might,' Rita admitted. 'But I'm not afraid of him anymore.' She smiled maliciously. 'There was nearly four hundred pounds in my account. I've taken it all. It is mine, isn't it?'

She glanced at Florence for confirmation, but Florence said nothing. She'd given her cousin shelter, but she was determined not to get caught up in her marriage disputes.

'I'll have to find a job, though. The money won't last forever,' Rita went on. 'The only thing I'm good at is shorthand and typing.'

Florence sat up straight as a brilliant idea struck her.

'I know just the job,' she told Rita excitedly. 'I've been nagging my boss, Barry Davies, for weeks to get me some help. I'm snowed under with work. It would suit you down to the ground, Rita.'

Rita looked excited, too.

'Put a bit of extra make-up on that bruise,' Florence suggested. 'And call at the office tomorrow morning. But, for goodness sake, don't let him guess you're married and expecting.'

Barry Davies was no pushover, as Florence knew. He took a lot of persuading, but finally agreed to take Rita on on a temporary basis. Florence and Rita were content with that under the circumstances. Within months their delicate conditions would be evident, and Barry would probably tell them both to sling their hooks.

Until then they were sitting pretty.

They were both in the office a week later and Florence was showing Rita the ropes. With her cousin's help she'd have the place working like a Swiss clock in no time.

Florence handed Rita a pile of invoices to type, but paused when she saw the strange, contemplative expression on her cousin's face.

'What's cooking, Rita?'

Rita looked up, tilting her head to one side, and smiling.

'I was thinking how ironic this is, the two of us working together again. Remember the solicitor's office? You couldn't get out of it fast enough.'

'I loathed it,' Florence admitted vehemently.

Rita gave a light laugh.

'It was be a hairdresser, or die, wasn't it? But it was the dream that died.'

Florence gave a sniff.

'No, my dream isn't dead,' she declared staunchly, her heart thumping. 'I feel it stirring again.'

'Oh, no, Flo!'

Florence smiled at Rita's dismay, and perched herself on the edge of the desk.

'Last night Greg and I went over to Sketty to look at the house he's buying. We could only view it from the outside as the owners are still there. They've having trouble getting a mortgage, or something.

'Anyway, we walked along Eversley Road afterwards and that's when I saw it. It's ideal!'

'What?'

Florence let out a long daydreaming sigh.

'A small hairdressing shop to let. Perfect, Rita, it's perfect. Oh, if only I had some money!'

Rita's cheeks turned pink, and she looked embarrassed.

'Flo, I'd lend you the money in a minute, you know that, but I've got to think of my baby. I'm going to need every penny...'

Florence jumped to her feet, embarrassed herself now.

'Oh, Rita, I didn't mean you, kid. No, I'm seriously thinking of tackling my mother again for a loan.'

Rita's eyes were as big as saucers as she stared at Florence in amazement.

'Dare you?'

Florence set her jaw in determination.

'It's partly my mother's fault that I married Cliff in the first place,' she declared briskly. 'If she'd invested in Terri's when I asked her, or even loaned me the money to buy the partnership, I'd never have married him, Rita.'

Rita looked sceptical, and she shook her head.

'Don't blame your mother, Flo. Face it! It was *your* decision to marry Cliff, no one else's.'

Florence gave a shuddering sigh of despair. Her cousin was right. She was far too ready to blame others, when in reality she'd brought all her troubles on herself.

Rita stood up and came to her, putting a hand on Florence's arm.

'Come on, Flo, love, cheer up. Things could be worse. But ... don't you think it's a risky idea to start a new business in your circumstances? Why don't you give up the notion of being a hairdresser?'

'Give up!' Florence was shaken at the idea.

Rita shrugged.

'After all, Flo,' she said persuasively. 'So far, it's brought nothing but problems for you.' She paused. 'Look, Flo, kid, you'll have your baby, and you've got Greg's love. He's a good man. What more do you want?'

Florence didn't reply. She recovered her composure, and lifted her chin stubbornly.

Perhaps she was too ready to shift the blame, but nevertheless, she *did* reckon her mother owed her something, despite what Rita said, and now she was ready to collect.

CHAPTER 34

Florence felt her heart race alarmingly as she stepped up to the back door of her mother's guest house. There'd been such bitterness between them over the last few years. And it wasn't over yet!

Her marriage to Cliff was over, finished. Soon she'd be making a new beginning. But without even knowing Florence's side of the story, her mother would blame her for leaving Cliff. Edie'd see it as a deep disgrace, and there'd be more recriminations, but Florence had no intention of apologising.

She paused with her hand on the door knob, fingers trembling, and was unable to hold back a sigh of regret. This wasn't going to be easy. She was playing into her mother's hands perhaps, as though proving Edie was right all along. That was the hardest thing to bear. But it couldn't be helped. She must swallow her pride. She'd done nothing to be ashamed of.

On that thought, Florence gripped the door knob firmly and let herself into the sweet-smelling kitchen, breathing in the tummy-rumbling aroma of newly baked bread.

The kitchen was empty except for a young girl at the sink washing plates, who turned to look at her as she entered.

'Guests are not allowed in here, madam,' she

said pertly. 'Guests must use the front entrance.'

'I'm not a guest,' Florence answered.

'Oh!' The girl grabbed at a cloth nearby to wipe her hands. 'Well, what do you want then?' she asked sharply and a touch suspiciously. 'No hawkers, mind.'

Hawkers!

Florence ground her teeth in anxiety, self-consciously pulling down the jacket of her utility two-piece suit. She hadn't been able to afford new clothes for a while, but did she look like a hawker, for heaven's sake?

'I'm here to see my mother, Mrs Philpots. Is she about?'

The girl's eyes grew round.

'Well, I dunno. She's very busy, mind.'

Florence realised she'd come at a bad time. The holiday season was well underway. The guest house was probably full of holidaymakers. Edie and her staff would be busy serving breakfasts.

'Look!' Florence said, feeling nervousness and anxiety get the better of her, and suddenly angry at putting herself in the wrong. 'I want to see her. Where is she?'

'It's all right, Gwen,' a calm, familiar voice said from the doorway.

Florence whirled around to see Edie standing there, her figure upright, and somehow com-manding, even in a flowered wraparound pinny, her plentiful brown hair piled up on her head, streaked with silver now at forty-eight.

Edie had a backbone of steel, Florence knew, but she also knew she could match that strength. The trouble was, and she had to admit it after all this time, she continually felt the need to prove it, over and over again.

'Mam! I want to talk to you...'

'Gwen, leave those dishes,' Edie interrupted, speaking to the girl again. 'Help with the breakfasts instead.'

She glanced at Florence without a welcoming smile, and Florence felt her heart sink low.

'You'd better come up to the back sitting-room,' Edie said. 'We'll have some privacy there.'

Following her mother from the kitchen Florence felt an ache around her heart at Edie's distant manner, reflecting that it was only when she decided to go her own way in life that things had gone awry between them. But it needn't be that way from now on. More than anything, she wanted to patch things up between them. She wanted to come back into the circle of love, especially now that she was expecting a baby, though she wouldn't reveal that yet.

It was obvious Edie wanted an explanation of why Florence had disgraced them all, and she was quite willing to explain. After all, Edie ought to be shown that she herself must take some responsibility for it, despite what Rita said.

In the quiet small back sitting-room, Florence took a seat opposite her mother.

'How are you, Mam?'

'Shamed, Florence, that's what I am, shamed,' Edie declared. 'Your father and I hardly know how to look our friends in the eye.'

'There's no need to exaggerate, Mam,' Florence retorted sharply. 'Anyone would think I'd murdered Cliff instead of leaving him.' She

507

paused. 'Aren't you going to ask how I am?'

'Don't be flippant with me,' Edie said. 'I want to know why. Why have you disgraced us like that?'

Looking into her mother's accusing eyes, Florence felt pain rise up from the very centre of her being, the familiar pain of being misunderstood and dismissed by the ones she loved most.

This was the root of everything that had happened over the last two years. She'd struggled to overthrow that, to prove she was equal and worthy in her mother's eyes. Had it all been in vain?

Florence sat forward, squaring her shoulders and raising her chin. She would quell the pain like she always had, and fight on. What she said now would probably work against her longings to be thought well of, but it couldn't be helped.

'I left Cliff because I don't love him. I never loved him.'

'Then why, in heaven's name, did you marry him?' Edie demanded.

Florence lowered her gaze, catching her top lip between her teeth. She had no adequate answer for that question, not without admitting a grave error of judgement.

'It seemed the right thing to do at the time.'

She wouldn't admit it was because she'd felt an obligation to him. Her mother would pounce at that as proof she'd been right all along.

'Cliff won't agree to a divorce,' she went on. 'But I'm hoping he'll change his mind later.'

'Divorce!'

Edie half rose from her chair, then sank back

again, seeming to shrink a little. She was staring at Florence as though her daughter had suddenly developed horns on her head and cloven feet.

'Don't look like that, Mam!' Florence cried out. 'It's not so scandalous today. Lots of people are doing it.'

'Not in *our* family, they're not!' Edie said, her voice rising. 'My God, Florence! You're only twenty years old...'

'I'll be twenty-one in September.'

'You're twenty now,' Edie said, her voice a little firmer, but still tremulous with shock. 'Hardly married a year, and thinking of divorce? You've always been irresponsible and scatter-brained.' She shook her head sadly. 'But this is beyond anything yet.'

'I'm not scatter-brained,' Florence retorted hotly. 'Leaving Cliff was the right thing for me to do, Mam. I have my reasons.'

Edie gave a deep sigh, and Florence knew her mother was hurt and shocked.

'If only you'd told us first, before rushing into marriage with Cliff; a man with a criminal record, too,' Edie said severely. 'We had to find out about it through your Aunt Sybil. Imagine how me and your father felt?'

Florence was silent. She'd always regretted and felt sorry that she'd locked her parents out of her life at that time. But she'd been so hurt at their lack of understanding and their mistrust.

'In my heart I knew it would end like this,' Edie went on, shaking her head. 'And now, too late, you're admitting you made a mistake.'

Florence bit back a retort. Yes, she'd made a

bad mistake, but she'd never admit it openly. It would be admitting she was wrong in everything else in her life as well.

'Circumstances change,' she said, trying to remain calm. 'Things happen that can't be foreseen. Not even by you, Mam!'

'What things?' Edie's voice was sharp now, clearly not prepared to believe anything her daughter said.

Florence saw the familiar look in her mother's eyes. She was misjudging her again, jumping to conclusions, as she always did where Florence was concerned.

'Has Cliff been ... unfaithful, Florence?'

Florence wetted her lips, nervous again.

'No. The truth is...' She swallowed hard. 'The truth is, Mam, I've met someone else myself. I've fallen in love; really in love.'

Edie looked appalled, staring at Florence with her mouth open.

'Oh, Florence! Don't tell me you've been carrying on, like a loose woman?'

'Loose woman!' Florence exploded angrily. 'That's the second time you and Dad have accused me of that! How could you even think it?'

Edie looked unrepentant.

'What else are we to think when you insist on going against conventional behaviour? In my day this sort of thing was unheard of. It's still scandalous and outrageous, Florence, no matter what you say.'

'Don't be so old-fashioned, Mam, will you?' Florence flared. 'Times change, but you don't change with them.'

She tossed her head, her mouth setting in anger at her mother's lack of sympathy.

'Mam, do you think you could give me the benefit of the doubt for once? Do you think you can drag yourself into the second half of the twentieth century to understand what I'm going through?'

Edie's nostrils flared.

'Don't you speak to me like that, Florence. I won't have it! If you can't keep a civil tongue in your head, my girl, you'd better go.'

Florence bit down on her lips, breathing deeply, trying to staunch her anger. She hadn't mentioned the real purpose of her visit yet. She'd get nowhere with that by angering her mother too much. Perhaps she was fooling herself? Edie was no more likely to help her now than two years ago.

'I'm in love, Mam. I haven't done anything wrong.'

'Who is this man, anyway? Where does he come from?'

Florence tilted her chin stubbornly.

'I don't want to talk about him. I don't want him mixed up in it. It would ruin his career.'

Edie raised her brows, looking at a loss.

'You've bitterly disappointed me, Florence,' she said reproachfully. 'And what your father will say, I don't know.' She shook her head sorrowfully. 'To think a daughter of ours could behave like this.'

'Well, it's partly your fault, Mam!' cried Florence heatedly, unable to restrain herself any longer. 'If you and Dad had helped me two years ago, I'd never have married Cliff.'

Edie frowned.

'Don't go blaming us!' she said tightly, shaking her head.

She paused, her eyes narrowing.

'It's preposterous! But, that's just like you, isn't it, Florence? You were always rash and flighty. You get yourself into a mess then look for someone else to blame.'

'I'm not in a mess, Mam,' Florence retorted. 'I know exactly what I want and what I'm doing.'

She raised a hand as Edie seemed about to interrupt.

'I'm not blaming Cliff, Mam,' she went on. 'He's been faithful, though he knew from the start I didn't love him. I can't go on being his wife. The pity is...'

'What?' Edie was staring at her expectantly.

'The pity is I've had to relinquish my partnership in the salon. I've had to abandon my most cherished dream, Mam.'

Florence paused, looking keenly at her mother. Now she was ready to reveal the purpose of her visit.

'Mam, it's true what I said earlier, whether you like it or not. I'm not entirely to blame.'

Florence held up a hand as Edie opened her mouth to protest again.

'Please, Mam, do me the courtesy of hearing me out.'

Obviously reluctant, Edie sat back in her chair. The skin around her mouth was white, and her hands were restless in her lap.

'When I left Cliff,' Florence went on. 'I had to leave the business, too. My dream, my heart's desire. I had it in my grasp then had to let it go.'

Florence swallowed hard, willing herself to be calm, and keep her tone resolute. It was important that her mother realised how serious she was, how intent she was on preventing her dream from slipping into oblivion.

'I'm absolutely determined to start again somewhere else. I've seen a ideal place for rent, and I've come here today to ask you once more. Mam, will you and Dad lend me the money to set up a hairdressing business of my own?'

Edie was silent, her features set, her figure stiff and unyielding.

'Don't you understand what this means to me, Mam?' Florence cried out passionately.

She felt her own jaw tighten in a renewed burst of determination. Her mother must surely see how much it meant to her.

'I won't give up my dream, I won't! You'll help me, won't you, you and Dad?'

Edie continued to sit silent and unmoving, her head turned slightly away. Her fingers had stopped fidgeting in her lap. They were now clasped together tightly, her knuckles showing white.

'If you won't,' Florence cried out again, desperately this time, 'I'll never forgive you! Oh, please, Mam, *please* help me!'

Florence stared helplessly at her mother's still figure for a moment longer, wondering why she'd bothered to come here at all. She'd not come with any real hope in her heart. Yet miracles do happen, she told herself, and surely Edie could not go on dismissing her?

Edie was sitting with her face turned slightly away, unwilling even to look at her, and suddenly Florence felt desperate for some sign of concern from her, some consideration.

'Please help me, Mam,' she cried out unhappily. 'If you won't, then you're no mother of mine!'

Edie turned her head slowly to stare at Florence.

'I never thought I'd live to hear a child of mine say that to me,' she said in a low, tremulous voice. Her eyes looked moist, revealing deepest hurt, and Florence felt a burst of remorse for her harsh words. She had wanted to patch things up. Now she'd made matters worse.

There was silence for a moment, then Florence rose to her feet despondently. It was all so hopeless.

'I'm going, then, Mam,' she said, feeling wounded, wretched and close to tears of disappointment. 'I'm obviously not welcome in this house anymore. Don't worry!' She burst out. 'I won't bother you ever again!'

'Sit down, Florence,' Edie said evenly. 'And stop being so melodramatic.'

Florence resumed her seat, too surprised to make a retort.

Edie looked intently at her for a moment more.

'So, again you're rushing headlong into a new scheme,' she said.

Florence sighed.

'It's not new. It's the same dream, and I want it

514

now more than ever.'

'Don't you ever learn, Florence?' her mother said, with a touch of irritation. 'Look what it's cost you so far. A failed marriage. A clerk's job not worth tuppence.'

Florence stared. Was there anything about her that Auntie Sybil didn't know and hadn't passed on?

'I've had some bad luck,' Florence said defensively.

'Bad luck!' Edie's tone was biting. 'Bad judgement is a better word.'

She was silent again for a moment, and Florence waited with bated breath, sensing there was more her mother wanted to say.

'Florence, I wonder how much you really want this so-called dream of yours?' Edie said, regarding her speculatively. 'I wonder how far you're prepared to go to get it?'

How far would she go? Florence frowned, unable to grasp what her mother was getting at. She thought back swiftly over the past two years. She'd striven, fought every inch of the way, and she'd achieved her goal, too, but fate snatched it away at the last moment. She'd gone too far to turn back now, hadn't she?

'Is that a trick question, Mam?' she asked tartly, suddenly irked that Edie was playing some game with her.

'You want me and your father to lend you money,' Edie jutted her chin resolutely. 'All right, we will!'

'Oh, Mam!' Florence leapt to her feet, hardly believing it was true. 'Oh, Mam, you won't regret it, I promise.'

Edie sniffed.

'Don't promise anything yet, Florence. You haven't heard our condition.'

'Condition?' Florence flopped back on the chair, the wind taken out of her sails. 'What condition? What are you talking about?'

'In exchange for the money, your father and I want you to return to your husband. We want you to have a second try at your marriage.'

Florence was dumbstruck for a moment, her mouth gaping open, but in a second or two her mother's words sank in, and she was outraged.

'*What?*'

'I can't say I shall ever approve of Cliff Longford,' Edie went on. 'But the damage is done now. You're his wife. You've made your bed, now lie on it.'

Florence was almost beside herself with fury. It was the second time her mother had given her that advice, and it was still unpalatable.

'I've never heard anything so ... so immoral in my life,' she gasped out. 'In exchange for my dream I have to sell myself.'

She paused as Edie gave her a startled glance.

'Yes, that's what your condition amounts to, Mam. Prostitution!'

'Ooh!' Edie looked scandalised. 'How dare you say that!'

Florence regarded her mother with narrowed eyes.

'You and Auntie Sybil have a lot in common, after all,' Florence said scathingly. 'She said something the same to Rita. Rita was being

516

beaten and abused by her husband and Auntie Sybil told her to put up with it in exchange for Ken's money and position.'

'It's not the same!' Edie spluttered, obviously knocked sideways by Florence's accusation.

'Yes, it is, Mam,' Florence said angrily. 'You and Dad can keep your money.'

She drew herself up to her full height, proudly holding her head high.

'Both of you have always had a low opinion of me, haven't you? Well, I've got news for you. I won't be bought ... not a second time.'

Edie was still spluttering.

'Florence, now, you listen here to me...'

'Why should I?' she snapped. 'I scrambled after my dream thinking success would get me into your good books, more fool me!'

Florence picked up her handbag, pushing it under her arm, and began pulling on her gloves.

'I've learned something here today, Mam, something I should have learned a long time ago. What you think of me doesn't really matter. It's what I think of myself that counts. I know what I'm worth, and so does Greg. He loves me just as I am.'

'Greg?'

Ignoring her mother's question, Florence stalked to the door, where she turned and looked back at Edie, still seated, staring at her.

'Goodbye, Mam,' she said tightly. 'Like I said, I won't come here begging again. Ever!'

Rita had the kettle whistling on the stove when Florence got back to their rooms in Westbury

517

Street. She flopped down, pulled off her gloves, put her elbows on the table and put her face in her hands.

She was still shaking inside with anger, and knew it would be a long time before she forgave her mother, if ever. She was still vexed at her mother's condition, made so casually, as if it amounted to nothing much. No matter that she'd be unhappy for the rest of her life with Cliff as long as her behaviour was conventional and didn't upset other people's sensibilities.

Well, to hell with that!

If ever she'd had any doubts about going to live with Greg, those doubts were now swept aside.

'It didn't go so good, then?' Rita asked, placing a cup of tea before her.

Florence took the cup thankfully, letting out a long sigh of dejection, and told Rita all that had passed between herself and her mother. She felt ashamed telling it. It put her mother in such a bad light, and she knew that deep down, Edie was more kind-hearted than that as a rule.

'Well, what now?' Rita asked.

'Nothing,' Florence admitted dejectedly.

'What about trying for a bank loan?'

Florence gave a bitter laugh.

'What bank in its right mind would lend money to a twenty-year-old, pregnant woman, who's left her husband and earns a pittance? No, I haven't a snowball's chance in Hades of getting a loan.'

Rita sat down, and was silent for a moment, while Florence brooded on the vagaries of fate.

'Flo, listen, kid ... now don't get angry with me ... but is it all worth it? This driving urge to be in hairdressing, this dream, whatever you call it, is it really any good? I mean ... well...' Rita spread her hands in a questioning gesture. 'Your dream has turned out more like a nightmare, hasn't it?'

Florence wasn't angry. Since her earlier confrontation with her mother, she'd secretly been asking herself the same question.

What was it all for? Why was she banging her head against a brick wall? Wasn't she just a mite sorry that she'd started it, defied her mother and gone her own way? It hadn't turned out as she'd planned and hoped. She was obviously no nearer to finding her mother's approval. Perhaps she *had* been going about it the wrong way all along.

'Flo,' Rita went on persuasively, 'you've got so much to look forward to at the moment. There's your baby, and there's Greg. He's a good man, Flo, and I can tell by just looking at him that he loves you, adores you. What else could any woman ask for?'

Florence smiled.

'You're right, Rita. You were always the sensible one, really.'

'Oh sure!' Rita shrugged, her expression rueful. 'I was very sensible, marrying Ken, wasn't I? But one thing I'm certain about. Love is the only thing that's important. More important than money or success. I know what I'm talking about, Flo. My mother is a cold, selfish, greedy woman without a cup of love for anyone, and I married a heartless beast. The only one who ever gave me love is my father.'

Rita's eyes looked shiny with tears, and Florence reached for her hand across the table, squeezing it in sympathy.

Rita recovered her composure quickly, flicking back her hair light-heartedly.

'That's all finished now,' she said bravely. 'I intend to make a good life for myself and my baby, and you must do the same, Flo. Happiness with Greg is there waiting for you. Grab it. Don't let it get away.' She shook her head sadly. 'It may never come your way again.'

CHAPTER 35

August 1951

'Do I show much, Rita?'

Florence tugged at her dress anxiously. No matter what she wore her condition was becoming more and more noticeable each day. Barry Davies was bound to spot it before long and then he'd give her the sack. She planned to leave Davies Wholesale soon, but she didn't want to be ignominiously booted out!

Did it matter? she asked herself. She'd be moving in with Greg any time, now that the completion of the sale had gone through and the previous owners had moved out.

Greg was collecting the house keys later in the day. He planned to show her their new home first, before going on to the pictures.

Florence was excited at the prospect of seeing the house, but tried to keep a lid on her feelings.

'Oh, I wish I'd bought that smock I saw in Peacocks,' she groaned.

'That would be a dead give-away,' Rita laughed.

Florence made a face.

'It's all right for you,' she said. 'You show hardly at all.'

'Better get a move on,' Rita warned. 'We're late. It's the bus for us today.'

With one more twitch of her dress, Florence grabbed her handbag and followed Rita down

521

the passage to the front door.

The ringing of the door bell startled them both, and they glanced at each other puzzled.

'Tsk! Who's this now?'

Florence opened the door and nearly fell over in surprise to see Marge Spooner standing there.

'Good heavens! Marge! Well, there's nice to see you,' Florence said, nonplussed for a moment, wondering why her one-time workmate was calling on her so early.

'Is it?' Marge asked flatly.

She didn't smile a return greeting, but lifted her chin and gave a loud sniff. It was a sniff of disdain, and Florence's smile faded. Marge's expression was none too friendly. But why was she here?

'Come in, Marge,' Florence invited uncertainly.

Marge gave another sniff.

'No thanks. I wouldn't have called but I thought you ought to know. Not that you'll be interested, I don't expect.'

Standing by, Rita looked at her watch.

'Hey! We're late for work, Flo,' she said, glancing meaningfully at Marge.

Florence was studying her former workmate closely. Marge's unfriendliness was perhaps understandable. She had a very soft spot for Cliff and probably couldn't understand why his wife had left him. Maybe she owed her some kind of explanation.

'You go ahead,' Florence said to Rita.

'No,' Rita said warily. 'I'll wait.'

'Well, are you coming indoors?' Florence asked Marge.

'I said no!' Marge snapped. 'I've just come to tell you about Cliff.'

Florence was astonished. 'Did he send you?'

'He's been in a road accident,' Marge rushed on. 'Smashed up his lorry. They had to cut him out of the wreckage. He's in hospital, badly injured.'

Her heart turning over in her breast, Florence's mouth fell open in horror, and she could only stare at Marge.

Marge stepped away from the door, her look almost triumphant.

'I know you've got a fancy man now,' she said acidly. 'But Cliff is still your husband.'

With that parting shot she turned on her heel and was off down the pavement.

Florence could only stand on the doorstep watching her go.

'Well!' Rita said, breaking the silence. 'There's a horrible woman. Who's she?'

Florence closed the front door and leaned against it. She stared at Rita dumbly as she tried to sort out her dazed thoughts.

Cliff was badly injured, so Peter and Tansy were alone. Peggy next door would look after them for the time being, no doubt, but had a job of work to go to. They had no one else but Florence.

'Rita, love,' Florence said at last, her tongue flicking over dry lips. 'Go on to work. Tell Barry Davies I've quit.'

'What?' Rita looked stunned. 'He'll be furious! What reason can I give?'

Florence shrugged.

'Tell him I'm having a baby.'

'Flo! For heaven's sake! What do you think you're doing?'

'Cliff's children,' Florence explained. 'They need me. They've no one else.'

Rita held out a restraining hand.

'Hold on a minute, Flo! I'm sorry Cliff's in trouble, but this is nothing to do with you.' She shook her head emphatically. 'You're separated now. He's not your responsibility.'

'Didn't you hear what she said?' Florence exclaimed heatedly. 'I'm still his wife. I owe it to him to take care of his children, at least until he comes out of hospital.'

'Now, Flo!' Rita said loudly. 'Don't go tearing off on impulse like you always do. Think! It's all over and done with between you and Cliff. You can't go waltzing off back to Catherine Street just like that.'

Florence pushed past her cousin, making for the stairs.

'Where are you going, Flo?'

'I'm going to put a few things I'll need in a suitcase.'

Rita's gaze followed Florence as she ran up the stairs.

'But, Flo!' she called anxiously. 'What about Greg? He'll be here this evening to take you to see the house. What are you going to tell him?'

'The truth.' Florence paused in flight to glance down at her cousin from the half-landing. 'It's only temporary, Rita. Until Cliff's back on his feet. It's the least I can do for my stepchildren.'

'I knew you'd come,' Tansy said confidently,

when Florence fetched her and Peter from Peggy's.

'I'm back only until your father comes out of hospital.'

'He's not my father.'

Florence placed a hand on Tansy's shoulder.

'He's all the father you've got, Tansy. All you've got.'

Florence packed the children off to school, then went round to the hospital to enquire about Cliff. All they would tell her was that he was comfortable, and that she could see him at visiting time in the evening.

The house in Catherine Street was quiet, and somehow alien. Making a pot of tea, she caught herself wishing fervently she was in her own rooms, or even grappling with the mountains of paperwork at the warehouse.

She didn't want to be here, but what choice did she have? In all good conscience, what else could she do but return? It *was* only temporary, she comforted herself.

At the same time she dreaded explaining her reasons to Greg. But he must understand!

He called at Catherine Street just after lunchtime. Florence had been half expecting him. As she opened the door to let him in, he removed his hat, his gaze unsure as it searched her face.

'Florence? What's going on?' He sounded edgy. 'I called in at the warehouse to tell you I'd be late. Rita told me what happened. Why are you here, darling?'

She led him into the living-room.

'Sit down, Greg. I'm here for the children, love,' she explained. 'They've got no one else. Only neighbours. I am their stepmother. What kind of a person would I be if I ignored them?'

He continued to stand, anxiously fingering the brim of his hat.

'For how long? We'll be moving into our house next week. Our own place, darling, where we can be together.'

Florence fiddled with the collar of her dress. He was on the point of being angry, she could see, and she couldn't blame him really.

She smiled up at him reassuringly.

'I know, Greg, love, and I can't wait.' She shook her head. 'It's only until Cliff comes home. One, two weeks.'

'Two weeks! What about us, Florence? Are we going to be able to see each other?'

He threw his hat on a chair, and stepping forward took both her hands in his.

'I don't want you to stay here. Take the children to Westbury Street if you must, darling.'

'That's not practical, Greg.' Florence released her hands from his, and turned away a little. This was more difficult than she'd guessed, but she understood his point of view.

She turned to him again, smiling.

'It's only for a short time. We'll have the rest of our lives together.'

'Florence … you're not having second thoughts about us, are you?' he asked with a worried expression.

Florence flung herself into his arms, clasping him around the neck, lifting her face to kiss him.

She loved him so much it hurt. She couldn't wait to be with him, to be loved by him, but she had to do her duty first. If she turned her back on Cliff's children now, it would haunt the rest of her life.

'Oh, Greg, darling, never doubt my love for you,' she murmured, clinging to him, feeling the warmth of his cheek against hers. 'We'll be together soon, and I'll be all you want me to be.'

He left reluctantly, on the understanding they would meet up later in a café near Hospital Square before she visited Cliff.

She could see Greg was still uncertain, and was sorry, but comforted herself with the thought that the time would soon pass. In two weeks, maybe three they'd be together in their own home.

Later, Florence stood in the hospital corridor with other visitors waiting for the ward doors to open. No one was allowed in a minute before time.

She dreaded seeing Cliff again, not only because of the injuries he'd suffered, but also because she didn't want to face his reproach again. She didn't want to feel sorry for him. It was that kind of thinking that had caused her to make the biggest mistake of her life. She was determined that they wouldn't discuss their relationship.

Cliff remained with his eyes closed as Florence sat patiently by his bed in the long narrow ward, listening to the buzz of conversation from the other patients and visitors.

He opened his eyes once, but closed them again immediately, completely unaware of her presence. A cage had been placed over his legs. Thankfully there were no injuries to his head or face, but he looked extremely pale and spent. It was obvious he'd been through a lot of pain.

When the bell rang she left.

When she visited him the following evening he was awake though he looked exhausted.

'They told me my wife had been in to see me,' he said to her, his tone hopeful. 'I couldn't believe it.'

'Nothing's changed, Cliff,' Florence said hastily. 'I'll take care of the children until you come home. When will that be? Have they told you?'

He shook his head. 'It was a bad smash, Flo.'

He obviously wanted to say a lot more about their separation, but Florence didn't want to hear it, and left well before the bell sounded.

The days and nights were long in Catherine Street. Over the week she visited Cliff only once more to take in some clean pyjamas, a towel and such necessities. She didn't stay to talk. As far as she was concerned they had nothing to say to each other.

Greg called that week, but upset Florence by trying to persuade her to give up her vigil over Peter and Tansy, and they had bitter words over it. It made her heart sore. She missed Greg so very much, and the time they spent together was too precious for argument.

It was on her visit the second week that the ward sister told her the doctor wished to speak to her. She was ushered into the sister's office.

'Mrs Longford?' A tall young man in a white coat, stethoscope dangling around his neck, motioned her to take a seat. Florence sat on the edge of the chair, clutching the front of her cardigan nervously. What was going on?

'I'm Dr Turner,' he said.

He momentarily glanced down at the open file on the desk, then looked up at her, his expression grave.

'Mrs Longford, please excuse my having to mention this, but I understand from your husband that you and he have parted.'

Florence sat up straight, suddenly nettled.

'That's our concern alone, Doctor,' she said sharply. 'You surely haven't brought me in here to discuss my private life?'

He looked at her steadily for a moment.

'In a sense, yes, I have,' he went on. 'You see, Mrs Longford, you may not understand the extent of your husband's injuries. He's suffered serious damage to his legs and also his spine. The grim fact is, it's unlikely he'll ever walk again.'

Florence was speechless with shock.

'He'll remain here for quite a few weeks yet,' Dr Turner went on. 'And will then have a period of recuperation elsewhere. When Mr Longford returns home he'll be in a wheelchair, and will need help and care. He has no other relatives and I understand he has two children.'

'I'm looking after them at the moment,' Florence managed to whisper.

She was still numbed by the doctor's revelation. Cliff, a cripple! She could hardly believe it.

'Doctor?' She leaned forward anxiously. 'Are you sure? Is there some mistake?'

He shook his head sadly, closing the file and adding it to a pile of others at the side.

'I'm sorry, Mrs Longford. I'm sure this complicates your life, but as his wife you must be informed of the seriousness of his condition.'

Florence swallowed hard against the sudden dryness of her throat.

'Does he know?' she murmured.

'Yes. He's taking it quite ... philosophically at the moment.'

Dr Turner stood up, and Florence rose too. Her legs were trembling, and despite the residual warmth of the August evening, she felt chilled to the bone. What was fate trying to do to her now?

'That is the situation, Mrs Longford, but of course, you must do as you see fit.'

The ward sister who had been standing by silently, opened the office door for her and Florence walked out into the corridor on shaky legs. She stood for a moment, swaying uncertainly, not knowing which way to turn, her thoughts in turmoil.

She had the desperate urge to run straight to Greg, throw herself into his arms and forget all the doctor had said.

What she couldn't do was face Cliff at this moment. She needed time to recover from the shock and to think what she must do next.

Florence left the hospital immediately, and returned to Catherine Street. The children were already in bed and Peggy Rees was babysitting until she returned. When Peggy was gone,

Florence retreated to the bedroom.

She threw herself face down on the bed, struggling not to burst into tears. She mustn't give way to emotion. She must stay calm and think.

She was in a trap! And at the same time she felt she was being torn apart. Her love for Greg was burning in her heart. She didn't want to hurt him; she didn't want to lose him. He was the gateway to a life of happiness for her.

But what of Cliff? She *was* his wife and the question of whether she loved him or not was academic now. He was in desperate need of help, her help. There was no one else.

It would be expected that she'd help. Others would blame her if she walked away now. Words from her marriage vows came into her head – in sickness and in health. When she made those vows she'd deliberately taken on the responsibility for the welfare of another person. How could she now, in all good conscience, brush that aside because it didn't suit her?

Florence sat up, feeling heavy and burdened. Swinging her legs over the edge of the bed, she looked at her reflection in the dressing-table mirror. It was like staring her conscience straight in the face.

If she turned her back on Cliff now, her reflection warned, it would be a totally selfish act, and no good would come of it. How could she be really happy with Greg with that forever on her mind? Her guilt might poison their love, and she couldn't bear that.

She was torn between what was right and her

531

own selfish desires, and the very fact that she was in a dilemma told her what she must do.

She must send Greg away.

There'd never be another man for her. Greg was the love of her life. What they had was beautiful and wonderful, and she didn't want anything to tarnish it. She'd rather lose him than have *that* happen.

Florence felt a burst of terrible remorse and pain, and cried out aloud:

'Oh, Greg! My darling.'

He would be devastated. How could she face him? How could she tell him?

Unable to bear it a moment longer, Florence buried her face in her hands, weeping uncontrollably. She cried at the pain of her own heartache and for the heartache she would cause Greg. That thought hurt most of all. She would be the instrument of Greg's pain. Perhaps he'd come to hate her and would wish they'd never met!

As soon as the children had gone to school the next morning, Florence hurried down to the telephone box just outside the hospital gates. Greg might still be at the police station in Alexandra Road. She'd never needed or dared to contact him there before, but felt this was an emergency. She'd made her decision, and wanted to explain this to him as soon as possible. At the same time she was afraid, afraid to meet the pain she'd see in his eyes.

Greg wasn't there, but she left a message to contact her, then returned to Catherine Street to wait.

It was lunchtime when he came. When she opened the door he stepped forward to kiss her warmly, his eyes bright with hope.

'You're coming home?' he asked.

They stood in the passage. Florence clung to him, pressing her cheek against his warm throat, as he held her, not speaking yet. She wanted to linger on this moment. He might never hold her in his arms like this again, not when he heard her decision.

'Come into the living-room,' she invited at last. 'Have a cup of tea.'

He followed her along the passage.

'Florence, why did you leave a message?' His voice was uncertain now. 'Has anything happened?'

'Sit down, Greg, love.'

But he remained standing, studying her closely. He could read her like a book; she knew that. He could probably read the turmoil in her face.

Florence put her trembling fingers to her mouth, too overcome for a moment to answer.

'It's Cliff,' she said at last. 'It's bad news. The accident has crippled him. He'll be in a wheelchair for the rest of his life, as far as the doctors know.'

Greg swept off his hat in a gesture of regret.

'I'm damned sorry to hear that, Florence.' He shook his head sadly. 'What bloody awful bad luck. What'll he do now?'

Florence darted towards the kitchen.

'I'll make some tea,' she said quickly, trying to delay the telling of her decision.

But Greg wasn't fooled. He caught at her arm,

pulling her back, giving her such a piercing look that she flinched.

'Florence, what does this mean for us?' There was apprehension in his voice, too. 'What have you got to tell me?'

Florence put a hand to cover her mouth again, trying to stifle a sob.

'Oh, Greg!'

In one long stride he came to her, gripping both her shoulders tightly. His face was pale, making the blue of his eyes more vivid than ever.

'You're planning to leave me!' he said, with incredulity and dismay. 'You're going back to *him!*'

'Not as a wife, Greg. As a … nurse.'

'You'll live in his house not mine, Florence, for God's sake, don't do this.'

Looking at the fear in his eyes, Florence thought for one split second that she *could* walk away from her responsibility with impunity. But it passed as quickly as it came. There was no escape. Both she and Greg must suffer for her folly and overriding ambitions of the past.

'I must. I'm his wife, Greg. I can't turn away from him now. My vows…'

He stared at her dumbly, his paleness turning to dull grey.

'Florence, you don't know what you're saying. You're upset.'

She shook her head miserably, biting her lip to stem the flow of tears. Oh, God! She'd give anything not to put him through this.

'I won't let you do it, darling,' he said hoarsely. 'I won't let you ruin both our lives. Please! Please

534

say you'll change your mind.'

When she shook her head again, he cried out:

'Florence, at least think again. Please, darling!' His hands on her shoulders were trembling violently. 'You can't mean it! You can't mean you're sending me away?'

He gripped her shoulders tightly as if he'd shake sense into her.

'Greg! Do you think this isn't tearing me up, too?' Florence blurted out passionately. 'I love you. I want to be with you. I know now that's all I ever wanted. Everything else I've been scrambling for all along was an illusion. Greg, I love you only.'

With a suddenness that shocked her, he pushed her away.

'Do you?' His voice was suddenly harsh, his eyes accusing. 'I don't believe it!'

'Greg!'

'You've chosen *him*,' he thundered, his eyes glittering like ice crystals, cold and distant. 'You've been stringing me along. Playing me for a stupid jug-head, and I fell for it!'

'No! Greg, no. Please believe me...'

'My God, Florence! You certainly had me fooled. You let me fall in love with you, really in love.' He stared at her, his eyes wide. 'I wanted to give you everything. Now you throw my love back in my face.'

He turned away abruptly and strode to the door.

'Greg! Don't go and leave me like this.' Florence ran frantically after him. 'I love you, Greg. Don't let us part with anger between us.'

He had the front door open.

'Greg!' Florence reached her arms out to him. 'My heart is breaking, too, darling...'

He swung round to stare at her, his face a mask of cold stone.

'You haven't got a heart, Florence,' he said, bitterness underlining every word. 'Otherwise you wouldn't be doing this to me ... to us.'

'I haven't a choice,' she cried despairingly. 'Please understand. Don't hate me, Greg! I couldn't bear that.'

'You've made a choice, all right.' He frowned in anger, the muscles in his jaw tensing. 'You've chosen *him*,' he said harshly. 'What more is there to say?'

He paused as a spasm of great pain crossed his face.

'Goodbye, Florence.'

CHAPTER 36

Rita took her time over her tea. It'd been chaos at the warehouse all day and she was weary. She missed Florence; it was lonely in Westbury Street without her.

Rita sighed dejectedly. The evening stretched endlessly before her. Never mind! She'd have the wireless on. She was in the mood for some cheerful music.

She was just about to clear the table, when someone tapped on her door. She opened it to find Mrs Percival.

'There's a gentleman to see you, Miss Bevan.'

Rita blinked, and before she knew it, Mrs Percival was elbowed aside, and Ken Henderson stood squarely in the doorway.

Rita fell back a step at the sight of him, consternation and sudden fright making her heart thump uncomfortably.

'Ken!'

'Surely you're not all that surprised to see me, are you?' he said testily.

Mrs Percival's head was bobbing behind him. He half turned.

'That's all, thank you!'

The landlady disappeared rapidly down the passage, and Ken pushed his way into the living-room.

He looked around scornfully.

'What a comedown! Obviously, you like slumming it.'

'What do you want, Ken?'

'I want you to stop being a bloody little fool, Rita. Who *do* you think you are, eh?'

'Get out!'

His lips drew back in a snarl.

'Did you think I wouldn't find you, you bitch? And what do you mean by sending me that letter, threatening me?' His eyes narrowed as he glared at her. 'Anyone who threatens me needs to be taught a lesson.'

Rita trembled at the gleam in his eyes, but lifted her chin defiantly. For years he'd terrorised her, humiliated and abused her. But that was over. She was free of him. She was standing on her own two feet. There was nothing further he could do.

'See it as a threat, if you like,' she said contemptuously. 'But I mean what I say. I want a divorce, and I want recompense for all you've put me through.' She ground her teeth in a surge of newly-found courage. 'And you've put me through hell, Ken. You're going to pay for that.'

'You stupid little whore!'

Rita gasped in outrage.

'Yes, whore,' he repeated savagely. 'Did you think Malcolm wouldn't tell me? You're expecting his bastard. He told me.'

'Oh!'

His name calling didn't touch her. He'd called her worse in the past, but his words labelling her unborn baby ripped right through her. Malcolm had betrayed her after all. Well, she wasn't really surprised.

She noticed that Ken was wearing kid gloves. She knew what that meant. Another beating! But he wouldn't dare, not here!

She gazed at his face anxiously. When he was in one of his uncontrollable moods his expression always alerted her. The corners of his mouth would turn down and dull red patches would appear on his cheekbones. Rita felt breathless as she saw these signs now, and fear rose like a tidal wave.

With new resolution she took a grip on herself. He'd punished her in the secrecy of their own home, but here he'd be exposed. Did he have the arrogance for that? Looking into his eyes, Rita knew he did.

She took a tentative step towards the door. He moved slightly, too. Cat and mouse! How he loved that power game.

'You've got no right coming here intimidating me, Ken,' she said, tightly. 'I'm not your wife anymore.'

'Oh, yes you are,' he answered with a sneer. 'You're my ... property, to do with as I like. And what I'd like now is to teach you a lesson you won't forget, you treacherous slut.'

Rita uttered a high-pitched, almost hysterical laugh, fear making her throat tight and dry.

'Call me what you like. I don't care. But if you lay a hand on me ever again, Ken, I'll have you in court. I'll drag you and the rest of the rotten Henderson family through the dirt. I'll expose you and your disgusting appetites...'

He interrupted with a coarse oath, staring at her as though he couldn't believe she was defying him, that she wasn't gibbering in terror as she usually was.

'I'm suing you for divorce,' she went on loudly.

She paused as the red patches on his cheeks deepened, and renewed fury flamed in his eyes. But she wouldn't stop now. She had to make a stand against him.

'You can threaten and bluster all you like, Ken, but you can't stop me now. I've already seen my solicitor.'

Suddenly she was angry that she still felt the paralysing fear he always invoked in her. She wanted to break free. She had her baby to protect.

'You're going to pay, Ken,' she cried out wildly. 'Pay! Pay! Pay! Or else I'll see you rot in prison.'

The flames in his eyes spurted out at her and with a snarl, he lunged for her. A scream ripping from her throat, Rita whirled and was at the door in a few steps, Ken right behind her. Somehow she got the door open, and fled into the passage.

She was vaguely aware of Mrs Percival standing half concealed in the alcove under the stairs, but she didn't dare stop and ask for help. Ken was in a towering rage and would be blind to everything except his thirst for revenge. He mustn't catch her. She *must* get to her bedroom, lock the door, and trust Mrs Percival would have the sense to call for help.

She was at the foot of the staircase and was racing up as fast as she could, emitting moans of fear between gasping for breath. She heard his pounding feet right behind her. She prayed, prayed that she wouldn't stumble, that he

wouldn't catch her and that she'd reach the
sanctuary of her bedroom in time.

On the half-landing he caught her.

He held her upper arms in a cruel grip, and
began shaking her until her teeth chattered, all
the while calling her filthy names.

Rita struggled wildly, screaming. She couldn't
believe this was happening all over again. All she
could think of was her baby. She must protect
her baby from any blows he would strike.

Suddenly one of her hands was free and with a
hiss like a wounded cat, she clawed at his face.

On an oath, he thrust her from him. It was
deliberate. For a moment of suspended time Rita
swayed on the very edge of the top stair. All she
could see was his face, contorted, vindictive,
wild-eyed. She felt his fist thud into her chest,
then she was falling, falling...

She gave a loud, terrified cry as she went, then
was tumbling, tumbling over and over; tumbling
and screaming...

'My baby! My baby!'

She crashed at the bottom of the stairs with a
terrible thud.

A great agonising pain ran through her entire
body like a bolt of lightning...

Florence's first thought on waking was of Greg,
and unable to control herself, she turned over
and cried into her pillow. It was terrible that they
would never be together again, but the agony was
worse that they'd parted with such acrimony and
bitterness between them. She felt torn in two
with the misery of it.

Eventually, she got up and went listlessly about the tasks of the day, getting the children off to school, cleaning the house, queueing for the rations. It struck her that she'd be doing these very same tasks for a long time to come, and the thought made her dismal. She needed to talk to someone, and decided she'd call on Rita.

It was half-day in Swansea, so the warehouse would be closed in the afternoon. After lunch Florence walked round to Westbury Street. Mrs Percival answered her knock, and then stared at her in surprise.

'Miss Bevan in?' Florence asked, managing a smile for the landlady.

Mrs Percival's eyes were round.

'You'd better come in, Mrs Longford.'

Mrs Percival paused in the passage and looked enquiringly at Florence.

'I'd have thought you'd have heard,' she said. 'You being her cousin, and all.'

Florence shook her head, puzzled.

'Heard what?'

Mrs Percival crossed her arms in front of her and lifted her shoulders.

'Miss Bevan or rather Mrs Henderson is in hospital,' she said.

'What?' Florence could only stare in confusion.

Mrs Percival lifted both hands in a gesture of disgust.

'Oh, Mrs Longford, it was terrible! That poor woman.'

Mrs Percival revealed what had happened while Florence stood struck dumb with horror.

'She came bump, bump, bumping down the

stairs, Mrs Longford, heels over head, screaming her lungs out.' Mrs Percival put both hands over her ears. 'I shall never forget it as long as I live.'

'Oh, my God!' Florence covered her mouth with her hand in horror. 'Her baby!'

'Hid myself under the stairs, see. Afraid, I was. And *him*.' Mrs Percival sniffed in disgust. 'He comes down the stairs, steps over her lying there, and walks out of the door.' She sniffed again. 'Well, I thought he murdered her. I went straight and fetched a bobby. Told him everything I'd seen and heard.'

She lifted her hands.

'Oh, what a rumpus then. The bobby, the doctor, the ambulance. Her things are still here, mind, and I need the rooms.'

Florence could think of nothing else but Rita all day. Had she lost her baby? She dreaded to learn the truth, but when visiting time arrived Florence walked down to the hospital and found the ward Rita was in. She paused at the ward door.

Towards the end of the room she saw Uncle Ronnie and Auntie Sybil already sitting at the bedside. She wouldn't intrude, and there was a strict rule anyway. Only two visitors at a time.

She retreated, pausing at the Ward Sister's office door. A woman in a dark blue dress, with starched white cap and cuffs, was sitting at a desk.

'Sister, I'm enquiring about Rita Henderson. How is she?'

The Sister looked up, rather arrogantly, Florence thought.

'She's comfortable,' the Sister said briefly, then returned to the papers on the desk.

'I'm her cousin,' Florence persisted.

The Sister looked up again.

'Did she lose her baby?' Florence asked urgently. 'Please tell me. I *must* know.'

The Sister averted her eyes, but a sad expression broke through her arrogance briefly. It told Florence all she needed to know.

'Mrs Henderson is comfortable,' the Sister said, and Florence left, weeping.

Rita had lost her precious baby, and the blame was Florence's. Her cowardice had ruined her cousin's life.

CHAPTER 37

October 1951

Florence queued in the small post office, impatiently waiting her turn. Her legs and back were aching. It was like a nagging tooth ache, but there'd be no chance to ease her body. When she'd cashed her postal orders, she'd be off to the small tobacconist's shop in Bryn-y-Mor Road to do a gruelling three hours behind the counter.

Absent-mindedly, Florence's hands strayed to her swollen abdomen. Eight months gone and she was huge. She knew that by this time she should've given up the job at the tobacconist. Apart from the strain of standing so long, it was getting more and more difficult to squeeze herself into the narrow space behind the counter. She'd struggled on because they needed the money.

Somehow, Cliff had managed to send her fifteen shillings in postal orders each week since he'd been in hospital. She got ten shillings a week from her part-time job. It was just enough to keep herself and the two children, and she wondered where she'd found the skill to make the money stretch.

Someone in the queue behind touched her arm, bringing her out of her reverie.

'How's your husband, then?'

Florence turned to see a regular woman

customer at the tobacconist smiling at her.

'He's coming home from the convalescent home tomorrow,' she answered, trying to match the woman's cheery smile. But she couldn't.

'That's good news, isn't it? Give him my best and tell him I was asking after him, won't you?'

Florence tried another smile, then realised it was her turn at the window and was glad to move away. The post mistress handed her the precious fifteen shillings, and she left the post office to trudge down to Bryn-y-Mor Road.

She dreaded Cliff's return, dreaded the life that faced her in the future. She'd struggled on from day to day since that awful last meeting with Greg, her darling Greg, and she'd not seen him since. She often wept bitterly at the thought that he hated her now. It was unbearable.

Her heart was empty, empty and without hope. Never in her life before had she known what it was like to be without hope.

Without hope? No, that was not true, she told herself. She did have one ray of hope. Her baby would be born next month. She longed for that time, yearned. Her baby would be her one consolation, her joy. She'd live for him. She just knew it would be a boy. She'd already chosen his name. William, after her father.

She thought of Rita then. Poor Rita. What she must be going through, having lost her baby. Florence's guilt still smarted painfully, and she tried not to dwell on it. She couldn't imagine the anguish Rita was feeling – or perhaps she could.

At least Rita had physically recovered from her ordeal, but Florence could only guess at her state of mind. One good thing was that Uncle Ronnie had at last put his foot down and had overruled a much subdued Auntie Sybil and, from what she'd heard, Rita was now back in the family home at Brynmill.

Florence wanted to see her cousin, but hesitated. If she appeared before Rita in her present condition, it would be like rubbing salt in her cousin's wounds. She'd wait until after the birth.

Florence had Cliff's bed brought down to the front parlour. She'd faced his homecoming with resolution, expecting him to be morose and resentful of his incapacity. But he was calm and appeared resigned to his life in a wheelchair.

It was she who felt the resentment, and tried to fight the bitterness in herself, as she viewed Cliff's own fortitude with suspicion. She couldn't help feeling that he was prepared to be philosophical about his helplessness because it was a rope to bind her to him, inexorably.

She could guess what he hoped and expected, but Florence made her status plain as soon as they were alone in the living-room the night he came home.

'Thank you, Flo, for coming back, and for looking after the children,' he said. 'It means a lot to me to have you here. I'm so glad you're back.'

Florence looked up from sewing a patch on the seat of Peter's short trousers.

Cliff was sitting in his wheelchair on the other side of the fireplace. She hadn't seen him since he'd gone into the convalescent home in Blackpill. He looked older and thinner. He'd suffered much pain, she knew. It was a wonder he wasn't bitter.

'What else could I do?' she said quietly. 'Legally, I am your wife and therefore responsible.' She hesitated. 'I'll take care of you, Cliff, for that reason, but we'll never be man and wife again. You do understand, don't you?'

He glanced down at his hands clasped tightly in his lap.

'I'm delighted about the baby, Flo. I was hoping...'

'No, Cliff. All that has ended,' she said firmly. 'I'm just a housekeeper now and a nurse. Make your mind up to it.'

In the silence that followed, Florence lowered her gaze to her sewing again.

Now that she'd had time, so much time alone to miss Greg, long for him, and time to consider her terrible choice, the more she regretted it. Now it was too late. Greg had finished with her, probably hated her. She'd sacrificed him and so much else for what she'd seen as her duty to Cliff.

Duty before love? She probably seemed a fool to many people. But at least she didn't have a guilty conscience to torment her. Only a broken heart.

A fortnight later Cliff surprised her with an offer. He was handing out the housekeeping money.

'It's lucky we have that piece of Terri's at our backs,' he said. 'It's my return from that that's been keeping us going.'

Florence said nothing, putting the money he'd

given her in her purse. The business was no concern of hers now. She hadn't thought about it for a long time.

'Flo, listen...' He hesitated. 'I've got some compensation coming. A tidy sum. I sorted it out when I was at Blackpill, see. And I've also got a small amount of insurance, as well.'

'We won't starve, then,' she remarked, not really interested.

'I've been thinking,' he went on. 'This life isn't fair on you, Flo.'

She did look at him then, surprised. What did he mean?

'Why don't we buy Lil out of her share of the business?' he suggested, making Florence's eyes open wide. 'I've heard she'd like to go abroad to live. Spain or some such. We'll buy her out and you can run the place. How would you like that, Flo, love? You'd be the boss of the whole shebang. It's what you've always wanted, isn't it? Your own business.'

Florence eased herself onto a chair nearby. A year ago she'd have given her eye-teeth for a chance like this. Now the idea left her cold, yet a little angry, too.

On the face of it it seemed a generous offer, yet Florence could see beyond to a hidden motive. It would be one more rope to bind her to him, one more obligation.

Florence set her jaw. No more blind ambition, though. She'd learned her lesson in a most cruel way. She looked at him soberly.

'Thank you, Cliff. It's generous, but I don't think so.'

He stared at her, genuinely astonished at her refusal.

'But why?'

Florence lifted her chin high, determined.

'As I told my mother when she made a similar offer – I won't be bought.'

'Bought? I don't understand what you mean, Flo.'

Perhaps he didn't. But she did. At last she was seeing clearly. All that she really wanted, a lifetime of love and happiness with Greg, was now totally out of reach.

Remembering her scramble to get to the top, the reckless race to score success, for recognition and esteem from her parents. She felt deep pity for the young precipitous fool she used to be; rushing ahead heedlessly; deaf to advice; angry at what she saw as interference from her parents. Now she was paying for her folly, and paying dearly.

'I've lost my ambition,' she said dully.

She'd lost everything. Except... Her heart lightened. Except her baby. Her baby was everything to her now, everything.

She'd decided that from now on she'd concentrate on that one thought. Her baby. Soon he would come and fill her empty life.

On the Saturday morning following Cliff's return home, Florence rose from bed feeling heavy and awkward. She had some difficulty getting down the stairs and knew her days behind the counter at the tobacconist were over. After breakfast she sent Pete around to the shop with a note explaining herself. They were probably expecting it and were no doubt relieved.

It was hard going that morning and she could do little but sit, only hauling herself off the chair later to make the midday meal. She felt ashamed and was glad her mother wasn't able to witness her weakness.

In the early afternoon, after the meal, she was left alone in the house and decided she'd go back to bed for a nap.

Peggy Rees, next door, and her Bert, had bought one of those television sets, and Cliff and the children went next door to gawk at it. Cliff said, if he liked it, he might use some of his compensation money to buy one. Florence privately thought it scandalously expensive and a complete waste of money. But it was his money.

She'd been dozing no more than an hour when persistent knocking on the front door roused her. With difficulty she hauled herself off the bed and down the stairs.

A woman, probably in her late thirties, stood on the pavement outside. She wore a camel-hair swing-back coat with a huge collar, over a flower-patterned dress. A small hat in red felt with black veiling perched jauntily on one side, over her shoulder-length blonde hair. Florence's expert eye saw that her hair colour came out of a bottle.

The woman stared at Florence with bold eyes, looking her up and down several times. Feeling suddenly self-conscious of her bulk, Florence drew the edges of her cardigan around herself protectively.

'Yes?' she asked sharply. She'd never set eyes on

the woman before, but instantly took a dislike to her.

'Is Cliff in?' the woman asked. There was a touch of insolence in her tone.

Florence raised her brows.

'No. Who's asking? Who're you?'

The woman lifted her chin, peering down her nose at Florence, her insolence more marked now.

'I was going to ask you the same question,' she answered contentiously.

Florence was nettled. She didn't like the look of the woman and she didn't want to be standing here with an aching back exchanging pointless chit-chat with a stranger.

'I'm Cliff's wife,' Florence retorted with spirit. 'He's not in, and I don't know when he'll be back. All right?'

Florence moved swiftly to close the door but to her astonishment the woman put her foot against it belligerently.

'Hey! Hold on a minute, will you!' she yelled at Florence.

Florence held the door, resisting, and shouted back.

'What do you think you're doing?'

'I'm coming in!'

The woman put her hand against the door, and gave it such a violent push that Florence was forced to yield. Did the woman really mean to force her way in?

'He's not in, I tell you,' Florence shouted, placing herself as a barrier.

'Never mind that now,' the woman said loudly.

'Out the way!'

She moved forward to step into the passage. She was no taller than Florence, but big-boned and vigorous, and Florence could do nothing more than fall back a pace, astonished and perplexed at the woman's persistence and audacity.

The woman was in the passage and closed the door behind her.

'Now,' she said, staring fixedly at Florence. 'Who did you say you are?'

'Get out!' Florence yelled. Sudden anger made her feel dizzy and she leaned against the wall for support. 'Get out!'

'I'm not going nowhere till I get this straight. I asked you a question, sunshine. Who are you?'

Florence bristled.

'I'm Mrs Longford. Florence Longford. Cliff's wife. Now will you get out? Or do I call a policeman to you?'

The woman stood still, staring at her for a moment or two. She had a short, uptilted nose and grey eyes. They looked as hard as any granite. Yet, for all that, they seemed familiar, and Florence's puzzlement deepened.

'Well, there's a bloody funny thing, isn't it?' the woman said in a measured tone, though her expression was surly. 'And here's me thinking *I'm* Cliff's wife.'

Florence did a double-take.

'*What?*' She blinked several times, wondering if she'd misunderstood. 'What did you say?'

The woman gave her another appraising glance.

'So, you're Cliff's fancy piece, then?' she said with a sneer. 'You're young and pretty, I'll give him that. I never thought he had it in him to pick up anybody like you. And a bun in the oven, as well!'

'Now look here!' Florence shouted, trembling in outrage. 'I'm not taking insults from you. I'm Cliff's wife.'

'You can't be sunshine, 'cos I am.'

'What?'

'I'm Connie Longford, Cliff's wife, and have been for the last thirteen years.'

Florence was speechless. She fell back against the passage wall, her eyes round and staring.

'But ... but you're dead...!'

'Dead?' Connie laughed harshly. 'That's a good one, that is. Dead? Hey!' She frowned and her bottom lip jutted aggressively. 'I don't like the sound of that.'

'But ... but...' Florence stammered. 'But Cliff told me ... told everyone you'd been killed in a road accident in Australia in nineteen-forty-nine.'

'The sly bugger!' Connie exclaimed. 'Don't he just wish!'

Florence stared wildly at the older woman, realisation bringing a wave of horror to wash through her. It couldn't be true, not after all she'd been through, not after all she'd sacrificed.

'But, we were married just over a year ago...' she gasped out.

Connie's eyes lit up in triumph.

'Married you? Oh, bigamy, is it? Well! Let's see him wriggle out of this.'

Bigamy!

Florence felt the breath catch in her throat, and she thought she'd choke as the enormity of what Cliff had done hit her like a ten-ton truck.

Her hands went to her swollen abdomen. Her baby! Her baby! Florence lifted a hand to clutch at her throat, her mind balking in disbelief at the truth about her unborn child. If this woman really was Connie Longford, then Florence's baby was illegitimate. No! No! That couldn't be true! No, it mustn't be!

Nausea was rising, and she felt faint.

'You're lying!' Florence cried out desperately, fighting not to let the weakness overwhelm her. 'Get out, damn you! Get out!'

But even as she said it she knew it was true. This was Cliff's legal wife. He said Connie was five years younger than himself. She was only thirty, but she looked at least thirty-eight, old before her time, aged by the life she had led. Florence had a sudden insight into the depths to which Connie had sunk, and felt revulsion.

'I know what *you* are,' Florence stormed, waving an arm. 'Get out of this house.'

'No bloody fear!' Connie's expression was resolute. 'I want what's mine. Where are my kids?'

She elbowed Florence to one side, and strode into the living-room. Once there she took off her coat and hat and threw them on a chair nearby.

'I'm Cliff's legal wife,' she said firmly, folding her arms across her chest. 'I have my rights. You're his fancy piece, and you look down your nose on me! Pot calling the kettle black, isn't it?'

'I married Cliff in good faith...' Florence stammered, outraged.

Connie's lip curled nastily.

'Well, don't get any big ideas about his money 'cos you haven't got a right to anything, see.'

Florence edged her way into the living-room. She felt terrible. Her head was swimming with the shock, and she felt sick. This was an awful nightmare.

'You deserted him,' she accused Connie. 'You gave it all up.' Connie sniffed disparagingly.

'That's only five years ago. I pushed off when he was coming out of the clink,' she retorted quickly. 'Not going to take any chances, was I? He's dangerous. He killed Tansy's father. You know that, don't you?'

'Cliff's been straight with me,' Florence said. 'He told me everything.'

'Straight!' Connie pulled a face, laughing loudly and scornfully. 'Oh yeah! Forgot to mention the little matter of being married already. He could go back inside for this, you know.'

Florence suddenly couldn't care less what happened to Cliff. He'd used her and deceived her. She didn't know why she was even bothering to argue with Connie. But beneath her distress at the turn of events, she was curious about the older woman's intentions.

'What are you doing here?'

'Like I said, I want what's mine.'

'Cliff's in a wheelchair,' Florence said stiffly. From what she knew of her, Connie wasn't the caring sort. 'He'll never work again. He needs looking after.'

'I know that, don't I?' Connie's lip curled disdainfully. 'I've been back in this country a month. Last week I heard about Cliff's compensation money from a chap I met in a pub.' Her eyes lit up covetously. 'I want my share, see, sunshine, and I'm going to get it. I'm his wife. I want a decent roof over my head, too.'

'What?'

'I'm living in digs and they're bloody awful.'

She flopped down in an armchair, crossing her legs.

'Why should I put up with that when I've got this place?' She smiled sneeringly. 'Cliff won't be much of a problem now he's banged up in a wheelchair, will he? And now I've got something on him, something real juicy. He'll do as I say or go back inside.'

Florence stared at her in disbelief.

'You want to live here?'

Connie stared around and shrugged at Florence's obtuseness.

'This is my husband's house, sunshine,' she said. 'This is my kids' home. Where else would I go?'

Florence eased herself into a chair, feeling her legs weaken and unable to remain standing any longer. She stared at Connie's grinning face through a haze of stupefaction.

Connie reached for her handbag that had been thrown on the floor, and took out a packet of Woodbines. She lit up, flinging the spent match carelessly in the hearth.

She took in a few breaths, letting the smoke glide up from her nostrils, all the while resting her foxy gaze on Florence.

'When Cliff comes back,' she said eventually, 'you can tell him how things stand. I'm back! He better not kick up or else.'

'Cliff won't stand for it,' Florence gasped.

'Well, he'd better!' she snapped harshly, flicking her cigarette after the match.

She stood up suddenly and reached for her coat and hat. She shrugged into the coat, and put on the hat, looking at her reflection in the mirror over the fireplace.

'I'm going now,' she said, looking at Florence through the mirror and smiling tauntingly. 'Tell Cliff I'll be back tomorrow with my stuff. I'm moving in.'

Connie turned then, looking her up and down superciliously.

'And you, sunshine?' she said with a jerk of a thumb towards the front door. 'You're out on your arse.'

Florence hauled herself to her feet. She was trembling from head to foot as dismay turned to rage that pounded in her head.

'I wouldn't stay in this house anyway,' she stormed, fury making spittle foam on her lips. 'Not with a common prostitute like you, and a callous conniving scoundrel like Cliff Longford. I'd rather camp out in the sand under Brynmill Arch. I'd rather die in the gutter.'

Florence sat slumped on the settee for a long time after Connie was gone, her mind in turmoil, not knowing what she should do next.

Her urge was to fling some things together and

run, but she had nowhere to go. She'd have to think of something by tomorrow. She never wanted to be under the same roof as Connie again, not even for a short time.

She wouldn't run, though not until she'd faced Cliff with the terrible thing he'd done to her. Not until he saw how much she despised and detested him.

The thing that hurt most, the most terrible thing, was the harm he'd done their child. Illegitimacy was a monstrous burden to place on an innocent baby, but Cliff apparently had had no compunction. She wasn't so worried about her own reputation. That paled into insignificance compared to her son's. The child would be hers alone and would use her name. Cliff had no claim. She knew that much about illegitimacy at least.

His deceit was most cruel and callous. He had no decency. When she left him why hadn't he told her then that she was free? She could have married Greg without any hindrance. Cliff's continued silence cost her the man she loved and adored. How heartless! How amoral! Cliff was a man without conscience, and now she hated him, hated him, with every fibre of her being.

Florence went upstairs and managed to get the small suitcase off the top of the wardrobe. She'd take only a few clothes from this house. Nothing else mattered.

She'd finished packing and had the suitcase on the landing when she heard Cliff come in from next door. With relief Florence realised he was alone; the children were still with Peggy.

Cliff was whistling cheerfully, and Florence wondered at the cold-bloodedness of him.

'Flo!' he shouted up the stairs. 'I've been down the chip shop. I've got us cod and chips for tea.'

Florence heard the wheelchair go into the kitchen. She came down the stairs slowly and carefully, on her legs that were so weak and shaky she was almost afraid to put her weight on them.

She stayed in the living-room, waiting, sitting on one side of the straight-backed chairs which gave her back more support. She felt suddenly chillingly calm.

Cliff wheeled himself back in a moment, still whistling. He glanced at her, then stopped.

'What's the matter, Flo? You look awful. The pains aren't starting, are they? It's a bit too soon.'

She stared at him, silently, breathing deeply. She wanted to screech at him, babble out all her fury and rage, but she held herself in check a moment longer.

'You've had a visitor,' she said, amazed at the steadiness of her own voice.

He moved the wheelchair to a position on the other side of the fireplace, and picked up the evening paper from a small table.

'Who was it?' he asked, sounding not very interested.

He unfolded the paper and looked at the front page.

Florence swallowed hard.

'You remember Connie,' she said slowly, her gaze fixed on his face. 'Your wife? Well, she's back from the dead.'

A split second passed before his hands clutched

560

convulsively at the paper. Struck dumb, he looked up at her slowly, his face draining of colour; his eyes stared at her as though he was seeing the very devil himself.

Florence still held on to her rage. If she let it go, she knew she'd become hysterical.

'Why did you do it, Cliff?' she asked tremulously, shaking from head to foot. 'You've stolen my life, and what's worse, you've stolen the future of my child.'

Cliff opened his mouth; his lips worked, but no sound came.

'You trapped me,' she cried out her accusation, her voice an angry rasp. 'You saw I was inexperienced. You spotted my weakness, my craving for success and recognition. You played on it, tempting me with the partnership. And I was hooked, then, wasn't I? Obligated. You disguised it all in so-called kindness. I thought you were my friend. What a laugh!'

'Flo! Please listen...' he said hesitantly, finding his voice at last. 'I love you.'

'Love!' Florence screeched out, unable to control her fury a moment longer. 'Don't mention that word to me! You can't possibly understand what it means, not after what you've done to me. All you feel is self-love. You didn't think of me at all.'

Florence heaved herself to her feet with difficulty, and stood there swaying. She felt such hatred for him now. With sudden insight she knew the same murderous fury that he must've felt the day he killed Tansy's father. It passed momentarily, but it was the measure of her feelings.

'I hate you, Cliff!' she screamed at him. 'My baby is illegitimate because of your treachery. My innocent baby!'

'Flo? ... listen...'

'I despise you!' Florence shouted at him, clenching her fists at her side, wondering where she was finding the restraint not to strike him. 'The rottenness that's in Tony is in you, too, only you hide yours under a façade. Oh, kind, generous Cliff! And all the time scheming how you could trap me into a loveless marriage.'

He gulped, manifestly shocked at her words and expression.

'Flo, I did it because I love you. I wanted to divorce Connie but I couldn't find her. I never thought she'd ever come back. I wanted you desperately. We could've been happy together...'

'No!' Florence shouted. 'Never! I felt sorry for you, Cliff, that's all. I was young, naive and grateful. I never loved you. I told you that. Now I loathe you.'

'Look at my side of it,' he said, defensively.

She could see by his recovering colour that he was getting over the shock.

'I loved you,' he went on. 'I could give you everything you wanted. I couldn't ... can't live without you, Flo, love. Please, please, find it in your heart to forgive me. We can start again. I'll divorce Connie. We can be married, legally married.'

Florence looked at him, astounded.

'I don't believe this! You're incredible!' she gasped. 'You deceived me, cruelly, callously for your own selfish ends, yet you don't believe

562

you've done anything wrong, do you?'

She stared at him, wondering why she'd never seen his true nature before. A little voice inside her told her she hadn't *wanted* to see. As Cliff said, he'd provided all she'd wanted. What a terrible price she now had to pay.

'Why didn't you do the decent thing when I left you?' she demanded to know raggedly, weakened by the deep emotions rushing through her. 'Why didn't you tell me I was free to love someone else? If it wasn't for Connie's greed, I never would've found out. I'd have spent the rest of my life anchored to you. And you talk about love.'

He stared at her dumbly, raking his dark, curly hair with shaking fingers.

She shook her head scornfully.

'There's not one shred of decency in you. You knew I loved Greg. Selfishly you denied me that one bit of happiness. You couldn't have me, so no one else should. Sheer maliciousness!'

'No, Flo, it wasn't like that. I love you.'

'I don't want to hear that, I tell you!' Florence screeched, covering both ears with her hands. 'I can't bear even to look at you. I've got my case packed. I'm going this evening. Right now!'

'Flo! You can't! The children, think of the children.'

Florence took one last look at him, her mouth a hard line.

'Connie is moving in tomorrow, she said. She'll take care of them.'

Anger crossed his face for the first time.

'Connie's not setting foot inside this house.'

'You'd better do as she says, Cliff,' Florence

warned dully. 'She knows you're a bigamist. That means prison. I wouldn't cross her. She's a nasty piece of work. You're made for each other!'

Without another word Florence turned on her heel went upstairs to fetch her suitcase. It wasn't heavy. There wasn't much in it.

It was ironic, she thought. She'd fought and pushed to be successful, to be the great business-woman, and all she'd ended up with was a damaged reputation, an illegitimate child, and a battered old suitcase full of the tatters of her life.

A chill went through her at the thought. She was pregnant, homeless, and with only ten shillings in her purse, more or less destitute. Where would she go? What would she do?

Cliff eyed the suitcase with panic, gripping the arms of the wheelchair as though he would rise up from it if he could.

'Flo, be sensible,' he appealed. 'You've got nowhere else to go. Stay with me. We'll fight Connie together. Stay with me please.'

Without looking at him or answering, Florence pulled on her coat. She said all she was going to say. There could be nothing more between them, not even anger and rage. She picked up the case, walked down the passage and out of the front door. She resisted the urge to slam it after her.

Florence got as far as Hospital Square before she stopped walking. It was getting on for five o'clock and already growing dark. There was a cold evening breeze blowing, too. She tried to pull her coat closer around herself, feeling the chill biting into her bones, but it wouldn't meet in the middle over the bulk of her abdomen. She felt so weary, now all her anger was spent, tired and helpless.

Where could she go? Even as she asked herself, her heart was telling her what her mind didn't want to acknowledge. There was only one place to go.

She must go home.

Florence felt a wave of hot shame and humiliation pass through her, but there was nothing else for it. She'd have to go home with her tail between her legs and her head bent low. She'd have to confess she'd been wrong from the start. She'd have to beg her mother for help one more time and pray to heaven that she'd receive some kind of welcome. She had to find a safe haven for her baby.

Florence felt the bitter tears of self-pity sting her eyes. What a mess she'd made of her life; what an awful mess!

CHAPTER 38

With dragging steps Florence made her way to the stop where she could take a bus to the Mumbles, feeling cold, tired and hungry, weighed down with depression and despair.

She'd always had such a clear idea of her future, always certain what she should do and how she'd go about attaining her goals, her dream.

Now her dream was dead, and the only decent thing to do with dead dreams was to bury them. Did she have the courage to do that, to own up that she'd been riding for a fall all along, helter-skelter into disaster? Did she have much choice? she asked herself bitterly.

She thought back to that day, now so long ago it seemed; her eighteenth birthday. She'd been rash and impulsive, foolhardy and strong-headed. She must confess that now. Even poor Rita had seen it and tried to warn her.

But she'd been blinded and driven. By jealousy of her sister and brother, perhaps? Florence agonised at the thought, but she had to be realistic if she were to scour herself clean of the mess that was her life now.

How could she face her mother again? Florence trembled at the prospect, her courage almost failing her. What could she say?

Everything Edie had asserted about Florence was true; everything her mother predicted had happened. Florence had failed, and failed miserably. Her lofty dreams were brought to nothing, and now she wondered if they had ever been worth the struggle, the pain, and the animosity that had grown towards her parents.

Even if she'd finally achieved her dream of running her own hairdressing business, would it've been enough? Would she ever have been happy without love? She knew now with certainty that she never would. And never will without Greg, she told herself, feeling anguish eating into her very soul.

Florence caught her foot on the cracked, uneven pavements and almost fell as a sob erupted in her throat. For all her scheming and planning, she was left without either success or love. She was alone and had nothing!

Oh, Greg! My love!

Overcome with memories of him, Florence stopped for a moment with a hand against a nearby wall to steady herself. All this soul-searching was taxing her spirit, already weakened by the loss of the man she loved. Could she find the strength to go on?

He'd probably moved into the house in Sketty by this time, she reflected. It must be hard for him living in the house he'd bought to share with her, and it saddened her to think of him there alone.

But perhaps he's not alone, a pitiless voice said in her head, perhaps he's already found someone else to share it with him, to share his love.

She felt a searing pain in her breast at the thought of Greg loving someone else. But what could she expect? She felt cheated, but what must Greg feel?

She'd been cheated by Cliff, yet at the same time her innate honesty made her face the whole truth. She must take some of the blame. So convinced she knew better, she'd ignored the sensible advice of older, wiser people and had ridden roughshod over other people's feelings, her family's, for instance. She could acknowledge this without any self-deceit, now that she was alone and left with nothing.

Was she really alone? Was that, too, a deceit? She still had her family, didn't she? They were all she had. Would there be any welcome for her? She couldn't blame them if they turned their backs. Heaven knew, they'd been patient enough.

What a fool she'd been from the beginning!

She was angry with her own naiveté. In the towering arrogance of youth, she was the architect of her own downfall. But knowing that was no comfort.

Florence boarded a double-decker bus at last and was glad to get a seat on the lower deck to relieve the weight on her aching legs. The bus sped along the Mumbles Road and the closer it came to its destination the more Florence began to quake inside.

She thought of her last meeting with her mother. Her mind echoed with the sound of her own bitterness and arrogance then. Hadn't she sworn never to come begging to her mother again? Yet here she was! In the deepest trouble, praying for their pity and help. Would her mother forgive her for what she'd said that day?

And her father, too. She'd been so very angry with him when he'd called at Catherine Street, accusing her of living in sin with Cliff. How ironic that was now.

If only she'd bitten back her anger and talked things over with her father sensibly and reasonably. But she'd dismissed him so summarily. Her own father, the kindest of men! Would he forgive her? Surely, surely he would find it in his heart now to pardon her foolishness?

The bus pulled up at Oystermouth Square in the village and Florence stepped down reluctantly. It was getting late. As she climbed the hill towards her mother's guest house she saw that most of the little shops in the Dunns and Newton Road had closed. Only the pubs were open.

Reaching the guest house at last, she stepped into the brightly lit reception hall as the sound of brisk footsteps came along the passage from the kitchen. Suddenly uncertain, Florence half turned away. The steps paused as her presence was noticed.

She was afraid to look at whoever was standing there staring at her. She tugged, self-consciously at the edges of her coat. What must she look like? She had a sudden unflattering vision of herself; hatless, in the coat her mother had bought her, totally unsuitable for a pregnant woman and clutching a battered suitcase. She must look like a refugee!

'Florence?'

There was a clatter as a tray was dumped down on the reception desk.

'Heaven's above! Florence!'

Florence turned at the emotion and shock in her mother's voice, straining not to burst into tears herself. Edie stood with a hand to her mouth, staring.

'Oh, Florence, my darling girl! I'd no idea...'

Edie hurried towards her, arms outstretched to embrace her, and Florence dropped the suitcase.

'Oh, Mam!'

Florence held out her arms, too, as she had as a child, longing for the warmth and comfort of that loving embrace. Then Edie was holding her tightly, kissing her cheek.

'Florence, lovey! Why didn't you let me know? I'm so pleased you're here, chick. Oh! There's glad I am to see you.'

Overwhelmed by the unreserved show of feelings from her mother, Florence burst into tears, sobbing uncontrollably against Edie's shoulder.

'Mam, I'm so miserable. Something terrible has happened. Something awful. I don't know how to tell you, it's so awful. I don't know what I'm going to do.'

'There, there, lovey,' Edie said comfortingly. 'You're home now. Everything's going to be all right.'

'I must tell you, though,' Florence sobbed. 'I want to tell you everything. Oh, Mam! I've been such a fool. I should've listened to you.'

Edie patted her back gently as she hugged her.

'There'll be time for talk later,' she said soothingly. 'Come along with me now. You look done in. You need a cup of tea, something to eat and then rest. Come on, my lovely girl.

Everything's all right now you're home again.'

She picked up the suitcase and putting an arm around Florence in support, led her towards the stairs.

'Can you climb the stairs, Florence?' Edie asked gently. 'Let me help you.'

The strain on Florence's legs was awful, but with her mother's arm around her, supporting her at every step, she made it to the top landing.

'Your old room is waiting for you,' Edie said, out of breath too. 'You'll be comfy there. Now don't you worry about anything, my lovely girl.'

In the familiar surroundings of her old bedroom, Florence sat on the bed wiping away tears with the heel of her hand, while Edie unpacked the few things in the suitcase.

'I don't want to be a bother, Mam,' Florence said haltingly. 'I didn't know where else to go.'

Edie bent down, taking Florence's face in her hands and gently kissed her damp cheek.

'Where else would you go, but home to your family, my chick?' she said. 'I've been so worried about you, lovey. We've heard nothing for months. I was making up my mind to come and see you.'

'Were you, Mam?'

Edie nodded, gazing lovingly at her and Florence could see tears in her mother's eyes, and felt a great welling of thankfulness in her heart for that love that never fails.

'Now you get into bed,' Edie suggested, gulping a little. 'And I'll fetch you a pot of tea, a soft-boiled egg and a bit of toast. How about that?'

Florence nodded, thankfully.

'My ration book's in my case,' she said weakly, almost too tired to speak.

'Never mind that now,' Edie said. 'After you've eaten you can tell me everything, if you want to. Your father's down at Woodville Street replacing a tap washer for Mam-gu.'

Edie gazed lovingly at her, her head tilted one side, her eyes shining with unshed tears.

'Dad's going to be very happy to see you, Florence. Not a day goes by when he doesn't talk about you, wondering how you're keeping.'

Florence felt tears start again.

'Has he forgiven me?'

Edie smiled.

'What's to forgive, lovey? You're our darling daughter, and we love you.'

Florence felt stronger after the tea and the food. Her mother's welcome was more than she'd expected; much more than she could have hoped for; more than she deserved. And alone in the quietness of the room, she said another prayer of thankfulness.

In a little while Edie came and sat on the edge of the bed, and Florence poured out her heart. When she told her mother about Cliff's deception over Connie, Edie looked very shocked and then angry, and Florence's voice faltered, suddenly afraid her mother would blame her.

'He's done a terrible thing to you, Florence,' Edie said in a hard voice. 'Such callous villainy!'

She took Florence's hand as it rested on the counterpane and squeezed it comfortingly.

'You're in no way to blame, Florence, lovey,' she declared firmly. 'You are the innocent party.' Edie was angry. 'And to think I wanted you to go back to him! He ought to be had up for it.'

'No, Mam.' Florence lifted a hand, urgently. 'I don't want anything done. I don't want a scandal, for my baby's sake. Besides, there's Pete and Tansy, the children. God help them if they're left to the mercy of that Connie. She's a vile woman!'

Florence pictured the avarice on Connie's face when gloating over the compensation money.

'Cliff will find punishment enough,' she said. 'And I'm just thankful for my beautiful baby.'

Edie's features softened.

'Oh, Florence, lovey, it'll be my first grand-child. When are you due?'

For the moment Florence forgot all her misery. Her face wreathed in smiles of joy as she answered:

'Mid-November. I'm so thrilled, Mam, despite Cliff and everything. It'll be a boy, I know it will!'

Edie laughed.

'You're as bad as Mam-gu. Boys are the be-all and end-all of everything. How will you feel if it's a girl?'

Florence was taken aback.

'Oh, Mam,' she exclaimed, shocked. 'I'll love her just as much!'

Edie patted her hand. 'I know you will, Florence. You'll make such a good mother, I know it.'

Florence held on to Edie's hand. She didn't know how to begin to say she was sorry; sorry for everything. Such pain and worry she'd given her parents. How would she ever make it up to them?

'Mam, I was wrong. I know it now.' She shook her head hurriedly. 'Not wrong in striving to better myself, but wrong in the way I went about things. I was brash and arrogant; a real "arrogant little twerp" as Gramps always says about youngsters today. I was too self-centred to consider your feelings or Dad's. That was very wrong of me.' She squeezed Edie's hand. 'Please forgive me, Mam.'

'We'll always love you, Florence, and love always forgives. Remember that.'

Florence thought immediately of Greg and wished that were true. But perhaps he hadn't loved her enough to forgive her. That hurt! Because she loved him above all else. But it was no good living in the past. She had to go forward for her baby's sake.

Florence tried to grin bravely at her mother, relieved that at least her mother's love for her was strong and unselfish.

'If I have a daughter next month, Mam, I hope she doesn't grow up like me, though.'

Edie leaned forward to peck a kiss on her cheek.

'I hope your child grows up exactly like you, Florence, lovey. You're our darling daughter, and your father and I will always stand by you.'

It was on the Sunday of the third week of November that Florence's baby was born. Holding him in her arms, close to her breast, she felt a rapture she never realised was possible for a human being to feel.

'Isn't he beautiful, Dad? Just look at him! He's so wonderful!'

'Yes, he's pretty special, all right,' her father agreed as he sat on the edge of the bed, gently touching the baby's little hand. 'Seen some babies in my time, I have, but my grandson tops them all.'

Florence had to laugh outright at the pride in her father's voice.

'I'm going to name him William, after you, Dad,' she said.

'That's nice.'

She was astonished to see him blush and knew he was really overcome at being a grandfather at last.

'William Philpots, the second,' Florence declared, laughing.

'No, Florence,' Edie said carefully. 'I don't think that's right. He's Cliff's son, and when he was conceived you believed you were married. He must take his father's surname. That's his birthright.'

Florence looked at her father. He nodded his head.

'Your mother's right, Flo, *cariad*,' he said gently. 'Never known her to be wrong.'

Rita came to see her and the baby three days after the birth. Florence was so pleased to see her recovered and looking fit, yet felt flustered and uncomfortable, wondering how her cousin could bear to look at the new baby.

Rita cradled him in her arms, and a lump rose

in Florence's throat as she watched. She still felt guilty and needed Rita's forgiveness.

'I'm so sorry I let you down, Rita; not telling the family about your awful situation. If only I had,' Florence rushed on, overcome. 'Then you wouldn't have...'

'You're not to blame, Flo,' Rita said quickly. 'I am, in a way. I should've told my father at the beginning. I was a coward and ashamed. But it's no good looking back and regretting.'

Florence's heart ached for Rita's loss. She'd been cruelly deprived of this wonderful joy that Florence had found in her newborn child.

'He's perfect, Flo,' Rita said, admiringly, touching a gentle finger to the baby's chin. 'Oh, look! He's smiling at me! Well, would you believe it!'

Florence hid a smile then. She wouldn't bother to mention wind at a moment like this.

'How are you, Rita?' she asked kindly.

'I'm fine.' She looked up quickly at Florence. 'Really, I am, Flo. No permanent damage was done. Thank heavens.'

'You've been to hell and back, Rita,' Florence said sympathetically. 'It's wonderful you found the spirit to fight your way through it.'

Rita nodded.

'We've both been through hell in our separate ways, haven't we?' she answered, looking at Florence earnestly. 'But it's over, Flo. Now we build our lives again.'

Florence was impressed by the energy in her cousin's voice. She'd found an inner strength at last.

She gave Florence a speculative glance.

'Things aren't too bad at home now, but my mother is very subdued. She relies on Da a lot now, too,' she went on. 'The whole thing has been a terrible shock for her. She hardly ever goes out now, thinks people are whispering behind her back.'

She shrugged.

'Perhaps they are, too. That's why I'm getting out, Flo. I'm leaving home. Going up to London to get a job as soon as Ken's trial is over. I'm finished down here. But don't say anything to anyone yet, will you?'

She stood and laid the baby in his cot at Florence's side, then went on:

'Have you decided what you're going to do, Flo?'

Florence shook her head. She couldn't take any interest in her own future. That driving ambition she'd once known, which had burned so brightly, giving her no peace, was gone. Not a spark remained. She must live for her baby from now on. Without Greg, there was nothing.

'When does the trial start?' she asked to change the subject.

'In the New Year. Attempted murder.'

Rita looked at Florence who saw the brief yet shocking flash of terror in her eyes.

'He meant to do it, Flo. He meant to kill me.'

Florence's eyes widened.

'Will he be hanged if convicted?'

'I don't know,' Rita said, dully. 'The police are very much interested in his other activities, as well...' Her voice faltered. 'You know what I mean? They're certain of getting a conviction there. All in all, Flo, Ken will spend a long time in prison. Perhaps for a man like him that's worse than being hanged.'

Looking at Rita, and knowing all she'd suffered, Florence felt vindictive.

'Couldn't happen to a nicer chap. I hope he rots!'

Florence was in the reception hall, placing young William into his pram ready for his usual morning outing: a walk down to the village and back.

'Wrap him up cosy,' Edie said as she came out of the guests' dining-room. 'It's nippy out.'

'Can I fetch anything for you while I'm out?' Florence asked. Edie shook her head.

'Are you all right for money, Florence?'

Florence nodded, putting a hand on her mother's arm and smiling at her.

'Thanks for lending me that money, Mam,' she said gratefully. 'Now I can get some Christmas presents for the family.'

'You're very welcome, Florence,' Edie said, then clasped Florence's hand. 'Oh, I *am* looking forward to Christmas this year, lovey,' she went on enthusiastically. 'It'll be just wonderful!'

Florence smiled fondly.

'You've always loved your family around you at Christmas, haven't you, Mam?'

'Oh, yes!' Edie's face was beaming.

Her mother looked so much younger these days, Florence mused. It gave her a warm feeling to know how much happier Edie was now she'd come back to the fold. She knew too, that Edie was besotted with the baby. William the Second, as she lovingly called him.

'And this year is special,' Edie went on, 'because you're with us, lovey. We've missed you so much these last years, Florence, so very much. We're so happy to have you and William the Second, too.'

'I'll have to find some way to repay you, Mam,' Florence said.

'Nonsense!'

Florence shook her head.

'I can't sponge on you forever.'

'It's early months, yet,' Edie assured her. 'You have your baby to look after. When he's older, you can think about it then.'

Florence pulled on a tam and wrapped a woolly scarf around her neck.

'Will you go back to hairdressing?' Edie asked tentatively.

Florence was thoughtful for a moment, surprised at the question. It sounded as though her mother was reconciled to it, if that was what Florence wanted to do.

'I loved that part of it, Mam,' she confided. 'Hairdressing is something I'm really good at. I would have been a success, too, if I hadn't made a mess of it all.'

She was thoughtful again. Was her dream really dead? Wasn't there just one faint spark left? Perhaps. But she wouldn't rush madly into anything ever again. From now on she had to be sensible. Her baby's future depended on her.

'Maybe, one day a good opportunity might

come my way,' she went on. 'In the meantime, I need to earn a crust somehow, keep my self-respect, Mam. And William will need things as he gets older.'

'Don't worry about that,' Edie declared resolutely. 'William the Second won't go without anything as long as me or your father are alive.'

'Now, Mam! You mustn't spoil him. I don't want him growing up to think he can have everything he wants. He hasn't got a father to fend for him; only me.'

Edie was silent for a moment.

Florence tucked the shawl around the baby, and pulled his woolly hat straight.

'Love will come again, Florence,' Edie said quietly. 'It did for me. And for all you know it'll be a better love next time.'

Florence looked up.

'No, Mam. Greg was the one; the only one. There'll never be anyone else for me. Greg is pure gold. And I sent him away.'

Florence pushed the pram to the front door and down the steps to the drive. Edie followed as if she'd something more to say, and stood shivering in the chill wind that tugged at her floral wraparound pinny.

'Don't stand out by here, Mam,' Florence advised. 'You'll catch cold.'

'I've been thinking,' Edie said hesitantly. 'This is only a suggestion, mind! Why not come into the guest house business with me?'

Florence's eyes widened in surprise.

'Me?'

'It would be wonderful to have my daughter

follow in my footsteps,' Edie said eagerly. 'You'd make a success of it, Florence. You know, lovely, we're alike, you and me. We're not clever people, but we both have bags of drive and energy and willpower.'

'Oh, Mam, do you really think so?'

Florence was thrilled to hear her mother's praise, to know she and her mother were alike, and she felt a great lightening of her spirits. She'd yearned for it to be true for so long.

'Absolutely!' Edie assured her. 'Think about it. But off you go now, and do your Christmas shopping. We'll talk later.'

Florence enjoyed the morning walk in the crisp December air, feeling absurdly proud when anyone passing would peep into the pram and smile fondly at William the Second sleeping soundly, already four weeks old, and as bonny as any picture.

She was looking forward to Christmas this year, too. A time for putting all her unhappiness behind her. She'd never stop loving Greg or forget him, but that part of her life was past and she must learn to live without him.

Doing her shopping she thought continually of her mother's startling suggestion of coming into the business. The more she thought about it the more it caught her imagination.

Her dream of three years ago was dead, but there was nothing to stop her building a new dream, she mused, feeling a spark of ambition ignite again. She must, once again, have a goal to strive for. The idea of working alongside her mother, learning the business from her, appealed to her greatly. What better way to gain her mother's approbation?

Florence pushed the pram energetically up Newton Road, her mind buzzing with possibilities. Now she couldn't wait to get back to tell Edie she would gladly accept. She'd begin in the New Year.

She hauled the pram up the front steps in such a hurry that baby William yelled in protest, furious that he'd been wakened from sweet sleep.

With a laugh of pure love for him, Florence lifted him into her arms and hurried upstairs to her parents' back sitting-room, impatient now to see her mother.

As she walked along the passage she heard laughter and lively conversation from the sitting-room, and wondered if her sister Amy had come home early from Oxford. Amy would fall in love with William the Second on sight.

Florence pushed the sitting-room door open eagerly, expecting to see a family gathering, but stopped dead in her tracks. Staring at the trio before her, she almost collapsed in shock and astonishment.

They rose to their feet as she entered.

'You're back at last!' Edie began, smiling broadly. 'Greg here, called just after you'd gone out. We persuaded him to wait.'

Florence stood still just inside the doorway, clutching her baby to her, blinking at her mother's use of his first name. Not a respectful Mr Lloyd, but Greg, as though she'd known him for years. Yet they'd only met a little under two hours ago. She hadn't been gone longer than that.

'You never told me Greg was a member of the Magnet Club,' her father said enthusiastically. 'He won second prize for his roses last year.'

Florence could only stare at Greg. His face had been smiling and animated as she'd entered. Now he looked suddenly strained, his skin paling, the blue of his eyes deepening.

She couldn't believe he was standing here in her parents' sitting-room as large as life. Was he a mirage that would blink out of existence if she approached?

She began to tremble as questions crowded her mind. Why was Greg here? Had he forgiven her? Had he come hoping for a reconciliation?

Hope flared and swirled in her heart for a brief moment until her thoughts flashed back to the day Greg walked out on her. How vividly she remembered the pain and anger in his eyes, and the implacable thrust of his jaw when he told her they were finished. No, she dared not hope for forgiveness. She'd hurt him too much for that to be possible. She wasn't even sure she deserved it.

If it wasn't forgiveness that brought him, then it must be Cliff's criminal offence of bigamy.

Fear replaced the hope in her heart then, and she quailed. Nothing must harm her baby son or his future. If that's why he'd come she'd have nothing to say to him.

The baby must've sensed the agitation and tension in her trembling body because he began to wriggle in her arms, whimpering. Edie came across the room swiftly, and took him from Florence.

'I'll see to him,' she said reassuringly. 'I've got

584

to see about lunch, too.'

She stepped past Florence to the door, then paused, looking back at Florence's father, who had taken his pipe out of his pocket and was obviously preparing to settle back down in an armchair.

'Got some pretty good roses myself, Greg,' William said rather proudly, putting the pipe between his teeth. 'You must come down to the gardens and look at them. Plenty of time before lunch, there is.'

'Will!' Edie exclaimed quickly from the doorway. 'Never mind about blessed roses now! Florence and Greg have a lot to talk about.'

William looked crestfallen.

'Oh, *Duw!* Of course!' He thrust his pipe into his pocket again, looking embarrassed. 'Sorry, *cariad,*' he said to Florence. 'Didn't think, see.'

'Dad!' Florence held out a hand to him, suddenly not wanting him to leave. If Greg had come about the bigamy charge she wanted her father by her side for strength and support.

'It's all right, Flo, *bach,*' William said gently. He clasped her outstretched hand and squeezed it, but Florence wasn't reassured.

When they were alone, Florence stared at Greg apprehensively while he was regarding her with a puzzled expression.

'Why are you afraid of me, Florence?'

There was deep concern in his voice, but Florence wasn't to be fooled by it. She swallowed hard, lifting her chin.

'I'll not give evidence against Cliff,' she said defiantly. 'He *is* my son's father. I'll not have my baby labelled, branded for life. Nothing you can say will persuade me or force me.'

The line of Greg's mouth hardened and his eyes glittered.

'Longford has committed a serious criminal act,' he said. 'He should be brought to justice. I...'

'Greg, please go,' Florence interrupted angrily.

It was breaking her heart just seeing him, after thinking she never would again. Couldn't he guess how painful it was for her? Was the love he'd once felt for her completely dead?

Greg took a deep breath, squaring his shoulders.

'You don't mean that?' he asked quietly. 'Not a second time?'

Confused, she flashed him a glance.

'You walked out on me, Greg,' she said stiffly. 'Remember?'

'Only too well,' he answered. 'And I've regretted it every moment since.'

Florence felt her heart flutter.

'What?'

'I couldn't believe you'd choose him over me,' Greg said. 'I couldn't forgive it.'

Florence turned away abruptly to walk over to the window looking out over the gardens. They were dug over now and bare, the hard, dark ground as empty of life as her heart. Had Greg come here today to punish her once more? What satisfaction did that give him?

'It wasn't a matter of choosing,' she said dully, without looking at him. 'There was no choice, Greg. It was all to do with vows and duty. I believed I was doing the right thing.'

'Sacrifice can only go so far,' he answered harshly. 'Then it becomes senseless and hopeless.'

Florence whirled around.

'Did you come here today to criticise and chastise me?' she cried out. 'You think I haven't suffered enough?'

'We've both suffered, Florence,' he said, but his tone was rebuking, she thought.

Florence put a hand to her forehead. The tension, the shock of seeing him again was making her head ache. This raking over of dead ashes was so useless.

'Greg, I see no point in all this. What's done is done. There can be no going back.'

'No,' he answered in measured tones. 'No going back, but ... but we *could* go forward.'

What was he saying? Florence looked up slowly, afraid she'd misinterpreted his meaning. She couldn't stand any more hurt.

'Look, Florence,' he said. 'I'm not here on official business today. There's no action against Longford at the moment. I only heard about what he did to you from gossip in a pub...'

'Gossip in a pub!' Florence was humiliated.

'That's part of my job, listening to gossip in pubs,' Greg said matter-of-factly. 'When I realised you weren't married I felt a tremendous relief...'

Florence gave a bitter laugh.

'*You* felt relieved!' she exclaimed loudly. 'That's rich! I'm left shamed, practically destitute with an illegitimate baby, but you're relieved.' She tilted her head, her tone sarcastic. 'I'm so glad...'

'Shut up, Florence, will you, and listen, for once!' Greg interrupted impatiently, raising his voice. 'You're twisting everything around!'

Florence was silent, staring.

Greg ran trembling fingers through his hair. Colour came back into his face.

'I'm not here because of Longford,' he went on more calmly. 'This is about you and me.'

'What?'

He took a few quick steps to reach her side. Florence gazed up at him, her mouth suddenly dry, afraid almost to breathe, afraid to let herself believe...

He reached out a hand to touch her then drew back, uncertain.

'We've been given a new chance, a fresh start,' he said, a huskiness in his voice. 'If we've got the courage to take it ... and if we love each other.'

She saw he was trembling with unspoken feelings, and deep emotion swept through her, too. If only it were possible for them to recapture what they once had.

'Greg!'

'I love you, Florence, darling,' he went on swiftly, eagerly as though afraid she would silence him. 'I never stopped, believe me.'

He grasped her hand and held it tightly.

'Please forgive me,' he asked earnestly. 'Forgive my pig-headedness in not trying to understand your motives. I was jealous of Longford and couldn't think straight. It drove me crazy!'

Florence reached up impulsively and took his face in her hands, kissing his lips eagerly.

'Oh, Greg! I love you more than you can realise. I've missed you so much.'

'Florence, darling!'

She was in his arms at last. His mouth was hungry and ardent for hers. She gave herself over to her emotions, feeling she was waking out of a long, dark dream.

He released her in a moment, looking down on her with eyes that were suspiciously bright.

'Let's get married by special licence,' he suggested.

'No,' she replied. 'I want a church wedding.' She almost added … this time. 'I want to dress up and have photographs to show our grandchildren. And my mother will never forgive me if I don't have my reception here.'

Greg gave a long sigh, holding her close.

'Anything you say, Florence. Just so long as you keep loving me.'

Their lingering kiss was interrupted by a knock and someone putting their head around the door.

'Ahumm!'

Greg tried to jump back guiltily, but Florence clung to him, preserving their embrace. She had nothing to be ashamed of now.

It was her father at the door.

'Pardon me,' he said, smiling. 'Flo, your mother sent me up to tell you lunch is ready.' Then he politely withdrew again.

'You will stay to lunch, won't you, Greg?'

Greg straightened his tie.

'I've already had my invitation,' he told her with a grin. 'I like your parents. I think they like me.'

Florence was sure of it.

Greg put an arm around her waist, ready to escort her downstairs, but Florence held back for a moment. There was something she needed to get straight.

'Greg, listen a moment,' she said. 'I can't wait for us to get married, but I'm not the kind of woman content to stay at home, you know, at the kitchen sink, like. We'll have kids, lots of them, I hope. But I want to *do* something, you know, darling, make a mark.'

Greg groaned.

'Oh-oh! What now?'

'I've decided to go into the guest house business with my mother,' Florence rushed on enthusiastically. 'She believes I can make a success of it. That's wonderful, isn't it? My mother believes in me! You don't know what that means to me, Greg.'

'And...?'

'Well, we'll be living up in Sketty, won't we, so ... I want to learn to drive a car.'

'What?' Greg released her, standing back to gaze at her with alarm. 'Oh, now Florence, hold on a minute! A woman behind the wheel of a car.' He shook his head doubtfully. 'I'm not sure I approve. It could be dangerous.'

'Women drove all the time in the war, no problem!'

'Er ... that's different,' Greg said uncertainly. 'Isn't it?'

'Right! That's settled then!' Florence said triumphantly.

The publishers hope that this book has given you enjoyable reading. Large Print Books are especially designed to be as easy to see and hold as possible. If you wish a complete list of our books please ask at your local library or write directly to:

Magna Large Print Books
Magna House, Long Preston,
Skipton, North Yorkshire.
BD23 4ND

This Large Print Book for the partially sighted, who cannot read normal print, is published under the auspices of

THE ULVERSCROFT FOUNDATION